MURDER AT BREEZE CANYON

MURDER AT BREEZE CANYON

by
Tony Spallone

MURDER AT BREEZE CANYON

Published in the United States of America by Long Walk Publishing.
www.TonySpallone.com / Tony@tonyspallone.com

ISBN-13: 978-0-9864271-0-7
ISBN-10: 0986427101

Edited by Stephanie J. Beavers Communications
www.StephanieJBeavers.com / 888-823-2283

Cover design by Slobodan Cedic

To my wife Patti

Acknowledgements

I owe special thanks to my wife Patti, who inspired me to write this novel. Without her enthusiasm and support, I would not have been able to write Breeze Canyon.

Thanks to my sister Rose Williams, whose editorial assistance and zeal for my story buoyed my interest in having this novel published; to Jenny Engleka, who shared her knowledge of writing; to my cycling buddy Mike Blackburn, with whom I had a real-life experience similar to one depicted in Breeze Canyon; to Gail and Sandy Lipstein and Lynn and Bob Ingersoll, who share and enhance our love of cycling; and to Stephanie Beavers, of Stephanie J. Beavers Communications, editor par excellence, whose expertise enabled me to present the best possible manuscript. She has taught me much about writing, and for that I hold her in high esteem. I look forward to a continued working relationship with her.

Prologue

Aldez Pass, the scenic roadway between Albuquerque and Santa Fe, has breathtaking views as it weaves through New Mexico's Sandia Mountains. Low barriers, severe elevations, twists, and turns alongside a deep canyon keep road traffic to a minimum.

Ordinarily it's tourists who use the roadway. For people in a hurry, the most direct and fastest way to travel between the two cities is Route 25.

Only a few strong cyclists take on the challenge of biking the eight miles to the top of the pass.

Alex Castillo was one of them. He had done it twice before in the last several years.

It was Sunday morning and Alex was climbing the pass again. Even he was unsure why he was doing it. What was he trying to prove?

Only that he could do it.

Slowly, steadily, he rode until he made it to the top. When he got there, exhausted and cramping after three hours of rhythmic pounding, he got off his bike, drank some of his remaining water, and sat on the stone wall that bordered the uppermost scenic overlook. He soaked in the magnificent views of the Sandia Mountains, proud of his masochistic success. He had made it to the top.

Again.

But the best part was yet to come: the descent.

It was a breathtaking descent.

He could reach fifty or sixty miles an hour if he wanted, but at that speed, he knew if he misjudged the angle of any of the switchbacks, he would catapult into Aldez Canyon with no chance of surviving the fall.

Alex was a careful rider. He controlled his speed. He maxed

out at forty-five miles an hour on other descents, but never any faster than that. He applied his brakes judiciously. He wasn't foolhardy.

After fifteen minutes of rest, he was ready to go back down the mountain. He mounted his bike and coasted across a short, flat section before beginning his descent. A car approached from behind. One of the few cars he had seen during his climb. *A tourist no doubt*, he thought. He pulled over to the side of the narrow mountain road, but the driver didn't seem to want to pass. Alex thought the driver was probably frightened by what lay ahead and was waiting to be certain it would be safe to pass.

The car approached dangerously close behind. Alex put his hand down to signal for the driver to slow down, to back off. Instead, the car got closer. *I have to get away from this crazy bastard.* He decided to pull into the next scenic overview to allow him to pass.

The car was now just inches behind.

"What the hell," Alex shouted. *Maybe he's lost his brakes.*

The car bumped his rear wheel.

It wasn't a hard bump, but Alex swerved dangerously close to the precipice. He panicked. *God almighty it's not his brakes, he's trying to kill me.*

The car hit him again.

"What the hell are you doing? Stop. Stop!"

The car rammed Alex one last time. His bike hit the barrier. He tried to get off but couldn't. He flew over the handlebars and down into the canyon, flailing and screaming all the way to the bottom.

His screams echoed off the canyon walls.

No one heard him.

Except for the driver.

Part I

Chapter 1

Cyclist Found Dead in Aldez Canyon: The body of Alexander "Alex" Castillo, 39, of Santa Fe was found Monday in Aldez Canyon northwest of Santa Fe. Police have concluded Castillo was riding his bicycle and failed to navigate a turn as he descended at high speeds from Aldez Pass, plunging to his death. An avid cyclist, Castillo had been missing since Sunday morning when he left his home in Santa Fe. Authorities began a search for him that evening after he failed to return home. There were no witnesses to the accident. Castillo leaves behind two children. Funeral arrangements are incomplete at this time.

Santa Fe mornings in early spring could only be described as crisp, beautiful. Hank Kincaid and Sam Bailey were out this Saturday, riding with a dozen other cyclists from the Canyon Cycling Club. The desert reflected gentle pastels and gold-colored sand against a cloudless blue sky. The brisk air belied the heat the riders would face a few hours later.

"You hear about Alex Castillo, the guy who was killed in Aldez Canyon on Sunday?" Hank asked his riding buddy.

"Yeah, I read about him," Sam said. "Did you know the guy?"

"Not well. I talked with him a couple times when he rode with the Club, but he stopped riding with us some time ago," Hank replied. "I happened to run into him on Canyon Road last week. I hadn't seen him in a while, and I asked him if he was still riding. He said he wasn't getting out much—just squeezing in a ride here and there. Said he was going to ride the Pass on Sunday and asked if I wanted to join him. I told him thanks but no thanks. Anyway, I'll be damned that's when he was killed."

"Does anyone know what happened? Did he get hit by a car?"

"No one knows for sure. There weren't any witnesses. A couple of hikers found him at the bottom of the canyon on Monday," Hank explained.

"Good God, what a helluva way to die."

"For his sake, let's hope it was quick."

"I would never ride a bike on that road. You can probably go fifty miles an hour on the descent," Sam said. "And it's got that low barrier. You can look right down into the canyon when you're up alongside it. Why the hell didn't they make the barrier higher? I can't even look over the side when I'm driving the Pass. It's like there's a magnet or something that wants to pull me over."

Chapter 2

Missing cyclist found dead in Santa Susana Pass: Tomás Pérez, 32, of Santa Fe, was found dead Wednesday in a remote section of Santa Susana Pass. Pérez had been missing for three days. An extensive search by the Park Search and Rescue team along with dozens of volunteers from the Canyon Cycling Club found the decedent's remains. There were no witnesses. Pérez, an avid cyclist, apparently plunged to his death from Dawson's Peak overlooking Santa Susana Pass. Drawn to the site by the reflection from Pérez's bicycle, searchers found him in a virtually inaccessible area of the canyon. Pérez is survived by his mother, father, and two younger brothers.

"That's the second guy who's died in the last couple of weeks. They were both killed the same way," Hank said. "That's a helluva coincidence, isn't it?"

"Why would anyone ride so damn close to the edge of a cliff? What the hell was wrong with those guys? Did they have a death wish or something?"

Hank shook his head as he usually did in reaction to some of the things Sam said. The two had become friendly soon after Sam joined the Cycling Club a year earlier. They often rode together on the club's Thursday afternoon and Saturday morning rides.

Hank was the stronger, more experienced rider of the two; he was lean but muscular, a handsome man of thirty-eight, six feet tall with thick, brown hair and a square jaw—some said he resembled the comic book character Dick Tracy. Married to Connie and the father of two young sons, he was one of twenty-four Assistant District Attorneys for the First Judicial District headquartered in Santa Fe. He had been cycling since the age of eighteen and was one of the fastest riders in the club, yet he was supportive, friendly, and patient with new riders such as Sam.

At thirty-four, Sam was an inch shorter than Hank, but did not possess his same lean cyclist build. Sam had a bit of a paunch, a round face, and a shaven head. In spite of his self-effacing personality, he wore a constant smile. He usually had a tale to tell or a joke to share, and interspersed salty language in every ribald story. Hank enjoyed Sam's company.

Riding side by side this late Thursday afternoon, Sam was unusually quiet. Hank tried to get him out of his mood. "You're really getting strong, Sam. It won't be much longer before you kick my ass."

The compliment worked. Sam turned to Hank and beamed.

"I'm curious, Sam. What got you started cycling?"

"I'm a recovering alcoholic."

Hank glanced over and expected a joke to follow, but instead saw a serious Sam.

"Are you bullshitting me again?"

"No. It all started when I was fired from my job a few years ago."

"What happened? What was the job?"

"Ah, I don't want to get into the gory details. My fault I got fired. But then I couldn't find another job. My wife got more and more pissed at me because she said I wasn't trying hard enough. She made me feel like shit, so I started drinking. I figured if I had a few pops starting in the morning maybe I could tune her out. But she stayed on me like flies on shit."

Hank was stunned at what Sam was telling him. As they rode along, he glanced at his friend from time to time. Hank wasn't sure he needed to hear every detail of what went on between Sam and his wife, but he listened.

Sam continued, "The drinking didn't work, though. It got her more pissed at me, and got me more screwed up, too."

Hank was not yet convinced his friend was being sincere, but Sam didn't stray from his tale.

"It's hard to tell you everything, but she made me out to be a criminal. Started telling people I beat her. But I swear to Christ, I never touched her, ever. After a while, she decided she wanted a divorce. By then, I didn't give a rat's ass, so I said fine, let's get it done."

It was obvious to Hank that Sam needed to talk about his marriage, his divorce, his drinking—he needed to unburden himself, to explain who he was to his new friend—a catharsis of sorts. "It must've been tough, huh?" Hank sympathized.

"You don't know the half of it. She was a major bitch. I think she turned psychotic."

"Any kids, Sam?"

"No. Thank God we didn't have any. You know the movie *Rosemary's Baby*? If we had a kid it would have grown up to be the devil itself coming outta her body," he said with sincere bitterness.

"*Rosemary's Baby*. God, she must have been something." Hank laughed.

"I'm not exaggerating, Hank. Honest to God, she turned psycho on me."

"Sounds like it was a good thing you got out of the marriage."

"Yeah, there's no question about that. I've talked to a few guys about divorce. It's always traumatic. But afterwards, one of two things happen: you either find a way to make your life better, or you say 'screw it,' and you fall apart and don't give a shit about nothing. I did the falling-apart thing. There's no sugarcoating the fact that I became a drunk. I didn't do drugs or nothing. I was just a stinking drunk."

"You're pretty hard on yourself."

"Yeah, I guess. But I'm okay now. Think about it. The life almost got sucked out of me. I get fired from my job and my wife claims I beat her. Then she leaves me, we get divorced, I become an alcoholic, and I come *this close* to drinking myself to death." Sam lifted one hand from his handlebar and put his thumb and forefinger centimeters apart to demonstrate how close he had been to dying. "I don't mean to bore the shit out of you, Hank."

"You're not. Go on."

"Okay. I'll make a long story short. One morning, I wake up outside the back door of my house. I remember I was curled up in a ball, stone-cold drunk, passed out. My house keys were still in my hand for Christ's sake, but I was too drunk to put the key in the lock to open the door. I was lucky a coyote didn't gnaw my ass off."

"I guess it was lucky for the coyotes," Hank said.

They both laughed.

"Anyway, that was when everything changed for me. When I realized I had spiraled totally out of control, I decided I had to do something about my drinking or it was going to kill me."

"Did you do rehab?"

"Yeah, I checked into a place in Alamogordo. Hank, I can tell you I would never want to do that again. That's the reason I'll never touch another drink. I went through DTs and stuff, seizures, nightmares, things attacking me. It was hell."

"But you did it, Sam."

"Yeah, I did, and I haven't touched an ounce of booze since."

"Good for you." Hank reached over his bike to extend his palm for an awkward high five. "What about your ex? Do you ever see her?"

"Are you kidding? I'd have to die and go to hell to see her again. I heard she was in a mental hospital for a while after our divorce. That didn't surprise me at all, but I think she lives in Albuquerque now. Since we got divorced, I haven't seen her except for one time—but that's another story. I'll tell you about it some time."

"Tell me now, man. You got me hooked."

"All right. You asked. It was about six months after our divorce was final. I was off booze, and I had a date with this girl. No big deal. I took her to dinner. It wasn't a fancy place or nothing. My date and me, we're sitting talking about different stuff, and all of a sudden, wham! She comes up behind me and hits me smack on the head with the pointy heel of her shoe."

"Who came up behind you, your date?" Hank asked, trying to be funny.

"No. My ex, Yvonne. She damn near knocked me out. Blood's running down my face. We're in the middle of this jammed restaurant, and she's screaming at me about how I abused her. I looked around and everybody is thinking I'm an asshole for abusing my wife. But as God is my witness, I never did a *thing* to her. They had to call the cops to get her out of the restaurant. I told the police I wasn't going to file charges against her. I thought, what the hell was the point? "

"What happened to the girl you were on the date with?"

"She buzzed out of that restaurant so fast the wind from her backdraft almost knocked me over. She said, 'Sam, when your life is settled, call me,' and she left. I never saw her again. I didn't blame her. She didn't want to have to put up with a crazy ex-wife."

Hank attempted to bolster his friend's self-esteem. "To get through all you've been through is something you should be really proud of."

"Yeah, I guess I'm proud that I've been able to pick myself up." Sam took a deep breath, inhaling an air of satisfaction. "By the way, you know everything I've told you is true—every last word—even the part about *Rosemary's Baby*." He laughed. "The fact is, I was to blame for a lot of what happened because I got fired, but I'm now the new me. I'm happy, I have a new job, I've made new friends, I love cycling. And I don't have a death wish like Castillo and Pérez did."

Chapter 3

Cyclist Killed: Michael Redfield, 45, of San Clemente Road, Santa Fe, was found late Monday at the bottom of Breeze Canyon off Via Encantado. Police believe he died during the afternoon of Sunday, June 14, and fell into the canyon while riding his bicycle. There were no known witnesses. Police continue to investigate and ask anyone with information about the accident to contact them at 505-222-9999. Redfield had owned and operated the Terrin Gallery on Canyon Road since 1992 and was active in community affairs. He was a past president of the Santa Fe United Way, Director of the Santa Fe Chamber of Commerce, and was well known for his involvement in many church and charitable organizations. He was a member of the Canyon Cycling Club. He leaves three children. His wife, Maria, predeceased him.

Thursday morning, before heading to the funeral for Michael Redfield, Hank decided to visit the Santa Fe Police Department. He walked out of the building where the district attorney's office was located, crossed the street, and entered the police headquarters building. He was looking for Detective Lawrence DeGarzia, the officer in charge of the investigation into Redfield's death. The desk sergeant pointed to DeGarzia. Hank turned and saw the detective sitting at one of several desks shared by detectives in the Criminal Investigation Division.

DeGarzia, of Navajo and Hispanic descent, appeared to be about forty-five. He had the high cheekbones of a Native American Indian and wore his straight black hair pulled back in a ponytail. He was nearly six and a half feet tall and weighed over two hundred pounds. His suit jacket could not hide his powerful physique. He had a deep voice, and his huge hand completely enveloped Hank's on their initial handshake. DeGarzia had the reputation in the district attorney's office of being a solid investigator in spite of his spiny, irascible demeanor.

"Detective DeGarzia, my name is Hank Kincaid. I'm with the district attorney's office. I was an acquaintance of Michael Redfield, the cyclist who was killed last Sunday."

DeGarzia looked at Hank briefly and went back to his paperwork. "Yeah," he responded with indifference.

"I'm going to his funeral in an hour. I understand you may be looking at his death as a possible hit-and-run. I'd like to talk to you about it."

DeGarzia looked up from his paperwork again. "You see all this shit on my desk? I'm looking into a dozen cases. Murders, assaults, you name it. Do I think it was hit-and-run? Shit no. The guy had an accident, plain and simple. But the captain wants me to investigate it anyway, like I have time on my hands. Why? Because Redfield was a big shot in Santa Fe. In my opinion, it was an accident, period. He had an accident and that's that."

Hank was surprised at DeGarzia's attitude, but did not relent. "Look, Detective, the reason I ask is that he's the third cyclist to have died in the last several weeks, all in the same way. That's a hell of a coincidence, wouldn't you say?"

"Look, Mr. Kincaid, I don't care—"

"Please. Call me Hank, Detective. I know how busy you must be. We are, too, and the DA will be pissed at me for even suggesting that Redfield's death was a crime."

DeGarzia hesitated. The lawyers in the district attorney's office were usually officious, so Hank's cordiality surprised him. He sat back in his chair and eyed Hank with suspicion, a bit perplexed. "Well, *Hank*, we think Mr. Redfield lost control of his bike and fell to his death in the canyon. Right now, we don't have any evidence that would support a criminal action like a hit-and-run. We've searched the scene of the accident and haven't come up with anything. We also knocked on the doors of the few houses on Via Encantado where Mr. Redfield was riding at the time of his death and asked if anyone had seen any cars at the approximate time he was killed, or anything unusual, like tires screeching, a speeding car, a car with kids in it.

"Via Encantado is very remote. It's a dead end, doesn't get a lot of traffic. Because it's so isolated, it's a hangout for kids drinking beer, smoking pot, or making out with their girlfriends. But even that doesn't happen a whole lot anymore. They run a patrol car out there a couple times a night to keep that stuff under control."

"Mind if I sit for a minute?" Hank didn't wait for an answer. He moved a hardback chair closer to DeGarzia and sat. The noise in the room was at a high decibel level with police officers, detectives, witnesses, victims, and suspects in and out of the room, everyone seemingly talking at once. "Do you have any witnesses to the accident?"

"No, not really," DeGarzia answered. He decided to answer Hank's questions after all, in the hopes he would drop inference to Redfield's death being a crime. "An elderly lady by the name of Carlotta Smith said she saw a pickup truck leaving Via Encantado about the same time as the coroner estimates Redfield died, but she couldn't remember what kind of pickup or what color it was. She thought it might have been black or dark blue, but she wasn't certain. No one else saw anything. We recovered some fragments of glass on the road in the general vicinity of the accident thinking that if Redfield was hit by a car or truck, maybe the glass on the road could have been from a broken headlamp. Our lab tested it and said it was broken glass from beer bottles."

"So you have no evidence he died from anything other than a fall?"

"Let's put it this way, I haven't totally dismissed the possibility that he was hit by a car, but I don't think he was. As I said, right now I gotta believe he lost control of his bike."

"The newspaper account said he was missing on Sunday, right? But he wasn't found until the next day?"

"Yeah, that's right. One of the employees at his gallery notified police that he was missing. Redfield didn't return from his bike ride on Sunday at the time he said he would. The employee said Redfield told him he was going for a ride on Via Encantado and would be back by six o'clock to close up. She said he rode his bike almost every Sunday afternoon for an hour or so."

"Detective, could it have been a suicide? Could he have killed himself? I mean, could he have jumped? Was there a note?"

"There's no note. We haven't found anything that would point to him being suicidal. By all accounts, the guy was a devoted father. He had three kids. He lost his wife to cancer three years ago, so he's been raising his kids alone. Nothing points to a suicide."

Hank pulled out his card and handed it to the detective. "Mind if I have one of yours?"

DeGarzia reached into his jacket pocket and extracted a card. He gave it to Hank, and nodded several times. "Look, I'm sorry if I came across like an asshole. It's never ending, you know. All this," he said, pointing to the stacks of paperwork on his desk. "Call me any time. My cell number's on the card. You can call me Deeg, okay?"

"Thanks for your time. And, Deeg—," Hank hesitated, "I probably wouldn't think anything of these three guys getting killed, but there hasn't been a single eyewitness. No one has seen what actually happened to any of those guys, no other cyclist, no hikers, no one in a car or truck, no one. That's strange, don't you think?"

"Hank, cyclists get killed every month in New Mexico."

"I understand what you're saying—you think they're all a coincidence. Maybe so. Hell, I don't know. But as a prosecutor, I don't like the word *coincidence.*"

"Yeah, I know. It's a word lazy cops use, right? You think it's an excuse word," the detective said with an edge.

"All I'm asking is that you consider the possibility."

"Fine, Hank, I'll keep their deaths on my radar."

"Detective, is it okay with you if I take a look at the accident scene? I know a little about cycling. Maybe I can spot something from a cyclist's point of view."

"Help yourself, man," he said with a forced smile, and returned to his paperwork.

Hank didn't bother to say goodbye.

Chapter 4

The Canyon Cycling Club, also known as the CCC, had nearly one hundred members. The skill levels of the cyclists ranged from expert to beginner—categorized A to D—and also included road cyclists and mountain bikers. In good weather, the Thursday rides started at six p.m. and the Saturday rides began at eight in the morning. There was no formal structure to the various ride groups. Everyone met at the East Santa Fe Middle School parking lot and assigned themselves to a group based on their own perceived cycling abilities.

The D group—jokingly called the "D-vorce" riders—was comprised of casual riders, mostly beginners, or out-of-shape or unathletic middle-aged men and women, half of them divorced and some widowed. Social chatter on these leisurely rides was at a maximum, as were stops for ice cream and scenic photo opportunities. The rides usually ended with pizza and beer at Jimi's Pizzeria on Eighth Street, followed by so-called *after-parties*, spontaneous get-togethers at someone's house where beer flowed freely and flirting was commonplace.

Widowed three years earlier, Michael Redfield had joined the CCC to meet women his own age. "Better than going to a singles bar," he explained to people who asked about his newfound passion for cycling. At the time of his death he was forty-five. He had been a handsome, dark-haired man with a perpetual wide smile that highlighted his white teeth against his olive complexion, and was well liked by everyone in his riding group. Women, in particular, had found him to be charming and gentlemanly.

A high mass was held for Redfield at the century-old Saint Joseph's Roman Catholic Church. Redfield's three children were seated in the first pew alongside their grandparents. Other family members and people who had known Michael from his many business, civic, and charitable activities sat toward the front of the church. Cyclists from the Club arrived wearing their colorful teal, red, and white jerseys over their shirts or blouses in a gesture of mournful solidarity for their co-rider and friend. They filled several pews toward the back of the church. Their grief was palpable. Etched on their faces was concern, too—concern that three Club cyclists had died in the same manner in a matter of weeks.

Although the two were not close friends, Hank and Redfield had been friendly toward each other and worked together on United Way campaigns. Hank was there to represent the District Attorney's office.

Father Patrick O'Hearn presided at the service. The ancient priest gave a moving tribute to Redfield's character, spoke of his active participation in charitable causes, his friendship to so many, and his role in the commerce of Santa Fe. "Only God knows why a good and kind man like Michael Redfield was taken from this earth. And only He knows why, over the past six weeks, two other men have lost their lives from bicycle accidents—three men too many. I wish you peace and I pray for the safety of all of you, and especially for all you cyclists."

A dozen mourners stood to eulogize Redfield's good deeds and magnetic personality. Grieving was unrestrained throughout.

After the service, small groups of mourners milled about outside the church, making small talk in an effort to lessen their grief. Hank stood with a group from the CCC. "Hard to believe this could happen for the third time in only a couple of months," one member said. Another of the fellow mourners, his club jersey taut over his dress shirt, whispered to Hank, "Have the police found out how it happened?"

"They're still investigating, but there were no witnesses that they know of," Hank answered. "We may never know how it happened."

"Someone said he may have committed suicide. Is that true?"

"I asked the police about that," Hank said. "It's highly unlikely. There wasn't any suicide note, but they haven't totally discounted that theory."

There were other rumors. One mourner offered, "I heard it might have been a hit-and-run. Someone said the cops were sweeping up broken glass from the scene. They probably thought that, if a car hit Michael, the glass could have come from a smashed headlight which they could then trace."

Another person said, "I heard that one of the cops said a neighbor saw a pickup truck speeding by at about the time Michael was killed."

"Frankly, I wouldn't be surprised if some kid did it," someone else declared.

"You mean, you think a kid hit Michael?"

"I don't know. It just sounds like something a kid would do."

"Why do you say that?"

"Maybe a kid was texting or talking on a cell phone and accidentally sideswiped Michael, then panicked and left the scene. It wouldn't be the first time a kid's been distracted while driving."

"There's always going to be someone out there in a car or truck who's not paying attention or doesn't like sharing the road with us," Hank said. "We've all got to be careful." He and the other mourners headed for their cars to queue up for the solemn drive to the cemetery.

Chapter 5

Hank returned to his office after Michael Redfield's funeral. He wanted to speak with his boss, District Attorney William Snider. Hank knocked twice on the door to his office and popped his head in. "Got a minute, Bill?" he asked.

Snider's desk and credenza were piled high with paper. By his furrowed brow, Snider appeared heavily burdened by the crush of cases, but he never refused a request to talk to one of his assistant district attorneys. His open-door policy was not one in name only—it provided his assistants with an environment of trust and mutual respect. "Come on in," he said, nodding for Hank to sit. He removed his reading glasses and set them down in front of him. "What's up?"

"The police don't believe Redfield was killed by a hit-and-run. The cop running the investigation, Detective DeGarzia, said they found no evidence that a car hit him. He thinks Redfield lost control of his bike and fell into Breeze Canyon. I disagree. And, even though he says he will, I don't think he's going to pursue this any further. No doubt he's overwhelmed with other cases."

Snider swept his arm over the dozen separate piles on his desk. "It's been tough these past several months. A lot of things going down," he said.

"I understand, Bill. But for my own satisfaction, I thought I'd look into his death, maybe take a ride over to the site of the accident later this afternoon and look around. Okay with you if I do? I'd also like to stay in touch with DeGarzia to see how this progresses. I mean, there've been three cyclists killed in a matter of weeks, all in the same way. That seems to be more than a coincidence. Frankly, I'm surprised this hasn't drawn more attention from the police."

Snider leaned back in his chair. He stretched his neck and

shoulders to loosen the tension which sometimes overwhelmed him. "Okay, but I don't want you to butt heads with DeGarzia. Do a quick review and keep me informed," the DA said. "You've got a heavy caseload, too. Don't let this interfere with the rest of your work."

"Absolutely. I won't."

*****

Mid-afternoon Hank received a text from Sam. *R U riding 2nite?*

Hank replied, *Riding 2 Redfield crash site on Via Encantado. Want to meet me there at 6?*

Sam responded, *See u there.*

*****

Via Encantado extended along a finger of land at the edge of Breeze Canyon. The canyon was aptly named for the constant breeze that funneled through it from the west. The remote road ran for nearly two miles and dead-ended into the desert. Because it was flat and had little or no traffic, cyclists used the road to ride intervals, wind sprints that helped improve their conditioning. Redfield rode there often, occasionally with friends from the Club, but on the Sunday of his death, he had been riding solo.

Hank pedaled slowly down the center of the road. The breeze was refreshing. There were no cars in sight. To his left, the desert was filled with flowering cacti—prickly pear, with their red and purple flowers, and large-spine orange and yellow chollas. To Hank's right, the cavernous Breeze Canyon was dotted with junipers and huge glacial boulders. Layered rock formations were stacked precariously, amazingly able to withstand the vagaries of time.

For over twelve thousand years, before the modern city was founded, the Anasazi Indian tribe lived in harmony with this harsh, yet beautiful, desert. Hank felt a connection, a kinship with these Pueblo peoples. It was a spiritual feeling, one he couldn't easily explain.

He got off his bike when he spotted ash remnants in the center of the road. These flare remains indicated he was close to the accident site. Ahead, Hank saw a cross on the canyon side of the road. It was spiked into the ground on the dirt shoulder and surrounded by several plastic vases filled with artificial flowers. He approached the area.

This is where he went over. Hank lowered his bike to the pavement and stood close to the precipice looking out over the canyon. After a minute, his gaze turned to the far end of the road, toward the desert dead end. The wind had picked up, whistling loudly through the canyon. He was deep in thought, unaware Sam had arrived.

Sam laid his bike down on the opposite side of the road. He made no sound as he crossed to where Hank stood looking out over the canyon. Without warning, he shoved Hank toward the cliff. "Goodbye, Sherlock," Sam said with a deep, raspy snarl.

Hank tensed and dug his heels into the dirt shoulder. Sam grabbed him around his mid-section and pulled him back.

"Jesus Christ, Sam. Are you crazy? What the hell's wrong with you?" Hank shouted.

Sam laughed. "For God's sake, Hank, I wasn't going to push you over."

"I don't give a shit. You don't mess around like that. You scared the shit out of me."

"That's what I was trying to do."

"You're an asshole, man."

"All right, I'm sorry." Sam was still laughing at his stupid, frightening attempt at humor and did not even try to mask his insincerity. "You didn't hear me coming, and I saw you trying to logic out what happened to Redfield like you were Sherlock Holmes or something. Isn't that how Sherlock and Professor

Moriarty ended up—both falling from a mountain or a cliff?"

Hank was still steaming. "Not fucking funny."

"I'm sorry, okay?" Sam extended his bicycle-gloved palm for a high five as a gesture of forgiveness. "But I did save your life, you know."

After a second's pause Hank cursed him again. "Asshole," he said, shaking his head before slapping Sam's palm with his own. He couldn't stay mad at the guy.

"If you're through screwing around, can we get serious?" Hank asked firmly.

"Okay, boss, what have you got?"

"Nothing yet, but it's interesting that on this entire road there's only a small section that doesn't have a roadside barrier—maybe twenty-five, thirty yards where the guardrail is down." He punctuated his observation by pointing to the three-foot-high, thick wire cable that lined the road, installed to keep cars from hurtling into the canyon.

"Yeah, and your point is?"

"Well, as you said when we talked about Castillo and Pérez being killed, why in hell would Redfield be riding this close to the edge of the canyon, especially here, where there's no barrier?"

"I don't know what you mean. If he was riding toward the end of the road, he'd be on this side," Sam argued.

"I understand. But the road is so wide, and the dirt shoulder is very narrow, so why wouldn't he be riding more toward the middle of the road? There's absolutely no traffic. Why would he have been riding so close to the edge of the canyon and risk falling? He had to have seen that the barrier was down."

"The only thing I can think of—the only obvious explanation—is that maybe a car was coming up behind him and he moved over to give the car room to pass," Sam suggested.

Hank walked the width of the road. "It's eight paces across. That's wide enough for two semis, and there would still be enough room for him," he said. "What else could have happened?" He thought for a moment before speaking. "What about a problem with his bike? A blow-out, maybe at high speed, or he lost his chain."

"Yeah, that could be it, Hank. That might make sense."

"I'm going to call DeGarzia to find out about Redfield's bike. He's the detective looking into Redfield's death." Hank pulled his wallet from the seat pack that was clipped to the underside of his bike saddle. He extracted the detective's card and dialed his cell phone. It rang twice before DeGarzia answered.

"Hey, Deeg, this is Hank Kincaid from the DA's office. We talked this morning. Do you have a minute? ... Good. I'll be quick. I'm at the scene of Redfield's accident with a friend of mine. We cycled out here to get a better feel for what Redfield may have done and we have a couple of questions. Can you tell me if either of the bike's tires was flat when it was recovered? ... The rear tire was. Do you know if it was a blowout?" Hank shrugged his shoulders and shook his head to indicate to Sam that the detective didn't know. "Okay, no, I understand. Can I take a look at the bike tomorrow? ... The police impound lot, okay. You'll clear it with them for me to take a look? ... I'll let you know if I come up with anything." Hank thanked DeGarzia and hung up.

"What did he say?" Sam asked.

"He said the rear tire was damaged, but he didn't know what caused it, whether it was a puncture or a blowout. Apparently, there was lot of glass on the road, and he felt it may have been a glass puncture, but he wasn't certain. If he's right, that could explain what happened. Anyway, I'll check the bike tomorrow to see if I can learn anything else. Damn. I meant to ask him where that woman lived," Hank said.

"What woman?" Sam asked.

"This morning he told me that a woman by the name of Carlotta Smith had seen a black or blue pickup drive past her house about the same time Redfield was killed. She must live in one of the houses at the start of the street. I'd like to talk to her. Maybe I can find out a little more about what she saw," Hank said. He looked out over the canyon. "But it's starting to get dark. I'll talk with her tomorrow."

Chapter 6

Early the next day Hank drove to the police impound lot. The garage was next to the sheriff's office on Camino Justicia, off Route 14 and across from the jail. Surrounded by an eight-foot fence topped with barbed wire, the lot housed vehicles towed by order of the police department for a variety of reasons: their involvement in accidents, drug confiscations, drunk-driving arrests, and evidence in other criminal cases. The lot also warehoused stolen bicycles waiting for their owners to claim them. Michael Redfield's bike was stored there along with several others. Hank identified himself to Sergeant Collins at the desk.

"Detective DeGarzia said to expect you," Sergeant Collins said. "Redfield's bike is in the rack toward the back of the lot. It has a tag on it identifying it as his. Here, let me show you. I'll walk you back there."

The two weaved their way through the lot of about fifty cars and reached a lone bicycle rack positioned along the far garage wall. Hank whistled when he saw Redfield's bike. "I don't know if you can appreciate this or not, but this bike was an Italian-made Colnago M10 S Carbon Fiber beauty. Very nice," he said. "You're looking at some major bucks here. I guess the art business is alive and well in Santa Fe." He thanked Collins and took out his cell phone to snap some photos of the bicycle from different angles. The rear tire and tube were off the rim, and the rear wheel was bent and heavily damaged. He examined the spokes. If any were broken, it might have affected the integrity of the wheel, possibly collapsing it and making it impossible for Redfield to control the bike.

The spokes were not damaged. Hank bent over the bike and found several scratches on the frame. He decided to call DeGarzia.

"Deeg, this is Hank Kincaid. I'm at the impound lot. Can you tell me where you found Redfield's bike? Was it at the bottom of Breeze Canyon or still on Via Encantado near where he fell?"

"Actually, it was hung up on some brush that was growing from the wall of the canyon—probably about twenty feet below the road," DeGarzia answered. "Why does that matter?"

"I think I may know what happened to him. I'm not a hundred percent certain, but I think he was hit from behind by a car or truck. I think he was rammed—killed by a hit-and-run."

"How the hell can you know that?"

Hank explained his theory. "Look, the bike's rear tire was bent like a pretzel. You just told me it didn't fall into the canyon, that it got hung up on some brush. That explains all the scratches I see on the bike and means that the bent tire wasn't caused by the fall. Don't you see? The wheel getting bent had to have happened before the fall, and the only logical explanation is that it was hit from behind. There is nothing else mechanically wrong with the bike. If I'm right, Redfield was hit by a car, and that would have spun him out of control. I think he may have been catapulted off his bike into Breeze Canyon. The damage to the bike couldn't have happened when it flipped into the canyon, but rather when someone rammed it from behind, maybe more than once. It caused the tire to deflate and basically explode off the bent rim."

"Okay, all right, I get it. What you're saying is possible, but that doesn't prove shit that the three bikers were killed by the same guy."

"Yes, you're right. I understand. But I go back to the fact that they all died in the same manner. Do we know if the bikes belonging to Castillo and Pérez were damaged the same way? If they were, it might prove we have one guy out there killing cyclists."

"I'll look into it," Deeg remarked impatiently. "I'm not even sure I can locate the damn bikes, but I'll check it out."

"Good. Let me know what you find. In the meantime, I'm going back to Via Encantado this afternoon to interview the woman you said saw the pickup truck go by. Do you have her address?"

"Carlotta Smith? Yeah, I'll look it up and text it to you. Tell me when you're going and I'll meet you there. I might as well hear what she has to say. Listen, I appreciate what you're saying about Redfield's bike, but—"

"I know what you're going to say," Hank interrupted. "Nothing I've told you about the condition of the bike is sustainable."

"You got it, pal."

"Yeah, I get it. But I'm fairly certain my theory is correct. The damage the bike sustained could not have happened when it went over the edge. It was damaged beforehand. The fact that it was hung up on some brush on the side of the cliff actually buffered it from being damaged even more—a kind of soft landing, if you see what I mean."

*****

Hank explained his observations to the District Attorney. Snider cautioned him. "Hank, go ahead and follow up with Smith, but you need to reach a quick conclusion." Hank's boss didn't mince words. "Detective DeGarzia is a pro. Take his lead, okay? I don't want you to waste your time on this."

Through his research on Carlotta Smith, Hank learned she was a native of Santa Fe, eighty-five years old, married once when she was twenty-one, but divorced five years later and never remarried. She was an artist and horticulturist noted for her work with daylilies. She had been living at 14 Via Encantado her entire adult life. Hank wasn't sure what to expect from her or how much light, if any, she would be able to shed on Redfield's death. If his theory was correct, however, she was probably the only person who could identify the hit-and-run driver or the vehicle the killer was driving.

Hank parked his car in Carlotta's driveway. DeGarzia arrived thirty seconds later and parked on the street. He greeted Hank with a perfunctory nod. It was obvious he felt he had better things to do. Carlotta was in her yard, wearing a wide-brimmed cream-colored hat, watering her plants and flowers with a garden hose. As Hank expected, she had the typical appearance of many older Santa Fe women; the high altitude and nearly year-round sun had weathered her complexion to rough, deep wrinkles. She stooped slightly but looked fit for her age. He sensed immediately that she was a spirited lady and that he would have to work to win her over. Carlotta looked up from her watering and immediately lowered her head again. In their suits, Hank and DeGarzia looked like religious followers canvassing the area. She turned her back to them without a greeting.

"Mrs. Smith, may we talk with you?" Hank asked.

"No." Her curt answer was an effort to preempt them. "Look here. I'm a Baptist, have been all my life, and I'm not going to change religions at my age. So I suggest you talk to someone else. Goodbye and thank you very much," she said and resumed her watering.

The two men looked at each other, surprised at the woman's feistiness. Deeg was not happy. Hank gestured to him that he would explain the purpose of their visit. "Ma'am, my name is Hank Kincaid. I'm from the District Attorney's office and this is Detective Lawrence DeGarzia from the Santa Fe Police Department. We're here to see if you can help us solve a case we're working on."

Carlotta looked back up at Hank and then stared at Deeg until recognition kicked in. "I remember you," she said. "You're the detective who was here before. If you're here to talk about that man who fell into Breeze Canyon, I didn't see anything. Detective, I told you before I didn't see anything, and I'll tell you again. I feel bad about him, but I can't help you."

As Carlotta spoke, Hank looked keenly at one of her flowerbeds. "Excuse me, but do you hybridize your *Hemerocallis*? You must have hundreds here," he said.

She looked at Hank. "Two hundred and fifty-three, to be exact. What do you know about *Hemerocallis*, young man?"

"They're my mother's pride and joy. She used to be in a garden club here. I remember she subscribed to the *Daylily Journal*, and won some gardening awards for her hybrids."

"What's your mother's name?"

"Joy Harrison. It was Joy Kincaid, but my father died and she remarried and now lives in North Carolina. She's still quite a gardener, and has nameplates next to each daylily as you do. She's got hybrids named after all her friends, each of my children, my wife, and me. Did you know her when she lived in town?"

Carlotta mellowed. "Actually, the name sounds familiar. We still have a daylily club, and it seems to me I remember that name from some time ago. But I'm eighty-five and my memory isn't what it used to be," she said, and forced a quick smile.

Hank asked, "Mrs. Smith, we were wondering if you could spare a few minutes to talk to us about that fellow—his name was Michael Redfield."

"I knew Michael." She looked back and forth at the two men. "All right, but let's at least get out of the sun. Come into the house, and I'll make us a pot of tea." Hank and Deeg shrugged at Carlotta's sudden change in attitude, and followed her inside. Her home was immaculately maintained. The walls of the foyer and living room were covered with photographs, Indian artifacts, Southwest art, and paintings. "Have a seat in there," she said, motioning to the living room. "I'll be back in a minute."

"Okay if I look at some of your artwork?" Hank asked.

"Help yourself," she answered, and went into the kitchen.

While Deeg scrolled through the text messages on his phone, Hank moved from wall to wall like a visitor to a museum, looking at photographs and assorted watercolor paintings signed *C. Smith*. His eyes were drawn to a Georgia O'Keeffe original hanging over the stone fireplace. A downlight highlighted the rich crimson and vibrant yellow of a single daylily. Hank was impressed at the beauty of the work.

Carlotta returned from the kitchen with a tray of cups and saucers, a pot of tea, and a plate of cookies. "We didn't want you to go to such trouble, Mrs. Smith," Hank remarked.

"No trouble at all."

Deeg continued to review his messages as Hank took the tray from Carlotta and placed it on the coffee table. He asked, "Tell me, how did you come to possess a painting by Georgia O'Keeffe? It's beautiful."

"She was a friend of mine many years ago. We met one day in Taos when I was painting a landscape, and she happened to stroll by and glance at my work. She lived in Abiquiú, about an hour and a half away, and went to Taos from time to time to paint. Don't know why, exactly, but we struck up a conversation, and our friendship grew and lasted until she passed away in 1986."

"How did you get her to sign her painting? I understand she seldom did that," Hank observed.

Deeg lifted his head and glanced at the painting before returning to his texts.

"Young man, you are, indeed, impressing me. First you talk about *Hemerocallis* and now you talk about the art of Georgia O'Keeffe."

"My art knowledge is limited, but I know what I like, and I like your artwork. I assume that C. Smith is you?"

"Yes, it is."

"Very nice, Mrs. Smith."

"Thank you," Carlotta said with a bright smile. She paused to pour the tea. "Now, gentlemen, what can I tell you?"

"We know you spoke to Detective DeGarzia once before, but as we mentioned outside, we're hoping you can shed some additional light on Michael Redfield's death," Hank said. "We're not certain, but we think he might have been killed by a hit-and-run driver. The detective hasn't found any evidence to support the theory, so we're doubling back and doing some more research. Mr. Redfield was an acquaintance of mine, so I have a personal interest in solving the mystery surrounding his death."

"I'm shocked to hear you think someone might have killed him. Couldn't imagine who would do such a thing to such a nice man."

"I can't either, which is why we're asking your help."

"Well, as I mentioned, I knew Michael." With her best coquettish lilt she added, "He was very sweet, a gentleman, and very handsome. I've been in his gallery on Canyon Road a number of times, and he carried some of my paintings over the years."

"I'm sure you can see why we want to clear up the cause of his awful death. We owe it to his memory to do that," Hank remarked.

"I understand."

DeGarzia put his phone away and took out a small note pad on which he had taken notes during his initial interview with Carlotta. He went right to the point. "Mrs. Smith, when I spoke with you right after his death, you said you didn't see anything you could connect with his death. But you mentioned you saw a truck leaving at roughly the same time that Michael died. You said it was a black or blue pickup truck. Do you remember about what time that was?"

"It was five o'clock last Sunday. I'm usually out about that time to water my flowers because, you know, the sun is not as severe. I remember Michael rode by on his bike and shouted out to me, 'Beautiful garden, Carlotta.' He started riding his bicycle here a couple of months ago. Sometimes he would stop and chat, but he didn't that day."

"Did you see him again after he first rode by the house?"

"No, it's funny you ask that. Sometimes when he rode here, he would go back and forth on the road pretty fast. I mean he would go fast one way then slow coming back. But that day I only saw him the one time. I didn't think anything of it. You know, maybe I didn't see him returning because my back was turned to the road."

"Let's go back to the truck. Are you sure it was a black or blue pickup?"

"Yes. I saw it as it was leaving."

"Anything else you can tell us about it? Sometimes, after a few days, specific details about an event start to work their way back into a person's mind," Hank said.

"Well, yes, that happens to me a lot now. I won't be able to think of something—a name, or a place—and later it suddenly surfaces."

"So, now you're sure of the vehicle?"

"Now I'm certain it was a black pickup. We don't normally get a lot of traffic on our road, so when I saw him go by I looked up."

"You said 'when I saw him go by.' So it was a man?" DeGarzia asked.

"No, I don't know why I said that. I didn't see who was driving."

"Did you notice any other cars that went by that day about the same time as that pickup?"

"No. Not at the same time, not that I can remember. The only other car I saw before I went into my house was one of those cars that almost scrapes the road. You see them circling around in the square in Santa Fe. What do you call them?"

"Lowriders."

"Well, whatever they're called, they're very loud."

"What time did you see that car?"

"It was much later. I first saw it about seven o'clock. There was a boy and a girl in it. They drove toward the end of the road, and I never did see them drive away. Lord knows what they do there." Hank thought he saw a slight smile crack Carlotta's lips. She knew exactly what they did at the end of the road.

Deeg spoke to Hank, "I don't think they could have been involved, as they didn't show up until well after Redfield was killed."

"Okay, getting back to the truck. Did you notice the make or model of the pickup truck? Was it a Ford, a Chevy, a Dodge?" DeGarzia asked.

"No, I'm afraid I didn't. I don't know much about cars."

"Could you tell if it was damaged in any way," Hank asked, "or if it had anything printed on it, like a phone number or the name of a company?"

"No, nothing like that. It was going fast, but it wasn't screeching fast, if you know what I mean. Not like some of the cars we get out here. Occasionally we have cars with kids racing back and forth. Drag racing, I think they call it. I've asked the City to install speed bumps to reduce that kind of thing from happening, but they haven't done anything about it." She shook her head and pursed her lips in displeasure. "Back several years ago, a car crashed into the canyon, and a couple of kids were killed. The driver had been racing another car when he lost control and flew into the canyon, but still the City doesn't do anything."

"I think I know where the car went over. I saw a stretch where the guardrail had been knocked down," Hank recalled.

"Detective, do you think you can talk to the City about the speed bumps?"

"I'll see what I can do." DeGarzia's promise was half-hearted, but he wrote *speed bumps* in his note pad.

Carlotta smiled wide. "That would be wonderful, Detective, if you could get the City to take care of that. You know, you have a wonderful bearing. You almost remind me of the subjects in the paintings by R. C. Gorman. Would you consider posing for me someday?"

DeGarzia turned crimson red. The teacup in his enormous hand looked like a child's toy cup. He set it down and glanced at Hank. He was embarrassed by Carlotta's suggestion and avoided answering her directly. His impatience with the elderly woman was growing, and harsh words crossed his mind, but he held his tongue and redirected her to the conversation. "Ah, I'm not sure I would make the best subject for you. If you don't mind, I'd like to get back to the truck for a moment. I wonder if you can remember anything else about it. You said it was going pretty fast, but you're not sure if it was a man or a woman driving. Did you notice anyone else in the truck besides the driver?"

"I guess it could have been a woman driving. But I'm certain there was no one else in the truck. I think the driver was wearing a baseball cap."

"Now that's something," Deeg said. "When I spoke with you last, you said you thought he, or she, was Caucasian, white."

"He was white, I'm pretty sure. I only had a glimpse of him. But, yes, I'm *almost* positive he was white, or maybe Hispanic."

"Anything else? Can you tell us what else he might have been wearing?"

Carlotta paused a moment and stretched her memory as she tried to recall anything more about the driver. "No, I can't say."

"Would you have seen his license plate?" Hank asked.

"No. The detective asked me that before. I know that would be helpful, but I didn't pay any attention to it. But, you know, there is another thing I remember about it. The back of the truck had an aluminum box in it."

"You mean a tool box?"

"Yes, I guess that's what it was. It was right behind the driver. You know, the kind of box a carpenter or someone like that would have. Do you know what I mean? Maybe if you put me under hypnosis I could remember more," Carlotta joked. "I'm an artist. I'm pretty good with details, but I apologize my recall isn't what it used to be. I'll remember more. I know I will."

When the interview ended, Hank and Deeg each handed Carlotta their card. "Mrs. Smith, you have been helpful. We really appreciate it. If you can remember anything else, please call either one of us, any time, day or night. Call us on our cell phone numbers. They're on the cards. And, by the way, you are one delightful young lady," Hank said. He meant it.

Carlotta offered a broad, flirtatious smile. "It's been a long while since anyone's called me 'young lady.' I've enjoyed your company, too. It's not often I get to have tea with such handsome young men. If I can remember anything more about that truck or the driver, I will be certain to call you."

"Mrs. Smith, one more thing, if you don't mind. I would love for my wife to see your beautiful gardens. May we come by sometime? I would call you in advance."

"Young man, it will be my pleasure to meet your wife, and no need to call. I'm always home. I don't go out much anymore. And, Detective DeGarzia, please think about posing for me."

Deeg reddened again and shuffled his feet like a clumsy teenager. "I will. Thanks for talking with us, Mrs. Smith."

Chapter 7

Sam and Hank gathered with the other members of the Cycling Club for their usual Saturday morning ride. Sam asked Hank, "Did you have a chance to interview that lady?"

"Carlotta Smith. Yeah, I did. DeGarzia and I talked with her yesterday. She knew Redfield from the art world and remembered him riding on Via Encantado the day he was killed."

"Did she actually see what happened to him?"

"No. She didn't see anything other than a pickup truck leaving Via Encantado at about the same time Redfield was killed. She said the driver was wearing a baseball cap, but she couldn't remember anything else about him or the truck other than the truck was black. She might be able to remember more over time."

"What about the bike? Did you check it out?"

Hank described his visit to the police impound lot and his discovery of the bent rear tire on the bike. "I suspect he may have been killed by a hit-and-run driver, perhaps that same pickup."

"Wouldn't the entire frame of the bike be damaged if that truck had hit him?" Sam asked.

"Look, you've got to understand this is all supposition on my part. But to answer your question, if Redfield was hit by a car or truck, the driver might not have been going all that fast. Could be he was tapping the bike, not hitting him hard, but kind of pushing him to the edge of the canyon—you know, toying with him."

"I'm not sure I buy that."

"Why not? Redfield may have first been riding on the opposite side of the road from the canyon, and the truck or car pushed him across the road a little at a time to that stretch with no guardrail. Maybe the guy gave him a final bump, a harder one that damaged his rear wheel and knocked him off the bike and into the canyon."

"Why wouldn't he have jumped off the bike before being pushed to the edge?" Sam asked.

"Maybe he felt the guy would run him over if he got off, or maybe he was locked in with his pedal clips and wasn't athletic enough to jump off. Think about it. Someone's bumping you, and you're trying to maintain control of your bike. If you get off or fall off, you have to think the guy is going to run you over. You would have to be quick to jump off your bike and out of the way of a truck under those conditions."

"So you think the guy was toying with him?" Sam asked.

"Yeah, maybe so. It wasn't enough for the pickup to just run him over. He wanted to punish him."

"That makes sense. Like he had some kind of grudge against him, and wanted to scare the shit out of him before ramming him over the edge."

"Sam, you might be onto something. Maybe the killer knew Redfield. Maybe it wasn't a random act. I'll ask DeGarzia to check out anyone who might have had a grudge against him. And if he finds one, we'll see if the guy owns a black pickup truck."

"Here's what we have: a beat-up rear tire on a bike and a sighting of a black pickup truck that may or may not have been involved in Redfield's death. It sounds like we're real close to solving this mystery," Sam said. The sarcasm in his voice was obvious. "After all, you've narrowed it down to a pickup truck. Let me see. There are about twenty-five million pickups in the state of New Mexico, including mine, and half of them are black, like mine. About ninety-nine percent of those drivers wear a baseball cap, as do I. Umm, I can see an arrest is imminent."

"Very funny. Man, you're a riot." Hank pretended he was pissed, but he knew full well that Sam's mocking was justified. "Why am I even telling you any of this? I know I need a lot more evidence before DeGarzia will believe this was murder. I'm going back over to where Redfield was killed to see if I can find anything else."

"Let me go along too, okay? This is starting to get interesting."

"Nah, you'll just be a wise-ass."

"I promise I'll behave."

"Look, Sam, I'm not a cop. I realize I'm way out of my element on this, but the way Redfield died doesn't make any sense. If you throw in the fact that Castillo and Pérez died the same way, in my mind, that's a hell of a coincidence. But if DeGarzia can't find anything that proves my point, I'll drop it."

*****

The two friends cycled to Via Encantado on Sunday afternoon. Hank pointed out Carlotta's house when they rode past. He hoped to see and introduce her to Sam, but she wasn't in her garden. They rode to the end of the road where it dead-ended with the desert.

"So what do you want to do?" Sam asked.

"Let's walk our bikes back from this point," Hank said, and handed him a quart-size plastic baggie.

"What the hell is this for?"

"If you find anything on the road like glass, cigarette butts, anything, candy wrappers, anything, pop it in the bag. You take the right half of the road and I'll take the section nearest to the canyon. Whatever we find, we'll turn over to DeGarzia. I'm hoping to come up with evidence to show that someone killed Redfield. Maybe he left some evidence along the way. We'll go as far as where Redfield went over the cliff."

Sam offered, "You know, since the accident, there have been dozens of cars on this road, so I'm not sure we can find anything that's gonna help us."

"I know. You're probably right," Hank said. "Look, you don't have to do this if you don't want to, but I need to keep digging. Something's not right."

"I don't mind. I'm only giving you my two cents' worth."

Rolling their bikes, the two men walked slowly, looking for debris on the road and the dirt shoulders along the way. Occasionally one would bend over, pick up a piece of glass, a cigarette butt or other refuse, and drop it in his plastic bag. Fifteen minutes later, about one hundred yards from the accident site, Hank bent down to examine something on the road. "Hey, Sam, look at this."

"What is it?"

"Look at this skid mark. It's too narrow to be from a car. It could be from a bike. And look, there's another mark up ahead in the middle of the road." The two men followed a chain of six rubber skid marks until they saw one final mark near the dirt shoulder, headed toward the point where Redfield went over. "If someone was hitting Redfield from behind, pushing him toward the canyon, Redfield's instincts would have kicked in and he would have applied his brakes. That's what I think these could be—skid marks from when he applied the brakes."

"You think the police would be able to match the rubber against the tires on Redfield's bike?" Sam asked.

"Yeah, they should be able to do that. And if they do, it would support my theory that he was driven off the road."

Sam wasn't convinced. "Hank, this all sounds like you're trying to make something from nothing. A bent tire on a bike and some skid marks on a road don't mean a whole lot. If you want to know my opinion, I agree with DeGarzia. I think the guy lost control of his bike."

*****

This first thing Monday morning, Hank appeared in front of DeGarzia's desk. He handed him the two plastic bags of road rubbish he and Sam had collected. "Deeg, I don't know if this will amount to anything, but I went out to Via Encantado with a friend and we collected all this. Maybe your lab can match something that will show if Redfield was murdered."

DeGarzia took the bags and gave them a cursory examination. He set them on his desk, visibly uninterested in their contents. "Yeah, thanks."

"I know you think this is all bullshit, Deeg, and that I'm trying to play detective here, but I'm more convinced than ever that Redfield was murdered. And there's something else we found—skid marks on the road leading to the spot where he went over the cliff."

"And?"

"It looks as though he was applying his brakes but wasn't able to stop or get off the bike. It's possible the pickup that Carlotta Smith saw was the truck that bumped him and eventually pushed him over the cliff."

"You're really into this, Hank," the detective said, shaking his head. "You're not going to drop it, are you?"

"There's something wrong with the way Redfield died. It doesn't make sense to me. I've been cycling for a lot of years, and I understand people are going to have accidents, but this doesn't make sense. Would you please consider one last thing for me? Is it possible someone had an ax to grind against him? Can you try to find out if someone had a grudge? I mean, everyone holds a grudge about something or other. Maybe someone was pissed at him badly enough to want to kill him— a jealous husband or a drug deal gone bad. Is it conceivable he was involved in drugs?"

DeGarzia shifted his large frame in his chair. "There's

absolutely no evidence that drugs played a part in this. The guy was squeaky clean. Listen, I agree a lot of people hold a grudge about something or another. Hell, I do, too. So, yeah, I'll check it out. But this is the last of it, Hank. My plate is full with a lot of other shit. If I don't find anything, will you drop this once and for all?"

Hank hesitated. "Yeah, okay. Deal."

DeGarzia shook his head. "I don't believe you."

"Will you let me know if the lab finds anything of interest in any of the stuff we collected?"

"I'll let you know." The detective picked up one of the bags, flipped it around in his hand, and dropped it back down on his desk.

"And will you check the skid marks on the road? They start about a hundred yards from where Redfield went over the cliff. Could you have them checked against his bike?"

DeGarzia didn't answer, but nodded his okay as he wrote down a few notes.

"Oh, one last thing—"

"I knew it. What now?" DeGarzia was clearly irritated by Hank's persistence. "Look, I really got a lot of stuff going on."

"Yeah, I know, Deeg, but have you given any more thought to the coincidence of three cycling deaths in a matter of six weeks?"

DeGarzia cocked his head and said, "Yeah, I have. I'm still looking into it." Hank was unconvinced by his response.

Chapter 8

That Saturday, Hank suggested to his wife that they take a drive to Carlotta Smith's house. "She's the one I told you about with the huge gardens full of daylilies."

Connie was a good gardener in her own right. "Sounds good. I'd love to. Do we need to call and tell her we're coming?"

"No, there's no need. She said we could stop by any time. She hardly ever leaves her house. Let's get a babysitter and go to dinner afterwards."

*****

Hank pulled his car into Carlotta's driveway. "I'll knock on the door to let her know we're here. I'm hoping she'll invite us in for some tea. Her house is like a Southwest art museum. And she's a good artist in her own right."

He knocked several times, but Carlotta did not come to the door. He rang the doorbell, waited, and rang again. He turned to face Connie and shrugged his shoulders before knocking one more time. "I don't think Carlotta's here," he said.

"Too bad. Maybe she's out of town. See her papers near that tree?" Connie pointed to a small pile of newspapers accumulated under a mesquite tree at the side of the driveway.

"I'm going to talk with her about stopping newspaper deliveries when she goes out of town," Hank said. "That's like an engraved invitation to a burglar to come in and help himself. I'm disappointed she's not here, but, what do you think of the gardens?"

"They're beautiful. Look at that one," she said, pointing to a lavender-colored lily. "And that pale pink one. My goodness, they're beautiful, aren't they? I'd like to come back when she's here so she can give us a tour."

Connie took close-up photos of several flowers. She was especially taken by a large, red lily with a yellow throat. "Look, this one has a nameplate captioned *Georgia O'Keeffe*."

"Apparently Carlotta and O'Keeffe were the best of friends," Hank said. "She seems to have named the grandest lily for her. She has a painting by O'Keeffe hanging above the fireplace. This lily might well have been the subject of that painting."

Hank and Connie strolled through the gardens for another fifteen minutes until Hank announced, "It looks like it's going to rain. Let's head off to dinner. We'll come back another time when we know she's in."

As they walked toward their car Hank stopped at the edge of the driveway and looked around the yard. He tilted his head as though listening for something.

"What's the matter, Hank?" Connie asked.

"Something's not right. It suddenly hit me. The plants need watering."

"Yeah, so, what do you want to do, water them for her?" she teased. "It's going to rain soon. Maybe that's why she hasn't watered them."

"No, listen. Carlotta's too fastidious about her garden—the same way she is about her house. She wouldn't leave without having someone tend to her flowers. And the newspapers over there. She would have stopped deliveries or have someone pick them up from her yard. I want to check something else." He went to the end of the driveway and looked in Carlotta's mailbox. "The mail hasn't been collected."

"What are you thinking?" Connie asked.

"There might be something wrong with her." Hank walked back to the front door with Connie right behind. He rang the doorbell, but again there was no response. He was concerned. "I wonder if she's okay. You know, she's eighty-five years old and I don't know if anyone ever looks in on her. Maybe she's sick or something." He tried turning the doorknob, but it was locked. "Let's go look around back."

"We could check with the neighbors to see if they know anything," Connie said.

"The nearest neighbor is a quarter mile away. Let's take a quick look. We'll be only a minute to see if she's all right."

The two walked along the side of the house on a gravel pathway lined with more daylilies. Hank peered through the windows to see if he could see anything of Carlotta. He could not.

When they turned the corner, they found the rear kitchen door ajar. "Should we go in?" Connie asked.

Hank didn't answer. He pushed the door open and yelled in, "Mrs. Smith, hello. Mrs. Smith, are you in there?" There was no response.

The two looked at each other, unsure what to do. "Maybe we should call the police."

Again, Hank said nothing. He was hesitant, but walked inside the kitchen, shouting another, "Hello, hello!" with each step.

Connie was concerned. "Hank, do you think we should we be doing this?"

Hank nodded and motioned for her to follow.

Carlotta's small kitchen was like her living room, meticulously clean and tidy, with photos and artwork throughout. There were no dinner dishes or cookware in sight and nothing was askew, although the silverware drawer was wide open. They walked through the kitchen and into the adjacent living room. Hank shouted again, this time much louder. "Mrs. Smith, this is Hank Kincaid from the DA's office. We met a few days ago. The back door was open. Are you okay?"

He stopped in his tracks, stunned at what he found. The Georgia O'Keeffe was missing from its perch above the fireplace.

"What the hell?" Hank pointed to where the painting had been hanging. "The O'Keeffe painting's gone. Something's wrong. I think she's been robbed. Connie, call 9-1-1."

"Maybe she's in the back room."

Hank noticed a cane near the front door. He grabbed it and held it firmly, ready to use it as a weapon if necessary. "Go ahead and call," he repeated.

Connie fished for her cell phone in her purse and made the call to 9-1-1. "Let's wait for them outside." She was getting nervous. "The operator said she would dispatch the police but that I should keep the phone open. Hank, she said we should leave the house and wait for the police outside."

"You go outside to the street and wait. I want to check the rest of the house."

Connie knew it was no use to try to stop her husband. "I'm going with you," she said. "But, please, Hank, let's be careful."

Without saying a word, they walked down a dimly lit hallway. Hank held the cane aloft, ready to use it against any intruder they might encounter. He hailed Carlotta again and paused to listen for a response.

There was none.

"There could be a perfectly logical explanation," Connie whispered. She tugged on Hank's sleeve. "Come on, let's leave. We shouldn't be doing this."

Hank stood at a closed door. "This is probably her bedroom." He listened for any sound from within, but heard nothing. He knocked loudly. "Mrs. Smith, are you okay? It's Hank Kincaid from the DA's office."

Again there was no answer.

Hank expected the worst. The door squeaked harshly when he pushed it open. Connie was startled at the sudden sound. Hank stepped in and looked around, but the room was empty.

They walked into a second bedroom Carlotta had

converted for use as her paint studio. A plastic tarp dotted with drops of errant paint stretched across part of the floor. Neatly arranged cans stuffed with brushes lined a shelf, and a number of paintings in various states of completion stood stacked against the far wall. Her stool sat alongside an easel that held an unfinished painting. Carlotta was not there, either.

Hank noticed the door to the hall bathroom was open a crack.

"Mrs. Smith, are you in there?" When he tried to enter, the door bumped up against something and wouldn't budge. He tried to peer in, but was unable to open the door wide enough to see what was blocking the entrance. "Damn. Something's in the way."

"What is it?"

"I think it's her. I need to get in there," he said, and nudged the door open wide enough to look in. He was relieved when he saw it wasn't Carlotta that was blocking the door. "It's not her. It's a rug that got bunched up when we tried to open the door."

Connie let out a deep sigh. "Thank God. I thought for sure it was her."

Hank reached around the bathroom door and was able to push the rug aside so they could enter. The bathroom showed signs of a struggle. The shower curtain was pulled partially off and a framed, autographed photo of Carlotta with Georgia O'Keeffe hung askew.

"Look, there's a kitchen knife in the bathtub," Connie said.

"That's not good. Maybe she had to use it to defend herself against whoever was in the house."

"What could have happened to her? Where could she be?"

Hank shrugged his shoulders. "Let's check the garage. That's the only place we haven't checked."

They walked back to the living room. Hank glanced at

where the O'Keeffe had been hanging a few days earlier and shook his head. "Gone. What a shame."

A door on the far side of the house led to a one-car garage. Hank opened it and flicked on the light. It was as immaculately maintained as the rest of the house. The floor of the garage was covered with indoor-outdoor carpeting, and an assortment of boxes and garden tools lined the wall shelves in an orderly manner. Carlotta's car was there. They walked around the car and looked inside to make sure she was not in it. "We'd better get outside and wait for the police," Hank said.

He opened the garage door just as a black and white cruiser was pulling into the driveway. Hank identified himself to the cop and explained their concerns. The cop told Hank and Connie to wait outside, and then went into the house through the garage.

Hank pulled his cell phone from his pocket and dialed DeGarzia. "Deeg, I'm at Carlotta Smith's house with my wife. Carlotta's missing and it appears her house has been burgled. We called 9-1-1. A cop just got here. I can't be certain, but this all may have gone down several days ago. I'm thinking it might somehow be linked to the Redfield death."

"Shit. Okay, stick around till I get there."

Chapter 9

Within five minutes of Hank's call to DeGarzia, another police car arrived at the scene, its lights flashing and siren whining. Fifteen minutes later DeGarzia arrived. He was in ill humor. He had been enjoying a quiet Saturday afternoon at home watching a baseball game on TV when Hank called. He skipped formalities and asked, "Where is she?"

Both Hank and Connie shook their heads. "Don't know. Deeg, this is my wife, Connie."

Deeg nodded in her direction but otherwise did not acknowledge her. "So, what's going on, Hank? What were you doing here?"

"I was showing Connie the gardens. Remember Carlotta said, 'Come over any time. You don't need to call. I'm always here.' Well, we came over unannounced. I rang the doorbell several times, but she never answered." Hank pointed to the mesquite tree and continued, "Connie noticed the newspapers piled up near that tree, so we walked around to the back and found the kitchen door partially open. We called for her, but didn't get an answer. I decided to go in to see what the matter was. We thought maybe she had fallen or was sick or ... or dead."

DeGarzia's silence was Hank's sign to continue. "We went through the entire house. We couldn't find her. When we got into the bathroom, we found a kitchen knife in the bathtub, and thought she might have been hiding from someone and was going to use the knife to defend herself. It was obvious there had been a struggle. Remember the Georgia O'Keeffe painting over the fireplace? Well, it's gone."

"Are you sure?"

"Of course I'm sure."

DeGarzia countered. "Okay, come inside with me while I check out the house."

He ordered one of the two cops on the scene to keep onlookers offsite while they investigated. The sirens had alerted the neighbors, and some of them wandered to Carlotta's house to see what was going on. DeGarzia asked the second cop to check around the outside of the house for evidence. "Bag anything you find—anything. You've got to hustle. It looks like it's going to pour, so put on your rain gear."

The overcast sky was getting darker in advance of the storm that threatened. Santa Fe was in dire need of rain, but any that fell could erase potential evidence located outside the home. Speed was of the essence.

Hank spoke briefly with Connie. "Why don't you go ahead and get something to eat? I may be here a while. I'll ask Detective DeGarzia to drive me home."

"No. If you don't mind, Hank, I'd like to stick around. I'll wait in the car so I don't get in anyone's way." She felt droplets on her arms. "It's starting to rain now," she said, and got in the car to wait for Hank.

The first drops of rain forced the neighbors to scatter back to their homes.

Deeg and Hank entered Carlotta's house through the kitchen. Suddenly, the rain came down hard. It pounded the tile roof of the adobe-style house. Deeg shook his head. "Shit. It's raining like hell. That'll take care of any evidence outside."

The two men walked through the house, retracing Hank and Connie's earlier steps, and ended in the garage. "Wait a second. What's this?" DeGarzia was looking at something on the floor. He removed a small plastic bag from his pocket and took out a pair of tweezers. He got down to one knee and picked up something that had been ground into the carpeting. "A spent match. Do you suppose she smoked?"

"I doubt it. There's no sign of it in the house. No ashtrays, nothing like that," Hank answered. "But I guess it's possible she only smoked outside."

"Look at this. You can see the match actually singed the carpet a bit. That doesn't seem like something she would let happen." DeGarzia took a yellow evidence tent card from his jacket pocket and placed it over the match burn for a later forensic review.

Hank followed the detective back to the kitchen. Deeg opened the back door and asked the cop outside if he had found anything. It was still pouring.

"Yeah, a cigarette butt. But it got rained on pretty good." The cop pointed in the direction of his find. "I marked where I found it over there. The butt's been bagged, but it's sopping wet."

"Anything else? Anything at all? Footprints?"

"No, sir. I doubt there'll be any footprints left with this rain, but I'll keep looking. Hey, Detective, what do we have? Is the lady dead or something?"

"We don't know if she's alive or dead. We don't know where she is."

DeGarzia and Hank walked back into the garage. They stood at the opened garage door and watched the rain pour down. Hank asked, "What do you think? Do you think this ties into the Redfield case?"

"You're still trying to make a point that Redfield was murdered, aren't you?" DeGarzia remained irritated at Hank's insistence on the matter.

"Yeah, I am," Hank shot back, equally annoyed at DeGarzia's attitude toward him.

"You're jumping to conclusions. Look, there have been some burglaries out this way over the past few months—not on Via Encantado, but they've occurred in this section of town.

Could be the same guys. Maybe Smith's notoriety made her an easy mark. A bad guy finds out about an old lady living alone, her house is in the middle of nowhere, so it's ripe for the taking."

"Well, if it was a burglary, Detective, they had to know something about art," Hank said. "For them to take the Georgia O'Keeffe painting, those guys knew what they were doing—that painting was worth a few bucks. And it doesn't look like anything else is missing."

"How do you know that?" DeGarzia asked. "The only way we can find that out is by checking to see what Smith's relatives say. Chances are she has a will scheduling her valuables. We'll check with the neighbors, too, to see if they know anything. "

"I'm telling you, I have a bad feeling about this. Right now, we should be trying to find out what happened to her. Where is she? Did someone take her? And if they did, why?"

Deeg's irritation boiled over. "I don't know what's happened to her. I don't know if it's related to Redfield's death. I don't know shit about what's going on here, and there's nothing more we can do right now. I'll keep a cop at the curb. I'll have forensics dust for prints and search for more evidence. We'll check the cigarette butt for DNA. But we can't do anything else. We can look for her in the morning, or maybe she'll show up. As for you, why don't you drop the detective thing? Why don't you take your wife out to a nice dinner and let me do my job? I'll let you know in the morning what we come up with."

Hank stiffened. "You know, you're pissing me off. From the beginning, you've talked down to me about Redfield's death, and now you're doing the same with Carlotta. You can go fuck yourself."

Deeg was taken aback by Hank's anger. He didn't respond. Hank moved to walk out the garage, but Deeg stopped him. "Wait. Listen, you're right. I've been a pain in the ass. I'm letting other stuff get to me."

Hank turned back to face the detective. "Look, Deeg, I respect you. I'm not trying to intrude on your investigation. I'm just trying to find out what the hell is going on."

DeGarzia extended his hand in apology. "Let's start over, okay?"

Hank nodded and shook Deeg's hand. "Deal," he said, and dashed to his car through the rain.

*****

The next morning Hank's cell phone rang. "Hank, this is Deeg. I'm at Carlotta Smith's house. We found her."

Chapter 10

Prominent Local Artist Carlotta Smith Found Dead in Breeze Canyon: Carlotta Smith, 85, was a long-time resident of Santa Fe. She was a friend and protégée of the late Georgia O'Keeffe, and a highly regarded artist in her own right. Police continue to investigate, and consider her death a homicide. Police are asking that anyone with information about Smith's death to call the Santa Fe Police Department at 505-222-9999. The Santa Fe Citizens Neighborhood Watch Organization is offering a $1,000 reward to anyone with information leading to the arrest and conviction of the individual or individuals involved in Smith's death. Funeral arrangements are pending.

Hank had feared the worst. "Where did you find her?"

"In the canyon behind her house. I'm here now. I'll fill you in when you get here." Deeg hung up before Hank could respond.

Hank headed out to Via Encantado. He parked behind a police car with its lights still flashing. An ambulance passed heading to the end of the road. Hank ducked under the yellow police tape, but was stopped by a cop who was standing guard at Carlotta Smith's front walkway. Hank showed his ID and explained that DeGarzia had called for him. The cop let him pass by.

In his usual terse style, DeGarzia briefed Hank. "This is what we have. This morning I had a couple of cops search to the end of the road and into the desert to see if they could find her. They didn't turn up anything. But one of the cops thought to hike down into the canyon. That's where he found her body—behind the house, but hidden from view. The medical examiner's down there now, said she was probably killed three or four days ago."

"Killed?"

"Yes. Her neck was broken. The ME thinks it was broken before she fell into the canyon."

Hank and Deeg walked to the edge of the canyon behind the house and peered over. Hank saw several officers close to the canyon wall looking for evidence. "The neighbors know anything?"

"One of the neighbors said she was walking her dog a few nights ago at about ten o'clock when she saw a car pull away from the curb in front of Smith's house. It was leaving, driving toward her. At the same time, a pickup passed her headed in the opposite direction, driving toward the house. She said the two vehicles drove past her at the same time, and they both had their high beams on so she looked away."

"Was she able to describe them at all?"

Deeg paused. "She said she saw enough of the pickup to know it was a dark color, maybe black, and it had a tool box in the bed."

"Damn it! The same damned type of truck Carlotta said she saw the day of Redfield's death. What about the other car?"

"A dark-colored sedan. She couldn't describe either car or their drivers in any detail. But she noticed that when the pickup got to the end of the road, it turned around and headed back toward Smith's house, and that it stopped and turned off its headlights before it got to the house."

"Anything else?"

"No. Other than that, no one noticed anything unusual at the house the past few days. It appears none of them liked the old lady very much. Said Carlotta was unfriendly and kept to herself, so no one even noticed she was missing."

The two men walked back into the house through the kitchen. "Deeg, what are you thinking?"

"Have to admit it looks like you were right all along. It could have been the same truck. The killer might have thought she was the only person who could identify him, so he kills her, throws her over the cliff, and steals the O'Keeffe painting for his troubles." He paused and looked directly at Hank. "There's one more thing I haven't told you."

"What's that?"

"The killer left a calling card. When I hiked down to see her at the bottom of the canyon, it became obvious that Smith's murder is tied to the Redfield killing. At this point, I'm not exactly sure how, but I think you'll agree they're related."

"Why? What did you find?"

"The killer put a bike helmet on her head before throwing her body into the canyon."

Chapter 11

Carlotta Smith's lawyer came forward after news of her death was first reported in the local news. As executor of her will, he stated that, to the best of his knowledge, she had no known relatives. Her considerable estate, which included her jewelry, car, artwork, proceeds from the sale of her home, and a large life insurance policy was to be left to the Taos Indian Pueblo, a tribe of American Indians for whom she had special affection. It was on their land that she did most of her landscape painting, and it was there that she had first met Georgia O'Keeffe.

Hank felt a nagging guilt over Carlotta's death. "Do you think she was killed because of the attention we were giving her?" he asked DeGarzia.

"Hard to say. My guess is that whoever killed Redfield saw Smith working in her yard as he sped away after the act. Most likely he considered her unfinished business and didn't want to take any chances that she could identify him."

*****

Funeral services for Carlotta were held at the Santa Fe Baptist Church. Given her age and reputation as a curmudgeon who did not suffer fools lightly, the only people in attendance were a few elderly church friends and members from her daylily club, and several others from the art community in Santa Fe.

Hank and Deeg attended the service. Afterwards, without identifying themselves, they engaged some of the mourners in conversation in hopes of determining if anyone had a particular interest in the manner of her death or a closer knowledge than otherwise should have been evident. The detail that the killer had put a bicycle helmet on Carlotta's head before throwing her over the cliff was a confidential and sealed fact of the case, a fact known only to DeGarzia, the investigating police officers from the crime scene, the medical examiner, the District Attorney, and Hank. That could become the most critical piece of information about the crime and help cement any case against the killer.

*****

The day after Carlotta's funeral, Deeg asked to meet with Hank and District Attorney Snider at the DA's office.

Snider pointed to the two chairs in front of his desk. "Have a seat, gentlemen. How did it go at the funeral? Anything raise your suspicions?"

Hank answered for both of them. "No. It was sad, actually. Very few people there—maybe twenty or so. Mostly old folks, and it hardly appeared any of them could have been involved in her murder. We chatted up a few, but no one gave any indication of knowing more than what's already been put out."

Deeg nodded in agreement.

"So where are we on this? We know Smith was murdered, but what about the cyclists? Do we have a serial cyclist killer on our hands, or were their deaths coincidental accidents?"

Hank looked to Deeg. "There's that word again, *coincidence*. I don't believe these are coincidental deaths."

"Mr. Snider, I understand how Hank feels about this and, yes, it's possible the cyclists could have all been killed by one person, but I'm still not convinced. There's nothing that links all three to Smith."

"What about the fact they were all members of the Cycling Club, Deeg?" Hank asked.

Deeg didn't answer him directly. "Look, I think Hank's right that Redfield and Smith's deaths are linked, but we don't have anything on the Castillo and Pérez deaths. Hank disagrees, I know, but I still think they died from biking accidents. I just don't think they're connected with Redfield's murder. We've been checking out the backgrounds of all three. We're trying to find out if there was anyone who might have a grudge against them all, and the only thing we've found of interest has to do with Redfield." Deeg took out his notepad and flipped through the pages. "A year or so after the death of his wife from cancer, he joined the same cycling club Hank belongs to. We understand he was a popular guy, especially with the ladies."

Looking at Hank, DeGarzia continued, "As Hank is aware, there are a number of divorcées and widows in the Club. The fact that a good-looking, successful guy like Redfield was popular among that group is not unexpected. It was rumored among the members he enjoyed the company of two married women—at the same time."

"You mean two married women from the Cycling Club?" Snider asked in point of clarification.

Deeg read from his notes. "Yes. A Stacey Keenan and a Heather Dorell."

Hank reacted with surprise. "You're kidding me. I know them both. Heather Dorell is drop-dead gorgeous, so I can see how he would be attracted to her. But that's surprising about Stacey Keenan. She doesn't seem to be the type. She's not especially attractive. I mean, she's not unattractive, but she's not in the same class as Heather."

"Have you talked to them?" Snider asked.

"Yes. I think it's possible they both could have had a motive to kill Redfield. You know, unrequited love, jealousy, passion, whatever. I talked with them individually this morning, and asked them about the rumors they were having an affair with Redfield. Keenan swore she was not. She said only that she knew him and that they biked together. She said that after their rides, some of the people go to Jimi's Pizzeria, drink a few beers, and have a bite to eat. From there, they go to what she called *after-parties* at someone's house. At first, I couldn't knock her off that story, but I told her that unless she owned up to the affair, I would identify her to the press as a person of interest in Redfield's and Smith's murders. That did it. She broke down and admitted to the affair, but of course, denied having anything to do with Redfield's death."

"What about Heather Dorell?"

"She admitted to the affair right off the bat," Deeg answered, "like it was no big deal. I asked her how her husband would react when he found out about it. She shrugged her shoulders and said she didn't care one way or the other if her husband found out, and that he probably wouldn't care anyway."

"She's a beauty, isn't she? But she's pretty hard," Hank said.

"Yeah, she's hard all right. Nothing seemed to faze her. She and her husband must have a strange marriage."

"Did you tell them you understood Redfield was bedding both of them at the same time?" the DA asked.

"No. I want to spring that on them when I question them further at headquarters."

"You have to consider their husbands as suspects, too," Snider said.

"Yes, sir, I agree. We're looking into the possibility that one of the husbands knew the wife was having an affair and killed Redfield. I told the two I had no choice but to bring their husbands in for questioning. Heather Dorell didn't care, but I thought Mrs. Keenan was going to have a stroke. She said she was scared what her husband might do to her. I mean, she showed genuine fear. But, she made her own bed, sort of speaking, and now she has to lie in it. Her husband is in Chicago on business and won't be back until Friday. I'll question him when he gets back. In the meantime I can interview Jake Dorell, Heather's husband."

"Did Redfield fancy himself a Casanova?" Hank asked. "I'm surprised he had affairs with two women who are polar opposites in looks and personalities. Any word if he was the kind of guy who tried to screw anyone wearing a skirt?"

"No, I don't think he fancied himself a stud," DeGarzia answered. "I can understand the attraction to Heather Dorell. But, you're right. I'm not seeing why he would be interested in Stacey Keenan."

"You never know about some people. Do you know if he had affairs with any women outside the Cycling Club?" Snider asked.

"We're trying to find out if that was the case, and we're also looking to see if he had any issues with people in the art world. Right now, all we can tell is that he only had a history with the two women from the Club," DeGarzia said. "Nothing else has come up."

Chapter 12

Seated in the stark, mirrored interview room at police headquarters, Jake Dorell fumed as DeGarzia advised him of his rights. "I don't need a lawyer because I don't even know why the fuck I'm here."

A carpenter by trade, he was stocky and rugged-looking, with closely cropped red hair. Adding to his scruffiness was a days-old beard. If he smirked or allowed himself an occasional smile, the gap from a missing tooth on the left side of his mouth was visible. His withering stare made him appear on the edge of anger at all times.

"Where were you on the fourteenth?"

"When the hell was the fourteenth?"

"A week ago Sunday."

Dorell had no alibi for the times Michael Redfield or Carlotta Smith were murdered. "I was home watching TV."

"What were you watching?"

"Sports. ESPN. The Dodgers in the afternoon, golf, women's softball, soccer, you name it, I watched it."

"Did you leave the house at all?"

"No. I had a couple beers and dozed off. It was a long week."

"Why? What happened that week?"

"Nothing in particular. Every week is a long week. I work my ass off. I'm a carpenter. You try working in this fucking sun every day."

"So you dozed off. When did you wake up?"

"Shit, I don't know. It was dark."

"How much beer did you drink?"

"I told you, a couple. What the hell difference does it make? What are you, the beer police?" he answered.

"Let me try this again." DeGarzia remained calm, but his

voice held an edge, "How many beers did you have?"

Jake shrugged his shoulders and pulled on his ear. "Maybe a six pack," he said.

"Six or maybe more?"

"Yeah, maybe more."

"Was your wife there when you woke up?"

"Yeah, I think so. Shit. I don't know."

"What do you mean you don't know?"

"She has her life and I have mine. I really don't know if she was there or not. She tells me I snore, so she don't sleep with me. Check with her. She'll tell you."

"I'll do that," DeGarzia said.

"What the hell is this all about? Why am I here?"

"We're investigating the deaths of two people: Michael Redfield and Carlotta Smith. Did you know either of them?"

"Never heard of 'em. Who are they?"

"Redfield was a friend of your wife's, and Smith may have been a witness to his murder."

"So, why am I here?"

Without missing a beat, DeGarzia said, "Did you know your wife was having an affair with Redfield?"

"You shittin' me?"

"No, I'm not."

"You mean, you think I killed those people because she was screwing some guy? Ha!" Jake roared.

"Do you read the newspapers?"

"No."

"You said you watch TV. It's been all over the TV."

"I don't watch the news. I got my own problems and life sucks, so I don't give a shit about who's doing what to who."

"You don't seem upset that your wife was having an affair."

"Trust me, I don't give a shit. It wouldn't be the first time. Me and her go our separate ways, you know what I mean? I can't control who she screws. Have you met her? She's always been a horny bitch. She's got legs that go up to her neck and an ass that won't stop swinging even when she's standing still."

"Where were you on June twenty-fourth?"

"What day was that?"

"Wednesday."

"I was working. Check with my boss. He'll tell you."

"What about that night?"

"No different than the fourteenth. Watching the Dodgers, drinking a couple of beers."

"Was your wife home?"

"I don't know. I don't know what the fuck she does all day. She don't get home until late on Thursdays. Is that when she was screwing that guy, Redman, or whatever the hell his name is, or was?"

"Do you smoke?"

"Yeah."

"Does your wife?"

"Yeah, like a chimney."

"What kind of a car do you drive?"

"A Ford F-150."

"A pickup. What color?"

"Black."

"Do you have an aluminum tool box in your truck?"

"Yeah."

"You have a problem controlling your anger, don't you?"

"No shit, Dick Tracy."

"Tell me about it."

"You already know."

"Humor me."

"I was arrested a few years back because I slugged an asshole at a Home Depot. The guy was pissing me off."

"About what?"

"I don't even remember exactly. He cut some wood for me, and it was the wrong length. He claimed he cut what I asked for, and we went 'round and 'round. So I cold-cocked him. I think the judge believed me, because he gave me a suspended sentence and had me go to some bullshit anger management thing."

"And what about when you hit your wife?"

"That was nothing. Ask her. She'll tell you. I slapped her because she was giving me some shit about somethin' or other, like she always does. So she called the cops on me. She dropped the charges. It was no big deal. Go ahead, ask her."

"So you're not upset that she was having an affair?"

"I ain't exactly thrilled, but, no, I don't really give a shit. I get some ass from her when I want it, so it's no big deal."

"So it sounds like you have a kind of open marriage."

"Yeah, somethin' like that. Whatever the hell that means."

"Let me ask you this. What kind of temper does she have? I mean, would she be capable of killing someone, like, for example, if she was having an affair with this guy and finds out he was having an affair with someone else at the same time?"

"You shittin' me? Is that what happened? Why in the hell would the guy want to screw around with someone else? She'd give him all he could handle."

"Would she be upset enough about it to, say, take her anger out on the guy?"

Dorell thought about it for a second, alternately shaking, then nodding, his head. "Nah, shit, I don't know. Yeah, maybe, but with her temper and that ass of hers, you don't think she's some kind of nun, do you? She could have any man she wants, anytime, anyplace, but God bless the man who ends up with her, because she's one royal pain in the ass."

"So you think she could kill someone for that reason?"

"Yeah, I guess so. We all got a break point, don't we?"

"Will you give us a sample of your DNA?"

"You already got it from my prior. But, yeah. Shit, I don't care. Take some more. I ain't done nothin'."

DeGarzia told Dorell he was free to go after obtaining a mouth swab for testing. "But don't leave Santa Fe."

"So I'm still a suspect?"

"Let's just say I don't want you to leave the city without my permission."

Chapter 13

Heather Dorell was exactly as her husband described. She was nearly six feet tall, with long, flaming-red hair and a voluptuous body worthy of immediate entry into the Playboy Mansion. Her high cheekbones, beautiful green eyes, and full lips made her the envy of many women. But she was also coarse, profane, and inarticulate.

"Where were you on the fourteenth?"

Heather rolled her eyes toward the ceiling and squinched her mouth. She thought for a moment, counting the days with her fingers as she worked them backward in her head. "I was home."

"Your husband doesn't remember you being home."

"Probably 'cause he was hitting the sauce again. I was home. Can I prove it? No, but that's where I was," she uttered through a cigarette-strained voice. "Where the hell else would I be?"

"Do you remember if your husband was home?"

"Yeah, he was. I don't remember for sure, but I think he was watching a baseball game. That's all he does most times. I went to bed early and didn't see him until the next morning when he was on his way to work. We sleep in separate bedrooms because he snores like a walrus in heat."

"Did he say anything to you?"

"You mean like 'good morning' or somethin'? He didn't say nothin'. Most times, we don't talk to each other. But I don't really give a flying fig if he never says nothin' to me, ever."

"Did he seem out of sorts?"

"Out of sorts? Nothing different than what he's always like. We've been married for eighteen years, since I was sixteen years old and he was nineteen. He's the same today as he was back then. Only I didn't know it back then. Otherwise, I wouldn't never have married the ignorant asshole."

"You both have such mutual respect for each other," DeGarzia said.

"If mutual means, like, *none*, then we got mutual respect," Heather laughed at her attempt at humor.

DeGarzia smiled. "How long were you having an affair with Michael Redfield?"

Heather squirmed a bit in her chair. Her reaction was not lost on DeGarzia. "I don't know exactly. Like maybe three, four months."

"How did you meet him?"

"At my Cycling Club last year. But I stopped riding over the winter and didn't see him again until this spring."

"Did you have any contact with him during the winter?"

"No. Everyone kind of hibernates in the winter. At least I do. When it starts getting a little warm, we all get together again."

"After you started riding again this spring, how did you hook up with Redfield? Was it at one of the after-parties you all go to after Jimi's Pizzeria?"

"Yeah, it was kinda building to that. Michael was a sweet guy, real polite, a gentleman, I guess you could say. I never really met a gentleman before. Did you know that *gentleman* means a *gentle man*?" Her eyes flashed astonishment at that knowledge. "Shit, I didn't know that's what it meant until I met Michael. That's what he was. A real gentleman. So sweet. One thing led to another, and we ... connected, you know what I mean?"

"What happened? Why did your relationship end?"

"Can't say." She shrugged and spoke with indifference. "Don't know. It just ... did."

"Would you be surprised if I told you Stacey Keenan was having an affair with Michael Redfield at the same time as you?"

"No way. You have got to be kidding me!"

DeGarzia thought she was overreacting. "You knew, didn't you?"

"I did not. Why, that little bitch. And she's supposed to be my best friend."

"She was having sexual relations with him during the same time period as you."

"No shit. Hey, can I smoke in here?"

"No. There's no smoking allowed in this building."

"Please. Just one." She spoke in a soft voice, hoping her charms would work on DeGarzia.

"No!"

Heather pursed her lips and sank back in her chair.

"So you're telling me you were not aware Redfield was having an affair with Stacey Keenan?"

"I already said I didn't know. How many times do I have to tell you? I don't even believe you."

"Believe it. It's true." DeGarzia eyed Heather. "You said Stacey's your best friend?"

"Yeah, I thought she was. I don't really have nobody else I can say is my friend. I met her when she started to bike. You know what we got in common? We got a couple of asshole husbands who enjoy beating the shit out of us."

"So your husband beats you?"

"He used to hit me, but not anymore."

"What about Stacey? You say her husband hits her?"

With arms folded on the table, Heather leaned in toward DeGarzia as if she were going to tell him a secret. She whispered, "Yeah, from what she tells me, he knocks her around all the time, the poor girl. But she don't do nothin' to stop him. Says he's always spoutin' off about what she should or should not be doin'." Heather raised her voice. "What an asshole. And when she doesn't do exactly like he wants, he hits her."

DeGarzia shook his head in sympathy. His mind took a momentary leap to his childhood and the beatings he used to receive from his father. "Why don't you and your friend leave your husbands if they're abusive? You know there are agencies that could help you, shelters that could house you."

"I ain't goin' no place. I ain't got a job. I left school when I was in the tenth grade. Jake makes a good living, and he lets me alone most times. I got a roof over my head. I got everything I need. I get pissed at him sometimes, but what woman don't get pissed at her husband? And he gets pissed at me, but I can take it. Now, Michael, he told me I shouldn't have to put up with my husband's shit like that anymore. So I told Jake, 'Don't never hit me again.' I told him if he ever did, I'd cut off his balls when he was sleeping. I told him that, and he ain't touched me since, 'cause he knows I would."

"Did Stacey go with you to the after-parties?"

"Not at first. She used to be a squirrely girl who never went nowhere. I had to talk her into going out to get pizza at Jimi's with the gang from the Club. I kinda felt sorry for her 'cause she started to tell me about her husband and what he was doing to her, and I told her mine tried to do the same thing. So we got to be friends."

"So you got her to go to the parties?"

"Yeah, after a while I did, but she never stayed too long. She always had to get home so she could talk to her husband. Nine o'clock. He travels a lot, so he calls her at nine o'clock every freakin' night, and like a bunch more times during the day. She was always scared shitless that he would call and she wouldn't be home. And that would be a reason for him to beat her when he got home."

"How would she have been able to hook up with Redfield if

her husband had her on such a tight leash?"

"I don't know. I didn't even know she was having an affair with Michael. If you say she did, then she did. But she never talked about him like she was having an affair with him. She would tell me she liked him. That he was a gentleman. I never would have guessed she was screwin' him. What a scuzzbag he turned out to be."

"Did you ever tell Stacey you were having an affair with him?"

"No. Never thought no one had to know, not even her."

"So you were pretty upset when you found out she was having an affair with him too?"

"I didn't know she was. You just told me. That's the first I heard. Stacey didn't tell me. Stop trying to put words in my mouth. I did not know! Get it?" Heather thrust her head back, looked at the ceiling, and spit out a loud, "Ha, ha. Why, that little bitch. I'm floored. I mean, little Miss Goody Two Shoes. She's always acting sweet and innocent-like. Hell, she ain't no different than me. I can't wait to see her again to tell her."

"Would she have been capable of killing Michael Redfield?"

"I wouldn't have ever said yes, but now I have to say I guess anything's possible."

"And what about you?"

"What about me?"

"Did you kill him?"

"Are you shittin' me? Why would I do that? I liked him. I even thought maybe me and him could hook up, you know? I mean, maybe I coulda left my jerk-off husband. I woulda done it, too, if Michael woulda asked me. I cried for days when I heard he was killed. I still miss him. He was the nicest man ever."

"Did you kill Carlotta Smith on the night of the twenty-fourth?"

"What? Who?" Heather sat back in her chair. "Oh, I know who you mean. I seen her in the news on TV. Hell, no. I didn't kill her. Why would I do that?"

"Because she witnessed you killing Michael Redfield."

"Bullshit. You're pissin' me off about killing Michael. First off, I didn't kill him, and second, since I didn't kill him, why would I kill her? Don't make no sense, does it?"

"Do you think your husband could have killed Redfield because you were having an affair with him?"

"Yeah, I guess, but I don't think so. You don't understand. He couldn't give a shit about me bein' with another guy. He does the same thing. He screws around too."

"Do you know if Redfield had affairs with other women from the Club besides Stacey?"

"Nope."

"Nope, you don't know, or nope, he didn't?"

"I don't know. I never asked him. But if he did, so what? I didn't own him. He did what he wanted to do. And I wouldn't care what he did. None of my business."

"What kind of car do you drive?"

"A Chevy Malibu."

"Your husband says he owns a Ford pickup. Ever drive it?"

"Yeah, if my car's on the fritz. Why?"

DeGarzia didn't answer. He ended the interview with the same request for a DNA sample that he had made of Jake Dorell, and also gave the same admonishment, "Don't leave Santa Fe, Mrs. Dorell. We'll want to talk with you again."

Chapter 14

Plain was the only way to describe Stacey Keenan. She was not extraordinary in any way—not by her looks, not by her brown hair worn in bangs, not by the way she dressed. Other than a touch of lipstick, she wore little makeup. She came across as prim and proper, painfully shy, and unsure of herself. She was, indeed, the polar opposite of Heather Dorell.

Stacey's interview was filled with tears, anguish, and remorse.

"I've never done that before. I know you don't believe me, but I never have," she said between sobs, her hands folded politely on her lap.

"Mrs. Keenan, I'm not here to judge your morality. I want to know: Did you kill Michael Redfield?"

"No. Of course not." She spoke softly. "Oh, no, I would never kill anyone. Ever since I was a little girl, my parents always preached to me to live a life of righteousness. Live the way of the Bible. And that's what my husband–Clyde–wants me to do, too. And I've tried to do exactly that my whole life. But I slipped. The devil drove me to temptation. Now look at me. You're accusing me of killing a man—a man I loved deeply. I am heartily sorry for my sins and for offending God, but I did not kill Michael."

"What about Carlotta Smith? Did you kill her too, to cover up your murder of Michael Redfield?"

"I don't know who you're talking about. I didn't kill anyone. I would never have thought of killing Michael. I loved him. And he loved me."

"How long had your affair with him been going on?"

"It was only a couple of months."

"How did it start?"

Stacey could not stop crying. DeGarzia slid a box of tissues across the table to her. Her efforts to compose herself were fruitless; she wept through all of her answers. "Clyde was out of town on business again. We don't have any children, so I thought I'd join the Cycling Club to get out to meet people and to fill my time."

"Is that where you met Heather Dorell?"

"Yes. I met Heather there, and she's my best friend now."

DeGarzia was patient through all of Stacey's ramblings. "Clyde wasn't happy to know I wanted to join the Club, but he finally gave his permission. To be honest, I was surprised he did. He wants me to stay in the house to cook, and clean, and live a life of purity. He always says God is pure, and God wants us to be pure in his image."

Deeg couldn't help but feel sorry for her. Her husband had sucked the life out of her, and she anguished over her infidelity. "Mrs. Keenan—Stacey—what happened between you and Michael Redfield? How did your affair start?"

"Michael and I got to talking one night after we all went to Jimi's, the pizzeria. And then we talked another time, and another, and the next thing I knew he was knocking at my door one night. It was right after I talked to my husband. Clyde always calls me when he's away, and always at the same times."

"I understand you always have to be home in time to answer his nine o'clock call."

"Yes. Every night, exactly at nine, Clyde calls to make sure I'm okay."

"You mean he calls to keep tabs on you?"

Stacey squirmed in her chair. "Yes, that too, I guess."

"Getting back to Michael Redfield. After you got to know him at the—I believe you call them after-parties—you're telling me you began your affair with him the night he knocked on your door?"

"Yes. At first I had no idea he was interested in me. He was such a handsome man, so nice and charming. I thought he was attracted to Heather, and I understood why. She's really beautiful. So I was surprised when he came to my house. He knew Clyde was away. It was my fault. I shouldn't have told him that, but I didn't care."

"So you think you led him on?"

"Yes, sir, maybe I did. I told Michael all about Clyde and the way he treated me, and he felt sorry for me. Detective, please don't tell my husband about this. Please. He'll kill me."

DeGarzia didn't answer. "Were you aware that Redfield was having an affair with Heather at the same time as his affair with you?"

Stacey was stunned, catatonic. Her expression froze and she didn't move. She stared at DeGarzia with her eyes opened wide in shock. "No. Oh my God! No! He couldn't have. I didn't know," she cried. "Oh, what a fool I've been. What a fool I am. I loved him so. Are you sure? Are you sure?"

"Yes, I'm sure."

"Oh no. Oh no. What have I done? Clyde will kill me."

"What did you do when you found out Michael Redfield was seeing Heather too?"

"I didn't know until now."

"Are you sure? I understand you knew." DeGarzia was lying.

"I did not. I am so naïve. I could tell Michael liked her, but I had no idea. And she's my best friend."

"Stacey, do you smoke?"

"No. I never have."

"Does your husband smoke?"

"God forbid, he would never touch a cigarette. Why are you asking?"

DeGarzia didn't answer. "I want you to understand, I do not

want you to leave Santa Fe without my express consent. Is that clear?"

"Yes, but, what about my husband?"

"I will need to talk with him when he returns from his business trip."

"What should I do? What do I tell him?"

"Stacey, that's between you and Clyde."

"He said if he ever found out I was with another man, he would kill me. What should I do? I'm frightened of what he'll do."

"You can get a restraining order."

"No, I don't want to do that. I don't know what to do," she wailed. "But it's my punishment and I will have to take it. I deserve it. I deserve it!"

"I will speak with him and warn him in the harshest tones that he is not to hurt you. I'll tell him we'll arrest him if he does. That's as much as I can do."

"Detective DeGarzia, please don't do that. It will only make matters worse."

"Listen, Stacey. I know about abuse, how difficult it is to escape from it. I've discussed it with Heather as well. You are both in abusive marriages. You don't need to be. Women who are abused feel entrapped. They say they have nowhere to go, can't make a living, the husband didn't mean to hurt them, whatever. But you know something? None of that is true. There are people who can help you get through the anguish and confusion of abuse. Maybe Michael Redfield made you happy. You have to understand that you can be happy again, but you need help. Don't let Clyde hurt you, no matter what you've done. You can survive without him. I want you to call me personally if your husband tries to hurt you," DeGarzia said. He pulled a card from his pocket. "My cell phone number is on this card."

She took the card and studied it for a second before tucking it into her pocket.

Chapter 15

Stacey first met Clyde Keenan while waiting for the Central Avenue bus to take her to the hole-in-the-wall souvenir shop where she worked. That particular morning, Clyde was on his way to a business meeting and was waiting for the same bus. He was a slight man, with pale skin and a deeply receding hairline. His wire-framed glasses etched a permanent line on the bridge of his nose.

Stacey smiled politely at him, which Clyde took as a sign to start a conversation. He spoke about the weather, and she nodded vacantly as he went on about the rain clouds that were forming. People at the bus stop were always talking about the weather. She didn't care one way or the other. Her day in the souvenir shop would be the same boring routine no matter what the weather.

On board the bus, Clyde asked permission to sit next to her. Stacey was sorry she had been so courteous to him at the bus stop, but nodded and gave an insincere smile to mask the fact that she much preferred he sit elsewhere. She looked straight ahead as he continued his discourse about the weather. He asked her what she did and where she worked. If he detected any sign of disinterest on her part by her simple nods and unembellished responses, he gave no indication.

When she stood to get off at her stop, Clyde said, "It was nice talking with you." She gave one final nod and stepped off the bus. As it pulled away, she glanced up at the window where she had been sitting and saw him wave to her. She quickly looked away.

That same afternoon, as Stacey was preparing to close the souvenir store for the day, she was surprised to see Clyde walk in. He smiled at her and explained, "I hope I'm not being too forward, but I was in the neighborhood and thought I'd ask you out to dinner."

Stacey didn't know what to say to put this man off. "Oh, ah, well, I won't be able to. I have to close up."

Clyde persisted. "I can wait for you."

"Are you sure?"

"Why, yes."

"Oh. When?"

"When what?"

"When did you want to have dinner?"

"As soon as you close up," he answered, "unless, of course, you have another appointment."

Although she had no interest in this man she had met only hours before, Stacey fumbled for words before stammering her stunned acceptance. "No. I'm, ah, okay. I mean, okay." She immediately regretted her decision.

"Good. There's a nice restaurant only a block away. I've eaten there before. Okay with you?"

"Yes, that would be fine." She fumbled with her key to lock the shop, wondering what she was getting herself into.

Stacey did not know what to make of Clyde. She was thirty-two years old—an old maid in her family's eyes—and under pressure to get married. Clyde appeared to be much older, given the grey at his temples and small wrinkles around his eyes. "You're not married are you?" she asked self-consciously.

Clyde laughed. "No, I'm not married. Never have been," he said, flashing his ringless left hand at her. I was close once, but it turns out the girl was not who I thought she was. I am a religious person who lives by the tenets of the Bible. She was not. What about you?"

"I'm Catholic," Stacey said, thinking that answered his question. He laughed again. "And, no, I'm not married either."

At dinner, Stacey listened as Clyde talked about himself, his job, his travels, and his religious beliefs. Even though she found him worldly, he was equally egoistic and boring, qualities she found utterly unappealing.

In the weeks that followed, Clyde asked Stacey out whenever he was home from his business travels. At first, she turned him down with a number of different excuses. But he was relentless and she too spineless to come straight out and say she was not interested in him. He showered her with flowers, small gifts, and boxes of chocolates wrapped in gold foil paper. Unaccustomed to such attention, she finally agreed to see him again.

One Saturday evening, six months to the day after they first met, Clyde proposed to Stacey at the same restaurant where they had their first date. He didn't get down on bended knee or ask her to marry him. Rather, he announced to her that he would marry her. "I will be proud to make you my wife," he told her, "to nurture you, to live our lives under God's dictates, and to provide for you so you will want for nothing."

Stacey anticipated Clyde was going to propose marriage, given that he was constantly quoting Bible passages on the relationship between husband and wife. She rationalized. *I'm thirty-two years old. I may never have another chance to get married. Is he really that bad?* She wanted to marry before it was too late to have children. And, while she did not feel thunderclaps of emotion toward him, his unremitting attention overwhelmed her, and she reasoned that love would grow through marriage.

In spite of her misgivings and apprehension, Stacey accepted Clyde's proposal. "Okay, I will marry you," was all she could say.

"Good," he said.

Neither showed emotion or happiness at what should have been a joyous occasion.

*****

They settled into his small, two-story house in Santa Fe. Clyde insisted Stacey quit her job. "You don't need to work. I will provide for you. You stay home and tend to the house. Become my wife in the manner in which the good Lord intended of women, for the parables recite, 'wives must submit to their husbands in all things.'"

She did not argue with his interpretation of the Bible. She was married, and she intended to be the best possible wife she could be, if that was what he wanted. She would devote her life to fulfilling his needs and, when he was ready, they would have the children she so desperately wanted. In the meantime, she would sacrifice for him. After all, he was providing her with a comfortable home and an allowance for food and household needs.

Stacey was a virgin when they married, and apprehensive about sex. How should she act? What was she supposed to do? Clyde would have to show her. He would be her teacher.

She vastly overestimated his bedroom skills. Awkward and seemingly devoid of any ability to show passion or tenderness, Clyde was concerned only for his own gratification. From the first night of their marriage, intimacy proved to be unapologetically painful and robotic for Stacey. After climaxing, Clyde invariably fell asleep while still on top of her, and he stayed that way until she struggled to roll him off.

She hated sex.

And she began to hate him.

Her life evolved into one of constant attention to Clyde's needs. He rebuked her when she was slow to satisfy his demands. At first, she accepted the scoldings as constructive criticisms. However, in the months that followed, his scoldings turned to anger, and his anger to rage. Eventually, his rage turned to physical abuse.

Constantly on edge, Stacey's stress diminished only when

Clyde was away from home on business. Even then she had to be available when he phoned her at prearranged times of the day. His anger reached fever pitch if she did not pick up within three rings. He would rant about how she was shirking her duties as his wife.

"But Clyde, I couldn't get to the phone in time."

"Don't give me that. You know what time I call. I do not have time to waste. I want you there to answer when I call. I don't want you gallivanting about someplace or another, or watching that godforsaken TV when I'm doing my duty to check on you to make sure you're safe and well."

Stacey remained obsessed with having children, but each time she brought the subject up, Clyde told her they had to wait. "You'll see I'm right," he said, dismissing her pleas.

In time he declared, "I've decided I do not want children. I told you before we were married that I didn't want any children. You had better make sure you take your birth control pills. Do you understand?"

Stacey was devastated.

"But, Clyde, you only said we should wait. You never said you didn't want any children."

"Well, I'm saying it now. And don't bring it up again. I'm tired of the subject. You've been harping on me since the day we were married. That's it. I'm through talking about it."

"But, Clyde—"

He didn't allow her to finish.

That was the first time he hit her.

Stacey was stunned. He had been so thoughtful to her before they were married, so kind and generous. What had happened to him? Why had she not seen this side of him? Why had she settled for someone like Clyde? Clearly, he was not the husband she had longed for or needed. All she ever wanted was someone to love her. She had been so weak, so naïve, and now she wanted to tell him how she felt, that she didn't love him, that she wanted to leave him, but she couldn't bring herself to talk to him.

She was frightened he would hit her again.

*****

Stacey's bicycle was her only diversion from the monotony and drudgery of her otherwise joyless, loveless life. She searched the Internet to learn more about cycling clubs in Santa Fe, and found information about the Canyon Cycling Club. For weeks, she debated whether she should join. How would Clyde feel? Should she tell him about it before joining? After much internal debate, Stacey summoned the courage to call the Club's membership chairperson who invited her to ride with the D group the following Thursday night. That would give her a chance to gauge her ability level. Although apprehensive, she agreed to go.

She arrived at the Club's meeting place behind the East Santa Fe Middle School dressed in tennis shoes, Bermuda shorts, and a tee shirt. Some fifty other people were already there, chatting with friends and organizing themselves into the various riding groups. Everyone was wearing colorful jerseys, clip-on cycling shoes, spandex shorts, and fingerless riding gloves.

Stacey stood out in her simple summer attire. She had to fight the urge to get back into her car and leave. Heather Dorell was the first to greet Stacey and introduce her to other D riders. The striking redhead was loud, profane, and unrefined, but she was also gregarious, funny, self-assured, and sexy—all the things Stacey was not. "Don't worry about a thing, honey," she said. "You'll be fine. You'll fit right in. Stick with me, and if anyone gives you a hard time, I'll kick the shit out of them," she announced and laughed out loud.

*****

Stacey was bolstered by both her own determination and the pep talk with her new-found friend. When Clyde returned home from his business travels the next night, she told him she had joined the Cycling Club. She was so excited and thought he would be pleased that she had met new people and was out getting exercise. She told him she had met the nicest girl, Heather Dorell, and that they were going to go shopping for cycling clothes together.

Clyde was outraged. "You did what? And you're going to go shopping for what? Without my permission? I didn't say you could do that."

"Clyde, the membership is only ten dollars a year."

He became more incensed. "All you want to do is spend my money. Ten dollars? For what? You can ride by yourself and it won't cost anything."

Uncharacteristically, Stacey stood her ground. She promised she would get a job to pay for her Club dues and cycling clothes. Clyde relented, but followed up with, "Your place is at home, not clerking in some store. Don't you think I can care for you? Is that what you think?"

"No, Clyde, that's not what I think. I do, however, think it would be good for me to get out of the house once in a while and get some exercise. That's all."

"Yeah, right. Go ahead and ride with that Club. But remember, I will have you out of there so fast your head will spin if you don't tend to the house. Understand? I don't like what you're becoming. Be careful you don't go too far. I don't have patience for my wife leading a wayward life. Understand?" he repeated.

"Yes, I promise," she nodded, and tried to give him a hug.

He shook her off. "Just remember what I said."

*****

Heather and Stacey continued to bond during Club rides,

the Thursday after-parties, and occasional lunches together. Although vastly different in looks and personalities, the two became inseparable, and when they shared intimate tales of their torturous marriages and abusive husbands, their kinship grew ever deeper.

Part II

Chapter 16

Michael Redfield lusted for Heather Dorell from the first time he laid eyes on her. He found her so very sexy in her tight spandex shorts and colorful cycling jersey. After the Thursday night rides, he always asked her if she was going to Jimi's Pizzeria, and then made sure he sat next to her in one of the red booths that lined both sides of the restaurant's main dining room. He laughed at her jokes and took advantage of every opportunity he could to brush his leg against hers, touch her bare arm, or softly rub her back.

Heather liked his attention. She was equally charmed and fascinated by Michael, his gentle ways, his intelligence, and knowledge of art. He was darkly handsome, polite, and well spoken—everything Jake was not.

Stacey noticed their mutual attraction and smiled. She told Heather that Michael seemed to like her. "Yeah, I like him too," Heather admitted. "He's a classy guy, really sweet, different from all them other bozos I've ever known."

At one of the Thursday after-parties, Heather excused herself and told Michael she was going out to the porch to have a cigarette. He followed her out. "Mind if I join you? It's getting a little stuffy in there. I could use some fresh air."

"Sure, come on out. I'd love your company."

The Santa Fe evening was moonless. They sat together on the porch swing in the dark. Michael made small talk to still his rapid breathing. "Beautiful night, isn't it? So calm and quiet."

"Yes, it sure is. Beautiful house, too, huh?" Heather turned to look at him, bumping her bare leg against his. "Oh, I'm sorry," she murmured.

"That's okay. I don't mind."

She didn't take it away.

They said nothing more for a few seconds. Heather could hear Michael's shallow breathing and knew.

"You want a cigarette?" she asked. She slowly rubbed her leg against his.

His eyes were drawn to her leg. "No, thanks. I don't smoke. Ever think about quitting?" Michael didn't know what else to say, short of coming right out and asking her to go to bed with him. His courage failed him at the moment—after all, she was married.

"Yeah, but I ain't got the will power. I mean about nothin', if you know what I mean."

"Nothing?"

"Yeah, I know it's bad for me, I mean smokin', but I don't care. I don't have that much to look forward to in my life," she said.

"You don't? Why not?" He casually rested his hand on her knee. Her skin was so soft to the touch. *God, she must certainly hear how fast I'm breathing.*

She put her hand over his and rubbed it softly. "I didn't mean to get heavy on you. It's just that I'm married to a real jerkoff, and I wish I wasn't."

"Lady, if I were your husband I would promise you the sun and the moon. You're a beautiful woman."

"You think?"

"Yes, *very* beautiful." Michael reached over and gently took the cigarette from Heather, flicked it to the ground, and turned back to face her. He looked down the porch to see if anyone else was outside. They were alone. "I would like to kiss you, if that's okay with you," he said.

"What's taken you so long?" Her voice purred and she leaned into his kiss. She moved her hand to his thigh. Their long, tongue-to-tongue kiss tasted like tobacco to him and a breath of spearmint to her.

The door opened. People were starting to head home, but in the dark no one saw the couple on the swing. Heather moved her hand slowly up Michael's thigh. His penis had become erect against his biking shorts. She stroked it gently, causing him to gasp. He reached for her breasts and caressed them softly, breathing deeply to control his heartbeat. Heather's breathing accelerated too. She could feel Michael's penis throbbing through his shorts.

The front door opened again and Stacey emerged. Heather pulled her hand away.

Straining to see her friend in the darkness, she spoke out, "Heather, I've got to get home."

"Okay, Stacey. Give me a second. I'll be right there. I promise I'll get you back in time."

Stacey went back inside.

"Good God, Heather, what are you doing to me?" Michael could barely speak.

"Let's go someplace."

He didn't hesitate. "Yes, please."

"But I've got to drive Stacey home before her husband calls. God forbid it if she's not there to take his call."

"I'll wait for you."

She gave him another kiss, a short one, but with full tongue. "Where do you want to go?"

"Do you know where my art gallery is on Canyon Road? I'll wait for you there. Park in the lot around back, and knock on the back door."

"I'll be there in half an hour," she said.

Heather dropped Stacey off a little before nine but didn't tell her anything about her planned meeting with Michael. She drove to his gallery and, as instructed, parked in the rear. Michael opened the door immediately upon hearing her knock.

"Hi. Good timing. I only got here myself." He greeted

Heather with a short but intense kiss. "Come on in and I'll show you around." Locking the door behind her, he guided her to his office and flicked on the lights. It was handsomely decorated with original artwork, a mahogany desk, and a large overstuffed leather couch. "I've got a shower in my office, if you want to take one."

"Wow, I'm impressed. A shower in your office? That sounds wonderful." She looked around and added, "We might have to try that couch out for size."

Michael felt himself get hard again.

Heather glanced down and saw his penis growing against his cycling shorts. "My God, Mr. Redfield, you're ready, aren't you? The shower's not going to be big enough for both of us."

"Probably not, but that makes it even better." He reached into the shower to turn on the water.

Heather did not hesitate. First off was her biking jersey, underneath which was a black sports bra. Without saying a word, she turned her back to Michael and removed her bra. When she turned to face him again, he stared at her and shook his head in awe of her firm breasts, flat stomach, and perfect figure.

She smiled knowingly and shimmied out of her shorts.

"Heather, you are, without a doubt, the most unbelievably beautiful woman I have ever seen." His penis was fully erect now. He was so excited he was concerned he was going to come. He pulled her close to him and held her breasts, then slid his hands down her back to her behind, where he softly massaged her firm ass.

"You're going to come, aren't you?" she said.

"Forgive the pun, but I'm trying hard not to."

She laughed.

Michael laughed too, trying desperately to not think of his pulsating penis.

"Well, let's get in the shower and see what we can do with you," she said, and deftly helped him take off his jersey. When he removed his biking shorts, his penis sprung free, fully erect.

Heather was pleased. Michael was toned, his penis rigid. "Not bad, Mr. Redfield. I think we can do something with that," she said with a wide smile.

He looked down at his penis and knew he wasn't going to last long. His look of uncertainty and rapid breathing gave him away. "Don't worry about that. It's been a while, hasn't it?" Heather said, fully understanding.

They stepped into the snug shower and hugged. Michael's penis was tight against Heather's belly. Her breasts squeezed close against his chest. Water cascaded over their heads. He pushed her wet hair off her face with gentle fingers. She liked his touch and closed her eyes. He held her behind and kissed her with an open mouth. She responded with her tongue deep into his mouth. She pulled back and reached for the bar of soap. She lathered her hands and slid them down to his penis, encircled it, moving back and forth gently, softly, knowingly. It was useless for him to try to resist. "It's okay, it's okay," she said. "Go ahead and come."

"I don't think I ... can ... stop ..." If ever he wanted to make the pleasure last, it was now, but he couldn't. He came in long, deep spasms of pure ecstasy.

She kept her hands around his penis until he was totally spent and kissed him gently on the lips. "Feel better?"

"Yes. You're unbelievable," was all he could say.

"Do you have any wine?" she asked. "It's my turn next."

*****

For several months, Heather and Michael met at his gallery on Thursday nights following the after-parties. Occasionally they met during the week after he closed his gallery for the night. Heather did not tell Stacey that she and Michael were intimate. He insisted she not tell anyone, and that worked for her. She fell in love with him. It wasn't only the sex; it was his refinement, his polite way, and his intelligence. Sometimes he walked her through his gallery and explained the nuances of art, and what made certain artists great. She learned he was particularly fond of Georgia O'Keeffe.

At first, Michael compared Heather's body to a work of art. The sex was beyond anything he had ever experienced with another woman. Heather was beautiful, and brazen, and unbelievably sexual. Over time, however, he came to realize he wanted a relationship based on more than sex. He grew tired of Heather's cursing, her smoking, and her inarticulate speech. His infatuation and lust for her diminished, and he viewed her as though she were a painting marred by a scratch. He longed to be with a woman who was more like his late wife, someone more gracious and gentle, and with whom he could carry on an intelligent conversation. He missed his wife. She was plain, and honest, and amazingly comfortable. That's what he wanted again.

*****

Heather suspected her relationship with Michael was winding down. It was not what it once was. Yes, she always got him excited, but she sensed a change in him.

"I'm not going to be able to see you tonight," he announced to Heather one Thursday. "I have an IRS audit I need to prepare for." He was lying and she knew it, but she didn't understand why. He gave the same reason the next Thursday and the next after that. She realized he had turned away from her. *Please don't let this be happening. I love him. I want to be with him.*

One Thursday night she followed Michael to his gallery. She was certain he was seeing another woman there. She parked out of sight and waited, but no one else appeared. When he emerged alone a half-hour later, he was showered and dressed in slacks and a golf shirt.

Maybe he's telling the truth. No one else was in there with him.

Curiosity got the better of Heather, however, and she wanted to know what he would do next. She was hoping he would simply drive home, confirming for her the reason he gave for not being able to see her.

She followed him, but he did not drive to his house.

From a distance, she watched as Stacey opened her front door. Heather checked her watch. It was quarter past nine. Stacey chatted briefly then opened the door wide to let Michael inside. Heather waited. She watched as the lights first went off in the living room and then on in Stacey's bedroom. It was half past nine.

Clyde was in Chicago.

*****

Michael made love in a way Stacey had never experienced with Clyde. He was knowing and sensual, never rushed. He pleased her and, at the same time, taught her how to please him. Stacey admitted she had never climaxed with Clyde, telling Michael that their sex was routine and painful, and without any foreplay. Michael was so different. He was passionate and sweet. He enjoyed the role he played, exploring every part of her body until she was fervent with desire. When she first climaxed, she screamed with such pleasure that it shocked Michael. He was delighted. He enjoyed being the assertive one.

*****

Heather felt betrayed. Before meeting Michael, she thought all men were like Jake—primal, crude, and boorish. Michael was kind, gentle, intelligent, and he treated her with respect. She had fallen in love with him and hoped they would have a future together. But now, the one man she thought was different from all the rest turned out to be exactly the same. Why did she fall so hard? And now he was cheating on her. He got what he wanted from her and was now taking advantage of Stacey.

Heather understood Stacey was not to blame. *It's Michael, the sorry bastard!*

Poor, naïve Stacey fell for his charms the same way she had. It was easy to do. If only she had told Stacey about her relationship with Michael. But she hadn't. Stacey did not know.

Michael was going to break her best friend's heart someday, too, the way he was breaking hers now.

I'm not going to let that happen to her, Heather promised. *I'm not going to let him do to her what he did to me. I hate him! Honest to God. I really hate him!*

Heather felt intense rage toward Michael and all men. Driven by obsession, she stalked him. She learned his daily routine. She followed him to Stacey's house, to his gallery, to his home, when he went on a bike ride with others, and when he rode alone. She learned he cycled on Via Encantado some afternoons, going out late and returning by six to close his gallery for the day.

She couldn't understand why he would want to have sex with Stacey. Maybe she was good in bed. *Better than me? No, I don't think so,* Heather reasoned. Stacey was plain, shy, and awkward. She had confided in Heather that she never enjoyed sex with Clyde.

I'll tell Clyde. I'll send him a letter. No. I'll disguise my voice and call him. That'll stop the affair. Yeah, that'll do it. Clyde swore he would kill her if she ever cheated on him. That's it. Then Michael will have to come back to me.

In her heart, Heather knew it wasn't Stacey's fault; it was Michael's. She knew what she had to do. She drove Via

Encantado to learn its bends and turns.
I'm going to kill that son of a bitch.

Chapter 17

As he did every Sunday afternoon, Jake Dorell was sitting in his small living room watching the Dodgers game on TV. Heather spied on him from the kitchen as she made dinner. Every so often, he got up to get another beer or go to the bathroom. They didn't utter a word to each other. That wasn't unusual.

After counting six empties, Heather crushed two Ambien sleeping pills and waited for him to go to the bathroom again. When he got up from his recliner, she quickly funneled the sleeping pills into his half-empty bottle of beer and swished it all around. He drank from the bottle unsuspectingly and an hour later was passed out. He wasn't going to wake for several hours.

Heather put on sunglasses and wrapped her long hair under Jake's Dodgers baseball cap. She grabbed the keys to his pickup truck on her way out and closed the door quietly behind her. After a twenty-minute drive, she reached the end of Via Encantado where she turned the truck around and parked. She lit a cigarette, and then another, and another while she waited. A half hour later, she saw a cyclist riding hard toward her.

It was Michael. He was alone doing a cycling interval.

Heather dropped down in her seat.

He made a turn in front of the truck and rode back, riding easily, out of breath, recovering from his interval. He hadn't seen her.

When he was a hundred yards away, Heather started the engine and followed him.

Michael heard the pickup before noticing it in the rearview mirror attached to his sunglasses. It was getting closer. He didn't think anything of it. He pulled to the far right to allow the truck to pass. But it didn't. It stayed behind him even as he rode close to the dirt shoulder. When he altered his direction, the pickup followed.

Damn it. The guy's playing games with me, Michael thought. He continued to cycle. The truck stayed with him.

Close.

Five yards behind.

Three yards.

Michael gave a hand signal that he intended to go left. He was going to move out of the way and let the driver take up the whole lane if he wanted. He wasn't about to pit his seventeen-pound bike against a two-ton pickup. He would get out of the way and let the guy pass.

Two yards.

Michael pulled to the left lane. Heather veered behind him. The sun reflected off the windshield making it impossible for him to see the driver. He was scared now, and lifted his right hand with his palm toward the truck as if to say, *What are you doing?*

One yard.

"Hey," he yelled.

Heather tapped the rear tire of Michael's bike with the bumper. Instinctively, he applied the brakes. His head snapped back, but his bike jolted forward. He skidded on the pavement, but stayed upright. He didn't know what to do. She hit him again. He fought to maintain his balance. He applied the brakes again.

Through her open window, she heard his guttural sounds of panic. "Uh ... uh ... uh." He was in the left lane when she hit him again. He veered onto the dirt shoulder close to the canyon's edge. *This is insane. The son of a bitch is trying to kill me.* Michael understood this wasn't a game. He was terrified. He couldn't evade the pickup.

He rode the shoulder now, dangerously close to the

canyon. Heather hit his rear tire again, this time harder than before.

He tried to brake but his tires slid in the dirt. He unclipped from his pedals but it was too late. They had reached the section of the road with no barrier.

She hit the bicycle hard one last time.

Michael flew into the canyon, arms and legs flailing as he tried to grab onto the brush that grew from the wall.

He bounced off the wall that barreled out from the side and was dead before hitting bottom.

She screamed from inside the cab of the truck. "You son of a bitch! It serves you right. You son of a bitch."

Heather knew she had to get home before Jake woke up. She sped past a house where she noticed a woman outside watering her flowers. Carlotta Smith looked up briefly, but immediately went back to watering her plants.

*****

On the drive home, Heather's mind whirred with clashing emotions as she tried to control her soaring adrenalin. She did not regret sending Michael to his death. After all, she had given him her heart, and he rejected her. He abandoned her for her best friend. He didn't even have the courtesy to tell her. He was no different from Jake. *Men are all the same. They're after only one thing.* Yes, she loved him, but she did not regret what she had done. But, then again, yes, she did. Maybe she shouldn't have killed him after all. Why couldn't she have just let him go? *Oh, my God, what have I done?* At first she whimpered. Then deep, racking sobs took over. She removed her sunglasses to wipe the tears from her eyes.

What about that woman outside watering in her yard? She looked up when I passed by. I shouldn't have been going so fast. Did she see me ram Michael over the cliff? Did she hear anything? I don't think he ever screamed, did he? I don't remember. What if the cops question her? I don't think she'd be able to tell them anything. She was too far away.

Heather would make sure to not leave any evidence behind. When she got home, she would check the front of the pickup for damage to the front bumper. The cops would believe it was just another accident. *Like Castillo and Pérez. Michael lost control of his bike. Ha!* She would go to his funeral and mourn him. *I'll show tears on the outside, but inside, I'll be smiling. He deserved it. The son of a bitch. He abandoned me. Flat out abandoned me like I was some piece of garbage he would leave on the curb.*

Anger, uncertainty, remorse, fear—her mind roiled. What should she say to Stacey? *Nothing. Why would I say anything? That would be stupid. I'm not even supposed to know about the two of them. No, I can't say a thing.*

And then, speaking directly to Michael, she said, "Why did you do it? Why? What was Stacey to you that I wasn't? It serves you right, you know. You abandoned me. It's been that way my whole life. I let you screw me, and boy, did you screw me. I told you I loved you. Did that scare you away? Yes, I did love you, but you played me for a fool. You can't blame me for killin' you. I did it for all the other women you played for fools, too. No, I'll be honest. I didn't do it for them. I did it because you hurt me so bad. You deserved it. It was your fault, not mine."

*****

Heather parked the pickup in the same place Jake had left it earlier. She searched the cab to make sure she left nothing behind and readjusted the seat to Jake's settings. The gas level had barely dropped. She got out and closed the door as quietly as possible. Still, it sounded loud. Loud enough, she thought, to wake Jake. She hurriedly walked around to the left side of the truck and glanced down. *Oh, shit, is that a scratch?* She reached down and touched a smudge where the bumper had met

Michael's tire. It was not scratched. *Oh Jeez, that scared me.*

Back inside the house, Heather saw Jake was still passed out on the recliner. A quick check made sure he was still breathing. The clock on the mantel showed she had been gone for a little over an hour. *I've got another hour or so until he wakes up.* She got a bottle of Windex from underneath the kitchen sink, pulled four sheets off a roll of paper towels, and went back out to the truck. She sprayed the towels with Windex and rubbed the bumper clean—not only the smudge mark, but the entire bumper.

Jake's truck was now clean of evidence that could tie it to Michael's killing. But wait. *Could they trace the dirt on the paper towels to Michael's bicycle tire? Maybe. That's what they do on TV. I have to get rid of the towels. I'll burn them. No, I have a better idea.*

Heather went into the bathroom, locked the door behind her, and ripped the paper towels into tiny shreds. Small bits. A thousand pieces. She put them in the toilet and flushed. *Shit, some didn't flush.* She waited until the water filled again. Every bit disappeared on the second flush. *That's it. It's over.*

She shrugged her shoulders.

I did what I had to do.

Chapter 18

Heather obsessed about the woman she had seen on Via Encantado. Had the woman seen her? Would she be able to identify the truck or her as the driver? Heather knew the woman had just a fleeting glance of the pickup. *She couldn't possibly recognize me now—I was wearing sunglasses and Jake's hat.* Still, Heather worried. *I have to find out for sure. I'll go to her house and tell her I'm lost. I'll know right away if she recognizes me by the way she reacts.*

Ten days had passed since Heather killed Michael. She knew it was foolish to return to the scene of the crime. She hadn't left any evidence behind. No one could suspect her. Yet the possibility of the old woman remembering something about her compelled her to return. *And if she recognizes me, what do I do, kill her? I don't know if I have any other choice. It's her fault for living out in the boondocks.* Heather made up her mind. She decided to go to Carlotta's on Wednesday after dark.

Just as she had done the day she killed Michael, she laced Jake's beer with Ambien, left the house once he was knocked out, and drove his truck to Via Encantado.

*****

The high beams from a dark sedan momentarily blinded Heather as she approached Carlotta's house on Via Encantado. She shielded her eyes from the light. "Asshole," she shouted, and turned on her own high beams in retaliation. Ahead, a woman was walking a dog and Heather wondered if she could be Carlotta. Blinded by the car lights, the woman turned away.

Heather drove to the end of the road, turned around, and inched back toward Carlotta's house. She doused her headlights and watched as the light of the dog walker's flashlight bounced down the road until it disappeared from sight. She waited another fifteen minutes to see if the dog walker would return, but she did not. *She wasn't the old lady.*

Heather took a deep breath and got out of the car. She walked to the front door of Carlotta's house, knocked, waited a few seconds, and knocked again. She had practiced what she was going to say. *I'm lost and I'm having a problem with my truck. It won't shift. It's stuck in first gear. Can I use your phone? I need to call my husband to come help me. Would you please give him directions how to get here?*

When no one answered, she peeked impatiently through the sidelights on both sides of the door. The front rooms of the house were dark, but there were lights on toward the back. *Be careful now. Don't leave any fingerprints.* She rang the doorbell with her knuckle, waited a few seconds, and rang again. This time she held the buzzer down for nearly five seconds. No one came to the door. *Where the hell is she?* Heather wondered.

In the moonlight, she noticed a stone walkway at the side of the house. She walked around to the back and saw the kitchen door was ajar. She pushed it open with her foot and stood tentatively outside the threshold. "Hello? Is anyone home?" she yelled. "Hello! I'm having car problems. I need your help."

No one answered. Cautiously, hesitatingly, Heather entered the kitchen. "Hello? Anyone home?" Her nerves were starting to get the better of her. "I need your help. I saw your lights from the street. Anyone home?" She went into the living room, then walked down the short hallway to the bedroom, being careful not to touch anything. Carlotta wasn't there. Nor was she in the spare room she used as her studio. Heather tried to open the bathroom door, but something was blocking it. She thought it could be Carlotta. "Is that you in there?" she asked quietly.

There was no answer. "Hello? I knocked but you didn't answer. I'm lost, and I came in the house to see if you could help me. Will you please come out?" She put her ear to the door, but heard nothing.

She didn't know what to do. "Listen, I need your help. Please come out. Are you okay in there?" This time she put her shoulder to the door and was able to push it open enough to peek in. A bunched-up rug blocked the door from opening.

"Damn," she cursed, and walked back to the kitchen and then into the attached garage. Carlotta's car was there, but she wasn't. The old woman was nowhere to be found.

Could that dog-walker have been her? No, she wouldn't have left her door open. Where the hell is she?

Heather took out a cigarette and lit a match, but decided against smoking in the garage. She blew out the match and dropped it onto the carpeted floor, grinding it with the sole of her shoe. She returned the cigarette to her pack and walked out the kitchen door to the backyard, where she waited impatiently.

After a few minutes, she went back into the house. Out of frustration, she shouted again. "Hello! Anyone home? Where the hell are you?"

No reply. Nothing. She looked around at all the artwork. "Wow, this house is kinda neat. She's got paintings all over the place. It's like Michael's gallery," she mumbled.

Heather noticed the Georgia O'Keeffe above the mantel. *Michael loved her work. If there's one thing I learned from him, it was to appreciate this kind of stuff.*

Heather stood on her tiptoes and carefully lifted the painting off its hooks. She went out through the kitchen, making sure to leave the door open as much as it had been when she arrived. She looked up and down Via Encantado and saw no one. After placing the painting face-up in the bed of the truck, she covered it with a blue tarp Jake kept in his tool box. She climbed in the truck and glanced at the dash clock. She had to get back before Jake woke from his Ambien-and-alcohol stupor.

Back at home, she was relieved to see Jake still passed out, snoring heavily. She carried the painting inside and into her bedroom where she wrapped it in a bed sheet and slid it under her bed for temporary safekeeping. She knew she couldn't keep it there for long but would figure out what to do with it later. Emotional exhaustion prevented her from thinking about it anymore.

She was happy the old woman hadn't been home after all.

I'm not going back again. From here on in, what happens, happens. I'll take my chances.

Chapter 19

Jake and Heather Dorell were the only two admitted smokers of the four persons of interest in the Carlotta Smith murder. Regardless, DeGarzia also collected a DNA swab from Stacey Keenan and planned to collect one from her husband when he returned from his business trip. The forensic lab would check all four samples against the cigarette found in Carlotta Smith's back yard.

DeGarzia offered Hank his opinion. "I think we're going to find Jake Dorell's DNA a match. He's the most obvious suspect. It's like he's ready to explode. I don't care what the hell he says. I think it bothers the shit out of him to know his wife screwed around with Redfield. And if it's not Jake, it's Heather. She could have been so pissed to find out her lover was screwing around with her best friend that she kills him."

Hank agreed. "You're right. It could be either. If it was Heather, though, you would think she would have killed Stacey to clear the field for herself with Redfield. But you know what? No matter who killed the guy, I think Carlotta Smith was an innocent victim in all of this. I really don't think she would have been able to identify the killer."

"Yeah, but the killer didn't know that."

*****

Hank resumed his normal caseload while waiting to hear back from DeGarzia on the DNA tests. That would be another several days.

On that Thursday night's Club ride, Sam brought up the subject to Hank. "I read about that lady, Carlotta Smith. Isn't she the one you talked to?"

"Yeah, she was the one."

"You hit it on the head when you said you thought Redfield didn't accidentally cartwheel into the canyon, that someone killed him."

"Yeah, but unfortunately, I may have ended up getting Carlotta killed too."

Sam was consoling. "Come on, Hank. You didn't get her killed. How would you know she was going to be a target?"

"You know what's sad about all this? The fact she didn't really give us any helpful information. She didn't see anything we could definitively tie to Redfield's murder. It's all a crying shame. Whoever killed Redfield probably murdered her too, but for no reason—none at all."

"You can't beat yourself up over this. It wasn't your fault," Sam repeated.

Hank's cell phone rang. He reached into his rear jersey pocket to see who was calling. "It's Deeg." He slowed to a stop and got off his bike. "Go on ahead, Sam. I'll catch up."

"I'll wait for you," Sam said. He stopped several yards ahead of Hank, but still within earshot. He straddled the top tube of his bike and waited while Hank took the call.

"Nothing, huh? Too bad ... No kidding? Let's see how she explains that." Hank listened a moment more and replied, "Okay, I'll check in with you first thing." He put his phone back into his jersey and got back on his bike.

"Was that about Redfield?" Sam asked.

"Yeah. DeGarzia thought some of the evidence we uncovered at Carlotta's house was going to point to a certain person as the possible killer, but it didn't. However, some of that stuff you and I found on the road has apparently proved interesting."

"Yeah? Like what?"

"Now, Sam, no more questions about this. I can't go into any more detail. I've already told you too much."

"Sorry, man. I didn't mean to butt in, but I'm hooked."

*****

The next morning Hank stopped in to see DeGarzia. "Okay, you couldn't tell who smoked that cigarette we found behind Carlotta Smith's house, but you said three of the cigarette butts we found out on the road belonged to Heather Dorell. Since we found them all in close proximity, she might have been stopped, waiting for someone, smoking the whole time."

"We're bringing her in again this morning. Her husband, too. But those cigarettes aren't enough, Hank. Right now it's all circumstantial."

"At least it gives us a direction to pursue. What about the match on the garage floor?"

"Nothing."

"And the skid marks on the road? Was the lab able to confirm it was from Redfield's bike?"

"Yes and no. They feel there was a good probability they were from his tires, but couldn't say so with a hundred percent certainty. The Michelin tires that were on his bike are apparently common on a lot of bikes."

*****

The Dorells each arrived at police headquarters in their own vehicle. DeGarzia spoke with Heather while Jake sat fuming in a separate interview room.

Deeg started. "Good seeing you again. How're you doing?" Heather said nothing.

"Can I call you Heather?"

She looked up at DeGarzia through mascaraed eyes and purred sensually, "Yeah, sure. Whatever you want."

DeGarzia stayed on point. "I understand you're a pretty good cyclist."

"I don't know who told you that. I'm okay. I've only been bikin' for a couple years, but I like it. It's fun. Why do you ask? Do you ride too?"

"Nah, with all these guys being killed, why would I want to? You ever worry about getting hit by a car?"

At that, Heather flinched, but recovered quickly. "No, not really. We ride back roads most times, so it's no big deal. You oughta try it. It would get you away from behind your desk. You're not married. I could show you how to ride," she said with blatant risqué intent.

"I bet you could," Deeg said, hiding his embarrassment at her suggestion. He looked directly into her eyes. "You're flirting with me, aren't you?"

"Yeah, I flirt with any man who's as big and handsome as you."

"Okay, that's enough," he said, firmly putting an end to her diversion. "Let's talk about the possibility of you or any cyclist getting hit by a car. We think that's what happened to Michael Redfield. Would you have any knowledge of that?"

"No. Why do you think he got hit by a car?" she said, and swiveled in her chair as she looked around the room.

"What are you looking for?"

"A sign that says you're not allowed to smoke in here. Last time you said I couldn't smoke, but I don't see no sign. You sure I can't smoke?"

"It's still no smoking. Look, we believe Michael Redfield was a victim of a hit-and-run. We have evidence such as skid marks on the road, the condition of the bike, that kind of thing."

"And you think I did it?"

"Yes, I do." Again she said nothing.

"Heather, I need to read you your Miranda rights. You have the right to remain silent. Anything you say may be used against you in a court of law. If you desire an attorney—"

"I don't need no attorney. I didn't kill nobody," she said. Her voice was calm.

"Do you understand your rights?"

"Yeah. I didn't kill nobody."

"Do you care to have an attorney present as I ask questions regarding the deaths of Michael Redfield and Carlotta Smith?"

"I told you no, I don't need no freakin' lawyer. I keep tellin' you I didn't kill nobody," she said, this time more forcefully. DeGarzia realized that, like her husband, Heather also had a short fuse. He would use that to his advantage.

"How do you explain the fact that your cigarette was found behind Smith's house?"

"What are you talkin' about?" She knew he was lying. "I know you're bullshittin' me. I ain't never been to wherever she lives. I don't know her, I don't know how my cigarette would have gotten there, and I didn't kill her."

"I didn't say you did."

"Then what the hell are you sayin'?"

DeGarzia didn't answer. "We also found several cigarettes on Via Encantado where Michael Redfield was killed. They had your DNA on them. What were you doing there?"

Heather's mind was racing. She remembered smoking several cigarettes and flipping them out of the pickup while she waited for Michael. She was shocked DeGarzia had found them and traced them to her. She fidgeted in her chair and continued to look around the room. "I wasn't there, and I don't even know where Via *Enchanto* is."

"Via Encantado."

"Via *whatever*. I don't know where it is."

"I don't understand how you can say you were never there when we found evidence that you were."

"You know, could be I've been there before. Sometimes I get in my car and drive to get away from my asshole husband. I've been all over. When I get to some place quiet, I just sit and look out at the scenery. I zone out. You know what I mean? I can't tell you for sure that I've been there, but if you say I was, it was because I was doin' that."

"Where else do you do that? Up in Aldez Pass?"

"Could be. I can't tell you for sure where I've been. I've probably pretty much been all over Santa Fe."

Deeg was frustrated. "Yeah, okay. When was the last time you drove your husband's pickup truck?"

"Are you kiddin' me? I can't remember what I had for breakfast, and you're askin' me when I drove my husband's truck. Shit, I don't remember."

"You have your own car, so why do you drive his?"

"If it's blockin' my car and I have to go someplace I take his. Is that a crime?"

"What if I told you that a neighbor of Carlotta Smith said she saw a red-headed woman in a pickup truck parked in front of Smith's house the night she was killed?" DeGarzia lied again. "The woman had long red hair like you."

Heather lashed back at the detective. "You know that's bullshit. If anyone saw a red-head there, it wasn't me." She was scared. *Could that dog walker I saw that night describe me? No way. It was too dark, and my hair was tucked under Jakes's hat. He's lying.*

"Mrs. Dorell, Heather, I don't think you understand. You are our prime suspect in the murder of Michael Redfield, and we believe you also killed Carlotta Smith."

"I understand. You don't have to keep sayin' it. I'm not fuckin' stupid." She had completely lost her calm. "I told you I didn't kill her—Carlotta, Smith, or whatever the hell her name is. And why would I kill Michael? Because I was havin' an affair with him? That don't make no sense. I was in love with the guy."

"No, that wouldn't make any sense. But you had motive. You were upset with him because he was also having an affair with Stacey Keenan. You wanted to get even with him for two-timing you."

"I didn't know he was dorkin' her until you told me the other day. And besides, it's a free country. He can screw who he wants. Okay, I want an attorney now."

DeGarzia immediately ceased his questioning and walked out.

*****

Hank had been observing the interview through the one-way mirror in an adjacent room. DeGarzia entered and asked, "What do you think?" He was irritated and unhappy with himself at the way the interview had gone.

"She's tough, Deeg," Hank shook his head. He was frustrated as well. "We don't have anything. The cigarette butts on the road don't prove a thing. We could make a case that they were there because she smoked them in advance of killing Redfield or Smith, but it won't hold water. Her alibi about getting away from Jake would be a bona fide explanation in the eyes of a jury. You've established a motive, but we don't have nearly enough to bring her to trial. The cigarette in Smith's back yard doesn't match Heather's DNA. It could have been smoked by anyone—a gardener, repairman, a visitor, anyone."

"Yeah, okay. Like I said all along, maybe Jake Dorell's the guy," Deeg said. "He didn't have an alibi for when Redfield and Smith were killed, he drives a pickup, and he has a major attitude. Could be he set her up for the fall."

"I agree, but what about Stacey Keenan? Or Clyde Keenan?"

"Stacey Keenan looks the least likely, but she's still a suspect. As far as Clyde Keenan goes, I'm going to go after him hard when he gets back Friday. In the meantime, I'll see what my buddy Jake Dorell has to say."

*****

"Mr. Dorell, as you know, we suspect your wife in the killing of both Michael Redfield and Carlotta Smith. There is sufficient incriminating evidence for us to consider charging her with their murders."

"So what do you want from me? You're costin' me another day's pay."

"Don't you care if your wife is guilty or innocent?"

"No, not really. She don't exactly get my vote for wife-of-the-year honors, you know."

"Can you help me understand how her cigarettes were found on the road where Michael Redfield was killed? She says she doesn't remember being there. If she's telling the truth, someone planted them there to incriminate her."

"How the hell would I know how her cigarettes got there?"

"Does she drive your pickup truck?"

"Sometimes. If my truck is behind her car in the driveway and she needs to go someplace, she'll take it. It pisses me off when she uses it. She leaves the fuckin' gas tank empty, and she has coffee cups and shit all over the front seat and cigarette butts in the ashtray. She's a fuckin' slob."

"Do you think she drove it on the fourteenth?"

"Shit, here we go, back to the fourteenth again. I don't know, yeah, she could have. I already told you I was asleep. I don't think there was anything of hers in the truck, so she probably didn't drive it. But like I keep sayin', I couldn't tell you where the hell she was that day."

"What about you, Jake? Can I call you Jake?"

"I don't give a shit what you call me. Just don't call me late for dinner." He grinned, exposing the gap where his tooth was missing.

"Did you kill your wife's lover and plant the cigarettes to make it seem as though she was there?"

"Let me get this straight. First you say my wife was the killer, and now you're sayin' I murdered those people so she could be blamed?"

"Yes, that's exactly what I'm saying."

"Man, you're really fishing. I fuckin' told you I didn't kill him. You may think I did, but I didn't. I don't give a shit about who she screws or doesn't screw. I didn't kill nobody on account 'a her screwin' around."

"You act like you don't care what she does or who she's with. But she's your wife, so I think you do care."

"Look. I've been married to her since she was sixteen. I don't know why we're still married, except she's as dumb as a fuckin' rock. If I kicked her out, she wouldn't be able to take care of herself. She'd be on the streets. I wouldn't do that to a dog, and I wouldn't do that to her. She's never worked a day in her life, and she wouldn't be able to do nothin' by herself if I left her. And besides, sometimes I like havin' her around. She takes care of my needs, if you know what I mean."

"Would you be willing to take a lie detector test?"

"Will that put an end to all this bullshit?"

"It might."

"Let's get it done."

*****

"Hank, Jake Dorell passed the lie detector test. It looks as though he didn't have anything to do with the killings."

Chapter 20

Jake was mad. He was always in a state of testiness and today was no different. He was angry he had to go to police headquarters to be questioned a second time. And he was angry he had to take a lie detector test to prove his innocence, even though he had passed. Late afternoon he confronted Heather in the kitchen. He had polished off a six-pack of beer and she was cooking dinner. "You whore. You were screwing that guy, weren't you?"

Heather looked at Jake but didn't say a word. She turned back to her cooking.

"The cops say they think you screwed him first then killed him."

"What the hell are you talkin' about? I didn't kill nobody," she shouted back.

"Were you screwing him, yes or no? It's a simple question, even for you."

"None of your fuckin' business. Why do you care what I did? You never cared before."

"I said, did you kill him?" Jake demanded again, his voice rising to a shout.

"If I did, I wouldn't tell you, you asshole."

"You did kill him. Well, I'll be a son of a bitch. You did kill him. I thought so. I can tell you did." He slurred the words. "You can't lie for shit. Maybe I gotta tell the cops."

"Go ahead and tell the cops, and I swear I'll chop your nuts off."

Jake set his bottle on the counter, staggered to where Heather was standing, and hit her with a glancing blow to the jaw. She was thrown back against the refrigerator, stunned but not hurt. He advanced on her, and tried to strike her again, but she slipped around him, grabbed a knife from the counter, and held it in front of her. "You're dead. I told you to never hit me again. You're dead!" she screamed.

"Right. Go ahead and give it your best shot, you whore. What're you gonna do, tell the cops I hit you? For sure I'll tell them you killed that guy."

Heather lifted the knife over her head. She lunged toward Jake, ready to drive the knife into his chest, but he grabbed her forearm as the knife descended. The tip of the blade caught his other arm. He winced. It was a superficial cut, but it spurted blood. He twisted Heather's arm behind her until she dropped the knife. He picked it up and shouted at her, "I ought to use this on you. Self-defense. That's what I'll tell them. Self-defense. You whore bitch. I should have left you in the gutter where I first met you, you ignorant tramp. You were nothin' then, and you're a nothin' now."

Heather was crying and screaming, "Let me go. Let me go." She tried desperately to free herself from Jake's grasp. It was hopeless. He released his grip on her only when she stopped resisting.

She turned to confront him, her long, red hair half covering her face. After brushing the tears from her cheeks, she spoke in a calm, clipped tone, measuring every word. "As God is my witness, I'm gonna kill you some day. I don't know where or when, but I'm gonna kill you." She said it with a viciousness he knew was real.

Jake locked his bedroom door that night.

*****

Heather called Stacey the next day. She wanted to visit to talk about Michael, but only if Clyde wasn't there. The two women hadn't spoken since their interviews with DeGarzia.

"Clyde is still in Chicago. He'll be back on Friday."

At the front door, they greeted each other with a tentative hug. "Heather, I'm so sorry. I didn't know you were seeing

Michael," Stacey said.

"I didn't know you were either," Heather lied.

"I thought you liked him, but you never told me you were, you know, with him. I mean, I didn't know," Stacey cried. "Why didn't you tell me? I wouldn't have … I wouldn't—" She couldn't finish. They sat facing each other on the couch in the living room.

Heather took Stacey's hand in her own. "I'm the one who should apologize to you. He must have liked you more than he liked me." Heather laughed. "Listen to us. We sound like a couple of school girls talking about a teenage crush."

"Heather, truly, I don't know why he liked me. I really don't. I can't hold a candle next to you. That was awful at the police station when they told us we were both seeing him."

Heather continued to lie. "Well, it was over a while ago with Michael and me. We only were together a couple of times. He wasn't nothin' to me. But for your sake, I'm sorry he's dead. Obviously, you were the one he loved. Look, maybe we're both at fault. We should have been honest with each other. But it's over now. We're still friends, right?"

"I loved him so much," Stacey sobbed. "He was so kind and gentle and honest."

Heather reached up and wiped the tears from her friend's face. "Stacey, I know you loved him, but I have to tell you the truth about him."

"What? What do you know about him?"

"Don't be mad at me for saying this, but Michael was no different than any other man. A man can be kind and gentle, but you know what? There is no such thing as a man who's honest."

"That's not true, Heather. Michael was honest."

"No, he was not. Listen, honey, you shouldn't never be fooled again by no man. Look at Jake, and what he's like. And

Michael, he goes to bed with us both. He wasn't honest either. I've been fooled a lot of times, but I ain't never gonna be lied to again. All men are assholes. They only got one thing in mind. You ever hear the saying that a man uses his penis for his brain? Guess what. It's true. Their minds ain't worth shit. It's their penis that decides what they do and who they do it to. Once you understand that about men, you'll know that you can't never trust any man, no more, no how."

"Maybe you're right about most men, but Michael wasn't like that," Stacey said.

"Yes, he was, Stacey. He was. What about Clyde? Did you ever think he would turn into an asshole, beatin' you all the time? And what do you think he's gonna do when he comes home and finds out about you and Michael?"

"I'm scared to death, Heather. I don't know what he'll do. I know he'll hit me. That detective said for me to call him if he did. I don't know what to do. Should I leave? I mean, should I pack up and go somewhere? But where do I go? I'm scared, I really am."

"You could come to my house, but asshole Jake will want to know why you're there and he'll make both our lives miserable. Maybe you should go to a hotel or somethin'."

"What did Jake do to you when he found out about you and Michael?"

"Last night was pretty bad. He was drunk again. I was in the kitchen cookin' dinner and he started callin' me a whore. I told him to go screw himself. I wasn't gonna put up with his drunken shit. So he hit me. That was the last straw. I grabbed a knife from the counter, and I was gonna kill him." Heather's eyes expressed her hatred for Jake. "Stacey, honest to God, I was that close to killing him except he took the knife away from me. He almost broke my arm. That's when I said, 'I don't know when or how, but I'm gonna kill you.' And he knows I'm serious. I been thinkin' about it for a long time."

"Are you crazy? You can't do that, Heather. There are places we could go that would take us in. That detective said the same thing. I think he's right. We could both go. Then we can start all over, together. You don't have to kill him to start a new life."

Heather did not hide her sarcasm. "Yeah, just like you plan to do, right? The truth is, I've tried to leave him. I told him a thousand times I was gonna leave him, but he laughs at me and says, 'Just you try.' He don't believe it. And he says he ain't gonna let me divorce him neither. He doesn't love me, that's for sure. Probably never did. He only married me so he could get some ass whenever he wanted it. He says I couldn't survive without him, that I couldn't take care of myself, but I'll show him. If he won't let me go, there's only one thing left I can do. I'm gonna kill him. I really am gonna have to kill him." Her eyes narrowed.

"You know, sometimes I feel that way about Clyde. No, not sometimes—" she corrected herself, "to be honest, all the time, anymore."

"You mean you've thought about killing him, too?"

"No, I don't mean kill him. I mean divorce him. If I ever meet someone like Michael again, you know, someone I can really love, I would leave Clyde in an instant." Stacey began to cry again. "But I know Clyde would be like Jake. He'd never let me leave. He's told me a hundred times that if I ever tried to leave him for someone else, he would shoot me. Honest to God, that's what he's said. I'm scared of him. But, yes, I have to be honest. Sometimes after he has sex with me, I pray that he dies right then and there. But I could never, you know, kill him."

"Yes, you could. I could kill Jake and never think twice about it." Heather wasn't sure how far to talk about her rage. She took Stacey's face in her hands, looked her in the eye, and said, "Let's do it. Let's do it, and then run away from here. Come on. If I do it, will you?"

"You're kidding me," Stacey said, grasping Heather's wrists. She looked intently at her friend. Heather didn't flinch. "You're not kidding? You're serious? No, you're crazy. We can't do that. I don't want to spend the rest of my life in jail."

"We won't go to jail if they don't catch us. I told you I've been thinking about it a lot. I know a house where we can stay for a while, and when the coast is clear maybe we can go to Mexico or wherever."

"What are you talking about? What house?"

Heather dropped her hands and stared at her friend for a moment, uncertain if she should disclose her plan.

"Tell me, Heather, what house?"

"Look, I didn't want you to know. I have a plan, and I'll tell you about it, but you need to promise you won't breathe a word of this. Do you understand?"

"Yes, okay, I promise."

"I found a place and I got food and stuff there already, enough food to last me for a couple of months. I'm gonna do it. I'm not gonna live like this anymore."

"My God, Heather, you can't be serious. We can find another way. You can't do this."

"Too late. I'm gonna do it and soon. I'm gonna buy me a gun and then it'll only be a matter of time. I will. I can't stand even lookin' at him no more."

Stacey was gripped by the thought. "Do you really think we can get away with it?"

"Yeah, we can. Don't you want a chance to be happy?" Heather's voice reflected her yearning.

"But we would need money. I've got a little saved up that we could use." Stacey's change of heart surprised Heather. She smiled, as this brought her plan a step closer to becoming reality.

"Me too. I've stashed some cash away, but we need more. I ain't got that much. What about Clyde?"

"Clyde's got a lot, but he won't let me get into the checking account. Maybe I could find a way. And I know where he keeps some money in the house. It's in a safe in his closet. I know the combination, too. I found it once when I looked through his desk drawer. I don't know how much he's got in there, but I know he's got some." Stacey's excitement was mounting.

"And I've got something, too. It's worth a lot of money. I don't know how much, but it's worth a lot. We could sell it," Heather said.

"What is it?"

"It's a painting by Georgia O'Keeffe."

"Where did you get that?"

"I can't tell you."

"Was it from Michael?"

"No, it's not important that you know. Now, please don't ask me." Heather was serious. "So, you're in with me, right? Are we gonna do it?"

Stacey wavered. Uncertainty set in. She shook her head, "I'm not sure."

"Don't say no right now. Think about it, okay?"

"Okay. I'm not saying yes or no. I'll think about it. But, tell me about the house. Where is it?"

"It's my safe house. It's in Golden."

Chapter 21

Clyde Keenan returned from his business trip early Friday afternoon. He was unaware of the Michael Redfield and Carlotta Smith murders or of Stacey's involvement in the case. DeGarzia was waiting for Clyde as he exited the airport terminal. He showed Clyde his badge and motioned to the open door of his unmarked police car, "I need you to accompany me to police headquarters to discuss a matter that involves your wife."

"What about my wife? Is she okay?"

"Yes, she's fine. We'll discuss it further at police headquarters."

"Tell me what's going on."

"I prefer to discuss it with you at police headquarters." DeGarzia escorted Clyde into the back seat of his car.

*****

The fluorescent light in the stark interview room made Clyde's thin, gray skin appear translucent. He spoke in his usual clipped, self-assured monotone. "Why am I here? And what does this have to do with my wife?" he asked.

"I need to ask you about Michael Redfield, a friend of your wife's. Where were you on the fourteenth?"

"The fourteenth? Let me recall." Clyde performed a quick mental calculation. "I was on my way to Chicago. My company's headquarters is located there. I had to be there for a monthly review of contracts that we have pending in Santa Fe, Albuquerque, and Phoenix. I travel quite a bit," he explained. "Who's Michael Redfield?"

"What do you do?"

"I'm a financial consultant for the R2 Corporation. Who's Michael Redfield?"

"I'll get to that in a minute. Where were you on the twenty-fourth?

"I would have been back in Chicago. That week we had company reviews."

"I assume your employer will verify that?"

"Yes, of course they will."

"Do you smoke?"

"No, I do not smoke, nor have I ever. It's a filthy habit which I do not condone," Clyde answered. He exuded an air of someone who believed he transcended ordinary people and their foibles. *Isn't he a prissy, holier-than-thou type*, thought DeGarzia.

"Do you own a pickup truck?"

"No, I drive a Prius and my wife has a Ford Focus. I will ask you again, Detective DeGarzia, why am I here? I have a right to know why I am suffering this inquisition. And I ask you again, who is Michael Redfield?"

"Michael Redfield was murdered on the fourteenth. And a woman by the name of Carlotta Smith was murdered on the twenty-fourth. We believe their murders are related. Do you know either of them?"

"No, I don't. Who are they?"

"Michael Redfield was a member of the Cycling Club your wife belongs to, and Carlotta Smith may have been a witness to his murder."

"I knew it. Against my wishes, my wife joined that *Club*. I knew nothing good would come of it. I don't understand what I have to do with them. And what does it have to do with my wife?"

DeGarzia hesitated. "Mr. Keenan, were you aware of your wife's relationship with Mr. Redfield?"

Clyde looked questioningly at DeGarzia. "What do you mean 'relationship'? I don't even know who he was, other than what you just told me about him belonging to my wife's Cycling

Club."

"Did you know your wife was having an affair with him?"

For a long moment, Clyde said nothing. He stared at DeGarzia, his eyes harboring shock and indignation. "Sir, you're speaking of an immorality my wife would never contemplate. She does not subscribe to such behavior. She has never, and would never, venture from the sanctity of marriage. I would not allow it. You most certainly are thinking of the wrong person. It could not be my wife. I do not believe you."

"Mr. Keenan, believe it. I do not have the wrong person. Your wife was having an affair with Michael Redfield."

He repeated himself. "That can't be. We have a good marriage, a wonderful marriage. She wouldn't do anything like that. When I return home, I will ask her about all this. I fully expect that she will vigorously deny your accusation."

DeGarzia was concerned for Stacey Keenan. He sensed Clyde's rage building and was certain it would erupt when he confronted his wife. "Mr. Keenan, I don't lie about such things. Understand, she admitted to the affair. Now, I need to know what you know about it."

"I do not believe what you are saying. She could not have been doing that. I will never, in a million years, believe that," he said. A moment later, he reversed his thought process. "Is it because I travelled a lot? Did she say that was why?"

"I can't answer that, Mr. Keenan. You'll have to find out yourself. So, are you telling me you had no suspicions about your wife?"

"That is exactly what I am telling you."

DeGarzia said nothing, waiting for Clyde to continue.

"Now, what else do you want to know? You don't really believe she killed those people, do you?"

"No, we don't. But we'd like to know if you did."

"Me? Certainly not. I did not kill anyone. Apparently,

Detective, you think I knew about her supposed indiscretions. I did not. Let me tell you about myself. I am a student of religions. I am fully aware that in certain cultures, if she were an adulteress, she and her lover would be stoned to death."

"We don't live in that kind of culture. Are you telling me I have to be concerned about Mrs. Keenan?" DeGarzia narrowed his eyes and leaned in close to Clyde. "Are you implying you will harm her? Should I take your comment as a threat?"

"No, sir. I am a Christian. I do not go around stoning transgressors, or killing them. No matter what the reason, I turn the other cheek. Nothing can drive me to kill—not even my wife—for her infidel—her *alleged* infidelities. I still don't believe it. She could not, and would not, do such a thing."

"Are you an abusive husband, Mr. Keenan?"

"Hardly. I live my life as the Bible dictates."

"Do you ever get angry at your wife?"

"What kind of a question is that, sir? Of course I get angry," Clyde said matter-of-factly. He pointed to DeGarzia's left hand. "I see you lack a wedding ring. As an unmarried man, you would not understand. Husbands and wives certainly have disagreements. Husbands get angry at their wives. It occurs during the normal course of a relationship."

"Does your wife get angry at you?"

"No. On the contrary. She is not allowed to be angry at me. She is a dutiful wife, as instructed to be pursuant to the teachings of the Bible."

DeGarzia shook his head. Clyde Keenan's razor-sharp anger was brewing inside. He beat his wife. There was no doubt he would hurt her—in the name of the Bible. "Do you have any idea where Mrs. Keenan was on the days Redfield and Smith were killed?"

"She was at home. I call her several times a day when I'm on the road. Always at the same time. I spoke with her as usual.

She did not indicate there was any problem at all."

"Every day at the same times?" DeGarzia feigned surprise at Clyde's mention of the phone calls. He wanted to confirm the truthfulness of Stacey's account.

"Yes."

"What times do you call?"

"Eight in the morning, twelve noon, four, and nine o'clock at night," he said, his pride apparent. "At precisely the same times every day, because, sir, I am precise in all aspects of life. It's what makes me successful in my profession. Precision and a goal of perfection is what I strive for."

"I don't get why you call her so often each day. What does that have to do with precision?"

"Of course you wouldn't understand. It's to ensure she is conducting herself in a Christian manner, toiling to keep idle thoughts at bay, and to be a constructive, dutiful, God-fearing wife."

DeGarzia stared at Clyde for a moment without saying a word. He was repulsed by this toad of a man. "What, exactly, do you do if she doesn't answer the phone?"

"That has never happened. She may be late on occasion answering my calls, but she is always there. The only time she goes out of the house is to run errands for the upkeep of our house. That, and I allow her to ride her bike with that Cycling Club."

"You *allow* her?" DeGarzia was incredulous. "She's not your child. She's your wife."

"Yes, she is my wife. But when she acts like a child, I must spank her for being a bad wife."

"Spank her? You *spank* her? You can't be serious."

"As I said before, you would not understand. We have a fine marriage. I do not believe anything you have said about her and Mr. Redfield. Somehow, you have been misled, and I forgive you for your assertions."

DeGarzia had heard enough. Incensed by Clyde's interpretation of the Bible as it related to marriage, there was little doubt in his mind that he beat his wife. "Mr. Keenan, I need a DNA sample from you. I can get a court order for it, or you can voluntarily offer a sample. It's up to you.

"I have no problem offering up a sample of my DNA."

"Fine. And I'll allow you to leave, but understand, until I confirm your whereabouts on the days Redfield and Smith were killed, I consider you a person of interest in our criminal investigation. You are not to leave Santa Fe under any circumstances without my specific consent. That includes going to your company's headquarters or to any other place of employment. Do you understand?"

"Of course I understand. I will seek a temporary leave of absence from my employer. I don't want them to know of my involvement in any of this."

"You do what you feel you need to. Just don't leave town."

"I would like to return home and see my wife now."

"I'll arrange for your transport home." DeGarzia turned off the video recorder and the two men rose from their chairs. DeGarzia towered over Clyde. With his back to the one-way mirror, he whispered, "Mr. Keenan, this is off the record, but I need to tell you, I despise spousal abuse. Despise it. I understand you're upset over your wife's affair, but I strongly suggest you control your rage. Work through your relationship as best you can. I promise that if you harm your wife, I will seek you out and deal with you. And I will make your employer aware of your tendencies. Do you understand?"

Clyde did not respond.

DeGarzia held out his hand to shake Clyde's. Clyde looked up at this huge man and reluctantly offered his soft hand in turn. DeGarzia squeezed it hard and didn't let go for five full seconds.

Clyde winced in pain.

"I said, 'Do you understand?'"

"I understand."

Chapter 22

Stacey's affair devastated Clyde. His perfectly controlled life had disintegrated into emotional chaos. His perfectly controlled wife had betrayed him. She had cheated on him. She was an adulteress. How could she? He had given her everything. All he asked for in turn was for her to be a good wife. A dutiful wife. To care for their home. To care for him. Was that too much to ask? He believed the Bible was clear about wifely obligations. He knew he could be harsh. But he had to be. He was teaching her how to be a good wife. Sometimes he got so mad at her that he struck her. He had to punish her more and more frequently, it seemed. It was infuriating when he called and the phone rang more than three times before she answered. He had always insisted that she pick up within three rings. "I am too busy to wait around for you," he would tell her. Now that he thought about it, he did recognize that recently she behaved differently toward him— not as diffident, perhaps a bit more audacious in her attitude.

Stacey was in their bedroom when Clyde returned from police headquarters. She was frozen with fear.

He called from the bottom of the stairwell. "Where are you?"

She responded with a faint "I'm upstairs." As though it would protect her against his rage, she held a pillow to her chest and listened to him climb the stairs.

"Why?" Clyde slammed the bedroom door shut behind him. "Why?" He couldn't control himself.

Stacey shook her head and didn't answer, paralyzed with overwhelming dread. She couldn't speak. She didn't want to say anything. She was unable to say how much she despised him, and how much she loved Michael.

"I said, 'Why?'"

Stacey braced for Clyde to strike. She hoped he would do it, get it over with, and not go on and on, screaming, lecturing, as he had done so often in the past when he accused her of some misdoing. He stepped closer to her, wrath visible in his eyes and on his face. His body was tense, his fingers tight, ready to slap her face, but he pulled back. She relaxed for a split second, unsure what Clyde would do next. In that instant he hit her hard on the side of her head with his open hand. She fell to the floor, dazed. She covered her head with the pillow. He kicked her in the side. She rolled up into a ball, but he kicked her again.

"Stop! Stop!" she screamed from under the pillow. But he didn't. He couldn't. He knelt on top of her and burrowed his knees into her chest. He slammed her head against the floor. "Please stop!"

He pushed the pillow into her face. He was smothering her. She writhed and bucked until he pulled it away.

"Please stop!"

He slapped her again.

She covered her head with her arms.

He wrenched them away. "Stop! Stop! I'm sorry, Clyde. I'm sorry," she said over and over.

"Why? Why would you do that, after all I've done for you?"

"Forgive me. Forgive me. I'm sorry."

"You're not sorry. I know you're not sorry." And Clyde was right. She wasn't. She loved Michael.

Clyde breathed hard, snorting like a wild animal. Stacey knew he was not through with her. He stood and went to his dresser where he rummaged through the top drawer. He pulled a small black case from underneath his clothes. He unzipped the case and removed a pistol. Turning back to face Stacey, he cocked the hammer of the gun. He stood over her, the gun tight in his hand. "I'm going to kill you for what you did!"

She lost all sense of fear. She was going to die, and she could do nothing about it.

Clyde dropped to his knees. He pressed the gun hard against Stacey's temple. "Lord, forgive me for what I'm about to do. My fate is in your hands."

"Clyde, no." Stacey begged for her life.

"I told you I would kill you if you ever did this," he screamed. "I told you I would kill you."

Suddenly, the ranting stopped and Clyde turned quiet. With controlled breathing, he got up and put the gun away. He went back to where Stacey was lying on the floor and gently lifted her up. He tried to wipe away her tears.

She didn't know what to expect. *When will this end?*

She sobbed loudly.

"Stop crying," he ordered.

"I'm sorry."

"I said stop. Stop it now! You're not sorry!" He held her in a tight hug, her arms limp against her side. She couldn't stop crying. He held her arms and shook her violently. "Stop crying!" She cried harder. He slapped her hard across the face. Her head snapped back. "Stop crying now!"

She knew what was coming. Clyde was going to rape her, as he had in the past. Without warning, he flung her onto the bed and screamed for her to take off her clothes. She didn't argue. He took off his pants and climbed on top of her. He drove his penis into her with violence. She gasped from the pain. He yelled, "You whore! Is this what he did to you? I wasn't good enough for you? I wasn't good enough?"

"No, that's not it," she answered. Stacey knew better than to disregard his questions.

"Then what was it?"

"Clyde, I'm not worthy of you," she said.

"You're a whore. Say it. You're a whore." He moved faster and faster.

"I am a whore."

"Say it again, louder," his breathing was intense.

"Forgive me. I am a whore."

"A whore," he muttered, and in an instant, he came.

Oh, God, please let him die, she prayed.

He buried his face in the pillow next to her head, exhausted from his rage. He was dead weight on top of her, spent, sweating. Stacey couldn't move. She couldn't breathe. The weight of his body descending on each exhalation crushed her chest. She had to control her panic. If she didn't do something she would suffocate under his weight. She tried to push him off but couldn't budge him. He was asleep. *God, please don't let him wake up.* Claustrophobia set in.

"Clyde, I can't breathe," she said in near panic. "Please get off." He was asleep, but he heard her and rolled off and onto his back. She couldn't get off the bed fast enough. Still gripped with fear, she raced naked from the bedroom and down the stairs. In the powder room, she splashed water on her face and used a hand towel to dab at a large cut alongside her ear. She was bruised and red, and her breasts were raw from his vicious groping. *I'll call the police,* she thought. Her mind whirred. *What should I do? The police can't protect me forever. He'll come back and hurt me again. I know he will.*

She looked at herself in the mirror. After a minute she felt composed. *Okay, get your clothes. Then go to Heather's. She'll know what to do.*

Clyde was now on his back, breathing normally. She glanced at him. He had a smile on his face.

A smile!

Stacey didn't hesitate. She went to the bureau, opened the drawer, and took out the pistol. She cocked it, went to the bed, and shot him in the chest. His arms shot up, then dropped to his side. His eyes opened wide—they stayed open, unblinking, unseeing.

She fired again.

Chapter 23

To cleanse the smell of Clyde from her body, Stacey took a long, hot shower. Afterwards, she sat at her vanity to dry her hair and put on her makeup. She pulled a frilly blouse and ruffled skirt from her closet and paraded around the bed naked. "I look good in blue, don't you think, Clyde?" She held the blouse and skirt up to her dead husband. "Do you like this on me? Michael did."

She felt free. Liberated at last.

Blood from Clyde's wound spread slowly across the bed. For a moment she thought about putting towels alongside his body to absorb the blood, but then laughed out loud. Her laugh was long and uncontrolled. She was free. She didn't have to worry about cleaning the bed or the blood. She was free to go anywhere, do anything, meet anyone she liked. She was no longer under Clyde's control.

"I'm sorry I killed you, Clyde. Ha! Just kidding. I'm lying, Clyde. I'm not sorry." She giggled. "I am not sorry. I said I was sorry, but really, I'm not. I loved Michael. You should have known him. He was so sweet and gentle. He made love to me like a real man. Not like you," she said. "I don't have to lie to you anymore, do I? Do you know how much you hurt me? A lot. A whole lot. So very lot." She wasn't making any sense and she knew it. She giggled again. "But I hurt you more, didn't I? Na, na, na, na, na."

Stacey took her time to finish dressing. She pulled two suitcases from the closet and filled them with carefully folded items of clothing. Each move was deliberate and precise. Downstairs in the laundry room, she pressed two of her blouses. She was in no hurry. She was enjoying her solitude without any possibility of control from Clyde. No phone calls, no painful sex, no living with the smell of his skin.

She called Heather. "Hey, girlfriend, can you come over to pick me up?"

"Sure. What's up?"

"Well, guess what. I did what you said I should do."

"What did you do?"

"I killed Clyde."

"Get the hell outta here. Have you been drinkin'?"

"Nope. I killed him, and I feel incredibly good about it. I wish there was a way I could kill him again."

"You have been drinkin', haven't you?"

"No, but I might enjoy a glass of wine until you get here. I've got my bags all packed and I'm taking whatever I can from him. I've emptied his wallet and the safe and I forged his name to a check so I can withdraw some money from the bank."

*****

Heather pulled up in front of Stacey's house fifteen minutes later. She didn't believe her friend had killed her husband. "Okay, I know you're bullshitting me. Where is he?" she asked. She wanted verification. "We talked about this. You said you didn't think you could kill him. What happened?"

"Look at my face. He beat me. He was vicious. Here, look at my body. Look at what he did to me." She lifted her blouse to show her friend the deep red bruises on her belly, breasts, and side. "I thought he was going to shoot me. He was so close to pulling the trigger. Heather, I have never been so scared in all my life. He kicked and punched me, and then raped me."

"He raped you?"

"Yes, he raped me."

"Oh, you poor, poor girl. You poor girl," was all Heather could say. Her eyes welled in sympathy and she hugged her friend. "Let me see him."

"You really want to see him? He's all bloody and everything."

"Yes, I do. I want to see."

Stacey led Heather upstairs to her bedroom. The door was closed. She swung it open and stepped in with a flourish. She gestured dramatically. "There he is, in all his glory."

Heather stepped into the bedroom and immediately turned away. "Oh, my God, Stacey." She covered her mouth and ran from the bedroom, sick from the sight of all the blood on the bed. She sat on the top step, ashen with nausea.

"Are you going to be okay?" Stacey sat next to her and rubbed her shoulders. "I'll get you a glass of water."

"Yeah, I'll be okay. Give me a second." After several deep breaths she regained her composure. "You've got to tell me every detail of what happened."

"I will. But let's go. I'll bring the gun."

Chapter 24

With Stacey's suitcases in the trunk of her Malibu, Heather headed back home. Along the way, she listened as Stacey detailed the events leading up to the shooting. Jake arrived in his pickup at the same time as Heather pulled in the driveway.

"Leave your suitcases in the car," Heather said. "We'll get them later."

"What the hell happened to you?" Jake asked Stacey upon seeing her facial bruises. He was more curious than concerned.

"I was in an accident. My airbag deployed," she lied.

He didn't care. He turned to Heather. "What's she doin' here?"

Stacey excused herself and went into to the kitchen to allow Heather to concoct a suitable excuse.

"We're goin' to the movies after dinner," Heather answered.

"What's for dinner?" he asked.

"I haven't decided yet." Heather turned and went to the kitchen.

"What the hell you been doin' all day? Screwin' somebody else?"

"Don't talk to me like that."

"Why the hell not? Are you gonna kill me like you killed your boyfriend?"

"You can say whatever you want to me, but don't talk like that in front of my friend."

"Screw you." Jake had already had several beers. He wasn't drunk, but he was close. He got himself another beer, sat down in his recliner, and turned the TV to ESPN. "Hurry up with dinner."

Heather mouthed to Stacey, "Where's the gun?"

"In my purse."

"Show me how to use it."

"You sure you want to do this?

"Positive."

"Okay, all you do is look down the barrel, aim it, and pull the trigger," she whispered.

"I ain't never shot a gun before." Heather was apprehensive. The sight of all the blood surrounding Clyde's body was still fresh in her mind. She had talked confidently about how she and Stacey should kill their husbands, but when it came down to shooting Jake, she lacked the same nerve she had shown when she killed Michael.

Several minutes elapsed. "What the hell you two doin' in there? Where's dinner?" Jake's speech was slurred. "Is it too much to ask to have dinner ready when I get home from work?"

"It'll be ready in a few minutes," Heather announced. She took the gun from Stacey, examined it, and wrapped it in a kitchen towel. She lowered her voice and asked, "Do I have to do anything with it? I mean, like, is there like a safety or somethin' I got to worry about?"

"No, it's ready to shoot. Just aim it and pull the trigger. That's all." Stacey sensed her friend's uncertainty. "Look, Heather, if you're not sure, don't do it. Just because I killed Clyde doesn't mean you have to kill Jake."

"No, I want to. Trust me, I do. It was my idea. I'm ready." She took a deep breath. "You go in and talk to him."

"About what?"

"Shit. I don't know. Whatever. Ask him about baseball. Ask him how the Dodgers are doin'. You need to divert his attention for a second. I'll be right behind you," she said.

"Are you going to be okay? One final time. Are you sure?" Stacey asked, now surprisingly the more assertive of the two.

Heather hesitated no more than a second. "Yeah, I'm good."

Stacey went into the sitting room and sat on the couch across from Jake. "When the hell is dinner gonna be ready? I been working my ass off all day and all I ask is for food to be on the table when I get home." He stared at Stacey's bruised face. "You're Stacey, right? What's your husband's name anyway?"

"Clyde."

"Do you have dinner ready for Clyde when he gets back from work?"

"Used to, but not anymore," she answered. "You never met my husband, did you?"

"No. No offense, lady, but from what I hear about him, I don't care to, either."

"Well, you won't have to worry about that," she said, and strained a smile.

"So when the hell is dinner gonna be ready?" he asked again.

"Heather told me to tell you it's almost ready. She said she wanted to make a real special meal for you. She said it would be ready in a few more minutes. Hey, Jake, how are the Dodgers doing?"

He turned to her and snarled, "What do you know about the Dodgers?"

"They're my favorite team, that's what."

Heather snuck into the sitting room with the gun still wrapped in a towel. "What the hell is takin' you so long?" Jake yelled. "Your friend said you're making me a special dinner tonight. What for?"

"For you to eat in hell!" She removed the towel and aimed the pistol at him with uncertainty. Her hands were shaking. Stacey leapt to her feet and moved further away from Jake. Heather fired the pistol at him. The bullet whizzed past his ear and thudded into the recliner.

Jake roused immediately from his near-drunken stupor. He jumped up and moved toward Heather with outstretched hand. "Heather, let me have the gun," he said with as much calm as he could muster.

Stacey stood by helplessly, not knowing what to do. She screamed, "Don't give it to him. Shoot, shoot!"

Heather held the gun unsteadily and backed slowly away from Jake toward the kitchen. She fired again. The bullet grazed his temple. His hand flew to the wound, but he kept moving toward her. She slowly backtracked into the kitchen. Enraged, he continued his advance and stopped a few feet in front of her.

"Let me have the gun, Heather! Now, I said." His voice was filled with panic, anger, dread.

"No way!" She took another step back. She bumped up against the counter, unable to retreat further.

"I said, let me have the gun," Jake shouted one last time, and sprang toward her. She fired again, this time hitting him in his left side. He staggered back and looked down at the blood spurting from his wound. "You bitch whore!" He tried to stem the flow of blood with his right hand. He stepped toward her again. She saw the blood oozing between his fingers, coloring his shirt and pants, and for a moment wanted to stop and help him.

"Shoot him," Stacey yelled, urging her friend on.

Jake flashed a look of loathing at Stacey and staggered toward Heather. "You killer bitch whore."

Heather shot again. The bullet hit Jake in his chest. His arms flailed, as if he were sparring against an invisible boxer. Blood trickled from the corner of his mouth.

He fell backward against a kitchen chair and crashed to the floor.

"Is he dead? Is he dead?" Heather asked.

Stacey checked his pulse and found none. "Yes, I think he's dead," she answered.

Heather looked at Stacey. "I hated him. I hated him, hated him."

"I know you did, Heather. I know you did. I hated Clyde, too."

Heather could not stop shaking. "I hate men. I hate them all. Hate them," she said over and over.

Stacey hugged her tightly. "Everything will be okay." She took the gun from Heather's limp hand and put it on the kitchen table.

"What do we do now, Stacey? What do we do now?"

Heather was in shock. "Come on, Heather. Help me move him into the garage so we don't have to look at him." They grabbed his lifeless arms and dragged his body to the garage, leaving a trail of blood across the kitchen floor.

Stacey closed the door behind them. "Heather, now look. We have to get going. All this happened so fast. Let's think. We have to get moving. You've got to pack."

"Okay. I'll go do that now."

Stacey was concerned. "Are you going to be okay?"

"Yes, fine. I hated him, Stacey. You know that, don't you?"

"Yes, I know. Now, listen. I've got to get to the bank before it closes so I can cash that check."

Heather stared at her friend and nodded vacantly.

"I'm taking your car. I'll be back as soon as I can. Will you be okay here by yourself?"

"Yeah, I'll be good."

Stacey returned in less than thirty minutes and found Heather in her bedroom packing. "I got a thousand dollars." She fanned herself with the bills, proud of her accomplishment. "And how are you doing?"

"I'm better. Look what I have," Heather said, half smiling.

She pulled the Georgia O'Keeffe painting from under her bed.

"My God, it's beautiful. Where did you get it?"

"I can't say, but we're gonna sell it. I know a pawn shop I think will take it that's open late. We should be able to get thousands for it. This will give us enough money to really help us out."

They put the painting in Jake's pickup and headed straight to Amos Green's pawn shop.

*****

"Heather, don't you think you should do this? I don't know what to do. I've never set foot inside a pawn shop."

"You'll be fine. Tell him you want ten thousand dollars. He won't give it to you, so settle for five or six. You won't have any problem. It's probably worth a hundred thousand."

"A hundred thousand? And I'm only going to ask for ten?"

"That's how these things work, Stacey. Look at it this way. It's not like we paid a hundred thousand for it, so we're not losin' any money. Any extra we can get now is bonus money for us. Now, go on in and get what you can."

Stacey was still hesitant but she carried the painting inside and laid it on the counter.

Amos Green was a pro without scruples. He would say anything to negotiate the best deal for himself. He examined the painting and asked, "How much do you want?"

Stacey knew she had to be assertive if she were to have any chance of success. She blurted, "Ten thousand dollars."

"You're kidding me. It looks to me like this is a fake. I'll give you a hundred dollars."

Stacey gasped. "A hundred dollars?" She didn't know what to say or do. Her inclination was to run and get Heather for help, but she realized she had to bargain on her own. "It ... it can't be a fake. I'm sure it's not. Let me have five thousand ... please."

Amos didn't hesitate. "Look, it's a forgery, but it's a good one, so I'll give you six hundred for it. Take it or leave it. That's my final offer."

She hesitated. *Maybe he's right. Maybe it is a forgery. I'd better take his offer. Something is better than nothing.* She agreed to Amos's offer, signed the receipt, and headed for the door.

"Don't you want your money?"

"Oh … yes." She raced back to the counter and grabbed the stack of cash. Back in the pickup, she told Heather what had happened.

"Holy shit. What the hell is wrong with you? That damn painting is worth a fortune and you only got six hundred dollars for it?"

Stacey burst into tears. "I'm sorry, Heather. I didn't know what to do. I told you you should have gone in instead of me."

Heather realized there was no use in yelling at her friend and calmed down immediately. They were in this together. "All right, don't cry. You're right. I should'a gone in, but it's done now. It's not your fault. It's gettin' late and we're both tired. I wasn't thinkin' straight. It's six hundred dollars more than what we started with so let's get the hell out of here."

Back at home, Heather pulled the pickup into her driveway alongside her car. "We got to hurry. We've got a lot to do. You get your suitcases from the car and put them in the back of the truck," she said, once again asserting her dominance. "I'll get mine, too, and then we're gonna take everything from the pantry that we can fit into the truck. Once we get to the house in Golden, we have to stay out of sight. We won't be able to show our faces in public until this blows over, and I don't know how long that's gonna be. It could be weeks."

After Stacey loaded her suitcases onto the truck, she went back to the kitchen, and got down her on her hands and knees to clean up Jake's blood.

"What the hell are you doing?"

Stacey was overcome with guilt. "I'm cleaning this mess. I might feel a little better if I don't have to look at it."

"Well, don't look at it then. Come on, Stacey. We got a lot to do."

Stacey started to cry again. "I can't believe we killed our husbands. Oh, my God, what have we become?"

Heather helped her friend to her feet and hugged her. "Listen, Stacey, we did it because we had to. There was no other way. You and I both know it. Now, you gotta pull yourself together. We just have to get out of here."

"I'm exhausted, Heather. I'm so tired."

They both were exhausted—emotionally and physically spent.

"I am, too. I am, too." Heather thought for a moment. "Okay, Stacey, listen. Listen to me. We gotta go. I know it's late, but you can sleep in the car."

"I can't. I'm so tired. I don't want to go. I'm going to the police and tell them what I did."

"No. You can't. What about me?"

"You go by yourself. I won't say a word," Stacey begged.

"Pull yourself together. We gotta go. What you did was the right thing to do. Clyde woulda killed you. You told me that. The cops won't care why you did it. You'll spend the rest of your life in jail. Is that what you want?"

"No. I ... I don't know what to do."

"Okay, all right, here's what we'll do. You're right. We're both really tired. Let's get some sleep here. We have to have our wits about us. We gotta think straight. No one knows what we did. It'll be days before anyone thinks to look for Clyde or Jake. We can take our time tomorrow, and pack everything we can think of. If we have to, we'll go to the store to pick up whatever else we might need. It'll be better if we leave at night, so when it gets dark tomorrow, that's when we'll leave. Okay?"

Chapter 25

"Hank, the painting showed up."

"The O'Keeffe? Where was it?"

"Sergeant Evans of our Robbery Division found it. He's here with me. I'll let him tell you. Let me put you on speaker."

"Mr. Kincaid, how're you doing? Sorry to bother you on a Saturday, but part of my job is to interface with the pawn shops in the city. I check in on them from time to time to see if I can spot any stolen goods from a list Robbery puts together. I was at a shop on Bridge Street last night and recognized the O'Keeffe painting from the description on the list. We're sure it's the one stolen from Carlotta Smith's house."

"I'm sure there aren't too many others like that floating around out there."

"The pawn shop owner is a shady character by the name of Amos Green. He's been receiving stolen goods for as long as I've been on the force and probably for twenty years before that. He fences stuff from lowlifes, gives them a penny on a dollar of real value. They can't argue too much about how much money he's lending them—I use the word *lending* loosely—because they usually have nowhere else to go. As you probably know, a legitimate pawn shop owner makes his money by charging interest for the money lent, and uses the pawned item as collateral. If the item isn't reclaimed in thirty days, the shop owner has the right to sell it. A thief doesn't come back. He pockets the money, and it's adiós, goodbye, see-you-again-when-I-have-something-else. Sometimes, we even catch the sons of bitches and they end up in a courtroom."

"I've prosecuted a few myself. What does Green do with the stolen goods?"

"He turns around and sells the stuff for huge gains. When I asked him about the painting, he said he got it last night. He paid six hundred dollars for it, but didn't know the real value of the painting or that it was stolen. Said he thought it was a forgery. He was lying, of course. And he knew the person who pawned it wasn't going to come back to reclaim it. He was probably going to ship it out of state to a middleman for fenced artwork who'd then sell it to a foreign buyer. That way, everybody makes a healthy buck except the person who stole it in the first place."

"Yeah, that's a pretty nice business model Mr. Green put together. Why don't we close him down?" Hank asked.

"We've tried to, but he's got a shyster lawyer who finds ways to beat the charges. His defense being that Amos didn't know it was stolen. Another reason we don't go after him hard is because it's good to know where stolen stuff is headed. We sometimes focus on Amos' shop when something goes down."

"Who pawned the painting?"

"It was a woman. The ticket was signed by an Evelyn Patterson. The name is bogus and the address she gave is an empty lot in the southeast section of town."

"So he actually had a receipt for it?"

"Yeah. He'd have no defense against a charge of receiving stolen goods if he didn't document every trade. He set the value of the painting at two thousand dollars."

"Two thousand dollars? You're kidding me. That painting was one of the few she ever signed. It might be worth up to fifty times that amount."

"Yeah, he knew it. When he saw me enter his shop, he tried to hide it behind the counter before I could see it. I got there probably only five or ten minutes after he made the transaction."

"Damn. You were that close to nailing our suspect in Carlotta Smith's murder."

"Yeah, I was close," Evans echoed. "We have a video from

inside the pawn shop. It's pretty grainy, but you can take a look at it when you want. The woman was wearing jeans and a baseball cap pulled tight over her forehead, so you can't really see her eyes. We tried to enhance it, but the quality of the video is so bad it doesn't help much."

"We're checking for fingerprints on the receipt she signed at the pawn shop," DeGarzia said.

Hank thought immediately of the prime suspect in Redfield's murder. "Heather Dorell's?"

"Hard to say for sure, but I don't think so," DeGarzia answered. "Heather's tall. The woman in the video looks to be much shorter."

"Did Green give a description?"

"From what he could see of her face under her hat, she was badly bruised, like she'd been in an accident or someone had smacked her around. He was going to ask her what happened, but never did, figuring it was none of his business."

"Anything else?" Hank asked.

"Yeah. Apparently the woman whined that the painting was worth more than what he offered for it. He told her to go to another pawn shop if she didn't like his offer. At that point she looked out the window, as if looking for someone to help her out or tell her what to do. He said she was so nervous, after she agreed on the price she started to leave without the money. You can see that on the tape. She was almost out the door before she remembered and had to go back to get the money."

"Any chance he spotted the car she was driving?"

"Said he didn't notice. But we're checking security cameras outside to see what she did after leaving the pawn shop. Given the high crime in that area, nearly all the stores on that street have a camera trained on the front of their shops."

Deeg added, "I'll let you know what we find out about the fingerprints."

"Okay. I'll fill the DA in on these latest findings."

*****

Deeg learned the fingerprints on the pawn shop receipt belonged to Stacey Keenan.

"You've got to be kidding me. Stacey Keenan?" Hank said. "She's the one who pawned the painting?"

Deeg added, "Yeah. At this point, we can say she was probably involved in Smith's killing."

"I agree. It's likely she was also involved in Redfield's murder. What the hell. I never would have guessed it. Stacey Keenan? Everything's falling into place."

"You never know in this business, do you?"

Chapter 26

Armed with an arrest warrant for Stacey Keenan, DeGarzia sped to the Keenan house accompanied by two backup squad cars. At the house, one of the cops went around to the back and another stayed with DeGarzia who pounded on the front door. "Police! Open up!" He turned the doorknob. It was unlocked. He drew his service revolver, held it aloft, and threw the door open. "Police! We have a warrant!"

There was no response. With guns drawn they walked to the kitchen where they opened the back door to let the other cop in. The three searched each room on the first floor and found no one. In the powder room, they discovered the bloodstained towel Stacey had used to dab her wounds.

They climbed the stairway to the second floor where they saw the door to the master bedroom was closed. They listened intently, but heard no sound from within. Deeg shouted, "Police! Come out with your hands up!"

No response.

Flanked by the two cops, Deeg threw the door open. They rushed into the room, pistols held high.

Clyde Keenan's body was on the bed encircled in dried blood. "God almighty," DeGarzia said. It was obvious Clyde had been dead a day or longer.

They searched every nook and cranny of the house, inside every closet, under every bed. When DeGarzia was convinced the house was empty, he called for the medical examiner and his team of forensic experts. Within fifteen minutes two other squad cars arrived, sirens blaring and lights flashing. An ambulance arrived a minute later.

DeGarzia called Hank. "It appears Stacey Keenan killed her husband. We found him in their bedroom, a couple of shots to his chest. She's nowhere to be found. Both cars are still in the garage."

"Could he have been killed by someone else?"

"It's possible, but I don't think so. It looks like she packed a bag and emptied the safe on her way out. She's on the run. Everything points to her being the killer."

"If both cars are still there, someone had to have picked her up."

"I'm on my way to Heather Dorell's now to see if she knows what's going on."

"Be careful, Deeg."

Chapter 27

Heather and Stacey slept fitfully and woke Saturday morning just before ten. Stacey felt an odd sense of curiosity and looked in the garage. She knew Jake's body would still be there, but she was drawn to check again.

"Stop looking at him, Stacey. He's not going anyplace."

"I know. I just ... wanted to make sure."

They took their time, carefully loading the pickup with every bit of food from the kitchen and every other supply they thought they might need. If they were stressed from the day before, it didn't show. Even so, Heather kept a close eye on Stacey, uncertain of her state of mind. Neither said much, but worked methodically throughout the day. When they finished packing, they covered the bed of the truck with a tarp, tying it down tightly for the trip to the remote town of Golden. They would leave at dusk.

Heather carefully tucked Clyde's pistol into the bottom of her purse. "It's starting to get dark. It's about time to go," she announced.

There was a knock on the front door.

The two women froze. "Who could that be?" Stacey whispered. She peeked around the corner from the kitchen to the front door. "Oh my God, it's that detective." DeGarzia waited patiently at the front door for someone to answer his knock. He rang the doorbell and waited.

Stacey was in a panic. She watched as DeGarzia headed for the driveway. "Oh no. He's looking underneath the tarp in the pickup. Now he's walking around to the back."

"Shhhh."

The phone rang. "Could that be him? Is he calling from the driveway? What do we do? What do you think he wants?" Stacey was completely unnerved.

Heather took the gun from her purse and quietly stepped outside around the corner from where DeGarzia was heading.

"What are you doing, Heather?" Stacey grabbed her by the elbow.

Heather shook loose from Stacey's grip.

Just as DeGarzia turned the corner, Heather fired.

The huge man crumbled to the ground, his cell phone dropping from his hand. After a second he rolled over and looked up, trying to focus on who had shot him. He recognized Heather and reached for the pistol in his shoulder holster. She stepped on his arm and ground down on it. DeGarzia was powerless to fight back. He was badly hurt. She yelled at him, "What are you doing here? Why don't you leave us alone?"

He looked up with glazed eyes. "Why?"

Heather waved the gun frantically at a helpless DeGarzia who lay at her feet and screamed, "You wouldn't understand. You wouldn't understand." Stacey approached and put her arm around Heather's shoulder. She pleaded with her. "Heather, please. Don't shoot him. He's only doing his job. Let's go. Please."

Deeg's head dropped to the ground.

Chapter 28

Deeg awoke in Santa Fe's CHRISTUS St. Vincent Regional Medical Center. He was breathing with the help of an oxygen line and fluids were being pumped into his body via an intravenous tube. His large frame filled the hospital bed. Twenty-four hours earlier, Heather Dorell had shot and nearly killed him. He blinked several times to clear the fog from his eyes. Slowly, he moved his head to the left, sensing others in the room. He saw Hank, his boss, Captain of Detectives David Ellsworth, and Police Chief Matthew Tremont.

The nurse tending to him spoke in a soothing voice, "You're going to be okay, Detective."

"What...happened?" he murmured. "What ... time ... day is it?"

Hank moved closer to his bed. "It's Sunday afternoon. You're at CHRISTUS. Someone shot you when you were at the Dorell's house yesterday evening."

Ellsworth asked, "Do you know who it was?"

They waited for Deeg to speak. Through dried, cracked lips, he said, "Heather ... Dorell."

"Deeg, we're going to get out of here," the chief said. "The doctor says you're going to be fine, but you lost some blood and it'll be a few days before they'll release you."

"I'll ... be ... okay," he said, mustering strength.

"We'll be back when the doctor gives the okay to talk to you. For now, get some rest."

Deeg nodded imperceptibly and fell back to sleep.

The three men stepped out of the room, and Ellsworth told a cop standing guard outside, "No one gets in without proper ID."

"Yessir, Captain."

"Hank, Chief, let's go down to the waiting room and I'll fill you in on what we know."

In the waiting room a dozen cops, most off duty and some still in uniform, stood waiting for news about DeGarzia. "Officers, first off, thank you for your concern. It was nip and tuck for a while," Ellsworth announced, "but Deeg's going to be okay. He's lost a lot of blood, but he'll pull through and be back to his usual pain-in-the-ass self in no time. Now, go home, all of you. And, please, be careful." He shook hands with each officer and accepted every condolence hug.

Hank, Tremont, and Ellsworth sat after the room had emptied. "As you can imagine, gentlemen, this is the toughest part of my job," Tremont said.

Hank and Ellsworth both nodded in understanding.

"Has Deeg's family been notified?"

"As far as we know," Ellsworth said, "he has no immediate family in the area."

Hank got right to the point. "So, what, exactly, went down leading to Deeg being shot?"

Ellsworth responded, "Here's what we know. The ME said Clyde Keenan and Jake Dorell were both killed sometime Friday evening. We found Dorell in his garage with gunshot wounds to the side of his head, torso, and chest. There was a confession note of sorts on the kitchen table at his house. It said, 'We couldn't take it anymore.' I'm not sure if their murders tie into the Redfield and Smith deaths, but if they do, it means Heather Dorell and Stacey Keenan are probably responsible for four murders."

"You may be right. The Georgia O'Keeffe painting turning up at the pawn shop seems to be the smoking gun that ties it all together. I'm now wondering if those two women were also responsible for the deaths of Alex Castillo and Tomás Pérez."

*****

The duty nurse phoned Hank first thing Monday morning. "Mr. Kincaid, Detective DeGarzia would like to see you. He had a restful night, and he insists on getting out of bed. The doctor cautioned him about doing too much too soon but the man is as strong as a horse and about as stubborn as a mule."

"I'll be right over."

When Hank arrived, DeGarzia was sitting in a chair, still connected to an intravenous tube, and wearing a sling to support his wounded shoulder. Captain Ellsworth was already there.

"Deeg, good to see you up. You gave everyone quite a scare. Are you up to talking?"

Deeg nodded. He strained his memory, not wanting to leave out any detail of the events of forty-eight hours earlier. In measured manner, he described what happened. "Most of it is coming back to me. I left the Keenan's while the forensics team was still there gathering evidence. I drove to the Dorell's to find out if Heather knew the whereabouts of Stacey and to see if she knew anything about Clyde's murder."

Hank affirmed Deeg's version of events. "That's right. That's the last time you and I spoke."

"Both the Dorells' vehicles were in the driveway, so I knew someone had to be home. No one came to the door when I knocked. When I tried opening it, it was locked. I went to the bay window and looked in, but couldn't see anything. I noticed there was a blue tarp covering the bed of their pickup, so I looked under it, and saw suitcases and groceries."

Deeg reached for the cup of water on the nearby table. "Sorry. My mouth is dry."

"We can come back later, Detective."

"No, Captain, give me a second."

"You are one strong dude," Hank said. "But don't push it."

Deeg nodded and continued. "Where was I?"

"You saw suitcases packed in the pickup."

"Yeah. I called the house to see if someone would answer. The phone rang a couple of times and the message recorder came on, so I hung up. I walked around back. Captain, all I wanted to do was find out what Heather knew about Stacey's whereabouts. I didn't suspect a thing at first. But something didn't seem right. Suitcases and food in the truck ... No one answering the door ... I decided to call for backup. I remember taking out my phone, turning the corner, and that's when I took a round. The rest of what happened is fuzzy, but I remember being on the ground and trying to pull out my piece. Heather showed up and ground her shoe into my arm to keep me from getting it. I'm sure she's the one who shot me. I remember looking up and seeing her standing over me waving a pistol. She was screaming, 'Why don't you leave us alone?' I couldn't do anything to defend myself. She was ready to shoot me again, but someone, another woman, told her not to shoot. The next thing I know, I wake up here."

"Who was the other woman?" Hank asked.

"I think it was Stacey Keenan, but I'm not positive."

"We found Jake Dorell's body in the garage," Ellsworth added. "He'd been shot three times. Ballistics showed he was shot with the same gun used to kill Clyde Keenan."

"Who was the shooter?" Deeg asked.

"We don't know for sure. The only thing we do know is that both wives are involved. One of them is the killer and the other is either a killer or an accessory. We also learned more about the activity at the pawn shop Friday night. A security camera from a neighboring store showed Stacey getting into Jake's pickup after exiting the pawn shop. We were able to read the license," he explained. "But we couldn't tell who the driver was."

"Heather?" Deeg asked.

"Don't know, but it probably was."

"And probably in the same pickup Smith saw leaving Via Encantado the night of Redfield's murder," Hank remarked.

"Again, it could have been. At this point, we have no way to know for sure."

"I'm curious, Captain. How did I end up here?" Deeg asked.

"A woman called 9-1-1, but she didn't identify herself. We have the recording. She said someone shot a cop, gave them the Dorells' address, and hung up. We've got a voice analysis expert checking the 9-1-1 tape."

"Maybe a neighbor," Hank suggested.

"Or Stacey," Deeg offered.

"Why her?" the captain asked.

Deeg shook his head. He looked first at Hank then at Ellsworth. "I'm speculating here, but when I questioned her about Redfield, it became obvious Clyde Keenan was an abusive husband. I told her I knew what she was going through." He hesitated, and stared at the floor. "My father was abusive to me, and I know how hopeless Stacey had to have been feeling. I told her to get help, to get away from her husband. Maybe she ... because ..."

Hank saw Deeg was getting emotional so he finished his thought for him. "Sometimes, when two people go through a similar type of traumatic episode, they bond. That happens in grief, too. If it was Stacey who saved your life by keeping Heather from shooting you again, it wouldn't surprise me that she was the one who made the call to 9-1-1."

"Any sign of either?"

"We have an APB out, but nothing yet."

*****

Heather pulled a small key out of her pocket and opened the lock on a rusty iron gate located at the entrance to a long, dirt driveway. She got back in the pickup, drove through the gate, and stopped again to lock the gate behind her.

They had driven an hour southwest of Santa Fe to arrive at a ranch situated between the ghost town of Golden and the small town of Cedar Grove. As the pickup made its way up the driveway, Stacey saw a small, adobe-style ranch house that looked over an unforgiving desert. A barbed wire fence surrounded the entire property which offered wide lookout vistas from every direction. "How in the world did you ever find this place?" Stacey asked.

"I looked for someplace where I didn't have to worry about nobody stickin' their nose in my business," she explained. "I went on the computer and I looked at, like, a hundred places, and that's how I found it. Hardly nobody lives down here. No one's gonna find us here if we play it smart. We keep the gate locked and we stay in the house. If we go out of the house, we go out back where nobody can see us from the road. That way, ain't nobody gonna know we're here. When I talked to the realtor, he said drug runners from Juarez used the house for smugglin' until the cops broke up their ring."

"How did you explain to the realtor why you wanted the house? I mean, it's in the boonies," Stacey declared. "He had to be suspicious."

"No. He didn't give a rat's ass. I made up a story that I was a writer and needed to be by myself so I could concentrate on writin' my book."

"And he believed you?"

"No, I don't think so, but he didn't care. It was a rental, and that's all he cared about. Nobody's rented this house for months, so he was just happy to have a taker."

"I couldn't imagine living here all the time," Stacey said.

Heather narrowed her eyes. "Well, get used to it, sweetheart, because this is where we're gonna be for the next couple a months."

After parking the pickup behind the house, the two women unloaded their suitcases and supplies. In the kitchen, Stacey opened every cabinet. "My God, look at all the food you've got here. How long did it take you to get all this out here?"

"I came here every couple a days."

"Didn't Jake realize your grocery bill was through the roof? Clyde sure would have noticed."

"He didn't have no clue. The important thing is, Stacey, we got to make everything last. We can't go out to a store or anywhere, even for a little bit. I figure the cops will be lookin' pretty hard for us for a while. Our pictures will be everywhere, you wait and see."

"You should have told me what you were doing. I could have helped you."

"I didn't know things would happen like they did. I didn't know how you felt about, you know, killin' Clyde."

"I still don't know, Heather. What I do know is that I'm going to hell for what I did."

Heather corrected her. "You ain't going to hell. Clyde's the one goin' to hell. He and Jake are gonna be there together."

Chapter 29

Cyclist Killed: Jordan Sanchez, 45, of Santa Fe, was found dead in a gorge in Iluminada Canyon on Sunday evening. His body was discovered by a motorist on an isolated stretch of Camino Hermoso near Nambe Lake. Sanchez was a partner at the law firm of Terwilliger, Smith and Sanchez. He had clerked for the late Supreme Court Justice William Rehnquist, was a trustee of the Santa Fe Indian School for Boys, a Second Vice President of the Santa Fe Bar Association, a triathlete, and Vice President of the Canyon Cycling Club. There were no known witnesses. He leaves a wife and two daughters. Funeral arrangements are incomplete at this time. Police are investigating the cause of his death as a possible hit-and-run. Anyone with any information is asked to call the police at 505-222-9999.

"I faced off against Jordan a couple of times in court. He was a good defense attorney, a good guy," Hank said to DeGarzia.

After a month's medical leave, Deeg was back at work, seated at his cluttered desk. Without looking up, he stated, "Those two women killed him."

"Heather and Stacey? How do you know?"

"I know at the very least the red-headed bitch was involved," DeGarzia said. His anger toward the woman who shot him was apparent. "Like you've said all along, it can't be just another coincidence. We found a cigarette butt near where Sanchez ran off the road, and the lab matched it to her DNA. I think it's beyond circumstantial now. Those two are serial murderers."

"Given the manner in which they all died … Castillo, Pérez, Redfield, and now Sanchez—it really does look as though they may have murdered all four."

"Add in their husbands and Carlotta Smith, their victim count stands at seven."

"Forget the husbands for a minute. There's got to be something that ties all the other murders together," Hank said. "We know about the affairs the women had with Redfield. Is it possible they had sexual relationships with those other men, too?"

"I will find a link. It might take time, but I'll find it. They're guilty as sin."

Hank recognized a change in Deeg. Since returning from leave, his emotions were ready to boil over in an instant—even more than usual. With a vendetta against Heather, he was hell bent on proving her guilty.

*****

The multiple murders made national news. Banner headlines on newspapers across the country read "Massive Manhunt Underway in New Mexico" and "Thelma and Louise Ride Again." Some in the media enjoyed paralleling vague similarities between the disappearance of Heather Dorell and Stacey Keenan and the *Thelma and Louise* movie in which two women cross the country after committing murder.

A dozen newspaper and TV correspondents converged on Santa Fe police headquarters to report on the progress of the case. Captain Ellsworth gave periodic updates and answered questions from the media. Where did they think the two women were hiding? How could they have eluded the search these past weeks? Did they go to Mexico? Could they still be in Santa Fe? Why cyclists? Were all cyclists in potential jeopardy, and, what could be the motive? Theories and speculation abounded.

*****

In the midst of the media frenzy, Deeg received an anonymous letter in the mail. Using letters cut from a newspaper, the sender had addressed an envelope to Detective Lawrence DeGarzia, Santa Fe Police Department, New Mexico. Deeg put on latex gloves and carefully opened the letter using a box cutter. He extracted what appeared to be a page from a newspaper. When he unfolded it, he saw it was the front page of a recent *USA Today* newspaper with an article that headlined the death of Jordan Sanchez. Deeg noticed a series of letters throughout the text of the article had been circled with a ballpoint pen. He wrote the letters on his notepad in the same sequence as they appeared in the article: *t – h – e – y – d – o – n – o – k – i – l – l – h – i – m – i – d – o – t – h – e – l – m – e.*

DeGarzia called Hank. "Hank, I got a letter I thought you ought to know about. It's a column from *USA Today* with the headline about *Thelma and Louise*, and it has a series of letters circled on the page. When I write the letters down in sequence, it reads, 'they do no kill him I do,' and it's signed '*Thelme*,' like *Thelma*, only ending with *e* instead of *a*."

"Where was it sent from?"

"It was postmarked Albuquerque. Could be a hoax. You know as well as I do that copycats and other sick people come out of the woodwork when these kinds of crimes occur. I had the lab check for prints, but it was clean."

"I don't know," Hank said. "There's something about this one that makes me think it might be legit."

Chapter 30

Nearly five weeks had passed since Heather and Stacey disappeared. Sam and Hank were on their usual Thursday evening bike ride.

"So, are the cops any closer to finding those two girls?"

"Can't say, Sam. It could be any day, or it could be weeks. No one knows where they went, and they haven't been seen since DeGarzia was shot," Hank said.

"So, let me get this straight. From what the newspapers are saying, they killed Redfield, then they killed that old lady because she was a witness, then they killed their husbands, then they try to kill your detective friend, right? And now Sanchez, too? I gotta tell you, it's getting to the point I don't want to ride by myself. What do you think, Hank? You think they killed all those people?"

"We're looking into it." He didn't elaborate any further, not wanting to get into the details of the police investigation.

The two were riding at the rear of a group of ten cyclists. The riders in this group were all strong cyclists, and each rode with the understanding no one would be dropped or left behind. Riding mostly in pairs, the cyclists stretched out for fifty yards on the lightly trafficked road outside the city. Hank and Sam were riding alongside each other as they often did. Sam was his usual talkative self. Hank didn't mind. Sam's jokes, trivia, or other news about something he had seen on TV or read in the paper always managed to amuse or interest him.

"Hank, I've got something to tell you. I've been debating for a while if I should. I know you'll be pissed, but I've gotta tell you anyway."

"Sounds serious," Hank said. He looked at Sam to see if he really was serious or about to tell him another tale.

"It's serious."

"Okay. Go ahead."

"If I tell you something in confidence, you can't tell anyone what I've told you, okay? Attorney-client privilege."

"You're not my client."

"Well, in some ways I am, because we're friends. Can I tell you something in secret?"

Hank was unable to fathom what Sam could possibly tell him that required an oath of secrecy.

"It can't go any further than between you and me. You can't tell DeGarzia, okay?"

"No, Sam, I can't promise you that. Tell me what it is, and I'll let you know if I feel I need to tell anyone. Are you in trouble?"

"No, nothing like that. At least I hope not, after I tell you what I got to tell you."

"Just tell me. What's up?"

"Back about four, five months ago," Sam hesitated. "I had a one-nighter with Heather Dorell."

"You're shitting me." Hank nearly collided with Sam upon hearing the revelation. "What the hell. Are you telling me the truth, Sam?"

"Yeah, true story."

"Why didn't you tell me before?"

"I was going to, after I read about her killing her husband. And then I didn't, and more time went by, and I knew you'd be pissed. I didn't think it was anything I had to admit to. It wasn't any big deal. I didn't think it was something I had to share."

"So why are you telling me now?"

"I don't know. Maybe it's because I shacked up with a killer and—shit, man, I don't know why I'm telling you now."

Hank was occasionally irritated by things Sam did or said, but this latest news angered him. "Sam, it might have made a difference," he said.

"Aw, come on Hank, a difference about what?"

"You should have leveled with me. I've got to tell DeGarzia."

"You said you wouldn't say anything."

"I didn't say that. I never promised you confidentiality. Do you know where Heather is hiding out?"

"Hell no. I don't know where she is. If I did, I would have told you. Look, I'm sorry I even mentioned it."

Hank did not respond. Sam saw he was upset. "All right, Hank, I'm sorry. Okay?"

Without a word, Hank took off on a hard interval and opened up a lengthy distance from the rest of the group. He reached the parking lot ahead of the other cyclists. Sam caught up to him as he was putting his bike on his bike rack. He apologized again.

"Let me buy you a slice at Jimi's," Sam said.

Hank glanced at Sam then looked away. "I can't. I've got to get home."

"Hank, I said I was sorry. Let me explain what happened."

"You either tell me you're going to talk to DeGarzia or you tell me here and now what happened."

"You're too pissed to listen. Let's sit at Jimi's, and I'll tell you everything you want to know. How 'bout it?"

Hank stared at Sam long and hard. Finally, he relented. "I'll go, but no bullshit. And no promise I won't tell DeGarzia, either. Understood?"

"Understood."

Sam followed Hank to Jimi's. Cyclists from the Club soon filled the small restaurant. A number of Heather and Stacey's former riding buddies greeted Sam and Hank as they entered. Sam, in particular, was the center of attention. He said hello to Jimi's wife, Dahlia, who worked the cash register, and spoke briefly to several others. Sam always had a funny story to tell. With his outgoing, affable personality, he was popular with everyone.

Most were talking about Heather and Stacey and their killing spree. A reporter from the daily local newspaper interviewed anyone who agreed to talk about the two women, either with accreditation or off the record.

In the back corner of the restaurant, a WKOB TV correspondent and her camera crew had set up lights and was interviewing Jimi Rodriguez, the owner and namesake of the pizza shop. At first he was not open to an interview, but he soon realized this newfound publicity could be a boon for business and agreed to answer the reporter's questions. Jimi offered his opinions of the cyclists who frequented his restaurant and was generous with his praise.

The reporter asked, "What can you tell me about all these cyclists?"

"They're all nice people," he said. "They come in every Thursday night, always laughing and joking, as you can see."

"Do you know the two women the police are looking for?"

"Yes, I know them. I mean, I don't know them personally. I only know them because they came in here a lot. I know the one woman, Heather—a very pretty lady. The other lady, Stacey, was quiet, but she was nice, polite, you know what I mean? She never stayed too long. She'd have a slice of pizza and sip a beer, and then she would leave."

"What about Michael Redfield?"

Jimi hesitated. "I didn't know him personally. But he seemed like a nice man, a real nice man, friendly. Who would have guessed?"

The reporter noticed the attention Sam received when he entered the pizzeria. She tried to pull him into an interview, but Sam politely refused. He knew it was best to meet with Hank away from all the noise and ruckus in the main dining room. The two men went to the rear dining room.

"You seem to know everyone. You come here a lot, don't you?" Hank said.

"Yeah, I usually do. You always go home to your family after a ride and I come to Jimi's for a pizza with the gang. We enjoy each other's company and sometimes it leads to other things."

"Like with Heather?"

"Like with Heather."

"And the after-parties? Do you go to them, too?"

"Yeah, most times."

"Tell me about you and Heather."

"We were at Victor Hewitt's house. I don't know if you know him. The after-party was at his house, so that's where it all started. The guy owns a big-ass house on Camino del Fuego."

"Yeah, I know him. Go on."

"There's really nothing to say. I hooked up with Heather that night we were at Victor's. She was in no hurry to go home, so we hung out. We were the last ones to leave. I'd hardly even spoken to her before that night. It was pretty obvious she had her eye on Redfield. Anyway, she had too much to drink, and I figured I'd see if I could get lucky. When everyone left, we kind of ended up together. I mean, the whole thing came out of left field. She'd never shown any interest in me before, you know? She was a knockout, and I didn't think she'd give me the time of day. I invited her to my house, not thinking she'd say yes. But she did. Then things kinda happened, all of a sudden. You know what I mean?" Sam paused, shaking his head as he recalled his surprising tryst with the beautiful Heather Dorell. Hank remained silent.

"She left her car at Victor's, and I drove her to my house. On the way, she was leaning her head back on the headrest, and I thought maybe she passed out or something. But when we got to my house, it's like she woke up and turned into a wild woman. Whew! I tell you. I mean, she wasn't in any hurry to go home, and stayed for a couple of hours. I guess eventually she sobered up enough she thought she should go home, so I drove her back to her car. Never said nothing. Didn't say goodbye, thank you, up yours, nothing. She got out of my car, climbed into hers, and drove off. It was like bang, bang, thank you ma'am. No fond farewells there. She just left."

"Did you shack up with her again?"

"No, just that one night. We never talked about it. She wouldn't even look at me afterwards. I'm pretty sure that's when she hooked up with Redfield. I'm telling you, she didn't pay any attention to me. But it didn't matter. I started seeing someone else, and I didn't care about her. As good as it was, I knew it was that one time only and, honestly, it was for the better. From what I understand, her husband was a mean-spirited asshole."

"She talk to you about Redfield or her husband?"

"That night? No, not about Redfield. Not at all. I asked her if her husband would worry about her. She said she didn't give a shit about him. Said she hated him, wished he were dead. She never said anything about Redfield, though. Look, Hank, I had a one-nighter. That was it."

"I still don't know why you didn't tell me about this earlier."

"You're right. I should have. I'm sorry. I really am. I promise I'll see DeGarzia and tell him what happened."

"I think that's for the best, Sam."

*****

Sam was uneasy as he entered police headquarters. He saw cops coming and going, suspects being questioned, victims giving statements, and detectives working mountains of paperwork or filing reports. A cop directed Sam to DeGarzia.

"Detective, my name is Sam Bailey. Hank Kincaid asked me to talk to you."

"Who did you say you were?"

"Sam Bailey."

Deeg moved some papers around on his desk and glanced up. "Hank Kincaid's friend? What did you want to see me about?"

"I need to tell you about something that happened between Heather Dorell and me."

"Okay, so what happened between Heather Dorell and you?"

"I had a one-night stand with her, like, five months back, and Hank thought you should know about it. Not sure why, but he said maybe you'd want to ask me some questions about her that might help you find her."

Deeg scribbled something on his pad, and asked, "Do you know where she is?"

"No."

"Not even a clue?"

"None."

"She ever mention anything to you about Michael Redfield?"

"No."

"Did she tell you she was going to kill her husband?"

"No."

"So what can you tell me that I would give a shit about?"

"Nothing." Sam felt uncomfortable. "I shacked up with her one night. I have no idea where she is. She never talked about Redfield. She said she hated her husband, but never said anything more about him."

"And that's it?"

"That's it."

"Yeah, thanks for coming in." Deeg jotted a few more notes on his pad and went back to his paperwork, ending their brief conversation.

Chapter 31

Stacey woke at six. She opened the bedroom door slowly, but was unable to keep it from squeaking. Heather stirred, rolled onto to her side, and fell back to sleep. Stacey marveled at how her friend could sleep so soundly in spite of all the tumult in their lives.

Stacey tip-toed out of the room and went to the kitchen to put on a pot of coffee. To stretch out the little coffee that was left she used only half the normal amount. She sat at the kitchen table while the coffee brewed and pondered her life. The two women had been hiding out in the one-bedroom house for three months. How did everything spiral downward to this point? She shook her head unconsciously. Even if she and Heather were able to avoid capture, she would live in fear every moment of every day, never able to lead a normal life. She was a murderer, but surprisingly did not regret what she had done. Clyde was a controlling, violent, and evil man who had hurt her deeply.

Why did I let him rule my life that way? I'm a sheep. I can't think for myself. What made me think he could take away my right to be happy? He was a brutal man. He hurt me and raped me, and I thought he was going to shoot me. And he smiled afterwards. He was pleased with himself. He smiled after he raped me. He would never have allowed me to leave. He would have tracked me down and, yes, he would have killed me. He came so close that last day, too.

Heather woke as the coffee finished brewing. She entered the kitchen and went straight to the coffee pot without acknowledging Stacey. She poured a cup and stood at the kitchen sink, vacantly looking out the window at the still and silent desert. From their first day in the house together, Heather had made it clear she was not a "morning person" and hated it when Stacey attempted to talk to her before she had had her first cup of coffee. Heather turned her back to any conversation. If Stacey spoke at all, Heather would walk out the back door to sit in one of the plastic chairs on the small, concrete patio where she could drink her coffee and smoke a cigarette in peace.

Stacey observed Heather. In some ways, she was no different from Clyde. Heather was her friend, but she was domineering and at times mean-spirited. Why could Clyde and Heather control her so easily? Michael was different. He loved her. She knew he did. He didn't try to control her. She had been so happy with him. They would have had a great life together.

"My God, how I miss him," Stacey blurted.

Heather turned from the window to face Stacey. "Miss who?"

"Michael. I loved him so."

Heather muttered, "Oh, no, not again," and turned back to look out the window.

"Heather, what should we do?"

She didn't answer. After three months in this prison of a house, their nerves were raw. They ate the same canned foods over and over, and were not able to see, talk to, or meet anyone else. The two women were on edge with each other. Some days, Heather went into a deep funk and would not speak a word to Stacey. If she did speak to her, her tone was prickly. Stacey cried often.

The stress of their solitary self-imprisonment was growing, but they had one lifeline to the outside world—a tiny TV with a rabbit-ear antenna they had to constantly adjust for any hope of ghost-free reception. Stacey and Heather watched incessantly—morning talk shows, soaps, news shows. The TV was rarely off. They never imagined their crimes would become national news and they would be labeled the new

Thelma and Louise, or worse, earn the sobriquet Serial Cyclist Killers. Their photos were shown on TV regularly and their crimes discussed on talk shows for weeks. They were the acknowledged killers of their husbands, but also deemed strong suspects in the killings of Michael Redfield, Carlotta Smith, Alex Castillo, Tomás Pérez, and Jordan Sanchez. The extent of their notoriety was amazing.

When news coverage of the murders had slowed and Heather and Stacey's celebrity waned, news of Jordan Sanchez's cycling death thrust them back into the limelight as the possible killers.

"Jordan Sanchez? I would've tripped over him and not known who he was." Heather bemoaned the fact they were also suspects in his death. "We ain't been two feet out of this house, and now we're supposed to be his killers?"

There was nothing else for them to do. They couldn't venture from the confines of their house during the day for fear someone would pass by and recognize them. On dark, moonless nights, they sat out front, unseen from the road, and watched cars drive by. It helped them feel a small connection with the world beyond the gates.

*****

"We need to do something. We're running out of food," Stacey said.

"Yeah? So what do you want me to do?" Heather snapped. "Grow a garden?"

"Don't be mean, Heather. We need to talk. I don't know what to do. I'm only saying we neeed to get some food."

"And I need some cigarettes. I'm scrounging for butts, for Christ's sake. There are only so many left in the ashtrays that I can relight."

Stacey was insistent. "We still have all our money. We're going to need to take a chance and get to a grocery store or a convenience store—somewhere we can buy some food and stuff. Are you listening, Heather? We need to go out. We've gone through almost all our supplies."

A month had passed since the Jordan Sanchez murder, and media attention surrounding his death had dropped off. Heather thought the time was right to head to Mexico, especially given the rapid depletion of their supplies. "What I do know is we've got to get the hell outta here. We can't stay here no more. We ain't got no food or cigarettes. We're goin' bat-shit, and we're gettin' on each other's nerves. It's time to leave."

"You mean for good? Are you sure we should?" Stacey asked. "I mean, we're safe here, but we just need to get more food."

"Stacey, we can't stay here forever. We got to go sooner or later. I ain't spendin' the rest of my life in this shack. We might as well be in a real prison. We're no better off here."

"I'm not so sure we should leave, Heather. I know you're right. We can't stay here forever, but they're still looking for us."

Heather became uncharacteristically philosophical. "Look, there's a life out there for us. We only got to find where it's gonna lead us. I don't know if you'll ever find someone like Michael again, but maybe you will." She stared through Stacey. "Maybe I will, too."

"I loved him so."

"Stacey, please, enough about Michael. I know you loved him. You've told me a thousand times you loved him and miss him, but please don't keep bringing him up. You'll find someone. I promise you will, but you ain't gonna find no one while we're locked away here."

"I know. I'm sorry. I promise I won't talk about him anymore. I don't want you to end up hating his memory because of me."

Oh, if you only knew. Heather turned her back to Stacey again and stared blankly out the window.

"Where should we go?" Stacey asked.

"Let's go to Mexico. That was my plan all along. I been thinkin' about how we can get away."

"How?"

"I'm thinkin' maybe once we get to Mexico, we split up."

Stacey was terrified at the thought.

"Calm down. Hear me out. I mean, they're lookin' for two women, right? They know we're together. Everybody in the entire country knows what we look like."

"Maybe being by yourself in Mexico would work for you. But I don't know any Spanish and I wouldn't know where to go or what to do. No, I don't like that idea at all. And, besides, we only have your truck. How am I supposed to get anyplace?"

"I'll take you to where you want to go. You'll be okay."

"Heather, I don't want to be by myself. I can't do it." Tears welled in Stacey's eyes.

"Oh, God, please don't go cryin' on me again. Okay, I won't leave you. We'll stick this out together."

Chapter 32

DeGarzia pursued dozens of leads. He was aggressive in his search for Heather and Stacey, but every lead proved to be a dead end. The women had vanished without a trace.

The sensational appeal of the killings had diminished, and even though there had been no further cycling deaths, the *Thelma and Louise* characterizations of Heather and Stacey continued to appear in sparse news accounts.

Although immersed in other cases, Hank kept in touch with DeGarzia regularly for updates on the investigation.

*****

Hank and Sam continued to cycle together once or twice a week. The flap over Sam's one-night stand with Heather was over. Sam told Hank that DeGarzia seemed uninterested in anything he had told him about his fling with Heather.

The annual Canyon Cycling Club Dog Daze ride was coming up. The event was huge, and typically drew some two thousand cyclists from throughout northern New Mexico.

Most participants signed up to ride the twenty-five, fifty, or seventy-five-mile routes, but nearly ninety planned on riding the century—a challenging ride of one hundred miles that looped south from Santa Fe to Cedar Grove, east to Stanley, and back north through Galisteo and Eldorado. Hank and Sam were going to ride the century.

Over the years, Hank had ridden many centuries and recognized that cyclists who rode the distance considered it a mark of accomplishment. He remembered his first century and how the achievement boosted his own self-esteem and confidence. Hank wanted Sam to enjoy that same feeling of satisfaction. He had come a long way since his marital and personal problems. Completing the long ride would be icing-on-the-cake toward Sam's personal rebirth.

*****

The day of the ride was a typical Santa Fe summer day—hot. Cyclists intending to ride the one-hundred-mile loop had to start no later than seven a.m., in part to beat the heat of midday. With little shade over large sections of the route, road temperatures would exceed one hundred degrees by early afternoon.

Riders needed to stay hydrated and fueled. Cycling Club volunteers manned six rest stops where riders would be able to refill their bottles with water or Gatorade and eat carb-replenishing snacks such as bananas, oranges, and peanut butter and jelly sandwiches. The first stop was at the twenty-five mile mark. Riders ate or drank what they needed to sustain themselves until the next stop.

Hank set the pace at fifteen miles an hour as he and Sam rode the first twenty miles. The terrain was relatively flat and Hank thought Sam would be able to maintain that pace. Hank's primary intent was to see Sam make it to the finish.

After refueling at the first rest stop, they started the second twenty-mile stretch. This second leg went south, past the ghost town of Golden on the way to Cedar Grove. It was difficult—more hills with less shade, and it was getting hotter.

Traffic was light for long portions of the Sunday ride. They passed small ranches along the way, most identified by a custom ranch sign at the dirt road entrance. An occasional dog yapped at the riders as they cycled past.

In time, the group of century riders spread out. Those wanting to finish with fast times attacked the course and easily separated from the others who weren't concerned with how long their ride took. The latter group was interested only in finishing. Hank stayed with Sam, patiently encouraging him, reminding him to drink and take nourishment. He broached a variety of subjects to keep Sam's mind off the ride. At Golden, they knew some riders were well ahead of them while others were far behind. The next rest area was still six miles away. Sam was going at a slower pace, and Hank calculated they'd be riding another half an hour to get there.

A quarter of a mile ahead, they watched as a black pickup truck drove the length of a dirt driveway from a small ranch house set back in the desert to a gate at the main road. The truck skidded to a stop a few yards from the gate. The driver got out of the pickup, opened the gate, and quickly got back in the pickup. Without even looking, the driver entered the roadway at the same moment Hank and Sam were passing by, nearly plowing into them. To avoid being hit, the two cyclists reflexively swung wide of the driveway into the opposing lane.

"Yo, lady!" Sam yelled, but the pickup quickly exited the drive with no apology from the driver. They watched as the truck initially headed south, but abruptly turned the opposite direction and sped away in the northbound lane. "Asshole!" Sam yelled after her. "Man, that was close. I don't know how she couldn't, but I don't think that freaking lady ever saw us."

Hank stopped, got off his bike, and turned back to look at the pickup. Sam stopped alongside him. "Did you see who was in the truck?" Hank asked. "There were two women, and I swear the passenger was Stacey Keenan. Honest to God, that's who it looked like. I think she recognized us."

"Are you sure? I didn't get a good look," Sam asked.

"No, not absolutely sure. It was too fast, but I swear it looked like her. Did you see how the driver changed direction when she pulled out? Like she didn't want us to get another glance at them."

"What do you want to do?"

Hank pulled his cell phone from his jersey pocket. "I'm going to call DeGarzia."

Several cyclists caught up to them as Hank was making his call. "You guys okay? Need any help?" One of the riders recognized Sam. "Hey, Sam, how're you doing? Is everything okay?"

"Hey, Chris, yeah. We just need to make a phone call. We're good," Sam responded. "We'll catch up with you at the next rest stop. Stay cool, man."

"Deeg, this is Hank. Sorry to bother you. I hate to screw up your Sunday, but I'm out on the Cycling Club's century ride. I know this is crazy and I'm probably seeing things, but I need you to check something out ... We're a couple miles south of Golden on our way to Cedar Grove ... Yeah, on I-14. Well, here's the crazy thing. A black pickup with two women in it sped out of a driveway and almost hit us. I think the passenger might have been Stacey Keenan ... No, I didn't get a good look at the driver. She had short black hair is all I could tell. It might have been Heather Dorell in disguise. It all happened so fast. I don't think she tried to hit us on purpose so much as she didn't see us ... She headed north ... Okay. She didn't lock the gate behind her so we can go up to the house to see what's there ... No, I'm with Sam Bailey. I'll be fine. I'll let you know ... No, I don't know the number. There's no mailbox or anything. The house sits quite a ways off the road on the right side as you head south. I'll GPS it on my cell to give you a better idea of where we are and I'll call you back after we check the house ... Yeah, I know, it's probably not them, but I guess stranger things have happened, huh?"

Hank suggested to Sam he hook up with the next rider and continue to ride the course. "Nah, I'm staying with you, Hank. If we don't finish, we'll ride another one some other time."

"Okay, if you're sure. Let's go up to the house and see if we can find out who lives there. If we don't find anything, we can get back to the ride. I'm sure Deeg will be all over this anyway."

The men walked their bikes up the dirt driveway. "It doesn't look as though the house is occupied," Hank observed. They saw no animals, no other vehicles, no gardens or flowerbeds at the austere ranch house. Hank knocked on the front door and shouted, "Hello? Is anyone home?"

When there was no answer, Sam looked in one of the windows on the side of the house. "It's empty. There's no one there."

They walked to the back entrance off the patio. "Look. The key's in the door," Hank said. He knocked again then used the key to unlock the door when it was obvious no one was going to answer. "Sam, make sure you don't touch anything. DeGarzia will want to check for fingerprints."

The kitchen had a small table and two cushioned chairs. It was clean and tidy. Dishes were in the cabinets, towels were folded neatly, and the refrigerator was empty except for a few condiments. The living room was furnished with a few essentials: a couch, two side chairs, a small TV, an end table, and a lamp. Sam next opened the door to the bedroom. He saw two single beds, both made up, and a bureau underneath a small window. The closets were empty. They walked back outside to look around. "Hank, look at that," Sam pointed out. "It's a pit filled with trash—cans and bottles and stuff. All their trash. If it was Heather and Stacey, they may have been here for weeks."

"I don't think we should jump to conclusions. I'm not certain it was Stacey I saw in the truck," Hank said. "But it sure as hell looks like they could have been here."

*****

"Hurry, Heather. Hurry!"

"What for? It's not like they're gonna follow us on their bikes."

"No, but they can call the police," Stacey warned.

"Okay, we don't know if they even recognized us. Calm down. Don't panic."

"What are the odds of us seeing people from the Cycling Club in the middle of nowhere?" Stacey asked. She could not believe the coincidence. "I recognized Sam Bailey, but I don't know who the other guy was."

"I know him. He's with the District Attorney's office. I seen him different times on rides. One of these days I'll tell you about Sam," Heather teased.

They rounded a curve and saw more cyclists headed in their direction. "Duck! Get down!" Heather quickly flipped her visor down, and raised it again when the cyclists rode past. "We're clear, Stacey. You can get up. I recognized Rob Young. The Club must be having some kind of cycling event going on, like a ride for cancer or somethin'. We'll probably see more riders. Duck down when we see someone comin'.'"

"Heather, I think you can slow down now."

Without acknowledging Stacey's caution, Heather slowed down to the speed limit. Each time they spotted cyclists, Stacey ducked low to avoid being seen. "Now we know. We can't go back to the house, and we can't keep goin' north. If they recognized us and called the cops, the cops'll be lookin' for us headin' toward Santa Fe. We have to get off I-14."

"Fine. But then what?"

"I'm gonna get on I-40 toward Albuquerque. I know a guy who's got a ranch in San Ysidro. Maybe he'll let us stay there for a couple of days."

"What makes you think he wouldn't turn us in?" Stacey asked.

"He's a really good guy, like in his eighties—a grandfather type. I love him to death. He ain't gonna turn us in."

Stacey wasn't so certain. "How do you know him?"

"I met him a couple of years ago when I ran out of gas right in front of his ranch. I don't even remember why I was in San Ysidro. Anyway, he stopped and asked if he could help. He gave me some gas and we got to talkin' about stuff, and we really hit it off. He has these political signs all along the front of his ranch. He's really into politics. I asked him why he had them, and he said he put them up because he thought most everybody in politics should be kicked out of office. And he don't like cops, neither. Said most politicians were communists and cops are on the take. He thinks our country is going to hell."

"So you think he's going to let us hide out there because you met him one time?" Stacey asked, her voice full of doubt.

"No. I've seen him plenty of times. I used to visit him every once in a while. We'd sit and talk. I'd bring him an apple pie or somethin'. We'd have some coffee, and I'd tell him about my problems with Jake. I even told him about you and Clyde. He probably knows from TV what we did. He's a smart man. I mean, I learned a lot from him. He knows more stuff about more things than you and me together. I really think he'll let us stay with him. Besides, unless you got a better idea, it's the only idea I got. We got to get off the road."

Chapter 33

Heather and Stacey drove undetected to Walton Turner's five-hundred-acre ranch.

"See what I mean about the signs?" Heather said. A half dozen crudely written signs adorned the front of Turner's property. Each was affixed atop a ten-foot pole, and each had a message for Congress. Stacey read two aloud. "Red or Blue, They Don't Have a Clue. Adjourn Congress—Permanently."

The old iron gate was open, representing more of a dare than a welcome to people to enter his property. Over the entrance hung a round, metal sign with a large *T* in the center that identified the ranch as the Circle-T. Heather entered and drove straight up the driveway, kicking up a stream of dust that followed them around a bend and up an incline to a ranch house situated out of view from the road.

The ranch was strewn with rusting hulks of ancient trucks, cars, and farm equipment. Trailer hitches, plows, and other harvesting machinery rested in the fields, and on one side of the house lay a chassis from an old Ford pickup, the cab of a dump-truck, and a 1940s Airstream camper. Junk everywhere. The house was in serious need of repair. Shingles were missing from sections of the roof; paint had peeled off over the years, exposing raw and rotted wood; and the front porch roof, supported in part by bowed two-by-fours at each corner, was on the verge of collapse.

The porch looked like the entrance to a backwoods hovel with a stuffed couch, ancient ringer-type washing machine, and unpainted plywood cabinet jammed side by side. Barn cats roamed the porch, periodically checking a saucer near the front door for food. A barn located fifty yards from the side of the house was also in grave need of repair.

Stacey looked around and observed the state of utter disrepair. "I'd hate to see what the inside of the house looks like."

"It's not pretty. Walton told me his wife died twenty years ago. He's an old-time New Mexican. Born and raised right here on this spread. He's too old to take proper care of the place. I told him he ought to think about movin' out. But he said he was born here, lived here, and was gonna die here. I asked him who checks in on him to make sure he's okay, and he said nobody— he never had any kids, and didn't much care for anyone comin' in anyway."

Walton's truck was not in the driveway. "It doesn't look like he's home. His truck's gone." Heather drove behind the house and parked. She removed the black wig and shook her head to loosen her hair. "I can only stand that wig so long. It makes my head itch." They waited.

An hour later, they heard a vehicle ramble up the driveway. A light blue, '92 Ford F-150 soon appeared.

"That's him."

Walton emerged from his truck. He was wearing a sweat-stained, beat-up, black cowboy hat and a red plaid shirt. A wide belt centered with a large silver buckle engraved with the insignia *Circle-T* was holding up his dirty jeans.

Heather and Stacey walked out from behind the house. "Hey, Walton," Heather yelled.

He was startled, but quickly recognized his friend. "Red! I'll be damned. How in blazes are you doin'?" He gave her a welcoming bear hug. Leather-skinned, with deeply rounded wrinkles from years in the sun, Walton was five feet seven and thin as a rail. He smiled, exposing a set of natural white teeth, and looked at Stacey with penetrating blue eyes.

"Walton, this is my friend, Stacey."

"Pleased to meet you, Miss Stacey," he said, politely tipping his hat.

"I guess you've heard about what's happened to us?"

"Sure have, Red. You girls been all over the newspapers and TV. They say you killed your husbands. Good reason, I suppose. And those bikers, too."

"Walton, our husbands, they beat us so many times that we couldn't take it no more," Heather said. "But that's not true about those cyclists that we supposedly killed. They're tryin' to pin those murders on me and Stacey, but we are innocent."

Walton didn't hesitate. "I kept tellin' you to leave that yahoo husband 'a yours, but I guess that's no-never-mind now. If you killed 'em, they had it comin'. I'm not about to judge you and your friend. Lord knows we have enough people in this country judgin' what you can and can't do. I'll leave that up to the good Lord to judge you. And if you say you didn't kill those other folks, I believe you. Period. I ain't gonna think about it for another second."

"We've been hiding out for a couple of months outside of Golden, but we think we got spotted and decided to come here. Any chance we could stay here for a while?" Heather tilted her head and squinched her face, hoping Walton would allow them to stay. "I mean, we don't want to cause you no trouble. And if you want us to go, say the word. But, please, you can't tell nobody we were here."

"Red, I could never say no to you. I'll tell you what. You can stay here as long as you like, but under one condition," he said, his voice serious.

Stacey eyed him with suspicion. Having just met Walton, she was unsure what he could possibly demand of them. Heather, however, did not hesitate, "Name it."

"You got to cook me an apple pie like you brought me other times you come to visit," he said, and grinned broadly. "We got a deal?"

"You bet we do," Heather answered. She was pleased he remembered her pies. "Walton, you got it. We'll make you an apple pie every day if you want."

"I haven't tasted as good an apple pie like the ones you make since my wife died."

"Stacey and I been thinkin', Walton. We can stay in the barn. That way, if they find us here, you can say you didn't know we were here."

"Like hell, you say. There ain't no police gonna come on my property without me saying so, and they know it. This is my property and I don't cater to no trespassers. They got no authority here on my land. I don't care what kind of police state they run. They can do whatever they want somewhere else, but not here. No ma'am, not on my property. You're staying in my house, Red. You'll have to fix up the bedroom for the two of you. I ain't too good at that stuff. The house ain't like it used to be since Martha died."

Finally, Stacey spoke. "We'll take care of the house for you, Walton. And we have money to help with groceries and stuff."

"That's true, Walton. We don't want to be a burden on you. We'll do whatever chores you need doin', and we'll do all the cookin' and cleanin'," Heather added. Their excitement grew as they realized they had found a safe haven.

"And bake apple pies," Stacey said with a smile.

"Where's your truck, Red? In the back? Put it in the barn, okay? And don't worry about no money. We'll manage okay. Bring your stuff into the house."

Heather and Walton exchanged another hearty hug.

"May I give you a hug, too, Mr. Turner?" Stacey asked.

"Only if you call me Walton."

"It's a deal ... Walton."

*****

"Heather and Stacey probably lived in that house the entire time after their killing spree," Deeg announced to Hank. "Their fingerprints were everywhere, and their DNA matched. There's no question they were there. Looks like they had this planned out for some time. They had everything they needed to survive for a couple of months without ever having to leave the house. We checked with the realtor who leased the place to them. He couldn't tell us much, though. He didn't recognize the two from the photos we showed him. He said the woman who signed the lease was an average type—tall, with short black hair and big glasses—no doubt a disguise. But Heather's fingerprints were all over the lease documents."

"Where the hell could they have gone now?" Hank asked.

"Can't answer that. You saw them heading north on 14, but we think they may have turned south again after that and headed to Mexico. That's only a guess. We checked with Border Patrol to see if surveillance video shows them traveling through the checkpoint to Juarez, which is only about a five-hour drive from the house. So far, they haven't uncovered anything."

"So we're back to square one."

Chapter 34

Captain Ellsworth announced the discovery of the hideout used by fugitives Heather Dorell and Stacey Keenan. He also announced the two women had once again eluded police. The national media covered the saga with renewed vigor.

"The newspapers are just not lettin' up on us," Heather said. "Every time someone gets shot in Santa Fe, they say it's us."

"Don't pay no never-mind to them," Walton said. He was angry. "Those newspapers and TV stations are owned by a bunch of flaming left-wing liberals. And the reporters are a bunch of commies. Mark my word they are. It'll come out one of these days. They ain't got an ounce of American in their blood. They're the biggest scams ever done to this country. It's plain pitiful, I tell you."

The women had been living at the Circle-T for nearly four weeks. They occupied most of their time cleaning, washing, scrubbing, and putting a woman's touch back where none had been for twenty years. Walton shopped for all the groceries they needed as well as supplies the women requested to brighten the house and make minor repairs.

Of the two, Stacey was particularly handy with a hammer and screwdriver. Heather was the better cook, so she generally made the meals. They knew they couldn't stay at the Circle-T forever. But for now, even though constantly vigilant, they felt a degree of security at the ranch. Walton became diligent about chaining and padlocking the front gate to keep accidental visitors out. He loved having Heather and Stacey there, and they reciprocated with warmth and respect as though he were their grandfather. Still, they knew they would have to leave one day—but when? And where would they go?

After dinner one evening, Walton suggested, "Let's sit on

the porch a bit. I need to talk serious with you gals." The sun was setting over the western sky and the air was clear and crisp.

"We'll be right out, Walton. Give us a minute to finish cleaning up." Ever the worrier, Stacey whispered to Heather, "I think he's going to ask us to leave. I have a bad feeling."

"Yeah, maybe. But I don't think so. He likes havin' us here too much." There was a chill in the air. Heather and Stacey each grabbed a sweater and headed out to the porch. The three sat in silence for a few minutes, taking in the desert evening under the wide New Mexico sky.

"See that sky? Ever since my wife died, the stars and the moon have been my family. As you know, Red, I ain't got no kids. Martha couldn't have none. And, other than those stars, I ain't got no relatives, no nieces, no nephews, no nobody. The way you treat me, you two are the closest thing I have to blood kin. You been my stars for all these weeks. It's like you're my kin now." Heather and Stacey looked at each other, unsure of where Walton was going. They let him speak. "I've made a decision. I'm going to turn over everything to the two of you when I die."

"Oh my God, Walton. You don't mean that, do you? We love you so much for all you've done for us already." Heather burst into tears.

Stacey bent over Walton and gave him an awkward but heartfelt hug. "Walton, all I ever wanted was to take care of someone. I wish you were forty years younger. I would have married you and taken care of you forever. You are the nicest, kindest man I've ever met." She, too, was crying.

"Well, I wish I was forty years younger. I'd drive both of you personally to some place where you didn't have no worries about the police. But now, the way I figure it, maybe you'll get caught some day. And if you do get arrested, you're gonna need money to defend yourselves, and not by some half-witted public defender wet behind the ears. You need good lawyers, like them that got that O. J. Simpson fella off after he done killed his wife and that fella she was with. If you got this spread, you can sell it and buy yourselves a good lawyer. Now, I don't know if anything here is worth anything to you, but land is land, and the good Lord don't make any more of it."

"Walton, I love you so much," Heather said. She buried her face in her hands and cried, overcome with emotion.

"I love you too, Red." A tear rolled down his cheek. He tried to wipe it away without being noticed, but the women saw, and knew he meant every word he said.

"We owe you everything, Walton. Everything," Heather declared. "We don't know what we should do. We know we're gonna have to go someday, but we don't want to. You know, until I met you, I hated all men. I hated them for what they can be like. But you make me believe, and Stacey too, you make us both believe there's some good people out there after all. We know we got to go, but we are gonna miss you—so much, so very much."

"I love you both. You can stay as long as you like. You decide best when it's time to go. Personally, I don't think you have to go anywhere. There ain't nobody gonna look for you here. But you gotta be the ones to decide."

Chapter 35

Heather and Stacey remained comfortably at Walton's ranch house another two weeks. They knew, however, their time was running short. Someday, somehow, someone was going to spot them. Maybe an old friend of Walton's would stop by, or the postman would need a signature on a letter, or the cops would stop by to check on the "old curmudgeon," as people knew him. If Heather and Stacey were found out, he would be arrested for harboring criminals, and probably end up in jail himself. The women liked him too much to allow that to happen.

One evening after dinner, Heather announced, "Walton, it's time we leave. We can't stay no more. Stacey and I have talked about it and decided we're gonna leave in a couple of days. We'll try to make it to Mexico. I wish we could stay here forever, but we know we can't, and we know you don't think we can either."

"We truly appreciate all you've done for us, but all we're doing is putting you in jeopardy," Stacey added. "Somebody's going to find us here, one way or another. We have got to go so we don't get you in trouble."

Walton shook his head a long time. "You know I don't care about being put in no jeopardy. I was hoping there'd be a way for you to stay."

"Me too," Heather concurred.

"Okay, now listen. I ain't gonna try to talk you outta leavin', but I don't want to know where you're going or how you're gonna get there. If the cops find out you been here, they're gonna try to get it out of me. So don't tell me no more. You gals need money?"

"We have enough to last us a while," Heather said, "but we have an idea. You don't have to say yes to it, but—"

"Tell me," Walton urged.

"Well, we were talkin', and we thought since, you know, the police are still lookin' for us, they're probably still lookin' for Jake's pickup. So we thought, what would you think about switchin' trucks? We take yours and you take Jake's?"

With an exaggerated grimace, Walton looked at Heather, then at Stacey, then back again at Heather. "You know, that gets me doggone mad," he said.

"It was just an idea, Walton. Please don't be mad."

"Red, let me tell you why I'm mad. I'm mad because I didn't think of that! Of course we can switch trucks. But my truck's an old lady. Maybe it won't get you to where you want to go."

"We have to take our chances, and we think drivin' a different truck would be our best chance," Heather answered.

Stacey voiced a concern. "Walton, here's the only problem I see."

"What's that?"

"What happens if they find out you're driving our truck?"

Walton thought for a moment. "First off, they ain't gonna stop me. There'd be no reason to. They're looking for a truck with two pretty women in it, not an old man like me." He removed his hat and rubbed his head, giving the matter some more thought. "I'll put a farm license plate on it from one of my old tractors. How would they ever know it's your truck? Besides, I only go back and forth into town for groceries and supplies. What could happen?"

Stacey had clearly thought things through. She suggested, "Here's what I think we should do. We make out two bills of sale: one for Jake's truck and one for yours. So, let's say the police stop you for some reason and ask you where you got the truck. You tell them you bought your truck from Heather about three, four months ago, and you have the bill of sale to prove it. You say Heather was an old friend, and she came by one day and said she needed some money. So you bought her truck because your pickup was broken down."

"And, Walton, all those murders they're accusin' us of, if the police were to ask you about them, you'd tell them you don't know nothin' about any of that."

Walton agreed. "Even if they wouldn't believe me, what are they gonna do, arrest me for being old? I ain't got too many more years to live as it is, so let them put me away."

Heather was genuinely concerned. "Walton, are you sure you'll be okay?"

"I'm telling you, Red, it's gonna be all right. I think it's a good plan. The cops ain't gonna stop me, but you gotta make sure you don't leave nothing behind that could make them know you spent some time here. Even if they take fingerprints and do all that other stuff, and they find out you been here, I'll tell them it's 'cause you both used to come visit me and we'd have coffee and talk. What do you think?"

Heather and Stacey smiled and nodded in agreement.

"You know, my truck's been around the block a time or two, but I've taken good care of her so I'm hopin' she'll get you to where you want to go without breaking down." Walton possessed a certain reverence for his old truck. "Don't drive it too hard. And you got to check the oil every couple hundred miles. It's been taking a lot of oil of late."

"We'll keep an eye on that."

"Sounds like we got ourselves a plan. But, one last request."

"What's that?"

"Would you gals make me one last apple pie before you leave?"

*****

Walton filled his pickup at the gas station. From there, he went to Walmart and bought a case of motor oil. As much as he loved Heather and Stacey and wished they could stay longer, he knew they were right. Sooner or later, the police would find them. They were taking a chance by leaving the Circle-T, but he wasn't going to try to talk them out of leaving. For now, however, he wanted to do what he could to help them. Walton hoped they'd be able to make another life somewhere else. One thing he knew for sure, Heather and Stacey were too young and too pretty to be stuck at the Circle-T taking care of him. *The cops are claimin' those poor girls are serial killers. Lord, I don't see how they could be. They're the sweetest girls I ever did know.*

On the day of their planned departure, the three spoke barely a word. Heather and Stacey were well aware of the seriousness of their situation, and understood that once they left the protection of the Circle-T, the police might find them at any time. It was imperative they find their new destination and get off the road as soon as possible.

They packed their suitcases and a five-gallon container of gasoline in Walton's pickup and covered the bed with a protective tarp. They also prepared sandwiches to hold them over for a day. With these few provisions, they would be able to avoid gas stations and other stops where they might be identified. The last item Heather packed was the pistol. She put it safely in the bottom of her purse and announced in a soft voice, "It's time to go." Once again, she was in disguise: short black wig, frumpy dress, and large, clear glasses. Stacey wore sunglasses and an old baseball cap tight to her head. The two did not look like serial killers.

Walton laughed when he saw them. "You gals look like different people altogether."

Stacey whimpered. She rushed to Walton and nearly knocked him over with a hug that pinned his arms. "I'll never forget you," she cried.

"Now, Stacey, you'd better not forget me. Maybe I'll get to see you again sometime, somehow," he said, even though he knew he probably never would.

"My turn," Heather announced. Stacey backed away and used the backs of her hands to wipe the tears from her face.

"Walton, if I'd 'a known there were people like you in the world when I was a little girl, who knows where I'd be today. I don't use the word often, but I love you more than you can ever know." Heather and Walton both cried unashamedly.

"Walton, we love you for all you've done. You've been unbelievably good to us," Stacey said. "I hope you know we're not the bad people the papers make us out to be."

"I know you're not. Understand, next to me losing my wife, this is the saddest day of my life. I'm gonna miss you gals—a lot!"

Chapter 36

The two fugitives departed at dusk on a Friday evening. They traveled the back roads they had mapped out, heading south toward Mexico. Where they would go and what they would do once they reached Mexico was still uncertain. Given their weeks and months on the run, an ultimate plan remained beyond anything they had been able to reason out.

Stacey was already second-guessing their decision to leave. "Mexico. What are we going to do there? Maybe we should have stayed at the Circle-T."

"Sooner or later we had to leave. You know that. We got to find a place we can go to where we can hide out and maybe try to lead a normal life. For God's sake, Stacey, we've been talkin' about it for weeks and weeks and now you're sayin' we should have stayed at the Circle-T."

"I know. I know. We had to leave. Only I wish it wasn't Mexico. I think we're going to stick out like sore thumbs. How are we possibly going to lead a normal life there?"

"We're gonna have to try. Enough, okay? If you don't want to go, I can drop you off along the way. But I'm taking my chances in Mexico."

Stacey brooded in silence for several minutes before being struck with an idea. She pounded the dashboard with her palm. "Chicago."

Heather was startled by Stacey's outburst. "What the hell is wrong with you? You scared the shit out of me."

"Chicago. That's where we should go. Don't you see? That's where Clyde and I went on our honeymoon."

"Are you freakin' crazy? What does your honeymoon have to do with anything? Why the hell would we go to Chicago?"

"Well, think about it. It's a big city and it's a long way from Santa Fe. People might have read about us, but it wouldn't be front page news like it is in New Mexico." Stacey's voice rose the more excited she got. "I don't know why I didn't think of it before. It was right in front of me. Don't you see, Heather? We won't be recognized like we would be in Mexico. People speak English not Spanish. We'll be like ordinary people there. We won't stick out. I can see us getting jobs, a place to live, and maybe live a normal life. We might even find someone, get married, have kids. And we can fit right in. Don't you see?"

"Whoa, girlfriend. You're gettin' carried away there." Heather laughed at Stacey's childlike exuberance.

"No, I'm not ... Well, yeah, I guess I am," she stammered. "But Heather, listen. I don't want to go to Mexico. You don't either. I know you don't. Let's go to Chicago. What do you think?"

Heather nodded deeply. "I like it." She glanced at her friend and smiled broadly. "I really like it," she announced, and turned the truck around to head north and east.

<h1 align="center">Chapter 37</h1>

Traveling north on Route 25 through New Mexico, Heather and Stacey drove for three hours without incident before crossing into Colorado. They took turns driving through the night, being careful not to push the Ford too much and always driving at or under the speed limit. Within another five hours they had crossed into Nebraska. As Walton had instructed, they stopped every few hundred miles to check the oil level. They ate their sandwiches, emptied the spare gas can, and chugged along at a steady pace, holding their breath every time they saw a police car. They navigated using an atlas Walton had left in the truck, and calculated another sixteen hours of drive time till they reached Chicago. They were in good spirits and felt giddily free of the notoriety that had haunted them in New Mexico.

"Let's get off I-80 before we get to Kearney and find some place we can stretch our legs," Heather suggested. "I'm obsessing about a cup of coffee and an egg McMuffin."

Stacey laughed, "Oh, my God. I was thinking the same thing. I'll take the next exit that says there's a McDonald's. I can't remember the last time I had an egg McMuffin."

Within half an hour, they saw a sign for McDonalds in Gothenburg. At the exit, they spotted a Nebraska State Patrolman parked on the side of the road watching for speeders. They instinctively looked away from him, and Stacey waited a full five seconds at the four-way stop at the top of the exit ramp before proceeding through the intersection. Within seconds, the trooper turned on his lights and pulled into the lane behind them.

"Shit. Slow down. Pull over," Heather ordered. "Did you go through that stop sign?"

"No, I didn't. I don't think I did anything." Stacey veered to get off to the side of the road.

The trooper pulled alongside their pickup. Heather casually put her hand to the side of her face to hide her appearance from the trooper. With her other hand, she reached into her purse to retrieve Clyde's pistol. At that moment, the trooper sped by, sirens whining and lights flashing. Up ahead, he caught up with a driver who had sped through the stop sign at the intersection.

"Oh, good Lord, my heart is beating a hundred miles an hour. I think I peed myself," Stacey said. She pulled back onto the road. "What were you going to do? You weren't going to use that pistol on him, were you?"

Heather didn't answer. She put the pistol back in her purse.

"Heather, please don't think of doing that again. Please. It's one thing that we killed our husbands, but I don't want to hurt anyone else."

"Okay, fine. Come on, let's find that McDonalds," she replied, and quickly brushed off Stacey's concern.

Chapter 38

The day after Heather and Stacey's departure from the Circle-T, Walton decided to venture out in Jake's pickup for the first time. He was low on supplies and had to get some groceries at the Safeway in town. The new-truck smell, powerful engine, and colorful gauges on the dashboard riveted him. *Maybe if a cop tries to stop me, I'll outrace him.* He laughed.

Within thirty minutes Walton had finished his shopping. He piled the groceries into the truck, climbed in, and started the engine. He was not yet accustomed to maneuvering this larger pickup, and did not see the Lexus SUV that was passing behind as he backed out.

Beep.

Thump.

"Shit."

He pulled the truck back into his parking space and climbed out. "What the hell's wrong with you? Didn't you see I was backing out? Are you an idiot or what?" Walton shouted at the well-dressed, middle-aged man standing alongside the truck.

"Sir, you hit me. It is your responsibility to back up with caution in a parking lot."

"Bullshit. It's your fault. Anyone can see that."

"May I have your name, sir? I'd also like to see your insurance information." The man kept his calm and spoke in a respectful tone.

"I ain't givin' you shit. You sound like one of them lawyers. So sue me. Move your car so I can get out of here."

"Sir, I'm not a lawyer. If you try to leave, I'll call the police."

"You can call the poh-lease, the governor, and the president, 'cause I don't give a rat's petuny. I'm leaving. And if you don't move your car, I'll ram it across the parking lot."

The man turned abruptly, got back into his car, and moved it out of the way. He called 9-1-1. "He's leaving without giving me his name. I'm going to follow him." The man gave the police Walton's license plate number and described the pickup. "He just left the lot, heading west onto Via Valdez ... No, he's an old man. Now he's turning onto Alamagorda Boulevard, heading north."

Within minutes, a police car raced to Alamagorda to intercept Walton. The officer driving turned on his flashers as he pulled alongside the pickup. Walton saw him out of the corner of his eye, but pretended not to. He looked straight ahead and did not stop or slow down. The cop sped ahead of Walton then abruptly stopped his car diagonally across the road. Walton slammed on the brakes and screeched to a stop barely three feet from the police car. With his gun drawn, the cop jumped out and hunched behind the hood of his car, aiming his pistol squarely at the old man. "Get out of the car." Walton did not move. "I said, get out of the car. Now!" the rookie cop screamed. "I want to see your hands *now!*"

Walton finally complied. He got out of the truck with his hands held high. "Is this high enough for you?" he said. "Boy, I bet you're a proud officer of the law today. You stopped an eighty-five-year-old man with your gun drawn because that eighty-five-year-old man bumped into a yahoo who wasn't paying any attention to what the hell he was doing." Walton looked around and spotted the Lexus. "There he is, over there, driving that fancy car. Hey, Mr. Lawyer, you happy?"

*****

"Hank, it's Deeg. I'm calling from San Ysidro. The cops here found Jake Dorell's pickup truck in the possession of an old rancher by the name of Walton Turner. He owns a run-down spread outside of town named the Circle-T."

"What was he doing with Dorell's truck?"

"He had an accident in the parking lot of the Safeway here and left the scene. The guy he ran into said Turner refused to exchange insurance information, so he called the cops when Turner left. Turns out, he was driving with an expired farm license plate, he didn't have any insurance, and the cop found an old registration in the glove compartment that belonged to Jake Dorell. The cop recognized the name and asked him how he knew Jake. When Turner gave him the runaround, the cop arrested him and impounded the vehicle. That's when the San Ysidro police contacted me."

"Did they find Stacey and Heather?"

"No. Not yet. They might be hiding out at his ranch. We're getting a search warrant now."

"What has he told you?"

"I only now finished questioning him, but I didn't learn a thing. He's a cantankerous son of a bitch. Doesn't like cops, that's for sure. All I could get from him was that he's owned Jake's truck for a couple of months and that he bought it from Heather Dorell. He had a signed bill of sale as proof."

"Did he say if he knew Heather before buying the truck from her?"

"I asked him, and he said he only knew her as a girl he called *Red*. He said she came by one day and asked if he wanted to buy her truck. She needed cash, her husband was dead, and he didn't leave her anything. She thought he might want to buy it. Turner said he didn't know she was wanted by the police."

"That's some story."

"They're going to have to let him go. The most they can do is charge him with a misdemeanor, leaving the scene of an accident. One of two things is certain. He either knows a hell of a lot more than he's saying, or he's an old busted rancher."

"I'll meet you at his ranch, Deeg."

*****

Hank pulled up the drive to Walton's ranch house. He saw Deeg's car, two San Ysidro squad cars, and another vehicle parked in front of the house. *The old man sitting on the front porch must be Walton Turner.* Two cops were in the barn looking for evidence. Deeg and a forensic investigator were inside the house.

Hank stepped onto the porch and nodded to the old man.

Walton looked up from under his cowboy hat. "What the hell do you want? If you're another of them yahoo police, I've a mind to blow you away. You're an illegal representative of an unconstitutional system of government. And you're trespassin'."

"Mr. Turner, I'm here to meet Detective DeGarzia. I'm not with the police. I'm with the Santa Fe District Attorney's office."

"That's supposed to make you better than them? What the hell do you want? I answered every question I been asked. When am I gonna get my truck back? I paid good money for it, and now I ain't got nothin'."

"Mr. Turner—" Hank tried to answer.

"Why do you still have my truck? I'll starve here without any food or nothin', and no way to get into town. Is that what you yahoos want? And what happened to all my groceries? I spent good money for 'em."

Hank attempted conciliation. "Listen, Mr. Turner, we'll get your truck and your groceries back to you as soon as possible. That's a promise."

"If you can do that, I'd be grateful," Walton responded, his voice mellowed. "Now, what do you want coming all the way here from Santa Fe?"

DeGarzia heard the voices on the porch and looked out the front door. "Hey, Hank. I see you've met Mr. Turner." DeGarzia rolled his eyes out of view from Walton.

"Yes, I have. I wonder if I could chat with him for a moment, Detective. Okay with you, Mr. Turner?"

"It's a free country. You can do whatever you damn well please so long as you plan to get the hell off my property."

DeGarzia went back to his work in the house. Hank pulled a plastic chair closer to Walton and sat. "Sir, my name is Hank Kincaid." Hank extended his hand and Walton reluctantly shook it. Hank noted Walton's callused grip and immediately knew this old man had led a hard life on his ranch. "Mr. Turner, I only want to ask you a few questions. When we're done, I'll look into getting your vehicle back to you as soon as I can."

Pretending to be accommodating, Walton said, "You're the only one around here makes any sense. You know, these police have been searching my house and my barn for Red. I told them she ain't here, but no, they wouldn't believe me. They had to waste everybody's time. I guess the police have to justify their existence, huh?"

Hank disregarded Walton's last comment. "Can you tell me how it is that Mrs. Dorell sold her truck to you?"

"Who the blazes are you talkin' about?"

"Red. Her real name is Heather Dorell."

"Oh, okay, Red. She ran out of gas once quite a bit back—I don't know, maybe a year or two ago, maybe longer, right here in front of the Circle-T. I gave her some gas and that was it. But she took a hankering to me, I suppose, because she would come by every once in a while to visit. Sometimes we'd sit and have a cup of coffee and a slice of pie. She'd bring me an apple pie or a nice card. Anyway, she was a sweet girl. That was the only thing I knew about her until she stopped by another time to ask me if I wanted to buy her truck. She gave me such a sweet deal, I couldn't pass it up. Said she needed the money." Walton took a breath before continuing with the string of lies he'd rehearsed. "My old truck was about to die on me anyways, and I needed a way to get to the Safeway. A man's got to eat, you know. My wife died twenty years ago, so I ain't got no one to care for me."

"I'm sorry about your wife. By the way, what kind of truck did you own?"

"A '92 Ford F-150."

"What happened to it?"

"What do you mean?"

"Well, you said it was about to die on you."

"I got rid of it."

"How?"

"I sold it for fifty bucks to a kid who, ah, wanted to work on it."

"What's the kid's name?"

"Shoot, I don't know his name."

"Are you telling the truth, Mr. Turner?"

"Yessiree, son. I don't lie."

"Were you aware the lady you know as Red allegedly killed her husband and has been running with another lady named Stacey Keenan, who allegedly killed her husband, too?"

"The police told me that when they interrogated me, like I was some kinda terrorist or something. I don't know nothin' about no husbands. But if these ladies did kill their husbands, those boys probably deserved it. All I know is that Red was a sweet lady."

"What about Mrs. Keenan?"

"Who you say?"

"Mrs. Stacey Keenan, the lady I mentioned that was running with Red."

"I don't know nothin' about another lady." Walton gave Hank a quizzical look. "Sir, I'm afraid you're a bit confused. Red was by herself when she came to sell me her truck."

"Do you have any idea where Red and her friend might have gone after they left?"

"Mister, I said Red was alone. What are you, deef or somethin'?"

"What did she do, walk home?" Hank asked. He didn't mask his sarcasm. "You said you bought her truck, right? What did you do? Drive her to a bus stop?"

"She walked down the drive to the road," Walton continued to fabricate. "She said a friend was gonna pick her up there."

"Why didn't her friend drive her car up the driveway and wait for her here at your house?"

"How the blazes would I know?" Walton started to show his nerves. He untied the red bandanna from his neck, took off his hat, and used the bandana to wipe sweat from the inside of his brim.

"Do you think her friend was Mrs. Keenan?"

"Who?"

"Mrs. Keenan, the lady who killed her husband."

"Okay, that's it. I ain't gonna talk to you no more," Walton shouted. He stood up and stepped off the porch. After taking a few steps, he stopped and turned back to face Hank. "Mister, you ain't making no sense at all. I suggest that you and those other yahoos get off my property right now. You're trying to trick me into telling you I know something about Red when I told you I didn't. Now, why don't you all get the hell off my property? You have no damn right to be here. None of you have no right to intimidate lawful citizens. That's what's wrong with this country. That's what things are comin' to."

DeGarzia heard Turner shouting and walked out to the porch. "What's going on out here?" he snapped.

Walton answered, "Look here, Mr. Big City Dee-tec-tive, this guy is asking me questions, trying to trick me into saying things he wants me to say. I strongly suggest you get the blazes out of my house and off my property before I kick your asses the hell off. You have no right to be here. You ain't nothin' but a bunch a' buffoons. And bring me back my truck."

"What did you call me?" DeGarzia lost his composure and stepped off the porch. "You old shit. I don't appreciate you calling me names."

"Well, tough titties. Ever hear of the First Amendment of the Con-stee-tu-shun of these United States of America? It's called freedom of speech, Bozo. Now get the hell outta here. Catch my drift? I don't want you here."

Deeg stepped closer to Walton.

Hank knew Deeg was angry. He jumped between the two men and cautioned Walton. "Mr. Turner, Detective DeGarzia has a warrant to search your property. It is his intention, and my own, to complete the search. I suggest you calm down, or we'll charge you with obstruction of justice."

"Well, go ahead and do it, young fella. I could give a rat's petuny about your threats." Walton waved the men off and headed toward the barn.

Hank spewed his frustration to DeGarzia. "That son of a bitch knows a hell of a lot more than he's telling us. Don't let him get to you, Deeg."

"Too late for that."

"What did you come up with in the house?"

"A lot of fingerprints. My guess is they'll be a match to Heather and Stacey's. Were they here? I bet you a hundred bucks they were, maybe even the whole time after they left Golden."

"What about the truck Turner used to drive?" Hank asked. "Any chance they switched trucks?"

"It's possible."

"He claims he sold it to some kid for fifty bucks, but doesn't know the kid's name. He's obviously lying. I think the women are driving it.

"Yeah, I think you're right. I'll get out an APB. We just may be getting closer to nabbing them."

Chapter 39

Heather and Stacey ordered breakfast at the McDonald's Drive Thru. They ate their Egg McMuffin sandwiches with zest, and agreed that coffee never tasted so good. For a brief moment, they felt normal—not like two criminals on the run.

It was Heather's turn to drive.

"Let's not get back on 80," Stacey said.

"What do you suggest?"

Stacey studied the atlas. "We may never get a chance to do this again. Let's take Route 30. It looks like it runs parallel to I-80 all the way through to Iowa. We stand a better chance of being spotted by the police on the interstate than we do on these back roads. So what if it takes us a little longer? Maybe we can find a place to stop later and spend the night. We're both exhausted."

Heather agreed. "I'm okay with that. We need gas anyway, so we can stop once we get on one of these back roads."

The windows were down and fresh air filled the truck as they rode along, relishing each sip of their coffee. It was going to be a warm day. Heather drove for twenty minutes before noticing a strange smell. She tilted her head toward her open window and took a deep breath. "You smell that?"

"No. What?"

"Smells like smoke, or burning rubber, or something. I hope it's in the air and not coming from the truck."

Suddenly, thick white smoke engulfed the hood, obscuring all visibility. Heather pumped the breaks and pulled over to the side of the road. The two women jumped out of the truck and moved several yards away, thinking it might burst into flames. Another pickup drove by, slowed, and pulled off the road, stopping just in front of where Heather and Stacey were standing. A farmer in overalls and an orange John Deere hat stepped out of the truck. "A little problem, huh, ladies?" he said.

"Yeah, really," Heather responded. "Can you help?"

The man took a rag from the floor of his truck, wrapped it around his hand, and carefully opened the hood. "Looks like a busted hose. It's blowing antifreeze over the exhaust system. Hate to tell you this, but you might have blown the head gasket."

"Is that bad?"

"Yep."

"Is there a garage around that could fix it?"

"There's one down the road a bit. I'll drive down and ask them to come and tow you to their shop."

"We'd appreciate that. Thanks for your help."

*****

Fifteen minutes later, a service station tow truck arrived. "Thank God we were on this road instead of 80," Stacey said to the tall, lanky kid who emerged from the truck. She noticed his name embroidered on his shirt. "Do you think you can fix our pickup today, Eddie?"

He spoke with a pronounced drawl. "We're pretty busy. My boss can tell you better. But if it's a head gasket, you might be looking at a couple of days before we can have it ready for you."

"A couple of days? And how much it will cost to fix it?"

"I couldn't tell you. My boss will tell you that, too. He's a pretty fair guy. He ain't gonna stiff you or nothing."

"Is there a motel someplace close by we can stay at while we wait?" Heather asked.

"Yes ma'am. There's the Darr Motel about a mile away. Let's take your truck to the garage first, so you can talk to the boss. Then I'll take you to the motel. Where you folks heading?" he asked, not really caring to know.

"We're on our way to Chicago, to a wedding," Heather lied. She concocted the tale on the spur of the moment before Stacey could say a word.

"Hope the wedding's not for a couple of days 'cause you might not get there in time."

"We're okay. It's next weekend. What town are we in?"

"Darr," he spelled the name for them. "*D* as in *Delta*, *A*, double *R*."

With Heather and Stacey crammed into the front seat of the tow truck, Eddie towed Walton's truck to Billy's Auto Repair Shop. An unfenced field full of wrecked cars and trucks spread out behind the shop. Billy was a plain-talking Nebraskan who showed sympathy toward the two women. He promised he would work on their pickup as soon as he could, but still expected the old Ford would need a couple of days to repair. Eddie transported the women to the Darr Motel and carried their suitcases into the motel office. Stacey attempted to give him a five-dollar tip, but he refused.

Heather checked in under the name of Elizabeth Buchanan and paid cash for the room. Stacey walked around to the side of the motel where she saw two boys fishing in a small pond. She waved to them, and they waved back.

*****

Darr was a small, out-of-the-way town in central Nebraska. The town's most frequent visitors were tourists looking for local flavor and an occasional long-distance truck driver. The motel was not elegant by any standards, but it worked for Heather and Stacey. They felt protected and safely out of the public eye.

"How are we going to pay for the truck repair, Heather?"

"We have more than enough cash, but we'll check with the garage tomorrow to find out how much it will be. We can always call Walton and ask him to wire us some money if we need more. I'm sure he'd do that for us."

With time on their hands, Heather and Stacey caught up on their sleep and passed the hours watching television or sitting out near the pond. They enjoyed watching the same two boys while away their Sunday fishing and skimming rocks over the water. Stacey continued to feel a nagging remorse about the children Clyde never let her have.

Heather and Stacey had been through much together. In spite of that, they had never really delved into their lives beyond the talk of their husbands or how they would survive going forward. The rustic setting helped them relax enough to open up and reveal long-forgotten details about their lives. Heather was introspective, more than she had ever been. She talked about her childhood in Albuquerque as the daughter of a power company lineman and a mother who worked as a maid. "I was the oldest of seven kids. I didn't care much for school. Never did. Did I ever tell you that kids teased me real bad the whole time I was growin' up? Those were the worst days of my life." She caught herself, "Well, maybe not the worst. Things have been worse. Anyways, high school was awful. I grew so fast. I was almost six feet tall by the time I turned fourteen. I was taller than most everyone in school, includin' the boys. And thin—I was thin as a pencil. Of course the kids would tease me about the color of my hair. They used to call me 'Olive Oyl,' like in the Popeye comics. Or 'carrot head.' I really hated that one. By the time I got to be sixteen, I filled out and all of a sudden, boys started to notice me, and that's when I met Jake. I remember the first time I met him was at a skatin' rink. He was a good-lookin' guy back then, and his hair was redder than mine. We kinda hit it off at first because of that. He was older than me. Three years older. Anyway, he dropped out of school, when he was, like, seventeen, so he'd been workin' as a carpenter, makin' good money, drivin' a nice pickup. I mean, I thought he hung the moon and taught it to shine.

"It didn't take no time at all before we were doin' it in his truck. And before you know it, he asked me to marry him, and I said yes right away. God, what a mistake, huh? But I didn't know any better. We decided to go to Vegas to get married, but then found out we needed my mother and father's permission. I shouldn't 'a worried about that, because they gave me permission right away. As far as they were concerned, I was one less kid they would have to take care of. So Jake and me got married when I was sixteen. It didn't take me long to find out he was an asshole, but the sex was good. That's probably why I stayed with him all this time—that plus I didn't know shit about nothin', so I relied on him for everything. He was makin' good money, and we bought our little house and were doin' okay. Now I wish I didn't do any of that. I wish I never met him."

✳✳✳✳✳

Heather fully expected the police would find them someday, but vowed they would not capture her alive. She had nothing to live for. She told Stacey she would take her own life rather than go to prison.

"Please don't say things like that," Stacey scolded. "If the police ever catch us, we'll tell them how bad our lives were with Clyde and Jake, how mean they treated us. Detective DeGarzia will believe us."

"Yeah, right. The detective I shot will believe us. Not a chance in hell," Heather replied.

"You're a good person. Remember that. Jake really had it coming. He was abusive to you, just like Clyde was to me."

Heather nodded as she replayed in her mind the horrible acts they committed in the name of friendship. She knew she was responsible for giving Stacey the idea to kill Clyde, but wished she had never suggested it. Stacey was a victim. She didn't have a mean bone in her body. Heather could only imagine what Stacey would think if she knew how Michael had died. At times, she was tempted to confess, but inevitably lost her nerve and ended up questioning the need to tell Stacey anything at all. But if the police caught them, Heather wanted to let them know Stacey was innocent. The need to explain the circumstances surrounding Michael's death pulled at her conscience. She picked up the pen and paper from the nightstand and sat at the desk to write.

"What are you doing?" Stacey asked.

"Nothin'. I'm writin' a letter to Walton," Heather lied.

"Oh. What are you going to say to him?"

"Just about where we are, in case he's wonderin'."

Stacey accepted Heather's explanation without question.

Heather filled sheet after sheet of the Darr Motel note pad. After twenty minutes, she finished then stuffed the letter in her suitcase.

To who it concerns: I am writing this letter so you can know the truth about what I did, I killed Michael Redfield. I used Jake's truck and pushed him into Breeze Canyon because he dumped me for my best friend Stacey Keenan. I thought I loved him, but then I was mad when I realized he took advantage of me. He was not the prince everyone thinks he was. I was going to kill that lady on Via Encantado too because I thought she maybe could indentify me but, when I got to her house she wasn't there, so I stole the painting by Gorgia O'Keefe. Honest to god I did not kill her. And then I had Stacey pawn it so we could have some money to live on after we killed our husbands. We did not kill any body else. Honest to god I shot Jake because he tried to kill me and I told him if he ever hit me again I would shoot him, so that's what I did.

And yes I shot that detective and I'm sorry I did. Stacey said he was just doing his job and I know she was right so I didn't shoot him again. She's the one who called 911 to tell them about the detective being shot. Stacey is the nicest person in the world. She would not hurt a fly. She killed her husband because he raped her and he was going to kill her first. She did it in self defence. He was a miserable bastard. I hope you remember that she did not kill no one except her husband. She's a good person. A really good person. I did not kill that lady and I did not kill any of those other bikers who were killed too, I don't know who killed them but Stacey and I did not. As god is my witness and as far as Stacey killing her husband I told her to kill him. He was an ass hole. If she gets caught by the police, she won't try to defend herself but it's the truth. He tried to kill her so please take that into consideration. If you read this letter I will be dead, I do not want to spend the rest of my life in prison. I have nothing to live for. I have been living in a prison my whole life with my jerk husband and don't want to live like that no more. Please tell Stacey how sorry I am that I killed Michael. I had no idea she was that much in love with him. I was wrong to kill him. Please tell her how sorry I am that I did that but I think he would have broke her heart too. I don't really know. Maybe not but it's too late to change what happened. I'm sorry.

Sincerely, Heather Dorell

*****

"Police! Come out with your hands up!"

Boom! Boom! Boom!

The pounding nearly rattled the door off its hinges. Heather and Stacey jumped off their beds, frozen with fear.

"What do we do?" Stacey was panicked.

"I don't know."

"We're going to have to give up," Stacey sobbed. "We have to."

"I'm not surrenderin'. I am not gonna spend the rest of my life in jail."

"We've got to surrender. We have no choice."

"You can go out if you want, but I'm not goin' anywhere. They're gonna have to kill me first." She emptied her purse on the bed, fishing for Clyde's pistol.

"Heather, you can't do that."

"You go out. I'm not."

"Please, Heather, no."

"Get out of here."

Stacey was desperate. "No. I'm staying with you."

They heard a shout through a bullhorn. "Open up! Now!"

"I said to get out, Stacey. You didn't do nothin' bad."

"Yes, I did. I killed my husband."

"He was a mean-spirited sonovabitch. They'll believe you."

"Your husband was, too."

"Yes, he was. But I want you to go. Now." Heather placed her right hand on the doorknob and held the pistol with the left. "I'm gonna open this door and tell them you're comin' out. Now go."

"I'm not going out without you."

"Yes, you are. Now get the hell out of here. Please. I'm so sorry."

"This is not your fault."

"Yes it is, Stacey. Yes, it is."

Stacey parted the heavy curtain to peek out the front window. "Oh my God," she cried. A half dozen cop cars were positioned in a tight semi-circle in front of their door. Police officers crouched behind the cars, guns aimed. Stacey ran to the bathroom, thinking they could slip out the back window, but the police were also guarding that escape route. "Heather, we've got to surrender. Please, let's go."

"Okay, okay. I'll go out with you." Heather cracked the door open and shouted, "We surrender. We're comin' out. Don't shoot. Don't shoot."

"Come out with your hands up!" They recognized DeGarzia's booming voice.

"Okay, Stacey, you go first. Keep your hands up."

Stacey walked out slowly. Scared. Sobbing. Her hands held high.

"Get down on the ground!"

Heather yelled, "I'm sorry, Stacey. Forgive me. It was all my fault. I killed Michael. I'm so sorry." She slammed the door shut behind Stacey.

"No, Heather. No!" Stacey shouted back. She turned to plead with Heather.

"Get down on your stomach!"

Stacey fell to the ground, terrified.

A single shot rang out from inside the room.

The police were uncertain if the shot was fired at them. They stood their ground but did not return fire. "Heather Dorell! Come out with your hands up!" DeGarzia shouted again.

There was no response. The SWAT team used a battering ram to break down the door. They rushed in with guns drawn.

Heather lay dead on the floor. She had turned Clyde's gun on herself.

Chapter 40

Thelma and Louise Crime Spree Comes To an End in Nebraska. Santa Fe Police Detective Lawrence DeGarzia announced the capture and arrest of Stacey Keenan and the death of Heather Dorell, the alleged serial killers of their husbands and five others, including noted Santa Fe artist Carlotta Smith. The women had been on the run for months. Keenan surrendered without resistance and is now in police custody awaiting extradition to New Mexico. The police allege Heather Dorell took her own life rather than surrender to authorities. An automobile mechanic in Darr, Nebraska, alerted the State Police to the whereabouts of the two women. Detective DeGarzia and a joint task force that included New Mexico State Patrolmen, Sheriff's deputies, and a SWAT team, made the arrest. Thus ends the case of two of the most wanted criminals in recent New Mexico history.

Stacey Keenan did not fight extradition from Nebraska and was back in New Mexico ten days after her apprehension at the Darr Motel. Television cameras highlighted her arraignment. Dressed in an orange jumpsuit, she stood at the front of the courtroom, scared, but attentive to what her court-appointed lawyer was telling her. She looked back and forth between her attorney and the judge, trying to follow their legal jargon. Stacey wanted to plead guilty to the charges of killing her husband and of being an accessory to the murder of Jake Dorell, but her lawyer, Patricia Appleton, had convinced her to plead not guilty. She would use battered-wife syndrome as her defense. Appleton was an experienced lawyer who had tried several such cases and had, with sympathetic juries, been able to obtain reduced prison sentences. Citing Stacey as a flight risk, the judge refused to set bail, instead remanding her to county jail. The date for her preliminary hearing had been set for three weeks out.

*****

Stacey sat at a table in one of the stark interview rooms at the county jail. Patricia Appleton was seated next to her and Detective DeGarzia sat across the table. A guard stood watch outside the door.

"I'm not going to ask you any questions concerning the death of your husband. While I certainly do not endorse your actions, if your version of the events is true, I don't condemn them, either." The hard-edged detective showed Stacey uncommon sympathy. "I am sorry you had such a difficult marriage."

Stacey teared up but nodded her head in understanding. "Thank you," was all she could say.

"My purpose, right now, is to inquire about the deaths of the four cyclists who were murdered over the past five to six months. I also need to ask you about a woman by the name of Carlotta Smith. I'm sure you've heard the accounts of her death?"

"I have," she answered, her voice barely audible.

"It's my understanding that, in the moments before Heather killed herself, she told you she killed Michael Redfield. What exactly did she say?"

Stacey looked to her lawyer who nodded her permission to answer. "She shoved me out the door at the motel. Just as she slammed it shut behind me she shouted 'I'm sorry, Stacey. Forgive me. It was all my fault. I killed Michael. I'm so sorry.' Those were her exact words. I'll remember them till the day I die."

"Did the two of you ever talk about Michael?"

"Yes. I told her how much I loved him. She admitted she had an affair with him, too. But she swore it was before Michael and I became involved, and not at the same time. She really didn't want to talk about him too much. And she never let on that she killed him. I still don't really understand why she did it. He was such a sweet man. He really was."

"Do you know about the letter the police found in her suitcase absolving you of any involvement in Michael's death?"

"Yes. Miss Appleton told me about it."

"She wrote that neither she nor you had involvement in the Carlotta Smith murder," he said, "but she did admit to stealing the Georgia O'Keeffe painting from Mrs. Smith's house. Were you aware she had stolen the painting?"

Stacey's attorney signaled to her client, "Stop. I don't want you to answer that. Any answer you give can incriminate you."

"Ms. Appleton, we are not concerned that Mrs. Keenan pawned the stolen painting. We just need to determine the facts surrounding Carlotta Smith's death. If it's true Heather Dorell didn't kill her, we need to find out who did and why."

"Under that premise, Detective, I'll allow her to answer. Go ahead, Stacey."

"Heather wouldn't tell me where she got it from. She said we were going to need money, and that she had this painting that was probably worth a lot of money. Until I read her letter, I didn't know where she had gotten it."

"Did she ever talk about, or in any way imply, that she knew who might have killed Mrs. Smith?"

"No, we never talked about her."

"It would appear, then, based on the disclosure in her letter, Heather went to Mrs. Smith's house to kill her. But she didn't find her there, probably because someone else had already killed her."

Stacey shrugged her shoulders. "I guess that's what happened. I don't know."

"So, after you both killed your husbands—"

"Detective, please. Your focus is on the other murders?" Appleton reminded him.

"Yeah, right." DeGarzia rephrased his question. "After the deaths of your husbands, you and Heather drove to the hideout in Golden, is that right?"

"Yes. Heather told me she had a place where we could hide out, but I didn't know where it was until we got there. She had rented the house and stocked it with food and everything she thought she would need to survive for a few months."

"So you stayed there the whole time?"

"Yes."

"Whose car were you driving?" DeGarzia was trying to discern a timeline for when Walton Turner had given Heather and Stacey his truck.

Appleton put her hand on Stacey's. "Don't answer that."

"Patricia, I'm trying to find out the role Walton Turner played in all of this."

"That's off limits, Detective. I think the interview is over."

"One last question. Stacey, did you and Heather kill Jordan Sanchez? We found a cigarette butt of hers at the site where he died. Why did she kill him?"

"She absolutely did not kill him. Absolutely not. And we didn't kill those other men, either. I know it was all over TV that we did—all that stuff about Thelma and Louise—but we didn't, and I don't have any idea who would have. It wasn't Heather and it wasn't me. We didn't set foot outside the house in Golden until we ran out of food."

"Detective, this interview's over."

Chapter 41

Walton stepped onto his porch early one evening. He sat in a straight back chair and looked out at nothing in particular. The events of the earlier weeks he had spent with Heather and Stacey flooded his thoughts. *I sure do miss 'em. I knew they shouldn't 'a gone, doggone it. I should've insisted they stay.* Several days had passed since the police visit to his ranch, and he was in anguish over everything that had occurred. Red was dead, Stacey was in jail, and he'd lost the truck—his only mode of transportation—in the process. He had no way of knowing how long it would take the police to finish processing it for evidence.

The police had charged Walton with harboring criminals but released him on his own recognizance. Without transportation he was moored to his house.

The sight of approaching headlights brought Walton back to the present. *Who in the hell could that be?* He went inside to retrieve his shotgun and leant it against the wall within reach. He sat back down.

"Hey, old man, remember me?"

"Get off my property. And I mean pronto."

"Why is it you always have a chip on your shoulder?"

"I guess I'm just lucky."

"Nah. I think you're *un*lucky tonight."

"I'm telling you one last time, get the hell off my property or I'll blow your head off." Walton grabbed his shotgun.

"No. I've come a long way to settle a score with you."

"What the hell are you talkin' about?"

"I'm here to put things right between us."

"I don't have a clue what you're talking about. Who's that in the car with you?"

"No one."

The man stepped onto the porch. Walton stood up and pointed his shotgun directly at the man's chest. "If you don't get the hell off my property right now, I'll blow you off of it."

"Go ahead and shoot." The man took another step toward Walton. With one quick move, he knocked the shotgun aside.

Walton pulled the trigger, but the shot scattered aimlessly toward the barn.

A moment later, laughter was heard from inside the car.

*****

"Hank, Walton Turner is dead."

"What?"

"Yeah, murdered. After my interview with Stacey Keenan, I decided to drive out to ask him a few more questions. I found him dead in his barn. The ME is doing an autopsy, but puts the timeline of his death at about forty-eight hours ago."

"Who could possibly have wanted him dead?"

"I don't know. But are you ready for this?"

"What?"

"The killer put a bike helmet on him."

"The same MO as Carlotta Smith? You've got to be kidding," Hank exclaimed.

"I wish I were. Yeah, just like Smith. Oh, and something else. The killer placed a cigarette butt on his chest. The lab is checking it for DNA."

*****

Walton H. Turner, 85, found dead on ranch. Police ruled Turner's death a homicide and are investigating the circumstances surrounding his murder. Turner lived in San Ysidro his entire life and was the owner of the Circle-T Ranch. A veteran of World War II, he was long known in San Ysidro as a political activist who railed against authority. He twice ran for governor of New Mexico in write-in campaigns under a platform espousing recalls of all elected state representatives and senators from New Mexico and the dissolution of the state legislature. Funeral arrangements are pending.

"No, no," Stacey screamed. "It can't be! No!"

The guard outside the interview room opened the door. "Okay in here?"

DeGarzia nodded yes and waved him off.

"Who killed him?" Stacey cried. "Why would anyone do such a thing?" She was hysterical upon hearing the news of Walton's murder. Patricia Appleton attempted to console her. Appleton was even more worried now about Stacey's fragile emotional state and voiced concern to DeGarzia, who alerted the warden to have her put on suicide watch.

"It's all because of me, isn't it? Someone killed Walton because we stayed at his ranch. Oh, my God, what have I done? All these people are dead because of me—Michael, Clyde, and now the kindest man in the world—all because of me."

"It wasn't your fault, Stacey," Appleton said. "Now take a deep breath and calm down. Detective DeGarzia wants to ask you a few more questions, but you need to compose yourself."

"I don't care what happens. I don't have anything to live for. I don't. I don't. Oh my God!" she said over and over.

Appleton looked at DeGarzia and shook her head. She wasn't sure she should allow the questioning to continue.

"I know this news has hit you hard, Stacey, but I need your help. Someone is out there killing innocent people like Walton. We need to stop whoever that is. But we can't do it without your help. I need to know about the relationship you and Heather had with Walton. Will you help me find his killer?"

Stacey looked at the detective and jutted her jaw. "Yes. Yes, I will. I'll tell you anything you want to know. I'll help you find the awful monster who's doing this."

"Stacey, look at me," Appleton said. Stacey turned and faced her lawyer. "I don't want you to say another word, especially about Clyde." Appleton turned to look at Deeg. "Detective DeGarzia, I'll allow my client to assist you in your investigation, but before she answers any further questions, I want your guarantee she'll receive due consideration in having the charges against her reduced from murder one to aggravated manslaughter."

DeGarzia hesitated before answering. "I'll discuss Stacey's cooperation with the ADA, but she must cooperate fully or any deal we make is off the table."

"To be clear, I will restrict my client from answering questions about her husband. Agreed?"

"Agreed."

Appleton fished tissues from her briefcase and handed them to Stacey. "All right, Stacey, go ahead and answer the detective's questions."

"First off, do you know of anyone who would want to kill Walton? Did he ever talk about anyone he might have had a feud with? Past or present?"

Stacey dabbed at her eyes. "No. He never talked about anyone. He didn't like lawyers, or the police, or anyone who had anything to do with the government. And in that whole time we were there, no one ever came by to visit. Of course, he locked the gate all the time so no one could get in. I really don't think Walton knew anybody, at least no one he wanted to be friendly with."

"Had you met him before staying at his ranch?"

"No. Only Heather knew him. I didn't. He helped her one time when she ran out of gas right in front of his ranch, or she had some kind of car problem, something like that, and he helped her. She said she would go back every once in a while and have coffee with him or take him a pie. He was a sweet, lonely guy. His wife died twenty years ago. Anyway, they knew each other that way. He really liked her. He called her Red."

"How did you end up at his ranch?"

"When we left the house in Golden, we were going to try to go to Mexico. But when we pulled out of the driveway, two guys from the Cycling Club were riding by at the exact same time. Heather never saw them. She almost ran into them. I remember screaming to her to watch out. She thought maybe they recognized us, so instead of driving south toward Mexico, we changed direction and drove north. We didn't know if they recognized us or not, but we were scared they did."

"What happened next?"

"We didn't know what else to do. We drove north for a while, but then Heather remembered Walton and thought he might let us stay at the Circle-T. So that's where we went. That was the first time I met him."

"How long did you stay with him?"

"Eight or nine weeks. We never stepped off the ranch."

"Never?"

"Never, I swear to you. We were sure we'd get recognized if we did, because our pictures had been in the news so much."

"It seems you were pretty safe at the Circle-T. What made you decide to leave?"

"We thought we needed to leave before someone, somehow, found us out. We knew we couldn't stay there forever. And we didn't want Walton to get in trouble if the police found us there. You know, harboring criminals or something like that. We loved him so. He was the kindest man we ever knew. He was like a grandfather to us. If only we had stayed, Walton and Heather would both be alive now."

"Walton's truck—how did you end up with his truck?"

"Heather was the one who came up with the idea. She thought if we switched trucks, the police wouldn't stop us. We made up a fake bill of sale to show Walton bought Jake's pickup. That way, if he was stopped by the police for some reason, he could say he bought the truck from Heather fair and square." Stacey paused. "Did something happen? How did you find out he had Jake's truck?"

"He was involved in a traffic accident and tried to leave the scene. He gave the cop a hard time, and when the police searched the pickup, they found an old registration card in the glove compartment that showed Jake Dorell as the owner."

"Oh. We never did go through the glove compartment."

"After you left the Circle-T, did you have any further contact with Walton?"

"No. We thought we might have to phone him to wire us some money to pay for the truck repair, but we never did, because—"

"That's when you were arrested."

"Yes, and when Heather shot—" Stacey was unable to finish. She broke down into tears again. Her attorney patted her on the back.

Deeg gave Stacey a minute to compose herself before continuing. "How did you end up in Nebraska?"

"Like I said, when we first left the house in Golden, we were going to try to go to Mexico. After we left the Circle-T, we thought we should go back to our original plan, but then changed our minds. We figured if we went north instead, away from Santa Fe, we would be able to get lost in a big city like Chicago. Our new plan was working until we had problems with the truck."

"That explains why you were in Nebraska. To reiterate, you're saying you didn't have any further contact with Walton once you left his ranch, and you knew of no one who had a grudge against him?"

"That's right."

"Are you aware we found documents among Walton's possessions saying he willed the Circle-T ranch to you and Heather? And now that she's deceased, you'll inherit the entire property?"

"Well, yes. He said he was going to leave the ranch to us. That way we could sell it and use the money to defend ourselves if we ever got caught. He said he didn't have anyone else to give it to, because he didn't have any children or next of kin."

"Did you have anything to do with his death?"

Stacey looked wide-eyed at DeGarzia. "Of course not."

"You didn't arrange to have him killed so you could inherit—"

Patricia Appleton stepped in. "Don't say another word, Stacey. Detective DeGarzia, don't be ridiculous. You're accusing my client of killing someone she held dear. And that's beside the fact she's been in jail for the past few weeks."

Deeg ignored the scolding. "Do you plan to sell the Circle-T?"

Stacey looked at her attorney. She leaned in and whispered a few words in her ear.

Appleton nodded to Stacey to go ahead and answer.

"No. The good Lord knows I deserve whatever punishment I get, but I'm not going to sell it. Even if it takes me a million years to get out of jail, I'm not going to sell it. I'm going to turn it into something good. After Walton told us of his plans, Heather and I talked about what we would do with the ranch. We didn't know how, but we thought if we got the ranch from Walton, we would make the Circle-T into a haven for abused and battered women."

"How were you going to do that? You were fugitives. How would you possibly have made that happen?"

"I don't know. It was stupid of us to think we would have been able to work all that out, but it was what we wanted to do. And now, even if I'm sentenced to prison, I will still try to make it happen."

Deeg nodded for a long moment. "Stacey, in all sincerity, if, down the road you're given a second opportunity, I promise I'll help you any way I can to make your dream come true. Counselor, this is off the record, but I have seen firsthand what abuse can do to people. Obviously, I can't change what happened between Stacey and her husband, but I will certainly put in a good word with the District Attorney about Mrs. Keenan's plans for the future."

"Thank you, Detective," Appleton said.

*****

The forensics lab informed Deeg that the DNA on the cigarette found on Turner's body matched the DNA on the cigarette butt found in Carlotta Smith's back yard.

"Hank, the problem is we don't know whose DNA it is."

"Yeah, but that makes sense, Deeg. Our killer put bike helmets on both victims, right? Similarly, it stands to reason the cigarettes came from the same guy."

"Yeah, but that doesn't get us any closer to finding out who's killing all these people."

Part III

Chapter 42

FBI Special Agent Mark Stephenson was seated at the head of a long table in a conference room at the police station. Hank entered and Captain Ellsworth introduced him to Stephenson. The two men shook hands. Hank glanced at Deeg who was at the whiteboard adding notes to several lists of data.

"Mornin', Deeg." The detective did not look pleased and gave only a cursory nod in response.

"You can probably guess why I've asked you here," the captain began. "I thought it would be helpful to have the FBI's help in profiling our so-called 'serial cyclist killer.' Special Agent Stephenson will assist us in developing a deeper understanding of the killer's personality and also his motives. I've spoken with Detective DeGarzia about my intentions and assured him that he will continue to lead the investigation. Special Agent Stephenson's role is purely advisory. I'll let him take it from here."

Deeg sat down next to Hank. He let out a long, deep sigh that Hank interpreted as exasperation at FBI involvement in his case. Stephenson chose to ignore it. He had faced similar reactions when assisting other police investigations, and recognized DeGarzia might be one more detective to have hard feelings toward him. No cop liked an outsider's perceived intrusion in his or her jurisdiction—it was part ego, part pride of responsibility. To handle it, Stephenson knew he would have to give Deeg credit at every turn.

Stephenson was a tall, lanky man with narrow shoulders, closely cropped brown hair, and angular facial features. He reminded Hank of the character Ichabod Crane from *The Legend of Sleepy Hollow*. Stephenson spoke in an articulate, clipped manner, as though reading from index cards. He turned to Hank. "Detective DeGarzia told me you were the first to see a connection with all these murders—commonalities, if you will. It's these common elements we'll focus on. Hopefully, they'll lead us to the person or persons involved."

Hank's ADA side came out. "I'm sure I don't need to remind anyone here of the importance of building a rock-solid case."

"Absolutely. That's everyone's aim," concurred Stephenson. "If I may, I'd like to give some information on my background. I've been with the bureau for twelve years. For the past two, I've been in the FBI Investigative Support Unit at the Academy in Quantico. Thanks to the popularity of all the police shows on television, we're commonly referred to as FBI profilers. As Captain Ellsworth mentioned, my sole objective here is to provide advice, specifically as it relates to the killer's tendencies. In other words, I'll be involved in the psychological or human behavioral aspects of the case. Detective DeGarzia will continue to lead the investigation. The bureau recognized some years ago that these kinds of serial murders are a strain on the resources of local police departments so they developed the Investigative Support Unit to assist in areas such as psychological profiling and advanced forensics techniques."

At the whiteboard, Stephenson began his review of the information Deeg had organized into five columns. Each column was headed by the name of one of the murder victims.

"Detective DeGarzia's briefed me on what's transpired to date. With his assistance, we've listed a series of notes, names, and places highlighting the common elements among the murders." In reality, Deeg had offered only reluctant assistance.

Pointing to the first column, the agent said, "Heather Dorell admitted to the murders of Jake Dorell and Michael Redfield. That much we know for near certainty based on her written confession and other verifiable facts in those cases."

Tapping the point of his marker on the whiteboard, Stephenson indicated the second column where Clyde Keenan's name was written. "And Stacey Keenan has admitted to killing her husband. We also know she provided Heather with Clyde Keenan's pistol, which makes her an accessory to Jake's murder. By all indications, however, Stacey was not involved in Michael Redfield's murder." As he spoke, Stephenson liberally underscored some names and circled others.

"Then we have Carlotta Smith and Walton Turner." He circled the names in the third column. "The killer left two of his signatures behind in both of these murders. One was to put a bike helmet on the victim."

"What do you suppose is the significance of that?" Hank asked.

"The killer wants us to know that, although Smith and Turner were not cyclists, their deaths are related to those of the murdered cyclists. At this point, we don't know exactly how."

"And the second signature would be the cigarettes left at the murder scenes."

"Correct. The killer left a cigarette on or near the site of each killing."

"Same question. What are the cigarettes supposed to signify?" Hank asked.

"We know the cigarette left on Turner's body had the same DNA—as yet unmatched—as the one found in Smith's back yard. What further complicates the picture is that Heather Dorell's cigarette was found at the site of Jordan Sanchez's death," he said, and pointed to the fourth column. "So we have two different sets of DNA at the sites of three different murders. If we believe, through her confession, Dorell had nothing to do with Sanchez's death, we can only assume someone tried to frame her for his murder."

Ellsworth interrupted. "So, do we take her at her word that she was not involved in Sanchez's death?"

"Yes, I believe we do. In fact, Stacey Keenan has already corroborated that Heather was at the ranch house in Golden at the time of the murder. The two never left the ranch house the entire three months they were holed up there. Since she's been forthcoming about all other facts in the case, let's, for the moment, assume she would not withhold information about Sanchez's death."

"If someone tried to frame Heather, is it conceivable that the cigarettes found at the Smith and Turner murder sites were also plants?" Ellsworth asked.

"It's possible. Or, they belong to the killer and he's mocking us. He could be saying, 'I'm smarter than you are. I'm giving you the smoking gun and you still can't find me.'"

Stephenson pointed to the last column on the whiteboard. "The other two cyclists were Castillo and Pérez. The timing of their respective deaths predates that of any of the other victims. There's no evidence they were murdered, but if they were, whoever killed Sanchez may have killed them too. Again, there is no concrete evidence to point to that. Because their deaths were deemed accidental, the police did not look for evidence such as cigarette butts at the scenes." He drew a two-headed arrow between the last two lists. "As you may have already concluded, since Castillo and Pérez died in the same manner as Sanchez, there probably is a link."

"So, let's talk about Redfield's death," Ellsworth said. "His appears to have been a copy-cat killing, committed by Heather Dorell, fueled by passion. I would say his death was most likely not related to those of the other cyclists."

"I agree. Given the fact she belonged to the Cycling Club, she would have heard about the deaths of Castillo and Pérez, and decided to kill her lost lover the same way. His death would appear to be just another biking accident."

"How do you explain the Smith murder? She was a threat only to Dorell, who wrote in her confession letter she didn't kill Smith. Why, then, was she murdered? And why was Walton Turner killed?"

"Good question, Captain. And one I can't answer. What I can tell you is this. Serial killers typically kill for one of three reasons: for the thrill; for sexual satisfaction; or because of some deep-seated, violent fantasy of dominance caused by a grudge, an insult, or some other kind of humbling experience. When the murderer kills, he feels dominant over the people who caused him to be hurt," Stephenson explained. "My guess is that these killings are the result of a grudge against the three cyclists, and it haloed to anyone who was in any way connected to the victims or to the killer himself."

"Which do you think it is?" Hank asked.

"I don't know," Stephenson answered with blunt honesty.

Deeg spoke up for the first time. "Do we have one killer for everyone or do we have multiple killers? The cyclists were all killed in the same manner, and Smith and Turner were killed in a different way. We don't know if it was one guy who killed them all, do we?"

"With the exception of Redfield and the two husbands, I believe it is one killer. Even though the Smith and Turner deaths were different from how the cyclists died, the two deaths are, nevertheless, associative."

"What the hell does that mean?" Deeg barked.

The captain shot an angry glance at Deeg, and Hank did a double take, but Stephenson dismissed DeGarzia's caustic tone and explained his theory in a matter-of-fact manner. "Yes, it's confusing, Detective. You're right. But the mind of a serial killer is confused and chaotic. Let's focus on Sanchez for a moment. He was killed in the same manner as Castillo and Pérez, yet we know there was an attempt to frame Heather Dorell for his death. The killer, whether consciously or subconsciously, tied himself to all the murders once he tried to frame her. And because of her connection to Turner, his death, in particular, was reinforcement that all the killings were done by the same person." Stephenson wrote *Heather* on the white board. He next drew a large circle around the names of all the victims, and then a line connecting the circle and the word Heather.

Ellsworth's look a moment earlier was not lost on Deeg. He addressed Stephenson in a civil tone. "If the cigarettes don't belong to the killer, and we determine who they do belong to, it would help us narrow down motive, wouldn't it?"

"Yes. We'd then need to find out why that person is being framed."

"Okay, so, what are we looking for?" Deeg asked.

"Consider this. Roughly eighty percent of the time, white offenders kill whites, blacks kill blacks, Hispanics kill Hispanics. Given that statistic, and because all three cyclists were Hispanic, the odds are they were killed by another Hispanic."

"Can you conclude the killings have ended? That the deaths of these people have satisfied his grudge, if that was, in fact, his motivation?" Ellsworth asked.

"I don't know that. The ring of possible victims could extend well beyond these people," Stephenson answered. He tapped his knuckles on the board. "Until we find this guy, we may never know. For right now, let's focus on the common aspects in the deaths of the three cyclists. In my discussions with Detective DeGarzia, he was able to identify quite a few commonalities."

Stephenson pointed to the list Deeg had written on the board. *Hispanics. Canyon Cycling Club. Friends. Alone. Low-traffic roads. Canyons.*

"The three men were Hispanic. They were past or present members of the Canyon Cycling Club. They were friends. Did something happen at the Cycling Club that would cause the killer to harbor a grudge against the three?" Stephenson turned to DeGarzia.

"I have a list of everyone who ever belonged to the Canyon Cycling Club, going back as far as they had records. I questioned every Hispanic on the list. None of them knew of any event where someone caused a problem. No one knew of any altercation of any kind with anyone, much less with the three guys who were killed."

"I can attest to that," Hank said. "I've been a member for several years, and I've never heard of any problems. Really, the Club is comprised of a cordial group of men and women. Everyone seems to get along."

"Have you ever heard any disparaging remarks made about Hispanics?" Stephenson asked.

"No. Never. To my knowledge, ethnicity has never been an issue. In fact, a lot of the time, we know each other only by first name, and so don't know if they're Anglo or Hispanic. Ethnicity is apparent for the blacks and Asians in the Club, but I could not tell you for sure who's Hispanic and who's Anglo."

Stephenson moved to a map pinned on the wall next to the whiteboard. The location of the canyon where each cyclist died was designated with a circle. "We also know the cyclists were all killed when they were riding alone in isolated areas, and that they fell to their deaths in various canyons. There does not, however, appear to be a pattern to these locations, from what I can see."

"I have a couple more things we should discuss," Hank said.

"Like what?"

"Jimi's Pizzeria for one. And the after-parties. A lot of the cyclists go to Jimi's after the Thursday-night rides, and from there they go to after-parties at different people's homes."

Stephenson added *Jimi's* and *after-parties* to Deeg's list. "Good. What do we know about these parties? For example, was anyone involved romantically with Castillo or the other victims? Did someone get their nose out of joint at one of these parties?"

"I'll try to find out. I'll ask Stacey Keenan," DeGarzia replied. "She used to go to the parties, and we know that's how her affair with Michael Redfield got started."

"Good," Ellsworth said.

DeGarzia took the opportunity to add, "She's remorseful and will probably do anything to cooperate. With her lawyer's blessing, she's been helpful throughout all this. Speaking of her lawyer, Hank, I told her I'd discuss the fact that Stacey's been cooperating, and that we would give her some consideration as a result. I hate to sound soft on her, but the fact remains, she was badly abused by her husband."

"I understand," Hank said. "If she continues to cooperate, I'll make certain the District Attorney is aware of it."

"Tell me about Jimi's," Stephenson said.

"It's a popular pizza joint—not only for cyclists, but for locals too," Hank said.

Deeg offered some personal observations. "I know Jimi Rodriguez fairly well. He's a second-generation Hispanic-American. Everyone in the Hispanic community knows him. And he employs a lot of Hispanics. Come to think of it, his wife, Dahlia is the only Anglo."

Captain Ellsworth gave Deeg his marching orders. "Deeg, question everyone who works at Jimi's, including his wife. Let's find out what they might know about the three dead cyclists."

"Will do."

"One last thing. Eventually, the killer will make a mistake. That's how the majority of these types of killings end. He becomes increasingly brazen and less careful, sloppy even. Maybe there'll be a witness or the intended victim escapes. As I said earlier, this killer might not be finished. It's imperative we figure out who the next victim could be, and when and where an attempt might occur."

Chapter 43

DeGarzia parked his car and entered Jimi's Pizzeria. Even though lunch hour was ending, the popular restaurant was still jammed. The cramped tables and booths in both the main dining area and small back room were mostly full, and the line of people waiting for take-out orders was six deep. Jimi's wife Dahlia peered around the customers in line at the cash register and greeted the detective with a smile. "Hi, Deeg. Good to see you," she said.

Behind the counter, Jimi was spreading a handful of cheese across a pizza. He looked up from his work. "Hey, Deeg, what's up? What can I get you?" he shouted over the din.

"A couple of plain slices," Deeg responded.

"You got it."

Deeg jerked his head toward the back of the restaurant and said, "When you have a chance." Jimi nodded.

"I'll be free in a couple," he said.

DeGarzia sat at a table for two and waited for his pizza. He observed the controlled frenzy of people ordering, eating, and paying their bills. Jimi was directing his workers, shouting out orders to be filled and orders ready for pickup, scolding one waitress he thought wasn't moving fast enough. Dahlia worked the register, giving each customer a sincere smile and a come-back-and-see-us-again thank you. Full-figured and pretty, her white skin was remarkably smooth. She wore her untamed blonde hair pulled up, adding to her sexy air. Her large breasts were apparent even though she wore a high-collared puffy blouse. DeGarzia noticed Jimi glancing at her often. *I wonder what that's all about.*

A waitress approached Deeg's table. She slid a paper plate with his two slices in front of him and expressed a perfunctory, "Enjoy" before wheeling around to wipe down the adjoining table. Deeg ate his slices and sipped his Coke while waiting for Jimi.

The lunch crowd dissipated. Only a few diners remained when Jimi walked over to greet Deeg. He tucked chairs under empty tables along the way and pointed out a table that needed cleaning. He reproached the waitress. "Eh! Get this table cleaned up." Jimi was the typical pizza parlor owner, in both looks and demeanor. He had black hair and was unshaven. Multiple burn marks, the hazards of working with a pizza oven, were visible along his arms. The white apron he wore around his wide belly was spotted with tomato stains.

"*Hola*, Jimi," Deeg said.

Jimi sat down across from him. "What's going on? How you doin'? We were pretty worried when we heard you got shot, but you look great."

"Yeah, I'm doing good. My shoulder's a little stiff, but I can't complain. I'm still kicking. Talk about kicking, looks like business is good."

"I can't complain, either. We get slow days but we're doing okay."

"That's great. That's great." Deeg took a sip from his soda. "Hey, Jimi, I need your help. You know about all these bikers getting killed, right?"

Jimi nodded.

"Well, the captain's making life miserable for me. It's like he expected me to solve the murders *hace una semana*, a week ago. So, now he brings in the FBI. One of their theories is that maybe a *Hispano* is behind all the murders. You know, a brother-on-brother type killer. And you, better than anybody, might be able to tell me who's behind this if it is a Hispanic. I mean, have you heard any rumors, any street talk about why these guys were murdered? Any of your compatriots have a grudge against them? Drugs? Anything?"

"To be honest, Deeg, I ain't heard nothin' about anybody having a problem with them. I knew all those guys. Didn't know them too good, but they seemed like ordinary people," Jimi answered. "Not Alex Castillo, though. He was a mover and a shaker. Smooth. I heard he did some running around after he divorced his wife, maybe even before he divorced. I don't know. He was too smooth for me. I didn't like him too much."

"What about you, Jimi, a good-looking guy like you? You ever run around too—like with those girls, Heather and Stacey?"

"Are you shittin' me? Look over there. See that beautiful girl?" Jimi nodded toward Dahlia. "That's my wife. *My* wife," he said. "I'm a short, stumpy guy who runs a pizza parlor who happened to get lucky and marry a beautiful girl like that. Why in the hell would I run around when I got her?"

"You got a pretty good marriage going, huh?"

"We have our moments like everyone else, but pretty damn good, yeah."

"So you don't know anything that can help me?"

"Afraid not, Deeg. But I'll ask around."

"Appreciate it. Hey, mind if I talk to Dahlia? I'd like to see if she's heard anything from the help. Maybe she's seen something that didn't look right. After all, you get a lot of bicycle types in here, and she's right in the center of it all."

Deeg sensed apprehension on Jimi's part.

"No, sure, of course you can talk to her. I'll get someone to take over the register and ask her to sit down with us."

"Let me talk with her alone, okay, Jimi? I won't be long."

Jimi forced a smile and nodded his assent. "Sure. I'll take over for her."

Dahlia Rodriguez was visibly nervous. "Hey, Deeg, Jimi says you've got some questions you wanted to ask me?" She stood, ill at ease.

"*Hola*, Dahlia. Have a seat. Please. No big deal. I just want to see if you can help me. I told Jimi we're trying to find out who's been killing all these cyclists. You get a lot of them coming in here for a slice and a beer, so I thought I'd find out what you know. You work Thursday nights when they all come in after their ride, right?"

"I work most every night, Deeg. Why?"

"Do you ever see anything out of the ordinary when the cyclists are here? Have you ever noticed anybody acting different, or anybody who gives you a bad feeling, like they're off base somehow, or mad at somebody? Ever hear any words or notice anyone looking cross-eyed at somebody else? Anything at all?"

Dahlia thought for a second. "No. Nobody ever tries to pick a fight or anything like that, if that's what you mean. Everybody always seems to enjoy themselves. They're always laughing and manage to get pretty loud after they've had a couple of beers. Most of the time, they all pick up and leave at the same time. I think they go from here to hang out at somebody's house—at least that's what I've been told."

"You speak Spanish, right?"

"Yes. Not great, but I get by." She gave Deeg a quizzical look.

"Ever hear any of the kitchen help talking about a vendetta against anyone—maybe because of drugs or their wives running around on them?"

She hesitated then shook her head. "No, never have."

"Dahlia, I'm sorry, but I've got to ask. Are you and Jimi okay? I mean, you've got a good marriage?"

"Yes, of course we do." Deeg noticed a barely perceptible twitch of her eye.

Deeg looked around to make sure no one was within earshot. He leaned in and whispered to Dahlia, "You ever think

Jimi runs around on you?"

"No." She was shocked at his question.

"What about you? You faithful to Jimi?"

Dahlia opened her mouth to speak.

"Now, think before you answer. This is between you and me. Don't lie. You know I can find out if you're lying. I know you like Hispanic types. I mean, you married Jimi, right?" Deeg looked directly at her. "You ever mess around with another Hispanic? Maybe one who belongs to that cycling club? Maybe one of those guys who got killed?"

Dahlia reacted with passion. "Never. What are you thinking? That maybe I'm running around and Jimi finds out about it and goes around killing them because of that? I'm sorry to burst your balloon, Deeg, but I never have, and never will. I love my husband. We have a great life together, I promise you."

DeGarzia studied Dahlia for a long moment. Tears welled in her eyes, but otherwise she was expressionless, her body stiff. He didn't believe her. "Dahlia, I'm sorry I had to ask. Now, listen to me. Behind that register, I know you hear and see things every day that maybe could help us. We've got a serial killer on our hands. Whoever it is, they don't like Hispanic cyclists. Why? We don't know. If you think of anything or hear anything, you call me right away. I don't care how picayune you might think it is. Okay?"

"Okay."

"We still friends?" he asked.

"Yes, of course."

He wasn't so certain.

Chapter 44

Another Cyclist Killed: Terrence Haverford, 54, of Camino Acantilado, was found dead in a gorge in Osvaldo Canyon on Monday evening. Missing since Sunday, he was discovered by a search party in the canyon near Osvaldo Lake. Haverford is the fifth cyclist who has died in the past five months in northern New Mexico. The deceased cyclists were all current or former members of the Santa Fe Canyon Cycling Club. Police have categorized Haverford's death as suspicious, and are conducting an investigation into the circumstances surrounding his death. Haverford was the owner of HEC Inc., an electrical contracting company. He was an active member of the Santa Fe Chamber of Commerce, an acolyte of the Saint Thomas Catholic Church, and a member of the Knights of Columbus. There were no known witnesses. He leaves a wife, three sons, and two daughters. Funeral arrangements are pending.

Terrence Haverford's death occurred two days after Special Agent Stephenson profiled the serial killer. Ellsworth, DeGarzia, and Hank met with Stephenson again to discuss the latest killing. Deeg was clearly angry. He explained what he knew. "We found a cigarette butt on the dirt shoulder a few yards off the spot where Haverford was killed. The killer scratched an arrow in the dirt pointing to the canyon and put a cigarette butt at the point of the arrow. The lab checked the butt for DNA. It matched the ones found at Smith's and Turner's, but we still don't know who it belongs to. We've checked the New Mexico and federal databases including the

FBI's CODIS data base, but we've found no match. I think this pretty much shoots a hole in the entire Hispanic theory."

"Haverford's murder certainly complicates things," Hank said. "This is the first time a non-Hispanic cyclist has been targeted. Damn it. What was wrong with him? Everyone's been warned about riding alone." He banged his fist on the table in frustration.

His outburst startled everyone.

Deeg offered, "I understand how you feel, Hank, but we were told Hispanics were the only people at risk—not the whole cycling world—not whites or blacks or anyone else, only Hispanics." It was not lost on all present that Deeg was directing his none-too-subtle comments at Stephenson.

The agent sat stone-faced, his gaze fixed on Deeg. Stephenson was confident his initial profile of the killer was accurate. He was not swayed by Haverford's murder. "I had no indication the race of the victims would extend beyond Hispanics. Now we know. I take full responsibility for not recognizing that. But, by all psychological indices, I'm still convinced the killer is Hispanic. I believe he may have expanded his killing field in an attempt to throw us off, but I still firmly believe a Hispanic is our killer, and we should continue to focus on that as a credible possibility."

DeGarzia bit his lower lip, lowered his eyes to the table, and said nothing. No one else said a word. Ellsworth needed to intercede. He was losing control of his team. They had become adversarial. He would admonish Deeg in private. But for now, he needed to make everyone's orders clear. "Okay, so we were unable to predict our next victim. Unfortunately, this is not an exact science. What we have to do now is communicate to every cyclist out there that no one is immune from this killer's actions—especially those who are or have been members of the Canyon Cycling Club. I'll hold a news conference to that effect to get the word out." In defense of Stephenson, he added, "As far as the investigation is concerned, until we have reason to believe otherwise, I want us to stay the course and concentrate on the Hispanic angle."

*****

"Mrs. Keenan—Stacey—I need your help," DeGarzia asked. "Another cyclist, Terrence Haverford, was killed the same way as Sanchez and the others."

"I heard about him. God, when will it all end?"

"We believe someone familiar with the Cycling Club is responsible for the murders of the cyclists over the past five to six months." He paused to gather his thoughts. "We're considering the possibility it could be someone who attends the parties after your Club's Thursday-night rides. We'd like to know a little more about those parties and the people who usually attend. I was hoping you could help us."

"Detective, why don't you interview the others who attend those parties," Patricia Appleton asked. "Why are you asking Mrs. Keenan?"

DeGarzia stared at the lawyer and responded firmly, "I'm asking Mrs. Keenan because I believe she has been, and will continue to be, truthful to me. She has nothing to gain by lying. Others might."

"Let's get this straight, Detective," Appleton said sharply, "we have been completely forthright with you, yet we still have no guarantee there'll be a quid pro quo from the District Attorney. Will the DA give Mrs. Keenan due consideration? Simple question. Yes or no?" Appleton demanded.

Irritated by the defense attorney's overbearing attitude, Deeg shot back. "Counselor, I told you I would discuss that with the ADA, and I have. He agreed to take her cooperation into consideration. Now, if you don't mind, I have four dead cyclists and an investigation to complete. May I continue with Mrs. Keenan? Yes or no? Simple question."

Stacey turned to her attorney. "Patricia, I would like to help if I can."

Applegate did not acknowledge Stacey immediately. "Fine. Let's continue, Detective. What more do you want to know?"

"A couple of things. First, Stacey, I need you to write down the names of all the people you can remember from those parties, as complete a list as you can give. Second, of those people, who were the ones who smoked? We know Heather smoked, but who else?"

"I can only give you the names of those who used to go to the parties when I did, but as far as identifying all the smokers, I'm not so sure. Most people don't allow smoking in their homes, so if anyone wanted to smoke they had to go outside. I don't think there were many and I can't really say I noticed every time someone went out for a cigarette."

"I understand. Do your best. Anything you can give us would help. Also, do you recall any non-cyclists attending those parties, say, friends of cyclists?"

"Yes, sometimes."

"Okay, I'd like their names too. And one last thing. Separate from your other lists, I'd like the names of all the Hispanics who attended the parties."

"There were a few. Why do you need that?"

"Without going into details, the FBI believes we need to focus on a Hispanic as the possible killer."

"Oh."

"Do you remember ever witnessing any arguments or fights? Or did you ever hear anyone make slurs against Hispanics?"

"No, there was never any problem. We all got along."

"What about the people from Jimi's? Any of the workers ever go to the parties?"

"Yes. I think Jimi himself was there one time. But I don't think he stayed too long."

"What about his wife? Did she ever go?"

"Dahlia? Yes, she went quite a number of times that I remember."

"Did she and Jimi go together?"

"No. Separately."

Chapter 45

Stacey's list of after-party attendees contained the names of twenty-one people.

"Are you sure this is everyone?" Deeg asked.

"No, not a hundred percent, but it's the best I can remember. Some people arrived at the parties after the time I used to have to leave. If you remember, I always had to leave pretty early to get home in time for when Clyde called me at nine."

"Right."

Deeg read the list. Alex Castillo was on it. The only other Hispanic was Jimi, and he was one of the few smokers. Pérez, Sanchez, and Haverford were not. Dahlia and Sam Bailey were on the list, too. And Stacey had listed Sam as one of the smokers.

*****

Dahlia fidgeted as she waited in one of the interview rooms at police headquarters. After five minutes, DeGarzia entered and greeted her with a friendly hello. Jimi was in another room waiting his turn to be interviewed.

"Dahlia, thanks for coming in. We asked you to come in to answer a few more questions. You are not being accused of anything, but we thought you might be able to tell us more about the people in the Cycling Club and your relationship with them."

Dahlia averted DeGarzia's eyes. "I don't have a relationship with them," she said.

"But you do, Dahlia. Don't you go to some of the parties the riders have after they leave your restaurant?"

She raised her eyes to look at DeGarzia then glanced over his shoulder at the one-way mirror, wondering who was behind it. Looking back at the detective, she answered, "Deeg, I only went a few times. Not that often."

Deeg was irritated. "You know, the worst thing you can do is to lie to me. So, please, think about your answers before responding." Dahlia fidgeted in her seat. "Why didn't you tell me the other day at the restaurant that you go to those parties?"

"I didn't think it was important, and you never asked about them."

"Does Jimi know you go?"

She hesitated again. "Yes, but I didn't tell him at first."

"Why not?"

"I knew he wouldn't be happy with me."

"So you went anyway?"

"Yeah. I wanted to get out. I wanted to socialize more. All I ever do is sit behind that cash register all day at the restaurant. I wanted to make friends with some of those people. They all seemed like nice guys and they all seemed to be having fun. It was harmless."

"You said 'nice guys.' What about the girls?"

"I didn't mean guys. I meant they all seemed nice—guys and girls."

"Does Jimi ever go?"

"Not that he's told me."

"Would you be surprised if I told you he's been to at least one?"

"He has?"

"Yes, Dahlia, he has. He's gone to one, maybe more, according to Stacey Keenan."

"Stacey Keenan the killer? You're going to believe her over me?"

"Yeah. Right now I believe her 'cause she's got no reason to lie to me about Jimi—or about you. Did you know he went to check on you, and when he saw you weren't there, he turned around and left?"

"No, I didn't." Dahlia was flustered by this newfound knowledge. Deeg suspected she knew more than she was telling him.

"I understand he would sit outside in his car and wait and watch for you." Once again, DeGarzia embellished what he supposed might have happened as he fished for a response. "I'll ask you again. Are you sure you didn't know about Jimi showing up at these parties?"

Dahlia squirmed in her chair. Her eyes darted around the room to avoid Deeg's glare. Finally, she blurted the truth. "Okay, yes, he told me he did that once," she admitted. "That's how he knew I was at the parties. He told me he followed me."

"What happened?"

"He was really mad. He wanted to know why I didn't tell him. He thought I was running around on him. I told him I wasn't, but that I needed to get out more. I was suffocating. We both were. We both needed to do something other than live and breathe pizza."

"I get the impression Jimi has a pretty bad temper, no?"

"He can get pretty mad, yeah. He can."

"How mad?"

"*Mad* mad. We argue sometimes like any married couple, and he gets mad at the people at work if they don't do things right or if he thinks they're stealing from him. You know, things like that."

"Jimi ever get so mad at you that he hit you?"

Dahlia hesitated. "No, never."

Deeg suspected he did. "He adores you, doesn't he? And sometimes he shows it by hitting you, right? He doesn't know what else to do. Isn't that right?"

She shook her head and began to cry. Tears gushed and she gulped in air with her mouth wide open. "Yes," she confessed. "But it's not his fault. He's a good man. I'm the one. But, Deeg, you've got to understand. Sometimes I feel like he suffocates me."

"When I talked with you at the pizzeria last week, I asked you if you were having an affair with someone from the Cycling Club. You said no. I'm going to ask you again, Dahlia. Are you having an affair with anyone from the Cycling Club?"

Dahlia looked at Deeg and was overcome with emotion. She covered her face with her hands and cried until she could no more. DeGarzia let her cry till she was spent. Finally, she raised her head, brushed the tears from her face, and reached for the box of tissues DeGarzia slid near her.

"Were you, or are you, having an affair with someone from the Cycling Club?" he asked again.

She looked at him and shook her head again.

"Tell me the truth, Dahlia. Are you?" Deeg was practically shouting.

"Yes, yes. Okay? Is that what you want me to say?" she cried out.

"With who?"

"Sam Bailey."

DeGarzia was stunned by her admission. "Sam Bailey?"

"Yes."

"Sam Bailey?" He couldn't believe what he was hearing.

"Yes. Sam Bailey."

"What about Alex Castillo?"

"Alex Castillo? No. I never had an affair with Alex."

"Are you telling me the truth?"

"Yes, I am. I knew Alex for a long time. I knew him before I knew Jimi. We were friends before I married Jimi."

"By friends, you mean you had a sexual relationship with him?"

Dahlia was embarrassed by Deeg's question. "No, he was a friend. That was all. Honest. I was married to someone else for three years before I married Jimi. I had an unhappy marriage and so did Alex. So we became friends and used to talk a lot."

"Who were you married to?"

"A guy by the name of José Creolos."

"What happened to him? Did he know about Castillo and Bailey?"

"No. He was killed in an automobile accident five years ago."

"I'm sorry to hear," Deeg said, his sympathy less than sincere. "So, what happened between you and Alex?"

"Nothing. We went our separate ways after José died. Alex got a divorce and I moved on, too."

"Is that when you married Jimi?'

"Yes, a couple of years after José died."

"Tell me about Alex."

"He came into the restaurant one night with his friends from the biking Club, probably about a year ago. He was surprised to see me. He said hello and told me about his divorce, and that he had just joined the Club. I told him it was good to see him."

"Is that why you began to go to the parties?'

"No. Not right away. One Thursday night, when Jimi was busy on the line, Alex joked to me that I should try to get away from my boring job for a while and go to one of the Club parties. 'We can catch up on old times,' I remember he said. I thought, what the heck, I'd go. There was no harm in it, so I found a way to sneak out. When the Club bikers left, I told Jimi I was going shopping."

"Did Jimi suspect anything going on between you and Alex?"

"No, not at the beginning."

"So you took up with Castillo again."

"No, I mean … I don't know what you mean. I told you I didn't have an affair with him. I didn't, Deeg. Sure, we talked about old times, but that's all we did—talk. He was more like a brother to me. I went to a couple more parties and, like you said, Jimi found out I was going, and that's when he thought Alex and I were having an affair. He saw us leave the party together one night, but we were both heading home, that's all. We weren't going anywhere together, but Jimi thought we were."

"What did he do?"

"He jumped out of his car, and he had this big chain in his hand. He swung it at Alex once, then again, and then a third time, but Alex was able to jump out of the way each time. I screamed for Jimi to stop."

"Did he?"

"Yes. He stopped and just stood there, staring at us. I was scared about what he was going to do to Alex. He said he was going to kill him."

"He said that?"

"Yeah, but he didn't mean it."

"What happened next?"

"Alex told Jimi nothing was going on between the two of us. He said we were only friends and some other stuff about how he was divorced and needed some advice from me. He said a bunch of stuff, and it was enough I guess, because Jimi got back into his car and left."

"What did you do?"

"I followed him home. I didn't know what to expect."

"And when you got home, what did he say?"

"Nothing. He cried. He just cried. I felt so bad."

"Did he strike you?"

"Jimi's a good man. He was mad I hadn't told him I was going to those parties. But I told him Alex and I were old friends from way back, and we were never anything more than that."

"Did he believe you?"

"No. He said he didn't want to talk about it and that if I wanted a divorce he would let me have it. But he didn't want one. He said he loved me."

"I'll ask you again. Did he hit you?

Dahlia looked away from Deeg. She bit her lip. Finally, she answered. "I deserved it."

"No, you did not deserve it. Don't say that. After that you stopped going to those parties?"

"Yeah, I stopped going. I called Alex to tell him I couldn't go anymore because I didn't want to hurt Jimi. That's when he surprised me. He said he hoped I would change my mind. He admitted he was hoping we could, you know, get together."

"What do you mean 'get together'? Have a sexual relationship?"

"That's what surprised me. I thought we were friends, but he wanted more than that. He said he'd always been attracted to me."

"What did you tell him?"

"I said I loved him like a brother but nothing more than that."

"And then? Did you tell Jimi what Alex had told you?"

"No. Jimi would have killed him."

"Do you think he did?"

"No. I don't mean he would *really* kill him, only that he would have been really mad, that's all."

"Did you ever see Alex again?"

"No, I never did. He dropped out of the Cycling Club, and never came back to the restaurant. When I found out he was killed in that accident up at Aldez Pass, I felt it was my fault."

"Why? Because you thought Jimi killed him?"

"No. I felt responsible because he was biking by himself. I mean, if he was still with the Cycling Club, maybe he wouldn't have died."

Deeg pursued the same line of questioning. "If Jimi has such a bad temper, it had to cross your mind that he might have killed Alex. Tell me the truth, Dahlia."

"No, honest to God, I never thought that. Jimi's not that kind of man. I know it sounds like he could have killed Alex, but I never thought he did. I thought it was an accident. I never even knew someone killed him. I thought he fell from his bicycle."

"Did you go back to any of the parties after Alex died?"

"Not for a long time. But after a while, I did. I really enjoyed being with those people. They were always happy. It gave me something to look forward to, you know what I mean?"

"Did you tell Jimi?"

"No. He wouldn't have let me go. I always made sure I got home before he got home from the pizzeria. I'd only stay at the parties for maybe an hour."

"Is that when you started seeing Sam Bailey?"

"No," she said. "Not right away. You have to understand, I don't have a very happy life. I want more out of life than being a cashier at a pizzeria. I want to get out and do more."

"Yeah, I get it. You're unhappy." DeGarzia felt no pity for Dahlia. "Go on."

"Deeg, I love Sam. I'm going to ask Jimi for a divorce. Sam and I have talked about getting married. I'm gonna tell Jimi."

"Aren't you scared what he'll do?"

"Yeah, I'm scared, but I love Sam so much that I don't—"
She couldn't finish.

"You don't what?"

"I don't care what Jimi does to me."

"He doesn't know about Sam?"

"No, I don't think so."

Chapter 46

Dahlia recalled how her affair with Sam had begun. She and Sam had been spending more and more time together at the after-parties. One Thursday evening, they were chatting at a party at the home of Dan Crill, one of the Club members, when Dahlia looked at her watch and said, "I've got to go, Sam. Jimi will be furious if I'm not there when he gets home."

"It's dark. I'll walk you to your car," Sam told her.

He was infatuated with her and she was attracted to him, too. They stood next to her car in the quiet neighborhood and he asked, "You okay to drive?"

"I'm good, Sam, thanks."

Although he felt awkward, Sam did not want to miss this opportunity to let Dahlia know how he felt about her. "Right. Ah, before you go...You know that, ah, I guess...you can tell I really like you."

She looked over his shoulders to see if anyone else was in view, and answered with a smile, "I guess you can tell I really like you, too."

He reached around to open the car door for her.

She put her hand on his shoulder. "Thanks. And you're a gentleman, too." Dahlia looked up at Sam and heard his breathing quicken. They were inches apart. He was still in his cycling clothes and smelled of sweat and cigarette smoke. She sensed he was getting aroused. She, too, was turned on. He pulled her close to him and kissed her softly. She couldn't help herself—the attraction was too great. She put her arms around his neck, pressing her breasts hard against his chest. He kissed her again. She felt his penis, taut against his cycling shorts, and her own strong sexual desire. They kissed long and hard, their bodies gently moving, rubbing against each other, exciting, titillating. Headlights coming up the street forced Dahlia to back away from Sam. She was fearful it might be Jimi coming to look for her. "I gotta go, Sam. I'll see you next week, okay?"

Sam lowered his hands self-consciously. Dahlia looked down and saw the outline of his hardened penis, highlighted by the car's headlights. When she realized it wasn't Jimi's car, she gave Sam a knowing smile. She got in her car and drove off, glancing at Sam through her rearview mirror. He stood at the curb a minute longer, trying to understand the meaning of her smile. As she drove home, her mind whirred in anticipation of their next encounter.

*****

The following Thursday, the ride group entered Jimi's Pizzeria en masse. Dahlia scanned the twenty-plus cyclists in their colorful jerseys and spandex shorts, looking for Sam, but he was not among them. She was crestfallen, and wondered why he had not come. Jimi's watchful eye noticed the subtle change in his wife's demeanor. After pizza and beer, the cyclists paid their checks and headed to their after-party. The restaurant cleared quickly and an hour later Jimi flipped the *open* sign on the front door to *closed*.

"I'll see you at home," Dahlia said to him. "What time you coming home?"

"I'll close up and be home in half an hour. Don't wait up."

Dahlia got into her car and turned on the ignition. A knock on the driver-side window startled her. "Hi, Dahlia," Sam mouthed.

She lowered the window and looked around to see if anyone else was near. "You didn't come in with the others tonight. I missed you."

Sam leaned on the car door with both hands. "Yeah, I went home to shower and change. I was hoping to see you after you were through work."

"I've been thinking of you—a lot." Dahlia placed her hand on Sam's.

"Me too," he said.

"I've got to go home. Jimi's going to be there in half an hour. I can't go anyplace tonight."

"Can I see you tomorrow?"

"Where?"

"Come to my house. I live on San Pedro. Number 2879."

She rubbed Sam's hand. "Maybe we shouldn't, Sam."

"Yes, we should. Come to my house tomorrow afternoon at one. I'll be waiting for you. Try to get away, okay?"

Dahlia looked into Sam's eyes and smiled again.

Chapter 47

Sam left his car on the street in front of his house so Dahlia could park her car in his garage, out of view from passersby. He stood in his driveway and looked at his watch. It was quarter past one. *Maybe she's not coming.* He worried, but then saw a car round the corner to his street. His heart raced when he saw Dahlia give him a furtive wave.

Sam looked up and down the street. No other vehicles were visible, so he motioned for Dahlia to pull in the garage. He immediately shut the door behind them. Dahlia stepped out of her car. She was anxious about their rendezvous. "Sorry I'm late." Sam thought she looked beautiful in her blue floral-print sundress.

"I was afraid you weren't going to come."

She smiled nervously.

Sam kissed her softly on the lips and they held each other in an awkward embrace. Dahlia sensed Sam's tension as well. "You okay?" he asked.

"Yeah. I'm good. A little nervous, I guess. That's all."

"Me, too," Sam admitted. "Would you like something to drink?"

"It's early, but I'll take a glass of white wine if you have it," she answered. "Oh, wait. I forgot—you don't drink."

"I bought a bottle just for you. Come on. Let's go into the house." Sam ushered her inside.

Dahlia looked around the kitchen. "You have a nice house." She was trying to calm her nerves.

Sam struggled to uncork the bottle of Chardonnay he had pulled from the refrigerator. When the cork finally popped out he laughed nervously. "I guess I'm out of practice." He poured the wine and handed Dahlia the glass, but she immediately set it back down without taking a sip. She looked at Sam with innocent eyes the entire time. He gently lifted her chin and kissed her on the lips. Intense desire overcame them both, and they kissed hard for a long time, their bodies pressed tightly together. Sam stroked Dahlia's back and slid his hands down to her firm behind. She felt his penis harden. Without saying a word, they knew they were ready. Taking Dahlia by the hand, Sam led her upstairs to his bedroom.

In spite of their intense longing for each other, they were overcome with awkwardness. They sat on the edge of Sam's bed. Without a word, Sam kissed Dahlia again and stroked her bare shoulders. His hand slid to her breasts. She purred faintly. Gently, Sam slid the dress straps off her shoulders, and eased the dress to her waist, revealing her large, silky breasts. He bent down and kissed her nipples. She held the back of his head close against her breasts, excited by the sensation of his tongue rolling over her skin. He pulled away and stood in front of her as he tenderly guided her to her feet. Sam pulled Dahlia's sundress down further and let it slip to the floor, completely exposing her porcelain-smooth, voluptuous body. "You're beautiful," he whispered.

Sam tore his clothes off and stood beside her, his penis fully erect. She reached for it and stroked it tenderly. He groaned and pulled away. There was so much more he wanted to do. He bent over and clenched Dahlia's nipples tightly in his lips, rolling his tongue over them and causing her to utter sounds of sensual delight. Her body was now taut with desire. She reached for him, and pulled him onto the bed alongside her, their bodies tight against each other. They kissed tongue to tongue, hard and long, as Dahlia continued to stroke Sam's penis. Murmurs of pleasure were the only sounds they made. He ran his hand over her smooth skin and fondled her breasts, gently messaging her nipples as they hardened to his touch. Her overwhelming desire was almost more than she could bear. She wanted him in her, but he pulled her hand away from his penis. "I want to kiss every part of you," Sam said.

He straddled her and kissed her lips softly. Slowly, he slid his tongue down her body, kissing her stomach first, then rolling his tongue titillatingly along the inside of her thighs, down to her knees, and slowly back up again. She moaned with tortured pleasure, her hips moving ever faster. Sam's tongue kept pace with her hips, faster and faster until she screamed with a climax stronger than any she ever remembered. He lay back down beside her, stroking her gently, waiting for her to open her eyes.

Sam was now ready, his desire explosive. He wanted to come inside of her. Dahlia knew what he wanted. She rolled over and sat on top of him holding his penis and guiding it into her wet vagina.

She moved faster and faster, beckoning him to go deeper and deeper. "Oh, my God" she screamed, and climaxed a second time. He groaned as he came with deep pulsating spasms. She stopped moving but he didn't want her to stop. "More, more, more," Sam urged until finally he was spent. Dahlia felt his warmth inside her, a wonderful warmth—she had never felt this way before.

Chapter 48

Jimi grew increasingly impatient with each passing minute. He paced back and forth in the small interview room while DeGarzia interviewed Dahlia down the hall.

After thirty-five minutes, Deeg came into the room. He looked the portly pizzeria owner up and down. "I never saw you dressed in anything except a pizza apron." Jimi was wearing tan slacks, a golf shirt, and a blue blazer.

"Yeah, I dress up for weddings, funerals, and being questioned at police headquarters by someone I thought was my friend. I like to clean up for special events like this." Jimi's prickly sarcasm was not lost on Deeg.

"Jimi, relax. I have only a few questions."

"Questions about what? Ask me what you need, so I can get going. I got a business to run, Deeg. What do you want to know?"

"About you and Dahlia."

"What about me and Dahlia?" he responded, his tone sharp.

"You told me the two of you have a great marriage, but Dahlia told me otherwise."

"Where is she?"

"She answered all my questions so I told her she could leave."

"What did she say?"

"Right now that's not important. What's important is for you to tell me what you know about Alex Castillo."

"Who?"

"Alex Castillo. Now please, Jimi, don't screw around with me. I'm a cop. I get to learn things about people I don't like hearing, but that's my job. I'm trying to find out who's going around killing people. Alex Castillo was killed by someone. It wasn't any accident. Tell me what you know about him."

"I don't know a thing about him," Jimi said.

"You're lying. If you want, I can arrest you for the murder of Alex Castillo and you walk out of here in cuffs or you can tell me the truth when I ask you a question. You tell me."

Jimi said nothing.

DeGarzia was bluffing and had no evidence to arrest him. At best, he had a possible motive. He gave Jimi time to let the threat sink in.

After a long silence, Jimi spoke. "Okay, so I knew Castillo. So what? I know a lot of people."

Deeg let out a big sigh and shook his head. He extracted a small card from his jacket pocket and declared, "I've got to advise you of your rights."

Jimi was dumbfounded.

"You have the right to remain silent. Anything you say can and will be used against you in a court of law." Jimi looked away, his tongue tucked in the side of his mouth as he waited for Deeg to finish. His irritation grew by the minute. "You have the right to speak to an attorney and to have an attorney present during questioning. If you cannot afford a lawyer, one will be provided for you at government expense. Do you understand your rights? Do you want a lawyer?"

"No, I don't want any freakin' lawyer, and yeah, I understand my rights. Hey, man, I thought we were friends. Why are you doing this?"

"Jimi, you and Dahlia both lied to me. Friends don't lie to friends."

"Yes, they do. Friends don't need to know nothin' about some things."

"Tell me what you know about Castillo."

Jimi shook his head and bit his lower lip. *What could Dahlia have told him? Why is he asking about our marriage?* Again, DeGarzia waited for Jimi to answer. Several times Jimi looked at him and then away. A long, uncomfortable minute went by. Deeg was in no rush. He knew the reward for patience was often a disclosure from a suspect. He would wait as long as it took for Jimi to answer. He would outwait him. Another thirty seconds went by before Jimi finally spoke.

"Look, Deeg, Dahlia and me, we've had our ups and downs. I didn't know Castillo personally, but I think he was a sleazebag. He tried to get in the pants of every woman he knew—didn't make no difference who it was. I'm glad he was killed. Dahlia said they didn't have sex but I don't know if I believe her or not. I don't know what to believe. She's naïve sometimes, I swear to God. I think he was trying to take advantage of her. He was a smooth talker. Me, I'm just a working stiff. She wants more than I can give her. I can't help who I am. But, I do know this. I'm a good husband—just not good enough for her. What else can I tell you?"

"So you don't know for sure if she was having an affair with him?"

"No, I don't. I followed her one night and saw the two of them together. I should have killed him then. They were leaving someone's house. I thought it was Castillo's. Turns out it was someone else's, and there were a lot of bikers there having one of those parties they have after they leave my restaurant."

Deeg wanted a confession from Jimi that would hold up in court. He phrased his next question carefully. "Then you admit to killing Alex Castillo on Aldez Pass because he was having an affair with your wife?"

"Shit, no, I didn't kill him. I said I almost did the night I found them together, but I didn't. No way, man. You're putting words in my mouth. I said I *almost* killed him the night I caught the two of them leaving that biker party. But then I'm thinking, why the hell would I kill a guy because maybe he's running with my wife? What, am I crazy? I'd end up in jail for the rest of my life. What for? For a woman who I can't make happy?"

"You're lying, Jimi. We know you killed Castillo and the other cyclists."

"Bullshit, Deeg. I didn't kill nobody."

"You smoke Marlboros, right?"

"Yeah. So?"

"We found cigarette butts where four different people were killed. We checked them out and found a match to your DNA." Deeg was lying again. "What I don't understand is why. Okay, so you had a reason to kill Castillo, but why the other guys?"

"You're crazy, man. I didn't kill Castillo. I don't know what you're trying to prove, but I didn't do nothin', and you're bullshitting me about the cigarettes. If you found my cigarettes, somebody put them there. Look, I admit, I got some satisfaction knowing he died. I'm not going to lie. The bastard maybe had an affair with my wife. I'll never know for sure if he did. Deep down I wanted to kill him, but I didn't. When he died, I thought, 'Man, there is a God. There is justice in the world.' I'm not ashamed to tell you I'm not sorry. I couldn't turn the other cheek, the no-good-son-of-a-bitch. But I didn't do nothin' to him, and I don't know nothin' about those other bikers who got killed. As God is my witness. I didn't kill nobody."

Deeg didn't mince words. "Was Dahlia unfaithful with anyone else?"

Another long period of silence. "I can't answer that. I don't know."

"What about Sam Bailey? Do you know him?"

"I know who he is, yeah. He comes into my place with the other riders—like Castillo used to, but I don't know him personally."

"Do you think Dahlia is having an affair with him?"

"No. Unless she says so, I don't think she is. He isn't her type. She only likes the Hispanic types."

"Jesus, Jimi, you're lying to me again. You and I both know the truth. She's been seeing Sam Bailey, hasn't she? In fact, ever since Castillo died, right?"

Jimi nodded once and dropped his head. He didn't want to get emotional in front of Deeg.

Deeg waited for Jimi to compose himself. "That hurts, doesn't it, to know your wife is unfaithful?"

"They don't know I know. I see the way she looks at him. When he comes into my place I want to spit in his face, but I don't do nothin'. He comes in like he's a big shot, all smilin' and laughin' and pattin' people on the back, like he's runnin' for mayor or something."

"What are you going to do about it, kill him?"

"Shit no. Let him have her. I don't give a shit no more. She's killing me. She'll end up doing the same to him that she's done to me. You know what? I think that's better than killing him. Let him live with the idea that he can't never trust her, that one day she'll do the same thing to him that she done to me. Fuck 'em."

"I'm sorry to hear all this going on with you, Jimi, but listen, I gotta know, what the hell did Walton Turner have to do with all of this?"

"Who the hell is Walton Turner?"

"You're lying to me again? Turner was the rancher from San Ysidro who was murdered."

"Oh, yeah, *that* guy." Jimi rolled his eyes. "My *best friend*. Shit, I don't think I've ever been to San Ysidro, and I don't know nothin' about him."

"Where were you on the night of the twelfth when Turner was killed?"

"Where was I? It don't make no difference what night it is. I work until ten o'clock every night, then I go home. Ask my sorry wife. She knows my routine. Or ask any of the people who work for me. I was working like I do every freakin' day of my life."

Deeg leaned back in his chair. Looking directly at Jimi, he spoke in a low voice. "Maybe that's something you should have changed. You know? Pay Dahlia some attention. Go to the movies. Go to a nice restaurant. Take her on vacation every once in a while."

"Yeah, shoulda, woulda, coulda. Too late now, ain't it? She ain't happy with me. She ain't never gonna be happy with me. You watch and see, she ain't gonna be happy with that asshole Bailey, either. She probably ain't gonna be happy with nobody. Who knows? I don't know what the hell makes her tick, and I'm tired of trying to find out. I can't trust her no more, so tryin' to make her happy now is not worth my time."

DeGarzia asked Jimi a few more question, but learned nothing more. Jimi made no incriminating comments or suspicious misstatements. Deeg left the interview room to talk with Hank and Special Agent Stephenson who had been observing the interview. "What do you think?"

"He's a prime suspect, but I don't see how we can hold him," Hank stated. "Let's see if he'll volunteer his DNA. If it's a match to the cigarette butts, we may have our killer. For now, I think we're going to have to let him go. Even though he had motive to kill Castillo, there's absolutely no evidence to support him being the killer and nothing to suggest he killed the other cyclists or Turner."

Stephenson agreed.

Deeg returned to the interview room and told Jimi, "You're free to go for now, but don't leave Santa Fe. I may need to talk with you again. If you think of anything that might help us with these murders, you've got to let me know, understand?"

"Leave Santa Fe. Yeah, like, where am I gonna go?"

"Do you understand?" DeGarzia's voice was harsh.

"Yeah, all right. I understand."

"And we need a sample of your DNA."

"Wait a minute," he said. "DNA? You want my DNA?" Jimi was angry. "So, you *were* bullshittin' me about finding my cigarette butts, weren't you?"

DeGarzia didn't answer.

Jimi shook his head. "Nice friend you are. You're freakin' unbelievable," he exclaimed. "You want my DNA? You can have it, and you can shove it up your you-know-what, *friend*."

Chapter 49

Agent Stephenson entered the conference room and dropped a folder on the table. "We think we may have our man," he declared.

"Jimi Rodriguez?" Hank guessed. "His DNA matched, didn't it?"

"No, it's not Rodriguez. It's a guy by the name of Emilio Arvelo. He used to be a patrolman with the New Mexico State Police. Everything points to him being our guy. Detective DeGarzia found a link between Arvelo and Castillo."

After their last meeting, Captain Ellsworth had dressed down DeGarzia and given him an ultimatum. Before speaking, Deeg replayed the captain's words in his head. *Either work with Stephenson or I'm pulling you off the case.* Deeg got the message. Looking directly at Ellsworth, he continued the explanation. "At Special Agent Stephenson's request, we retraced our steps to the beginning, to try to make sense out of the killer's motivation. I first looked deep into Castillo's background. I talked to his ex-wife, his friends, his family, his business associates, and found out about an incident that occurred a few years ago. Castillo was out cycling with a couple of friends when Arvelo cited him for disorderly conduct. It just so happens those friends were Jordan Sanchez and Tomás Pérez."

"Are you kidding?" Hank was astounded at the disclosure.

Stephenson answered, "Nope, I'm not kidding. I think it'll become clear in a minute why we think Arvelo's our guy." The folder he had brought in contained Arvelo's State Police personnel file. Stephenson leafed through the documents in the file and pulled out a single sheet.

"We found this incident report from a few years ago. I'll summarize. Arvelo was in his police vehicle with flashers on and windows open. He said he was on his way to the scene of a domestic disturbance to back up a fellow patrolman when he passed Castillo and the others on their bikes. When he drove by, he heard Castillo swear at him and saw him throw a water bottle that nearly hit his car. Arvelo stopped his car to deal with the matter. He got Castillo's name and address, and told him he was going to have a citation issued for disorderly conduct. He got back into his car and drove off to assist the other officer. According to Arvelo, the entire episode lasted about a minute."

"That doesn't make any sense. Why the hell would he have stopped if he was on his way to help another cop who needed backup?" Hank asked.

"Stupid, huh? The fact is, there wasn't a call for backup, and there was no domestic disturbance. He made the whole damned thing up."

"Why would he do that? Is there any more information on record?"

"Yes. Arvelo had a citation sent to Castillo ordering him to appear before a district judge. And apparently Castillo showed up, along with a lawyer and his buddies Sanchez and Pérez as witnesses. When Castillo took the stand, he admitted to swearing at Arvelo but denied throwing a water bottle. The witnesses corroborated Castillo's account."

Stephenson pulled more papers from the folder. "Here's Castillo's version of what transpired. Take a minute to read it." He slid copies of the documented testimony to Hank and the captain.

Two other cyclists and I were riding single file on Estrella Road when Patrolman Arvelo drove by us in his police car and nearly sideswiped us. His siren wasn't on and he wasn't driving like he was in a hurry to get to the scene of a crime. It was as if he was trying to run us off the road. I yelled at him, and called him an asshole. I know that was not a smart thing to do, but I was angry, as he had almost run us off the road. Patrolman Arvelo heard me swear at him because he stopped immediately, turned on his flashers, backed the car up, and jumped out. He ordered us off our bikes. He demanded to know who cursed at him. At first, none of us said a word. He then put his hand on his pistol, as if to threaten us, and asked the question a second time. That's when I admitted I was the one who cursed him.

The patrolman lost control. He became mad beyond reason. He accused me of throwing my water bottle at his car. I told him I did not, and pointed to the water bottles still in the cage on my bike. I also indicated the water bottles of the other cyclists were still on their bikes. That's when he asked me for my driver's license.

I thought he was joking. I said to him, "You're kidding me, right? I don't need a license to ride a bike." At that point, Patrolman Arvelo got even angrier. He swore at us, so angry that spittle flew out of his mouth. He said he was on his way to back up another patrolman on a domestic dispute, and if that patrolman got killed, the three of us would be considered accessories to his murder.

I said, "Don't you think you should be on your way to back up your partner instead of standing here screaming at us?" I admit again not the best choice of words under the circumstances. He drew his pistol and said something like, "You don't tell me what to do." He didn't aim his revolver at us, but held it down at his side.

He said he was going to look us up after his shift was over, find us, and "beat the shit out of us." He also said that if any of the veteran cops on the force were with him, they would have already beaten the crap out of us.

Patrolman Arvelo was totally out of control. The other cyclists and I were scared. No question about it. He finally got back into his car, turned off his flashers, and drove away casually. If he was supposed to be backing up another officer, his actions didn't seem like it. After he left, the three of us wondered what the hell that was all about. We thought he was crazy.

"What about Arvelo's testimony?" Hank asked.

"There wasn't any. He never testified. When it was his turn to present his case, he announced that the State of New Mexico was dropping the charges against Castillo and that the whole thing was a misunderstanding. It was bad enough he lied in his report, but at least he was smart enough not to testify under oath and perjure himself. The judge accepted the State's motion to drop the charges, but he lashed out at Arvelo. I have his comments here. They were short and sweet." Stephenson read from the court transcript.

I was a police officer before becoming a lawyer and a judge. If I had a nickel for every time I was cursed at when I was a cop, I wouldn't be sitting on the bench now. I'd be enjoying myself on a tropical island. Patrolman Arvelo, you've been on the force for several years but obviously still have a lot to learn. Are you not aware that the First Amendment to the Constitution allows for freedom of speech? If Mr. Castillo cursed at you, shame on him, but it's not against the law. I suggest you develop a thicker skin. I have some suspicion that you fabricated this incident. I believe Mr. Castillo did not throw anything at your car and, quite possibly, you've fabricated the story about a domestic dispute. I intend to send a report of these proceedings to your District Commanding Officer.

"After the proceedings," Stephenson continued, "when everyone was exiting the courtroom, Arvelo accidentally-slash-intentionally put his shoulder into Castillo's shoulder and whispered loud enough for the others to hear, 'You're all going to pay for this.' Castillo's lawyer overheard the threat and confronted Arvelo. He said, 'Did I just hear you threaten my client and his friends?' The lawyer went right back to the bench and informed the judge of Arvelo's threat. He said he would press charges for threats made to his client and his attempt to intimidate. He said the patrolman was not fit to wear that shield."

DeGarzia added, "What followed was a police departmental trial overseen by an administrative judge. After hearing the facts of what transpired, the judge made a recommendation to the chief of the New Mexico State Police who ruled that Arvelo be discharged from the force for cause."

"Castillo and the others got him discharged? For probable cause?" Hank said.

"Yes, we think so," Stephenson summarized. "Well, that's it. That's what we have." He pulled a photo from Arvelo's file. "Here's his picture on the day of his appointment to the State Police force." He slid it across the table for the others to see.

Hank flinched when he examined the photo.

"Look familiar, Hank?"

"I can't be sure, but, yes, I think I know who this is. He's older now, of course, but I swear the man in this picture looks like my riding buddy, Sam Bailey."

"Are you sure?" Deeg asked.

"Ah, it can't be." Hank moved to slide the photo back to Stephenson, but pulled it back to take another look.

They all waited for Hank to finish examining the photo.

"Yes, it could be him. If it isn't, he's got a clone. I'm not positive, but it sure looks like Sam." Hank was dumbfounded by the finding. "What do you think, Deeg? You've met Sam. Do you think it's him?"

"I do. Absolutely it's Bailey. The guy was right under our noses the whole time."

After a moment of silence Hank said, "I'm shocked. I don't know what else to say. Could this be a mistake? Do you know anything else about him?"

"He was with the State Police for nine years," Stephenson said. "From the information in his personnel file, he had a history of intimidation of suspects and using strong-arm tactics, beyond what he did to Castillo."

Ellsworth didn't want to lose a minute. "Let's move on this. If you both think Sam Bailey and Arvelo are the same guy, get an arrest warrant right away, before he kills somebody else. Get a DNA sample and check his fingerprints. Hank, I want to hold him a few days on suspicion until we get his DNA results."

Hank nodded. "Holding him should not be a problem, especially if he admits to being Arvelo."

Stephenson asked, "Can you shed any more light on Bailey's background, Hank?"

"Not a whole lot. But one thing for sure, if Sam is Arvelo, he's never exhibited the kind of temperament you described. Sam's a big, strong guy, but he's like a teddy bear, always cracking jokes, seems to get along with everyone." Hank paused and shook his head. "I'm not yet one hundred percent convinced that this is the same guy. I'd like to be here when he's questioned."

"How long have you known him?" the captain asked.

"A little over a year, I guess."

"Where he's from? What's he do for a living? Is he married? Does he have family?"

"All good questions. Frankly, I don't know much about him at all. We don't really hang out. He's just a guy I've been riding with," Hank clarified. "All I know is that he's divorced, sells insurance—but don't ask me who he works for—and, yeah, he said he was fired from his job a few years ago. But he never explained what the job was or why he was fired. And I never asked. It seemed he wanted to keep all that in the past."

"He never talked about being with the State Police?"

"No. But there is one other thing. He said he started drinking after he lost his job—claims he became an alcoholic. He told me he and his wife had a good marriage, but after he lost his job he lost control of his life, and his wife turned on him. He said she finally decided to leave him."

"Has he ever asked you about the investigation into the killings? Anything that, in retrospect, would make you think he was, maybe, *too* interested in what you know about the case?"

"We've talked about it sometimes, but nothing confidential, just what was reported in the papers." Hank thought some more. "No, there's really nothing else. Although, Deeg, remember he helped me collect evidence from Via Encantado before we knew for sure that Michael Redfield had been killed? And he was with me when we saw Heather Dorell and Stacey Keenan leaving their hideout in Golden. So, yes, I suppose he's shown some interest, but he's never tried to grill me about what I know or don't know. He knows I'm not at liberty to divulge anything about the case, so he's never pushed it."

"Where does Haverford fit into all this?" Ellsworth asked. "I understand the motive of revenge against Castillo, Pérez, and Sanchez. But, why Haverford, and why Walton Turner?"

"And Carlotta Smith?" Hank asked.

It was obvious from the blank expression on Stephenson's face that he had no answer. "I don't know where they fit in. Assuming Arvelo is the killer, I don't know what his motives were in killing them. Until we talk to him, there's no way to know."

"Gentlemen, I've heard enough. Bring in our Mr. Sam Bailey now."

"You know, I would have sworn it was Jimi Rodriguez," Stephenson said, perhaps more to himself than to the others.

Chapter 50

The only sound in the interview room was the drumming of Sam's fingers on the table. He was nervous and uncomfortable, and knew they were observing him through the one-way mirror. He had been behind the mirror a few times himself as a patrolman. Some minutes later, the door opened and Detective DeGarzia walked into the room. The detective had been seated at his desk the first time the two had met, and Sam was surprised to see how large and powerful Deeg was.

"Mr. Bailey—Sam—we meet again."

"Detective, yeah, uh ..."

"DeGarzia. My name is Detective DeGarzia. You came to see me once to tell me about your affair with Heather Dorell."

"Right."

The door opened again. This time, Hank entered. He nodded a greeting to Sam and stood against the wall behind him.

"Hank, what's this all about?" Sam turned to look at him. "They say they think I murdered all those cyclists."

Hank said nothing and looked away. He was angry at his friend's deception, and wanted to ask him a hundred questions. *Why did you deceive me? Why didn't you tell me you had been with the State Police? All the stuff you told me about a divorce, losing your job, and the drinking—were they all lies?* He knew Sam was going to undergo intense questioning. The facts pointed to him as the one with clear motive to kill. Alex Castillo had caused Arvelo to lose his job, and now Castillo was dead, probably murdered. So were Pérez and Sanchez. Sam Bailey and Emilio Arvelo were probably one and the same. It wasn't a case of mistaken identity. It all added up. He had to be the Cyclist Killer.

Sam turned back to face DeGarzia. "What makes you think I'm involved in these murders?"

"You're Emilio Arvelo, also known as Sam Bailey, aren't you?"

At that, Sam's demeanor changed and he stared right through the detective. He was perspiring and squirmed in his chair. He didn't answer.

"We know who you are, Sam. Let me tell you why we think you're involved in these murders."

"Okay, go ahead. Tell me." Sam was testy.

"Would you prefer I call you Emilio?"

"No. Sam will do. Emilio was my name from another life."

"So you admit you are one in the same person?"

"My birth name was Emilio Arvelo. I changed it to Sam Bailey."

Hank grimaced. The truth was out.

"Are you leading two lives, Sam?"

"No."

"I'm going to advise you of your Miranda rights, and know, too, this interview is being video recorded."

"I know my Miranda rights. You don't have to give them to me."

"Do you want a lawyer?"

"I don't need a lawyer. I haven't done anything."

"Sam, the fact is, we know who you are, and we know your background. Based on evidence we found at the scenes, we know you killed Alex Castillo, Tomás Pérez, Jordan Sanchez, Terrence Haverford, and probably Walton Turner and Carlotta Smith, too."

"I didn't kill those people. Ask Hank, he'll tell you. Tell him, Hank." Sam turned again to look at Hank, expecting a show of support.

Hank looked at Sam, but did not acknowledge his plea.

"Detective, on what basis are you accusing me of murder?"

"Forensics." DeGarzia exaggerated. "Evidence we've accumulated. We understand your motive for killing Castillo, Pérez, and Sanchez, but why the others?"

"I don't know what evidence you're talking about. I didn't kill anyone. For Christ's sake, I'm a cyclist, too. Why would I want to kill other cyclists? That's insane—absolutely insane! Okay, yes, I admit my real name was Emilio Arvelo, but now I'm Sam Bailey. I changed my name—legally."

"Why?"

"Because Emilio Arvelo doesn't exist anymore. Sam Bailey is a different man. Sam learned from Emilio's mistakes. I know it sounds like I'm leading dual lives, that I'm crazy, but I'm not. I like Sam Bailey, the man I am now. I didn't like the man Emilio was."

Hank stepped from behind Sam and sat down next to DeGarzia.

Sam flashed him a pitiful look, an appeal for understanding. Hank nodded, but still said nothing.

"Sam, do you smoke?" DeGarzia asked.

Sam glanced at Hank, embarrassed that he would have to disclose the truth about his smoking. "Yeah, I smoke every once in a while. Crazy, huh, Hank? With me cycling and all?"

"What brand of cigarettes do you smoke?"

"Marlboro."

"How do you explain your cigarette being found at the site of the murder of Terrence Haverford?" DeGarzia asked.

"Shit if I know. Maybe I flipped one out of my car window when I passed by before he was killed."

"Not likely. We found your cigarette placed at the end of an arrow you scratched out in the dirt shoulder."

"What are you talking about? I didn't do that."

"How did your cigarette butt end up on Walton Turner's body? Did you flip that one out of the car, too?"

"I've never—repeat, never—met or been anywhere near that guy. I didn't know him one little bit. All I know is that he lived in San Ysidro, which I've been to once, maybe twice, in my life."

"I'll ask you again. How did your cigarette butts get to be at the sites of both killings? And what about Carlotta Smith? We found your cigarette there, too. Does Emilio take over every once in a while, or is it Sam who does the killing?"

"That's not funny. Just because I changed my name doesn't mean I'm a psychopathic killer. And why the hell would I kill someone and then leave that kind of evidence behind? That doesn't make any sense. Someone's trying to frame me or maybe you're bullshitting me right now," he said. Sam's agitation was growing by the minute. "How do you know they were my cigarettes?"

"We know." Deeg was insistent.

"Will you give us a sample of your DNA, Sam?" It was the first Hank had spoken. "If it doesn't match the cigarettes found at the crime scenes, it'll go a long way toward exonerating you."

"Yes, I will, Hank." Looking directly at DeGarzia, Sam added, "So you've been bullshitting me. You have no proof. You have nothing. You're making me out to be a killer only because I happened to know those guys who were killed? Shit, you could accuse anyone at the Club. A lot of people knew those guys. Why me?"

"You're getting angry, Emilio. Were you this angry when you killed those cyclists?"

"Stop calling me Emilio. I'm not angry. I'm upset at your accusations. And, yes, I used to have an anger issue, but I've gotten over that. It's taken me a while, but I have," Sam said.

Hank repeated his question. "Will you volunteer the DNA?"

"Yes, of course. I didn't do anything, Hank."

DeGarzia pushed with more questions and accusations. "I understand you have a history of drinking. When you killed Alex Castillo, Emilio, had you been drink—"

"I didn't kill Castillo, and I haven't had a drink in over three years," Sam shot back.

"Let me try again. When you killed Alex Castillo, had you been drinking, Emilio?" Deeg insisted on calling Sam by his birth name.

"Look, I didn't kill him. I know I should have told someone. Hank, I should have told you I knew him. I'm sorry. You can't know how much I've appreciated your friendship. I never lied about Castillo. I just never volunteered that I knew him."

"Can you tell us what happened between you and Castillo?" Hank asked. "I want to believe that you're not responsible for any of these killings, but you've got to help us understand what happened."

"You mean when I was with the State Police?"

"Yes."

"I'm sure you've already read my State Police personnel jacket."

"I've read it, but I'd like to hear what happened from you," Hank said.

Sam bit his lip, looked up at the ceiling, and spoke, "There's no other way to say it. I was a hot-headed S.O.B. Back then, Castillo wasn't the only guy I tried to intimidate. I wasn't a bad cop. I mean, I never took a bribe. I didn't get involved in drugs, never anything like that. But the truth is, I was a mean-spirited asshole. I lied about what happened between Castillo and me. It got me discharged from a job I loved and was good at, and I was lucky I didn't end up in prison for the shit I pulled. By the time of my run-in with Castillo, I should have been fired at least a half-dozen times because of my intimidation tactics. That's what I did. But no one ever had the balls to stand up to me—except for Castillo. I respected him for that. He was a good guy. I was the bad one."

"Did you ever try to get even with him after you were fired from the force?" Hank asked.

"No. As God is my witness, absolutely not. Castillo was the furthest thing from my mind. When I got canned, my life headed south. Everything went into a tailspin. I didn't lie about any of that. I told you everything. I never even thought about Castillo. What was I gonna do, kill him because it was my own fault I was fired? I hit rock bottom with my drinking and I lost my wife. But after a while, I swore I would never take a drink again, and I haven't. I swore I would never lose my temper again, and I haven't. I'm proud of those things. Real proud," Sam said. He unconsciously puffed out his chest.

"Proud? Are you? Are you *proud* of the fact that you're having an affair with Jimi Rodriguez's wife?" Deeg asked sarcastically. "What about Jake Dorell's wife? Are you *proud* of the fact that you had an affair with his wife, too? You're apparently *proud* of the fact that you've been able to sleep with other men's wives. Who else have you slept with? Any other wives of unsuspecting men?" DeGarzia asked.

"No. That's it."

"Dahlia Rodriguez and Heather Dorell. That's everyone?"

"Yes."

"So you're proud of that, huh. Nice guy that you are. You're a changed man." Deeg was trying to bait Sam, to make him angry enough so he'd say something incriminating. "You're proud of all that, huh?"

Sam kept his composure. "That's unfair, man. Look, Heather Dorell came on to me. I told you what happened. One, she hated her husband, and two, I don't know any man who could resist her. She was gorgeous. As for Dahlia—she's a really wonderful, sweet girl. She really is. I think the world of her. I love her. And she loves me. Dahlia's the first girl I've met I think I could really settle down with. She's the kind of girl my ex-wife never was or ever could be."

"Tell me about your ex," DeGarzia said.

"She was a nut job. I can't explain how bad she treated me after I lost my job. She went off her rocker."

"What does that mean, Emilio—'she went off her rocker'?" Deeg baited him. "That's a little demeaning, isn't it?"

"Yeah, well, I'm sorry. But she went crazy. I couldn't believe how she changed. It started after I got canned. No matter what I did, I was wrong. Honest to God, it was like I was living in a war zone every minute I was with her. She came up with shit that was off-the-wall crazy. I don't know how else to say it. She accused me of running around, of hitting her, abusing her. Every kind of rotten thing she could think of."

"You did run around on her, didn't you Emilio? And you hit her too, didn't you," Deeg demanded. "It makes sense that you did. You're that kind of person."

"Did I run around on her? Absolutely not. Did I hit her? No, never. I swear on the Bible, never."

"I don't believe you. Did you want to kill her like you killed Castillo and the others?"

"Hell, no. I didn't want to kill her. I never touched her. Ever. If I did, there would be police reports, right? Check it out. She never filed a single complaint to the police. Not one. If I was such a bad guy, wouldn't I have some kind of charge against me?"

"Maybe she was afraid to report you to the police. We'll check it out. Either way, I don't believe you." DeGarzia leaned across the table and looked Sam straight in the eyes. "The fact that you don't have any complaints on record doesn't make you a saint. It's enough that you admitted you were a bad cop."

"Bullshit. I told you before I was not a bad cop. I'll say it again. I was not a bad cop." Sam's voice was louder now, his anger growing out of frustration with Deeg's insistence.

"Yeah, so you say. But after you got fired, you said Castillo never crossed your mind, even though he's the guy who got you fired in the first place. I find that hard to believe. The three guys who were witnesses against you are all dead now. I don't think that's a coincidence. You killed them all. I think you're an inveterate liar and a psychopathic killer."

Sam shook his head and dropped his chin to his chest. He was disconsolate. It was clear the circumstances surrounding the serial killings were compelling. "I'm invoking my rights. I want a lawyer."

DeGarzia pushed his chair away from the table. He stood over Sam and declared, "Emilio Arvelo, a.k.a. Sam Bailey, you are under arrest for the murders of Terrence Haverford, Carlotta Smith, and Walton Turner. You are also under suspicion of murder in the deaths of Alex Castillo, Tomás Pérez, and Jordan Sanchez." DeGarzia opened the door and motioned to the cop standing guard to escort Sam to the booking room.

As the cop put handcuffs on him, Sam spoke directly to Hank, his voice pleading, "Hank, I swear, I did not kill Castillo or any of those other people. I'm sorry I didn't tell you about my past, but I'm innocent. You've got to believe me."

"I wish I could," Hank said. "I really wish I could."

*****

Captain Ellsworth and Special Agent Stephenson were waiting for Deeg and Hank outside the interview room. "Gentlemen, until we match his DNA, we don't know if he's our man," Ellsworth said. "Probable cause is one thing, but forensics will prove us right or wrong."

Hank was subdued.

"You okay, Hank?" Deeg asked.

"Yeah, I'm fine. I can't believe it, though. I don't want to rush to judgment. I've been riding with him all this time, and I never suspected him. If he's the killer, it's like he's a Jekyll and Hyde. I want to believe he's innocent, but I understand—he had motive. Still, there's something not right about all this. Let's see what the DNA test shows."

"We'll have to wait for the court to appoint a lawyer before we can question him further," Ellsworth said.

Deeg did not spare Hank's feelings. "You know, all that stuff about turning over a new leaf after he was fired, it doesn't ring true to me. Sorry, Hank, but Emilio Arvelo is guilty as sin."

Chapter 51

The Santa Fe police crime lab tested Sam Bailey's DNA against the cigarettes found at the murder scenes. To no one's surprise, the results came back positive.

In front of police headquarters Chief Tremont, Captain Ellsworth, and Detective DeGarzia stood facing a dozen print and TV reporters in a hastily called news conference. Tremont announced, "Today we have received evidence that a suspect we have in custody may be the so-called Serial Cyclist Killer. We allege that Emilio Arvelo, also known as Sam Bailey, a former New Mexico State Patrolman, is the person behind these killings. We are still working out the details of his alleged involvement in these killings, but evidentiary analysis strongly points to Bailey as the killer. We will keep you informed as our investigation continues. So as not to compromise the continuing investigation at this point, we can disclose no further specifics about the case.

"Captain David Ellsworth and Detective Lawrence DeGarzia of the Santa Fe Police Department were the lead investigators on this troubling case. Captain Ellsworth will answer a few questions in just a moment. First, however, I want to thank Special Agent Mark Stephenson of the FBI and Hank Kincaid of the District Attorney's office for their tireless assistance in helping solve these horrendous crimes. Special Agent Stephenson will be returning to Quantico, Virginia with our sincerest thanks. He accomplished what he was sent to Santa Fe to do—help with the apprehension of the Serial Cyclist Killer. We wish him Godspeed."

*****

The judge assigned David Thackery as Sam Bailey's public defender. At his arraignment, Sam pled not guilty to the charges against him. Thackery requested to have Sam released on bail, but the judge, citing the obvious flight risk as well as the heinous nature of the crimes, denied the request and ordered him held without bail.

*****

Sam and Thackery sat in silence as they waited for DeGarzia to enter the interview room. Sam's wrists were free of their binding handcuffs, but his ankles remained shackled. Hank observed Sam from the adjacent room. Another five minutes passed before DeGarzia entered. He nodded to Sam and Thackery.

"Emilio, I need to remind you of your Miranda rights. Everything you say may be used in court against you. Do you understand your rights?"

"Yes." Sam's voice was barely audible.

"Speak up. Did you say you understand your rights?" DeGarzia asked again.

"Yes. Yes, I do, Detective," he answered, this time with raised voice. Sam insisted on his innocence. "Look, I want to cooperate with you. I want to show you I had nothing to do with those killings. I am totally innocent."

DeGarzia first asked Sam the usual series of identifying questions: name, address, age, occupation. He paused before moving on to the case-relevant questions. Sam tried to get comfortable in his seat, but the ankle cuffs limited his movements. DeGarzia had him where he wanted him— nervous and compliant.

"Mr. Arvelo—Emilio—do you smoke?"

"Yes, I do. And my name is Sam Bailey, not Emilio Arvelo."

Deeg did not acknowledge his comment. "Did you know Terrence Haverford?"

"Yes. He rode with the Club, but I didn't know him very well. He didn't ride with us that often, but he was a good rider."

"How do you explain the fact that one of your cigarette butts was discovered at the scene of Mr. Haverford's death near Osvaldo Lake?"

Sam looked at David Thackery for guidance. He shrugged his shoulders to indicate he didn't know the answer to Deeg's question.

"Tell him that."

"I can't answer that, Detective. I told you before I have no clue how my cigarette butt could have been there. Are you sure it was mine?"

"Yes. It was yours. DNA tests confirmed it."

"Then someone had to plant it there," Sam protested.

"And why would someone do that?"

"Hell if I know."

"Does anyone have a grudge against you?"

Sam thought for a second. "I've been thinking about that for the last few days, but haven't come up with an answer. Maybe Jimi Rodriguez, because Dahlia and I—" He didn't finish.

"Because Dahlia and you are having an affair? Is that what you were going to say?" Deeg asked.

Sam hesitated before answering. "Yes. That's what I was going to say. He's the only person I can think of who might want to frame me. I'm not saying he did. I'm answering your question who might. That's all."

"How would he, or anyone else for that matter, have gotten your cigarette butts?"

"I have no clue. I suppose from wherever I would've been smoking. I don't know how else."

"Did you smoke at Dahlia Rodriguez's house?"

"I've never been to Dahlia's house."

"I'm surprised you smoked and cycled too. You ever hear smoking is bad for you?" Deeg preached. "Those two acts seem to conflict with each other."

Sam overlooked the sarcasm. "I only smoke a few a day. Usually the only place I smoke is at my house and once in a while in my truck. You can't really smoke anyplace else in Santa Fe."

"You knew Alex Castillo. Did you kill him?"

"Yes. No. I mean, yes, I knew him."

"Detective DeGarzia, please don't ask questions in that manner," Thackery said.

"What manner?"

"Using a statement of fact followed immediately by an incriminating question. My client is cooperating with you here, but you're trying to trip him up so he'll incriminate himself."

"I really don't know what you're talking about, counselor."

"Mr. Bailey's agreed to meet with you to discuss why he's innocent, but if you continue with this manner of questioning, we're going to end the discussion. Do you understand?"

DeGarzia didn't answer. He was irritated by Thackery's inference of misconduct, and directed his attention back to Sam. "So you knew Castillo, right?"

"I already told you I knew him. But, no, I didn't kill him. I told you he was the reason I was fired from the State Police, but I didn't hold it against him. It was my fault I—"

"You've answered the question. No need to go into any more detail," Thackery said.

"Besides the cigarette of yours we found at the scene of Terrence Haverford's murder, there also was a cigarette butt, a Marlboro—the kind you smoke—in Carlotta Smith's backyard, and one on Walton Turner's body. They all had your—"

Thackery interrupted. It was now his turn to inject sarcasm, and he was good at it. "Detective, the fact they are the same brand is hardly corroborating evidence now, is it? The same brand? Marlboros? The largest-selling brand of cigarettes in the world? And you're accusing my client of killing someone because Marlboros were found at the murder scenes?"

Deeg did not answer right away. He had had previous encounters with David Thackery. Their mutual dislike for each other was obvious. "Counselor, if you had let me finish, I was about to tell Mr. Arvelo that his DNA was found on all the cigarettes. I'm not accusing your client of murder because we found a cigarette butt at the scene of a crime. I'm accusing him of murder because, one—we found cigarette butts with his DNA at the scene of multiple murders—and, two—he had motive to kill Alex Castillo and the other victims. He's claiming he was framed. If someone framed him, who could have done it, and when and where would the killer have gotten hold of his cigarettes? If your client doesn't want me to pursue this any further, we're done here. Mr. Arvelo also happens to be an acquaintance of ADA Hank Kincaid, who I respect personally and professionally. In large part, I'm asking these questions out of courtesy to him. For some reason, he wants to believe Mr. Arvelo's innocent. So, if he is, I advise you to advise him to cooperate with me so I can help him."

"Detective, my client is innocent. I'm pleased that his friend thinks he is too. But I've been appointed as Mr. Bailey's lawyer, and I intend to protect his rights to the fullest. You asked to meet with us so we could help you solve these murders, and we're here. Now I'm telling you that if you continue to badger my client, we'll end this conversation."

Deeg recognized the session had become adversarial. "I have one last question."

"Do you remember the names of the witnesses Alex Castillo brought to court after you cited him for disorderly conduct?"

"Yes, I know their names."

"Quite a coincidence that they also were killed during the past several months, don't you think?" Deeg wanted to get the parting shot in at Thackery. "It makes quite a compelling case against your *innocence.*"

Sam turned to his lawyer. He shook his head for a moment, trying to control his temper. When he looked back at Deeg, he answered firmly but calmly, "I know who they were but I did not kill them. I - did - not - kill - them!

Chapter 52

Sam's arrest caused a short-lived flurry of media coverage. News about the case died down quickly, partly because it was old news and partly because no other cycling deaths occurred while Sam was in jail awaiting trial.

Dahlia Rodriguez visited Sam often. He steadfastly maintained his innocence to her, and although the circumstantial evidence against him was overwhelming, she believed him. Dahlia was, perhaps, the only person convinced of Sam's innocence.

Hank visited Sam two weeks after his arraignment. He immediately noticed a change in his former cycling buddy. Sam's normally ruddy complexion had turned pallid and he had lost weight. His once-light demeanor was now somber.

Sam pleaded. "You have to believe me. I know the facts are stacked against me, but honest to God, I had nothing to do with any of those murders."

"Sam, because of our friendship, I've recused myself from your case. I'm not allowed to discuss any details with you, either. I have to be careful about what we talk about."

"I understand. I don't want to get you in trouble, Hank, but I will tell you this. I'm the Sam you know as your riding partner, not the Emilio I was in the past. You've got to believe me."

Hank looked for a betrayal of truth so often evident in the eyes of the guilty. He didn't see that look in Sam.

"Let me ask you this. Why would I leave my own cigarette butts at the scenes of the murders, knowing they would eventually be traced to me? It doesn't make sense, does it? I may be dumb, but I'm not that dumb. Don't you see? Someone's framed me. I don't know who, but someone has. Maybe it's someone I arrested when I was with the State Police who might be holding a grudge against me. Maybe it's someone like that."

"Such as?"

"I don't know. I just don't know. I've been thinking about it as long as I've been here, and I can't think of anyone. I was hard on a lot of people, so it could be anyone. I can't point to any one guy, Hank. I may have strong-armed a few people, but I never caused anyone to go to prison who didn't deserve to go."

"What about your ex-wife? You think she could shed some light on who would want to frame you?" Hank asked.

Sam thought a moment before answering. "Yeah, maybe. Maybe she could."

"Any idea where she lives?"

"Last I heard she was in Albuquerque, but I don't know for sure. For all I know, she could be married again and have a different name or maybe even go by her maiden name, Yvonne Consuego."

<h1 style="text-align:center">Chapter 53</h1>

With information retrieved from a database at the District Attorney's office, Hank located Yvonne Consuego, the former Yvonne Arvelo. He drove an hour to her home on the outskirts of Albuquerque to question her about Sam.

Unannounced, he rang the front doorbell, raising the ire of a dog inside. A few seconds later, the door was pulled open the few inches the security chain would allow.

"Yes? What is it?" asked a female voice from inside. Her tone was angry and unpleasant.

"Are you Yvonne Consuego?"

The woman peered through the opening to see who was asking. A Jack Russell terrier yapped incessantly through the opening until the woman ordered it to stop. "What do you want?"

"I'm with the Santa Fe District Attorney's office," he said, and showed his card. "Are you Emilio Arvelo's ex-wife?"

"Yes, I'm sorry to say."

"I'd like to ask you a few questions about him."

"Do you have a subpoena?"

"No, I don't. I can obtain one if necessary and interview you in Santa Fe."

Yvonne removed the chain and opened the door to Hank. Using her foot, she brushed the dog aside to keep him from running out when Hank entered. She studied his card more closely. "You know, Mr. Kincaid, I was wondering when someone was going to come around and ask me about him. We might as well get this over with."

The Jack Russell jumped up and down to greet Hank until Yvonne finally corralled him and put him in a room off the foyer. She escorted Hank to her small living room and indicated to him to have a seat on the couch. She sat across from him in a straight-back chair.

Hank looked discreetly around the room. It was immaculate. He observed that, apart from a few rubber toys for the dog, the room was devoid of any feeling of warmth or comfort. There were no photos of family, no artwork, the drapes were drawn, and the light was dim. The air was suffocating, heavy, and stale.

"I appreciate your taking the time to talk with me, Ms. Consuego. Have you been following the case of the Cyclist Killer in Santa Fe?"

She nodded yes.

"Are you aware that Sam, or as you know him, Emilio, is accused of killing several people?"

"Yes, I'm aware of what he's done." Yvonne didn't hide her scorn for her ex-husband. She was petite, not unattractive, but wore her dark hair wound in a tight bun which gave her a dour look. She had brown, penetrating eyes and did not look directly at Hank when she spoke but rather cocked her head, as if looking at something behind him.

"As you probably know, he is currently awaiting trial on those charges."

"I read he changed his name to Sam Bailey. It doesn't surprise me he killed those people. He never could control his temper. He was always close to rage."

Hank recognized anger welling within Yvonne—intense anger.

"You know, of course, that he was fired from the State Police because of an incident he had with a guy by the name of Alex Castillo and two other cyclists. Mr. Castillo has since died and we suspect he was murdered. Did your ex-husband ever talk about Mr. Castillo?"

Yvonne hesitated to answer. She stared at Hank, her expression frozen.

He repeated the question. "Mrs. Arvelo—Ms. Consuego—did Emilio ever speak of Alex Castillo after he was fired from the force?"

She squinted as she recalled the past. "Yes, as usual, he ranted and raved. He was always ranting and raving about something or other. Emilio said Alex Castillo was a rich, spoiled little boy who rode a bike dressed like a clown and looked down his nose at him because he was a cop. He called him a *Gabacho*. You know what that means? It means Mr. Castillo was Hispanic but tried to act like a gringo."

"Did he ever say anything about getting even with him, or that he was going to hurt him, anything like that?"

"I remember a couple of times when Emilio was drinking he said he hoped he would run into him again."

"Did he say what he would do if he did?"

"No, he didn't. He had a terrible temper is all I can tell you."

"Did he ever show his anger toward you?"

"Yes, he did—to me and to a lot of other people, to anyone who disagreed with him or who he thought was crossing him. He was paranoid. It didn't make any difference what or who it was. It could be a clerk in a store or a ballplayer on TV. It didn't make any difference. He would get mad. He got more than one warning when he was with the State Police, but he kept doing it. And that's what finally got him fired from his job. Mr. Kincaid, all I can tell you is that he walked around all the time with a chip on his shoulder, and he would dare anyone to knock it off."

"So you think he was capable of killing those cyclists he's accused of killing?"

"I'm probably the wrong person to ask, but let me put it this way. I wouldn't put it past him," she said.

"Ms. Consuego, I have to tell you, I'm surprised to hear you say he exhibited that kind of anger. I've known him for a while. We've cycled quite a bit together, and he's always come across as a big bear of a guy who likes to laugh and tell jokes. For the time I've known him, he's always been popular with everyone."

"That's hilarious. There's no way you're describing the same man I was married to. Are you sure we're talking about the same man?"

"We are."

"You know, when I first met Emilio, he reminded me of my older brother—a big, strong, sweet guy. But I don't know what happened. When he lost his job, he started to take it out on me."

"You mention a brother. You have family in the area?"

"Yes, my older brother Larry. I haven't been well, and he looks after me."

"You're fortunate to have help nearby."

"Yes, I am."

"Any other family?"

"No, not living. Eric, my other brother, died when I was a little girl."

"I'm sorry to hear that. How did Eric die?"

"It was sad. He died on the streets of Los Angeles of a drug overdose."

Hank saw tears welling and changed the subject.

"Sam said the two of you had a good marriage, but that things fell apart after he was fired."

"Yes, that's true. Please, his name is Emilio, not Sam. And, yes, he started drinking and did nothing to find another job. He sat on his behind and did nothing. I mean *nothing*. We went from being happy together to being miserable in a matter of months. He started to take things out on me. He hit me a lot when he drank. He got meaner and meaner." Yvonne's ire was on the rise.

"You know, Ms. Consuego—"

"Please, call me Yvonne."

"Thank you." Hank was pleased she was warming up to him. "Yvonne, Sam—ah, I mean Emilio told me he wasn't proud of a lot of the things he did, but when asked by our detective if he ever hit you, he said he never did."

"That figures, doesn't it? Of course he isn't going to tell you he abused me. But that's far from the truth. He is the biggest liar in northern New Mexico. I'm telling you, you shouldn't believe a word he says—about anything."

Hank recalled Sam's account of his marriage to Yvonne. Doubt crept in. Yvonne was intense, but credible. She was telling an altogether different story about Sam's character than the one Sam recounted, and she had no reason to make any of it up. Hank wondered if Sam was, indeed, an inveterate liar.

"Emilio also told me that, one time, after you and he were divorced, you assaulted him in a restaurant when he was with another woman. He said you hit him in the head with the heel of your shoe and that the police had to be called to the restaurant to restrain you. Did that happen?"

"No, Mr. Kincaid, that's baloney. Did we have a terrible fight in a restaurant? Yes. But I didn't attack him. He started it and I fought back."

"Do you mind telling me what happened?"

Yvonne took a deep breath before speaking. "I was in the restaurant alone having dinner. I had no idea he was there. My back was to him. I first saw him when the hostess walked him and his floosy girlfriend past my table on the way to theirs. That's when he made a loud comment about me to his girlfriend. He said something like, 'There's the bitch I was married to.' He called me a bitch. Well, I'm no shrinking violet, so I shouted after him, 'What did you say?' He came back to my table and said, 'You heard me. I said you were a bitch.' Everyone heard him say it. I mean, he said it really loud. So I stood up. I picked up a glass of water from my table. And I threw it at him—right in his face."

"What happened after that?"

"Your Mr. Nice Guy pushed me really hard and I fell against a table of people seated behind me. That's when the manager of the restaurant called the cops on him."

"That's a far cry from what he told me."

"Yes, I'm sure. Believe who you want. That's the way it happened. I was so embarrassed."

"Yvonne, if I may, I'd like to ask you one last question."

She nodded.

"Is there anyone you might know who disliked Emilio enough to frame him for all those murders?"

She thought for a moment.

"A lot of people, but I can't think of anyone in particular." She shrugged her shoulders and shook her head. "It could be anyone. But you know what, Mr. Kincaid? You're grasping at straws."

"What do you mean?"

"You've got the right man. No one framed him."

Chapter 54

The following day, Hank met with DeGarzia. "I located Sam Bailey's ex-wife. Her name is Yvonne Consuego and she lives in Albuquerque. I paid her a visit to see if she knew of anyone who might have motive to frame Sam. She couldn't come up with any specific names, but said there were a lot of people who had a grudge against him."

"Surprise, surprise."

"It would be an understatement to say she doesn't like Sam very much. She painted a grim picture of their marriage. Claims he abused her after he got fired from his job, so she left him."

"I believe her over him."

"I'm headed to the jail now, Deeg. I want to confront Sam about what she told me."

*****

"Sam, I spoke with your ex yesterday."

"You found her? What did she have to say for herself?"

"A lot." Hank couldn't hide his anger. "She told a pretty convincing story about how you turned on her after you were fired and how you were violent toward her. She made no bones about the fact she thinks you killed Castillo and the others. You've been lying to me, haven't you?"

"No. God, no. She's the liar. I swear."

"You know, I went there to see if she knew of anyone who would want to frame you. She said there were so many, she couldn't name just one. What's worse, she doesn't think you were framed. She said you're the killer."

Sam felt hopeless. "I'm sorry she feels that way. I'm sorry for many things I've done in my life, but I've never killed anyone. I don't know what else I can say."

"Why would she tell me you were an abusive husband?" Hank asked. He watched Sam's reaction closely. "She said you used to hit her when you drank."

Sam slammed the table with his fist, startling Hank. This was the first time Hank had ever seen Sam explode in anger. He wondered if Sam was overreacting to the accusation.

"That's absolute bullshit. I never, *ever* laid a hand on her. I never bumped her or shoved her or pushed her, or did anything to her. Never, Hank, never. You've got to believe me. I never even raised my voice to her. I loved the woman until she turned on me."

Hank didn't know who to believe. Both Sam and Yvonne told convincing stories.

"When we were going through our divorce, I know she told people I'd abused her—that I was violent and threatened her. It was all bullshit. Did she tell you about her abusive father?"

"No, she didn't. What does that have to do with anything?"

"You know what? I don't think she ever lied to me about her father."

"What do you mean?"

"I think that whatever happened to her when she was a young girl, she lives like it's still happening to her. She and her brothers had a terrible time growing up, and I think it poisoned her mind. But that was when she was a girl. It didn't happen in our marriage. It had to have taken a toll on her. Hank, she's making it sound like I abused her, like I was her father and not her husband, and I was the one that did it to her. I swear I never touched her. She even accused me of hurting her brother, Eric, but I never even knew the kid. He died when Yvonne was young. How the hell could I have hurt him? I think she's a sick woman."

Hank listened intently, studying Sam's face, eyes, body language. He did not discern Sam to be lying. Yvonne told her tale with sincerity. So did Sam. Both came across as credible, but one thought nagged Hank. *Sam weaves tales, exaggerates, and spins events for effect.*

"Yvonne told me about your melee at the restaurant. According to her, you started it when you called her a bitch. She said she retaliated by throwing a glass of water on you, at which point you pushed her, and the cops were called to break it up."

"Hank, I don't what else I can say. I'm telling you, she came up behind me and hit me with the heel of her shoe. I have the scar to prove it. Look." Sam leaned forward and pointed to a scar on his head. "I know you're having a hard time believing me. What if you talked to that girl I went out with that night? She could tell you what happened."

"What's her name?"

"Lauren Lycoming."

Chapter 55

DeGarzia received a second anonymous letter. The envelope was addressed to him in block letters similar to the one he received after the Jordan Sanchez murder. As with the earlier mailing, it contained a column from *USA Today* detailing Sam's upcoming murder trial. Once again, the sender had circled specific letters with a pen. Deeg wrote them out: *I – d – i – d – i – t – 6 – d – o – u – n – t – w – o – t – o – g – o – t – h – e – l – m – e.*

"Hank, I got another mysterious letter."

"Like the one you got after the Sanchez murder? What does it say?"

"It reads, 'I did it. 6 down,' with *down* spelled *d – o – u – n.* Then it says, 'two to go.' And they signed it 'thelme,' with *Thelma* spelled like they did before, *t - h – e – l – m - e.*"

Hank repeated, "I did it, 6 down, two to go, thelme. Someone's definitely playing games with us, Deeg. What do you think?"

"Yeah, that's my guess. There's no way to know who sent it. The lab checked for prints and came up empty. You know, there's always a whack job out there who tries to get in the act with something like this. It's probably a hoax. Anyway, I thought you should know."

"Thanks, but, you know," Hank thought out loud, "there's something about those letters—" He didn't finish his thought.

"I wouldn't make too much of it. I know you don't want to believe it, but everything still points to Emilio as being the killer. Facts are facts, Hank."

"Yeah, I know you're right. But as I've said before, I don't understand how I could have cycled with him for so long and not know what he was all about. You would think he would have slipped up somehow. I don't know how I could have misjudged him. I guess I still want to believe he's innocent."

"Mark my words. He's guilty as sin."

"Maybe, Deeg, but I still think Jimi Rodriguez could be the guy. He had motive too."

"Look, I get it. You want to free your friend. But on what basis? Just because Jimi Rodriguez has a bad temper or is a jealous husband doesn't mean he's a killer. That charge would never stick."

"I just don't think we should rule it out as a motive. If, in fact, Jimi kills all the cyclists he thinks Dahlia might be having an affair with, wouldn't that be one way to control her? I think you should bring them both in again, and push Jimi hard."

"Not sure I agree, but I'll do it. I'll call them back in. One thing for sure, that'll really piss him off."

*****

"Dahlia, thanks for coming back in. We appreciate your cooperation," DeGarzia said. He was going to take his time with her, and make Jimi cool his heels in one of the other interview rooms. "I need to ask you some more questions about Emilio Arvelo. If you still care for him, you need to be truthful."

Dahlia looked at him quizzically.

"I understand you've been visiting him in jail. You really care for him, don't you? Are you sure you're not jumping from the frying pan into the fire?"

"What do you mean by that?"

"I mean, going from Jimi and his bad temper to Emilio, the alleged cyclist killer."

"Deeg, his name is Sam Bailey. He changed his name. He doesn't want to be identified as the person he used to be." Dahlia's defense of Sam never wavered. "And, no, I don't think I'm going from the frying pan to the fire." Before DeGarzia could respond, she added, "I love Sam. He says he didn't kill all those people and I believe him. I'd do anything to help prove his innocence."

"Anything?"

"Yes, anything."

"You and Jimi are separated now, isn't that right?"

"Yeah. I told him about Sam, and he asked me to move out—gave me a day to get my stuff out of the house."

"Did he hurt you?"

"No. He screamed and yelled at me, said I was making a mistake, that I would regret it, and that I didn't know what I was getting into. He said Sam was a bad guy. He promised he would try to be a better husband in the future and he begged me to reconsider. He kept saying he would make things better, that he would change."

"What did you say?"

"I told him it was too late. I told him I wanted more out of life than to sit in a pizza shop all day. I said he deserved someone better, too—someone who could be a better wife to him."

"Did he threaten to harm Emilio?"

"No."

"Where are you living?"

"I found an apartment on Via de Vargas. Sam wanted me to move into his house, but I didn't feel right about that with him being in jail and everything."

"We think there's reason to believe Jimi may have tried to frame Emilio for the murders of those cyclists. You have to be careful. He could turn on you, too. Is your apartment secure?"

"Yes, it's alarmed. I'm not worried, though. I don't believe Jimi would hurt me. Besides, I don't think he has anything to do with all those people dying. I know he's got a bad temper, Deeg, but I don't think he would go that far."

"Let's review the timeline of when you first started seeing Emilio. It was after Castillo died, correct?"

"Yes, I started seeing *Sam* after Alex was killed, maybe a month. I don't remember exactly."

"So, it was after Alex Castillo's death, but before Tomás Pérez was killed?"

"I think it was, yes. But, wait—" Dahlia raised her face to the ceiling, closed her eyes, and tried to recall. After a moment, she said, "Yes, I'm almost positive it was before he was killed."

"Did you have an affair with Tomás Pérez?"

"Absolutely not."

"Did Jimi think you did?"

"I don't know. I don't think so. There was no reason for him to think that."

"Has Emilio told you he's been married before?"

"Yes, he's told me everything."

"Did he tell you why he changed his name?"

"Yes, he told me everything," she repeated. "After we started seeing each other, he admitted what he did when he was with the State Police, and about his drinking and divorce and everything. That's one of the reasons I love him. I trust him. And I trust that he wouldn't kill anyone. We talk. We talk about everything. He doesn't hold back. He's as honest as can be. It's nice to be able to share your life with someone like that. Do you have someone like that you can talk to, Deeg? It's important, you know."

Deeg started to shake his head but stopped himself. He looked away self-consciously.

Dahlia continued, "I'm not saying Jimi was a bad husband. But all he ever wanted to talk about was his pizzeria. Sam's different."

*****

"Jimi, thanks for agreeing to talk with me again."

"What do you want from me now?" Jimi was agitated. "I'm getting pretty tired of this routine. You're startin' to piss me off."

DeGarzia got straight to the point. "I'm going to ask you one more time. Did you kill Alex Castillo because you thought he was having an affair with Dahlia?"

"And I'll tell one more time, no, I didn't kill nobody."

"When did you find out Dahlia was having an affair with Emilio Arvelo?"

"You mean Sam Bailey? I don't remember."

Deeg leaned across the table—close enough that Jimi felt the warmth of his breath as he spoke. "What do you mean you don't remember? Was it last week, last month, last year?" Jimi pulled back. "Answer my questions, Jimi. What are you trying to hide?"

"Hide? I'm not hidin' shit, Deeg. I don't remember when. Like, maybe, three, four, six months ago. I don't remember."

"Did you know Tomás Pérez?"

"I knew him, yeah. What about him?"

"What about Jordan Sanchez? Did you know him too?"

"Yes."

"Did you kill them both so you could frame Emilio?"

"No!"

"Did you kill them to get even with Emilio because he was having an affair with Dahlia?" Deeg raised his voice. "Answer me truthfully, Jimi. Don't lie to me."

"Listen to me, Deeg. My whole life is turned upside down. The girl I once adored, my wife, turns out to be having an affair. I don't know, maybe even two affairs, maybe three. She said she didn't love me anymore. She said maybe she never loved me. That's what she told me. You know how bad that hurts to hear someone say that to you?" He wiped away a single tear that had rolled down his cheek. "It tore my heart apart to hear her say she never loved me. I don't think I'll ever get over it. I'll never feel the same about any woman again. But, Deeg, I did not kill anyone over it. We're going to get a divorce and I hope she has a good life. And I hope all the killings are over. All I want to do is run my little business and stay out of trouble. Honest, that's all I want."

"Did you know Emilio smokes?"

"No, and I could give a rat's ass if he does. I hope he has cancer and dies, the no-good sonovabitch."

"You know where he lives, don't you?"

"Yeah. So?"

"Ever go through his garbage to find cigarette butts so you could frame him for murder?"

"I followed Dahlia one time to his house. That's how I know where he lives. Did I go through his garbage? Shit no, I'm not a garbage picker. I didn't kill nobody, and I didn't frame nobody."

"Then how can you explain—"

Jimi stood. "That's it. I'm through. Either you arrest me right now or I'm walkin' out of here. I've had enough of this shit. I don't know how many times I've gotta tell you—I didn't kill nobody."

Chapter 56

The anonymous letters Deeg received continued to haunt Hank. *What do they really mean?* While driving home from work two days later, it hit him. Hank dialed DeGarzia's cell phone and made an immediate U-turn to return to police headquarters. "Deeg, I've got it."

"Got what?"

"I know what the letters are all about. I'll be there in ten minutes."

Inside police headquarters Hank didn't bother to wait for the elevator. He ran up the three flights to Deeg's office taking two steps at a time.

Deeg was curious. "What do you have, Hank?"

Hank was unable to hide his excitement. "I think I've got the answer. Let me see those letters again."

"Slow the hell down, Hank. Hang on." DeGarzia put on latex gloves and pulled the letters out of his desk drawer. Each was sealed in a clear plastic bag.

Hank also donned a pair of gloves and removed the letters from the bags. "Deeg, each message is signed the same way, *T – h – e – l – m - e*. We've been thinking it was a misspelling of the name *Thelma*, but it's an anagram for *helmet*, like in the helmets the killer put on Carlotta Smith and Walton Turner when he killed them. It's one of the killer's signatures."

DeGarzia stared at Hank and nodded at his eureka discovery. "Son of a bitch," was all he could mutter.

"Deeg, if I'm right—and I believe I am—the killer is not Sam Bailey. He couldn't have sent the last letter while sitting in jail. The killer is the only one who knows about the helmets on Carlotta Smith and Walton Turner. Sam's telling the truth. Someone is trying to frame him."

DeGarzia did not get caught up in Hank's excitement. "Okay, suppose you're right. If you are, that means the killer is planning to kill two more people. Four cyclists are dead, plus Smith and Turner make six, as in $S - i - x - d - o - u - n - t - w - o - t - o - g - o$. But then who and why?"

"I don't know the why, but Sam's got to be one of the two."

Not totally convinced, Deeg said, "I buy the helmet thing, but I'm not sure I buy that Bailey is the intended victim. He's already in prison and the evidence is stacked against him. The letters won't be enough to get him released. If the killer intended to frame Bailey, he's accomplished his goal."

"You're right. The letters won't be enough to get him released. There's a solid case against him, unless ..." Hank pondered a moment.

"Unless what?"

"What, exactly, would get him out?"

Deeg shook his head, "I don't know. What?"

"Another cyclist gets killed the same way as the others. That would get Sam out. That would show the killer couldn't possibly be Sam. The next cyclist, whoever it might be, would be one of the two final victims."

Deeg considered Hank's hypothesis, and surmised, "So then, once Bailey's released, the killer targets him as the second of the two remaining victims?"

"Yes, Sam's the final victim."

DeGarzia shook his head, but did not respond.

"Look, Deeg, I'm not saying you have to believe Sam's off the hook, but I do think there's reason to believe he's not guilty. Personally, I'm now convinced he's not the killer. I'm going to discuss my theory with the DA. He'll have to disclose the existence of the letters to David Thackery." Deeg shot Hank a sharp glance upon being reminded of the name of Sam's defense attorney. Hank nodded and continued, "Thackery will likely file a motion to dismiss the charges, of course, and the judge will have to consider the motion, but it won't be enough to have the charges dismissed."

"And if Bailey's not the killer, who is?"

"I don't know," Hank answered. "But Jimi Rodriguez is still the one with motive."

"Jimi Rodriguez."

Chapter 57

Jimi was counting receipts in the back office of the pizzeria when he heard the front door open and close. He checked the clock on the wall. Ten o'clock. Dahlia had been there an hour earlier with papers for him to sign, but she had left by nine thirty. The employees had all checked out for the evening.

Who the hell could that be? He opened his desk drawer and extracted a revolver he kept there for protection. He got up from his desk, revolver in hand, and yelled out, "Who's there?" He peered out from his office. "Oh, it's you again. What the hell do you want?"

"Nothing. I want to tell you I'm sorry about all the stuff that's happened. I hope you'll forgive me."

"Yeah, I forgive you, like when pigs can fly."

*****

James Anthony "Jimi" Rodriquez, 34, found dead. Rodriguez, owner of the popular Jimi's Pizzeria on Eighth Street, was found dead inside his office early Friday morning. Police announced Rodriguez was a murder victim but would release no details of his killing other than to say robbery was not a motive. Rodriguez was married to Dahlia Rodriguez, friend and reputed lover of Emilio Arvelo, a.k.a. Sam Bailey, the alleged Serial Cyclist Killer. Rodriguez was found dead by his employees when they reported to work Friday morning. Police are questioning his wife and employees, and ask anyone with knowledge of the crime to contact them at 505-222-9999.

"Hank, Jimi Rodriguez was killed last night."

"You're shitting me." Hank was both shocked and disheartened by the latest murder. "Where was he killed? How?"

"At his restaurant. One of his employees found him around seven o'clock this morning when he arrived at work. There was no sign of forced entry into the pizzeria, and the worker claimed the door was unlocked and all the lights were off. He said he knocked on Jimi's office door, and when he didn't answer, he walked in. He found him sitting at his desk. Here's the clincher, Hank. He had a bike helmet on his head."

"Son of a bitch. The same MO."

"Yes, I'm afraid so," Deeg answered.

"Did you get hold of Dahlia?"

"Yeah, she's taking it pretty hard. And she's scared, thinks the killer might be after her next. The ME says he was killed about ten o'clock last night. Dahlia said she visited him at the restaurant at nine, right after closing so he could sign some divorce papers, and stayed till about nine thirty. She said everything was normal, he was okay, their meeting was amicable, and nobody else was around. She didn't see anyone lurking, or strange cars, or anything unusual."

"Could it have been a robbery?"

"No. There was money in the register and his office safe was open, but the cash was untouched. It was definitely not a robbery. Our killer's still out there."

"Damn."

In a matter-of-fact way, Deeg added, "Look, Arvelo probably doesn't know about it yet, but if you want to tell him, go ahead. I think you finally have the evidence to get him released. The helmet thing cinches it. He's innocent. But I'll tell you this. We're running out of suspects."

*****

Hank met with Sam and David Thackery at the prison. "Sam, Jimi Rodriguez was murdered last night," he said.

Sam was stunned. "Is Dahlia okay?" He panicked at the thought of what might have happened to her. He looked back and forth between Hank and Thackery, waiting for an answer.

"Dahlia's okay. She's fine." Hank reached across the table to pat Sam's hand in a gesture of reassurance.

Thackery voiced some optimism, "Sam, I'm sorry to learn of Jimi's death, but the good news is that it proves you're innocent. The circumstances of Jimi's death were the same as when Walton Turner and Carlotta Smith were killed."

"Who did it? Who killed him?"

"We don't know."

"Are you sure Dahlia is okay?"

"Yes, we're sure. She's scared, but I'm going to ask Detective DeGarzia to assign a cop to keep an eye on her."

"Any suspects yet?"

"None. At this point, the investigation is back to square one," Hank answered. "We thought Jimi may have had the motive to frame you, but obviously that wasn't the case."

Thackery added, "I have already petitioned the court to have all charges against you dropped. I'll be talking with the DA as soon as I get back. I think you can be out of here by tomorrow, once the judge acts and the paperwork is done."

*****

Sam was released from jail the following day. He walked out of the Justice Department Building accompanied by David Thackery. Waiting reporters asked how he felt about having been wrongly accused of murder.

"I can only say I'm thankful the truth was uncovered—that I'm innocent. Thanks to my attorney David Thackery, who believed in me, to my friend Hank Kincaid, who stood by me, and especially to my fiancée, who lived through this nightmare with me. I'm only sorry the real killer is still out there and still killing innocent people."

"Are you worried that the killer might be aiming for you next?"

Sam showed no emotion. "Not really. I can't live my life in fear."

Thackery put his arm around Sam's shoulder as a sign the interview was over and ushered his client away from the microphones.

Chapter 58

j – u – i – s – t – o – n – e – t – o – g – o – t – h – e – l – m – e

"Another letter. It says, 'Juist one to go,' and it's signed 'thelme' again. It was postmarked two days ago," Deeg said. "Arvelo got out of prison yesterday and already I get another letter."

"We've got to put him in protective custody, Deeg. I'm positive he's targeted to be the last one," Hank said.

*****

"Sam, you've got to go under protective custody until we find the killer."

"I appreciate what you're saying, Hank, but I'm not doing it. I can protect myself. I've got a licensed 45, and I'm not afraid to use it."

"Will you at least stay off the bike? I mean, why tempt fate?"

"Yeah, I'll do that, but don't worry about me. The way I figure it, if I was a target, the killer would have done me in a long time ago. I think he's playing games with me. First, he frames me. Then he finds a way to get me released from jail. And now he tries to scare me. I don't think I'm the target. I'm more worried that it may be Dahlia, so I'm not letting her out of my sight. Maybe I'll take her away from Santa Fe for a while until you guys find the killer."

*****

"Deeg, remember Sam said he was assaulted by his ex-wife one night at a restaurant after their divorce?" Hank asked.

"Yeah."

"And then I interviewed the ex in Albuquerque, and she gave a completely opposite version of what happened?"

"Yeah, he probably really was a wife beater," Deeg said. "I have a hard time believing his side of the story."

"I'm not so sure. But I'd like to know who's really telling the truth."

"It doesn't make any difference, now that he's off the hook for the murders."

"It may be moot as far as Sam's concerned, but I'd like to talk to the woman who was Sam's date that night to find out what really happened."

"Why bother?"

"Out of curiosity, if nothing else."

"Do you know her name?"

"Lauren Lycoming. I'm going to look her up and pay her a visit tomorrow."

"I wouldn't waste my time if I were you, Hank. Whether Arvelo lied or his ex-wife lied doesn't make a freaking bit of difference to me. There's a killer still out there. If it's not Emilio Arvelo, I need to find out who it is and stop him. I don't give a shit about this Lauren Lycoming."

Chapter 59

Lauren Lycoming was watching TV in her apartment when she heard a knock on the door.

"Yes? Who is it?"

"My name is Hank Kincaid. I'm from the District Attorney's office. I have some questions to ask you about a former boyfriend of yours."

"Show me your badge or an ID," she demanded. "Put it in front of the peephole." He did as requested. "Okay, come on in." Lauren was a tall, dark-haired woman of about thirty.

"Lovely apartment," he said as he walked in. He was carrying a nondescript shopping bag.

Lycoming watched with curiosity as he set the bag down.

"Don't mind me. It's a gift for my wife. I'm just taking an extra step of caution. I don't like leaving things visible in my car, and my trunk's full of golf clubs."

She turned off the TV. "Okay. So, how can I help you?"

"I'm trying to find out about a man by the name of Sam Bailey, or Emilio Arvelo, however you know him."

"I know Sam Bailey. He's the one accused of killing all those people." She quickly added, "Just so you know, I only dated him a couple of times."

"Can you tell me why you broke it off?"

"Yeah. I didn't want to get caught up in the problems he was having with his ex-wife."

"What kind of problems?"

"The last time we went out, he and his wife had a huge fight at a restaurant when we were there. It was a doozy."

"Do you remember what happened? Who started it?"

"Yes, I remember exactly what happened. She started it. I remember seeing this lady come up behind Sam when we were having dinner. I didn't think anything of it. I thought she was trying to squeeze behind him to get to her table. Then, out of the clear blue, she takes off a shoe—it had a high heel—and she smacks it against Sam's head. I mean, she reached back and cracked him one. I remember the look on his face, like, what the hell just happened? She was going to hit him again, but he turned around in time to grab her arm."

"She started it?"

"Oh, yes."

"Are you absolutely certain?"

"Absolutely. Why would I make something like that up?"

"What happened from there?"

"He pushed her away and she fell onto a table. Knocked it over. She kept screaming and cursing at Sam. Finally, a couple of guys who were in the restaurant stepped in to break it up."

"And then what happened?"

"The manager of the restaurant took her by the elbow and rushed her out to the lobby. Sam just stood there. He was dazed and had blood running down his head. I used a napkin to try to stop the bleeding and told him we should go to the hospital to see if he needed stitches. He refused and said he would be okay. He apologized to the people in the restaurant. We heard more shouting coming from the lobby, so Sam and I went out to see what was going on. The cops had gotten there and were restraining her. Sam told them he didn't want to file charges, so they escorted her out of the restaurant and warned her not to return. That was it."

"What did you do?"

"I told him I was sorry for what happened to him, but I was leaving. I told him he could look me up again when his personal life was in order. He was a really nice guy, but that was the last time I saw him until he shows up on TV, you know because of the serial killings."

"Ms. Lycoming, it's been a long day. I wonder if you would mind getting me a glass of water. I have a few more questions, and I'll get out of your hair."

"Of course," she said, and turned to go to the kitchen. At that moment, there was another knock on the door. "Now who could that be?" she said under her breath, and went to check.

From the other side of the door she heard, "Ms. Lycoming? My name is Hank Kincaid. I'm from the District Attorney's office. I have a few questions I'd like to ask you about Sam Bailey."

In an instant, DeGarzia stole behind Lycoming and covered her mouth to keep her from crying out. With his free arm, he lifted her by the waist and carried her toward the rear of the apartment. She kicked and struggled to get loose from his grasp.

He hissed, "Shhh," and squeezed tighter.

She was able to reach up and scratch the back of his hand. She tried to scratch at his eyes, but DeGarzia slid the crook of his powerful arm around her neck and squeezed even harder, cutting off her air supply. Within seconds she stopped struggling. DeGarzia held her lifeless body for a moment then lowered her quietly to the floor. She was dead.

Outside, Hank thought he heard something—footsteps, whispers—and leaned toward the door to listen. *She's in there. Why isn't she answering?* He knocked again. "Ms. Lycoming, my name is Hank Kincaid. I'm from the DA's office," he repeated. "I need only a few minutes of your time. Are you in there?" Again, he thought, *I'm certain I heard something from inside.* He knocked one last time. After waiting another thirty seconds with no response, he took out a business card, wrote on it *Please call me*, and slipped the card under the door.

DeGarzia tiptoed to the door, looked through the peephole, and watched as Hank stepped into the elevator. He retreated to the apartment window and parted the curtains to watch Hank get into his car and drive away. When he was certain Hank was gone, he picked up the card Hank had slipped under the door, read the message, and stuffed it in his pocket.

He lifted Lycoming off the floor and sat her on the couch. He gently smoothed the hair away from her face and kissed her on the cheek before removing a bicycle helmet from the shopping bag he had brought in with him. He placed the helmet on her head. "Why did you have to lie to me?" he said, and buckled the chinstrap.

Deeg wiped his prints from anything he had touched and looked out the window. He left the apartment and used the stairs to exit the building. On his way to his car, he looked around nonchalantly to be certain no one was in sight. Convinced no one had seen him, he drove away slowly, unaware Hank was following him at a safe distance.

Chapter 60

Hank was confused. He was certain he had heard scuffling in the apartment. *What was Deeg doing here?* A million thoughts ran through his mind. *Did Deeg try to question Lycoming too or was he in the apartment building for another reason? He told me not to waste my time. He wasn't interested in what she might tell me about the incident at the restaurant. Something's not right.*

Deeg drove at a leisurely pace. Clearly, he was in no hurry to get home. He studied his rear view mirror regularly but did not spot Hank. He stopped at a convenience store to pick up some milk. Hank pulled onto a side street to wait, and turned away when Deeg came out of the store and glanced in his direction.

At home, Deeg pulled into his garage and closed the door behind him. Several lights were already on in the house.

Hank decided to find out what Deeg was up to, and pulled into his driveway. He walked up to the front door and knocked.

Deeg opened the door and was surprised to see the ADA. "Hank. What are you doing here? Are you lost or something? How did you know where I live?"

"I saw you leave Lauren Lycoming's apartment building."

"What are you doing, stalking me?" Deeg tried to make light of Hank's comment but his smile was insincere. "Well, come on in."

Hank hesitated, but then entered Deeg's starkly furnished house. "Okay, for a minute. So, were you able to talk with her? I was there, but she didn't come to the door. I'm sure someone was in there, though. I heard some noise, but no one answered."

"Maybe she has a cat."

"Yeah, maybe." *That was no cat.*

"I tried to talk to her, too. I wanted to ask her about that melee at the restaurant with Arvelo. I knocked, too, but she never came to the door."

"You and I must have passed each other."

"I took the steps up," Deeg said.

"Right. I took the elevator. But, Deeg, I didn't realize you were going to talk to her. You told me not to waste my time going over there."

"Yeah, well, it was on my way home, so I decided I'd pop in to ask her about it. You piqued my curiosity. Hey, how about a beer?"

"No, I've got to get home."

"What the hell … one beer," he insisted.

Hank studied Deeg's face. He was certain he was holding back, and sensed he was lying about his visit to Lycoming's apartment. *But why?* "All right, one beer." Hank was unable to put his finger on his suspicions, but his gut was telling him something was definitely not right. He wished he had waited to confront Deeg at Police Headquarters instead of at his home.

Deeg went to the kitchen to get the beer. Hank noticed the detective's service revolver, badge, handcuffs, and wallet on the foyer table. He noticed something else, too. *That's my business card. What's he doing with my card?* He picked it up, turned it over, and read the note he had written to Lauren Lycoming before sliding the card under her apartment door. *Please call me.*

For a brief moment, the significance of his discovery did not register. Then—*That was Deeg in the apartment. Why is he lying about this?* Hank's instinct was to turn around, leave as fast as he could, and sort things out later. He fished his phone out of his pocket and started toward the front door, but it was too late. Deeg returned from the kitchen, beers in hand.

"Hey, where you going, Hank? Here's your beer. Who are you calling?"

"I need to get going. My wife sent me a text. I'm going to have to take a rain check on the beer. I've got to call her to tell her I'm on my way home," Hank said. He hoped Deeg had not seen him pick up his card from the table.

But he had.

Deeg set the beers down and snatched his service revolver. He pointed it at Hank. "Let me have your phone," he said.

"What are you doing, Deeg?"

"I said, let me have the phone."

Hank gave it to him. DeGarzia glanced at the phone and saw Hank had not dialed his wife. He waved his gun toward the couch. "Sit over there."

"What's going on, Deeg? I don't get it." Hank was stunned by DeGarzia's actions.

"I'm sorry, Hank. I didn't expect you would go to Lycoming's apartment today. You said you were going to talk with her tomorrow, not today. I thought I'd beat you to the punch and get over there before you did."

"Okay. But why are you pointing your gun at me?"

"I'm sure you know I was there. Your card—that was stupid of me to take it, wasn't it? I should have left it in the apartment."

"What happened there?"

"Nothing, really. I talked with her a little."

"And what happened?"

"I had to ... restrain her," he said, and shrugged.

"What do you mean *restrain* her?"

"I really don't want to get into it."

Hank was insistent. "Why? What the hell are you saying? Tell me what you did to that girl."

"I had to keep her quiet."

"Where is she? Is she okay?"

"No, I'm afraid not."

"Is she hurt?"

"Yes. She's dead. It was her fault, really. When you showed up at her apartment, I told her to be quiet but she kept fighting me."

"You were in there with her when I tried to see her?"

"Yes. We heard you knock."

"Why didn't you let me in?"

"Because she would have lied to you, too, like she lied to me."

"You killed her because you thought she lied to you? You've got to be kidding. Was it about Sam Bailey and his ex?"

"Yes. She said it was my sister who started the fight at the restaurant."

Deeg's statement hung in the air.

"Your sister?" Hank was dumbfounded. "What do you mean, your *sister*? Are you telling me Yvonne Consuego is your sister?" The revelation struck him. "You're her brother. You're her older brother Larry?"

"Yes, Yvonne's my sister. Surprised, huh? We've kept it a secret. My real name is Lawrence Matias Consuego-DeGarzia. Yvonne's always called me Larry. My stepfather's name was DeGarzia. Yvonne changed her name back to Consuego. I should have, too." Deeg's expression was sad.

"Oh. I see," Hank said without conviction.

"Yvonne told me about your meeting with her. She said I shouldn't trust you." Deeg's tone conveyed uncertainty.

"Of course you can trust me. You know me, Deeg."

"Don't call me Deeg," he insisted quietly and firmly. "My name is Larry."

"I thought you wanted me to call you Deeg, but I'll call you Larry if that's what you want. I still don't understand, Larry. Help me understand."

"Understand what?"

"What happened in Lauren Lycoming's apartment? Why did you kill her?"

"I told you. She lied about my sister."

Hank shook his head. "You killed her because of that? I must be missing something. Did you ever think that maybe she wasn't lying, that maybe it was your sister who was lying to you?"

"No. Yvonne doesn't lie. It was that girl. Trust me, she was the liar."

"Let me ask you something. What do you have against Sam Bailey?"

"First off, his name isn't Sam Bailey. And second, I have a lot against him," Deeg responded.

A female voice called out from the stairwell. "Mr. Kincaid, you're getting my brother upset. Maybe I can tell you what he has against him."

"Yvonne?" Hank watched as she entered the living room and stood alongside her brother.

"Hello, Mr. Kincaid. I've been listening to you from upstairs."

"Why didn't you tell me Deeg was your brother?"

Yvonne held Deeg's arm. "Larry didn't want me to tell you. And you heard him. His name is Larry, not Deeg." She looked up at her brother and smiled. He smiled back. Although Deeg towered over Yvonne by more than a foot, Hank saw the resemblance between siblings as they stood side by side.

"Mr. Kincaid, you asked what Larry has against Sam Bailey? Let me tell you. Sam Bailey's a liar, a fake, and a bad, bad man," she said. "You know that too, don't you? And how about this— did you know his real name *isn't* Emilio Arvelo?"

"It isn't? What is it then?"

"José Consuego."

Hank looked at Deeg for clarification but none was forthcoming.

He turned back to Yvonne. "I thought Consuego was your maiden name. Did he have the same last name as you when you married him?"

"Is he dumb or what, Larry?"

Larry shrugged.

"I'm not dumb," Hank said. "Excuse me for not understanding, but I don't get it. Sam Bailey is Emilio Arvelo, right?"

Yvonne didn't answer.

"And now you're telling me he was also going by the alias of José Consuego when you were married to him?"

Yvonne shook her head. Her voice full of disbelief, she asked, "What makes you think I was married to him? He wasn't my husband. He's my father. I wouldn't marry my father. I hate him. He hurt us all so bad—all the time."

Hank was reeling at Yvonne's revelations. He found them incredulous. "Who did he hurt?"

"Larry and me. And he hurt my brother Eric, too."

Hank was having difficulty comprehending everything Yvonne was saying. He looked toward Deeg again for an explanation. "Is that true, Larry?"

Deeg stood silent.

"But, Yvonne, you told me about Eric and how he died. What did Emilio have to do with his death? I didn't think he knew Eric."

"Of course he did. Emilio was Eric's father. Why wouldn't he have known him?"

Hank didn't argue at Yvonne's convoluted tale. "Tell me how he hurt him."

"He shamed him all the time. He belittled him. He scolded and yelled at him. He made him cry. He was always making him cry. Then, one day, Eric couldn't take it anymore and he ran away from home and never came back. He was only fourteen. We found out later he died on the streets. And when he died, Emilio said that's what he got for running away. That he should have stayed. And the truth is, he ran away to get *away* from Emilio, and then died *because* of him."

"How did Emilio hurt you, Yvonne?"

"In so many ways. So many ways. So many times." She whimpered and buried her face in her brother's shoulder.

Hank was coming to realize that brother and sister perceived Sam to be their father. He wondered what had really happened in their childhood. How did their perception become their reality? Why had Yvonne and Deeg transformed their deep-seated hatred for their own father into hatred toward Emilio?

"Yvonne, I asked Emilio if he ever hurt you."

"And what did he say?"

"He said he never did. That he never touched or harmed you in any way."

"He said that? Well, there you go. He lied again. He did hurt me."

"What about you, Larry? Did Emilio hurt you, too?" Hank asked.

Deeg had been silent for several minutes. He stood impassive as his sister described Emilio's abuse, but got agitated with Hank's question. His eyes swelled. "Yes. Sometimes I heard him in the kitchen yelling, making mother cry. He'd come to my room and put a strap to me. He would say to me, 'Bad boy. Bad boy. God will punish you for being a bad boy.'"

Hank thought Deeg was going to cry. "I'm sorry if I'm upsetting you both, but Sam Bailey—or Emilio Arvelo—could not possibly be your father. He's not José Consuego. And,

Yvonne, I'm sure Emilio never hurt you or Deeg." Hank tried to reason with them, hoping his logic would penetrate their veil of psychosis.

Deeg pushed Yvonne away from him and stepped toward Hank. "I said, stop calling me Deeg!" The look on Deeg's face turned to anger and he smacked the barrel of his gun against Hank's temple. "I am not Deeg!"

Hank's head snapped back from the sudden attack. His hand flew to his head. Blood trickled slowly down his face and turned sticky on his hand. "Why did you do that?" he shouted. "What the hell's wrong with you? I called you Deeg by accident. I know your name is Larry. I just forgot for a second."

Deeg did not apologize.

Yvonne tugged on her brother's arm, trying to calm him. "It's okay, Larry. He'll behave now. Won't you, Mr. Kincaid?" she said, and smiled weakly. "I'll get you a wet cloth for your head. Now, don't get any blood on the couch," she said.

She rushed to the kitchen and came back with a wet towel.

"Thank you," Hank said.

"Do you think you'll be okay?" she asked.

"Yes, I'll be fine."

"Now, Larry, Mr. Kincaid, that's enough, okay? I want you boys to behave yourselves."

"Let me ask you something else," Hank said. "I'm still confused. Was Emilio married to you or to your mother?"

Yvonne put her hands to the sides of her head and shook her head violently. "Why are you are confusing me? I don't want to talk about it anymore. I was so little. I can't remember everything. I can't." She sobbed uncontrollably.

Larry pulled her toward him and hugged her tightly. "Shhhh. It's okay now. Everything is okay."

Hank tried to sound as sympathetic as possible. "I'm so sorry you were all forced to grow up like that."

Between sobs, Yvonne explained, "Sometimes it comes back to me. Some things. Nightmares. I wake up screaming, 'Don't hurt me. Don't hurt me.' I get scared he's still going to hurt me."

"Nightmares of your father?"

"I know it's him. But his face is always covered with a mask. The only thing I see are his eyes. Just his eyes. Sometimes I think I can see who it is but I wake up and can't remember. All I remember is his eyes. They're always looking at me. I can't run away from them. No matter where I go, they follow me. They scare me so much."

Deeg again tried to calm his sister. She was limp in his arms, pitifully seeking comfort in his strength. "Stop asking all those questions. Don't you see how upset she gets?"

"I'm sorry, Larry. I'm only trying to learn what you and Yvonne went through. And, Eric—how horrible for him to die that way."

At the mention of Eric's name, Yvonne steadied herself. She pulled away from her brother, wiped the tears from her face, and smoothed her blouse. "Yes, and it was all because of your friend, Emilio. He even drove Larry away."

"What happened, Larry?"

"I told my father it was not my fault Eric died," Larry said. "But he said that it was and he hit me. I had taken so much from him and I snapped. I punched him back. I remember standing over him and punching him … punching him, and punching him, and punching him." Spittle flew from Deeg's mouth as he recalled what he had done. "I wanted to kill him, but mother wouldn't let me."

As suddenly as he showed anger, he reverted to calm. "After that, the only thing I remember about that night is kissing Yvonne goodbye and leaving home for good." He strained to regain contact with reality but was unsuccessful. "I left that night and never went back."

"That had to be pretty tough on you," Hank empathized, unsure what the volatile Deeg would do if he continued to ask questions. But he had to know. In a calm, casual manner, he asked. "How old were you?"

"Eighteen. And, yeah, it was tough leaving my baby sister and my mother, but I knew I could never go back."

"I was only six or seven years old, and I was so frightened when he left," Yvonne said.

"What did you do after you left home, Larry?"

Yvonne answered for him. "He joined the Army. You should have seen him, Mr. Kincaid. He was a big, handsome man in his Army uniform." She nodded her head and boasted, "He could have been a movie star. I still have his picture."

"Hardly," Deeg said. He self-consciously scratched his neck in embarrassment.

"When he got out of the Army, he finally came back to New Mexico. I was so happy to see him. I hadn't seen him in twenty years. That's a long time. I begged him to stay. I told him about my life with Emilio after he left. He felt so bad for leaving me, and he said he would never let anything bad happen to me again. He promised me he wouldn't ever leave me again. And he hasn't. You promised me, right, Larry?"

Deeg nodded. "Yes, Yvonne, I promised." Hank was unaccustomed to seeing Deeg so submissive.

"So is that when you became a cop? Right out of the service?"

"Yes."

Yvonne stroked her brother's back. "He's a good cop, isn't he?"

"He's the best cop on the force." Hank hoped he sounded sincere. "We're a pretty good team, aren't we, Larry?"

"Yeah, we are for sure," Deeg answered.

"Larry, I'm your friend. You know that." Hank's mind went into overdrive. He needed to concoct a plan that would divert both brother and sister. "I think the three of us should team up to put Emilio behind bars. He's out of jail now, but we can charge him with abuse and put him right back in. You know we can do that." Hank was doing what he could to convince them he had their interest at heart. "I guess I never really knew Emilio after all. I see what you're saying about him now, about him being a liar."

"Well it's about damn time, Hank." Hank thought he sensed sympathy in Deeg's voice.

"You know, Yvonne, we can do a lot of good for other people who have suffered abuse, for those who have gone through the same things as you and Larry."

She tilted her head, confused at Hank's words. "What are you talking about?"

"I'm saying we can establish a precedent on behalf of all abused children if we take on Emilio. Think about it. I could represent Eric and both of you in court when we charge Emilio with manslaughter for killing Eric. We can put him away for twenty years, maybe thirty. It's worth trying. What do you think? I'll be there to help push the case through the District Attorney's office. Larry and I can partner on this, the same way we've been working together all these months."

Neither sibling answered. They didn't argue either. They looked at each other, and for a moment said nothing. Hank took their silence as a sign of hope.

It was false hope.

Chapter 61

"Why not let me have your gun," Hank said. He spoke in a soft tone and reached out for the service revolver Deeg was holding loosely in his right hand. "I'm on your side. Yvonne's, too. I want to see justice done against Emilio. I'm certain we can file charges against him."

"I can't, Hank. And you know, I really don't want to kill you, but we have to."

"Kill me? What the hell are you talking about? I'm the only one who can help you get Emilio."

"We have to."

"You don't want to kill me, Larry. I'm on your side," Hank replied, trying to mask his desperation. "You're my friend."

"Yeah, Jimi Rodriguez thought I was his friend, too. But if he was my real friend, he'd still be alive."

"What does that mean?"

"Nothing."

"Did you have something to do with his murder? Is that what you're saying?"

Deeg turned to Yvonne and did not answer.

"You're kidding me. You killed Jimi? Why?"

"You really don't know, do you?" Yvonne smirked. "He really doesn't know, Larry."

"Tell me, Larry. Why did you kill him?"

Yvonne looked up at her brother and squinched her face. "Should we tell him, Larry? Should we?"

Deeg shrugged his shoulders at his sister's playful suggestion. "Sure. Why not? It doesn't matter now. You can tell him."

"Okay, Mr. Kincaid. First off, you should know that we killed Alex Castillo," she announced. "Well, not we. I mean, *I* killed him."

"Oh my God. You didn't," Hank exclaimed. He could not believe what he was hearing. "Tell me you're kidding."

"No, I'm not kidding. Want to know how I killed him?"

"Yes, okay. Tell me what happened to him." Hank was numb with the revelation. None of what he was hearing made any sense. *Deeg killed Lauren Lycoming. Then they tell me their psychotic tales about Emilio and their father. And now Yvonne's saying she killed Castillo?*

"I really didn't plan it, you know, Mr. Kincaid. It just kind of happened. I was driving to Santa Fe to visit Larry when I saw Alex Castillo riding his bike on Aldez Pass. I hadn't seen him for years, but I recognized him right away, even with his helmet on. At first, I only was going to scare him. You know, ride close to him, almost hit him, pretend I was going to hit him. He was all by himself and no one else was on the road, so I drove right behind him, really close. And you know what he did? He told me to slow down. He yelled at me. Like he owned the road. That wasn't too smart. It got me mad. So I bumped his bike from behind. It wasn't a hard bump, but he wasn't so cocky anymore. He was swerving all over the road trying to get away from me. You should have seen him. It was actually kind of fun to see him panic and scream like a schoolgirl." Yvonne laughed at the recollection.

"That's when I rammed him really hard and he went over the cliff. He flew right over the barrier. His bike, too. I stopped my car and looked over. I saw him at the bottom of the canyon. And you know what, I felt good about what I did. He got what he deserved."

"Got what he deserved?" Hank asked. "What did he do to you that you would kill him?"

"Didn't you know Castillo was the guy who got Emilio fired from the State Police? And if it wasn't for him and his two friends, Emilio wouldn't have started to drink and take it out on Larry and Eric and me."

"Emilio? You don't mean Emilio. Yvonne, he's not your father. Damn it. Listen to me, both of you. Emilio Arvelo is not your father," Hank repeated. "Emilio was Yvonne's *husband*. Emilio and Sam Bailey are one in the same person, but he's not your father. He's not José Consuego."

"You don't know what you're saying." Deeg's anger rose. "And don't call him Sam. He's not Sam."

"Yeah, fine, okay. I won't. I won't. Tell me about the others. Did you kill all them, too?"

Yvonne nodded. "Yes, we did—Pérez and Sanchez and Haverford, and all the rest."

"And Carlotta Smith and Walton Turner?" Hank asked.

"Yes and yes!" Yvonne answered.

Brother and sister are the serial killers. Hank thought it implausible, but it was true.

"But, why? I don't understand." Hank wanted to know why the circle of victims had encompassed so many disparate people.

"Do we have to spell it out for you?" Deeg said. "You know, you're pissing me off. You don't listen very good, do you? We had to kill them. They were all in this together. I didn't realize it at first, but Yvonne explained it to me. They were all out to get our father fired. Then, after they did that, our father turned on us kids."

"And you think Carlotta Smith and Walton Turner knew your father?"

"They did," Yvonne insisted. "They used to visit in our house. I remember them talking and laughing in the kitchen. Larry didn't remember them, but I did."

The dynamics between the two was becoming increasingly clear to Hank. Deeg was the enabler, but Yvonne the manipulator, the one who directed Deeg. She lumped together everyone she perceived as having conspired both with and against Emilio. She targeted them all.

Why didn't they target me? I was Sam's friend. Hank decided to distance himself from Sam. "I'm glad I didn't know your father. From what you've told me, I wouldn't have liked him."

Deeg sneered at Hank. "Don't lie to us. You know him, all right. We know you've been going on bike rides with him."

Hank didn't respond. He wasn't sure what more he could do to free himself from these psychopaths. Brother and sister were killers—confused, illogical, and living in a dark haze of hatred, revenge, and paranoia. Hank knew he had to stay calm and keep them calm, too. Perhaps then Deeg would then revert to reality from the psychotic world in which he and Yvonne existed. Deeg's transformation from a strong, resolute cop to an incoherent schizophrenic stunned Hank.

"Do you want to know about Pérez and Sanchez?"

"Of course. But I wasn't sure you wanted to tell me."

"I don't mind," Yvonne said, all too eager to vent. "After I ran Castillo off the road, I told Larry what I'd done and asked him to help me get Castillo's friends, too. I wanted all those people to pay for the misery they caused us."

"Because Castillo, Pérez, and Sanchez testified against your father, you felt you had to get even with them?"

"Yes. Exactly." Yvonne clapped energetically, although her hands barely touched or made any sound. "You understand now. Good for you. You really do understand."

"And you planted Emilio's cigarettes at the crime scenes to implicate him in the different murders?"

"Yes!"

"Why?"

Yvonne looked directly at Hank without saying a word. She was giving him time to figure it out on his own. Hank finally realized the answer to his question. "Because it was your way to kill two birds with one stone, right? You killed the people who got your father fired, and at the same time, you made sure your father was accused of murdering them," Hank said. "That way, you could have revenge against your father for his abuse toward you when you were kids."

"Yes, yes, yes. That's right!" Yvonne was nearly giddy upon hearing Hank's reasoned response.

"I wasn't sure you really understood. But I think you finally do," Deeg said. "The first cigarette we planted was in the back yard of that old lady you loved so much."

"Carlotta Smith."

"Do you remember when we found it?"

"Yes, I remember. But I'm surprised about her. I thought you liked her."

"Nah, I didn't trust her. I knew what she was trying to do. She pretended she didn't know me, but she did. Yvonne said she saw her lots of times at our house. Do you know she tried to stab Yvonne with a kitchen knife? Can you believe that? She was a sick old lady. We chased her through her house and finally cornered her in her bathroom. That's when she tried to stab Yvonne. We'd gone to visit her to ask about Emilio, and she lied to us and said she didn't know who we were talking about. She lied to us. I don't like people who lie."

"So you killed her and threw her into Breeze Canyon because you thought she lied to you. The same reason you killed Lauren Lycoming? For lying?"

"Yes. We had to."

"Why did you have to?"

"We didn't want her to tell Emilio we knew about them."

Hank shook his head. He realized the more they discussed the murders, the deeper brother and sister plunged into their paranoia. He had to keep them talking. He needed time to come up with an escape plan.

"Why did you frame Heather Dorell after killing Sanchez? She didn't kill Sanchez, did she? You did."

"Yes, that's right. We did," Yvonne admitted proudly. "You want to know why? Because she shot Larry. He almost died because of her. Because of her, I almost lost my big brother. I wanted to kill her for what she did, but Larry said it was better if we made it seem like she was the one who murdered Sanchez and his friends. That way everyone would think she was the serial killer. It worked for a while didn't it?"

"You killed Sanchez the same way you killed Castillo and Pérez, running him off the road."

"Mr. Kincaid, do you know, Sanchez was even more fun than Castillo or Pérez?" Yvonne turned to her brother as she spoke. "Larry, how long did we have to follow him before we finally found him alone?"

"It had to be a month. We put a lot of time into him, didn't we?"

"But it was worth it," Yvonne smiled. "You should have seen him when he realized we were going to knock him over the cliff. He was pretty athletic. He jumped off his bike and landed on his feet. He was like a gymnast or an acrobat. He tried to run from us, but couldn't get very far because of those funny shoes you bikers wear. He was slipping and sliding down the road. We were laughing so hard. Finally, Larry caught up to him and hit him with his car, and he screamed all the way to the bottom of the canyon."

"I bet you're wondering about Terrence Haverford, too, aren't you?" Deeg asked. "He wasn't a buddy of Castillo's, so you've got to be thinking, why kill him?"

"Yes. Why him?"

"You remember Stephenson's profile of the killer? Remember he said Hispanics kill Hispanics, whites kill whites?"

Hank nodded. "I do."

"I didn't appreciate it when the captain brought Stephenson in to take over the investigation. *My* investigation. He thought he was so smart. Well, we decided we wanted to prove him wrong about his *profile*, so we killed Haverford, a gringo, to throw him off track. Clever, huh? It worked, didn't it? Stephenson got confused. I couldn't stop laughing."

"Yeah, right. But why Haverford?"

"Yvonne picked him. It could have been any gringo, but Haverford was the lucky guy. We even thought about killing you."

Hank didn't want to discuss that possibility, so he continued on the topic of Haverford.

"So you planted another of Emilio's cigarettes with Haverford. How did you get them?"

"That was easy. From his house. Yvonne still has his house key. We emptied one of his ashtrays one day when he wasn't home. We still have a few left."

"But, you know, Larry," Yvonne said, "we really only need one more cigarette—just one."

"For Emilio, I presume," Hank said.

Larry and Yvonne looked at each other and snickered. Then, in unison, they said, "No. For you."

"Me? Why me?" Hank did his best to keep his anxiety in check. He knew it was only a matter of time before they might act against him.

"Yes, you. Isn't that ironic? You get Emilio out of jail and he turns around and kills you. Then he turns around and he puts a gun to his head. At least, that's what the evidence will show," Yvonne exclaimed. "That's right—he's not in jail anymore, thanks to you."

"What do you mean, thanks to me?"

Deeg and Yvonne looked at each other again, smug in their explanations.

"Yvonne thought if we put a bike helmet on Carlotta Smith and sent those newspaper clippings signed by Thelme to Detective DeGarzia it would confuse everyone. Then we decided to kill Walton Turner and put a helmet on him, too. It did confuse everyone, didn't it?"

"Yes, it did. But, tell me about the letters, Larry. Yvonne sent the letters to you, but why?"

"To throw everyone off."

"So your plan was to have me solve the riddle of the Thelme anagram—which I did—and that would eventually get Emilio out of jail."

"Yes, that's right. You see, Mr. Kincaid, once we killed Jimi Rodriguez, you would realize only the real killer knew about the helmet. And since Emilio was in jail, he couldn't possibly be the killer," Yvonne explained.

"You planned to kill Jimi after Emilio was in jail all along. That would prove Emilio innocent, and he would have to be freed because the killer was still out there."

"And you thought Jimi was the killer. Were you wrong or what." Deeg smirked.

Hank got up from the couch. He realized he wasn't going to talk Deeg or Yvonne into reality and was no longer afraid to let his anger show. "What's so funny?"

"Sit down," Deeg shouted. He waved his revolver at Hank.

"You think it's funny you were playing me for a fool? You know what, Deeg? I don't give a shit anymore. Yeah, your name is *Deeg*. I don't care who you killed or why you killed them—"

"I said, *sit down!*"

Hank had had enough. He tried a different tack. "Screw you! You want to kill me? Go ahead. Kill me now." He got angry, and tried to penetrate Deeg and Yvonne's psychotic pall with aggression. He tried one last time to convince them that Sam and their father were two different people. "Listen to me. I understand what your father did to all of you. But Sam Bailey is not your father. Your father abused you, not Sam. Your father was a bad man. Sam never hurt Yvonne. I'll say this one last time. It was your *father* who hurt you—not Sam. Either put the gun away or kill me. I don't really give a shit anymore. I told you I would try to help, but if you don't want my help—"

Deeg interrupted. "If you don't sit down, I'm going to put a bullet between your eyes." He aimed the revolver at Hank's head. "You keep calling our father *Sam*. I told you not to." Deeg spit out the words with viciousness. Hank knew he had to back off. "One, two ..."

Hank sat down. He felt helpless.

Yvonne shook her finger at Hank. "Now, Mr. Kincaid, look what you've done. You've made Larry angry. You shouldn't do that. Please behave. He has a bad temper, I'm sure you know."

Hank sank back on the couch and let out a deep sigh. *Stall. I've got to keep stalling them.* Looking first at Deeg, then at Yvonne, he asked, "What would you have done if I hadn't solved the Thelme riddle?"

"If you hadn't come up with the solution, Larry was going to say he solved it."

"You first wanted Emilio to sweat it out for a while in jail, right? And once he was out of jail, you were going to kill him?"

"Yes. Exactly. Very good, Mr. Kincaid. Very good." Again Yvonne showed her approval with silent clapping.

"But now you're not going to kill him. You're going to kill me, instead. Is that what you're saying?"

"No. We're going to kill both of you."

<h1 style="text-align:center">Chapter 62</h1>

Hank's cell phone rang, startling everyone. Deeg pulled it out of his trouser pocket to see who was calling.

"I should answer it, Larry. It could be my wife worried about me."

Deeg read the screen. "It's not. It says Sam Bailey—Emilio."

"I'm supposed to be riding with Sam tonight." He was lying. "Let me tell him I'm not going to be able to make it."

"No. Shut up."

"I'm telling you, he'll know something is wrong. I always answer my phone. Always."

"Larry, let him answer. He'll tell him something came up and he can't ride with him. Nothing more. Do you understand, Mr. Kincaid?"

Hank nodded. Deeg handed him his phone. "Make it quick and hang up."

"Hey, Sam. What's up?"

"Put it on speaker," Deeg whispered.

Hank pretended to push the speaker button, but did not. He continued to talk. "Listen, I can't ride with you tonight as we planned. Something's come up." Hank risked Deeg's ire. "I'm with Detective DeGarzia at his house."

On the other end, Sam answered, "What? I didn't know we were riding tonight. I thought you said I shouldn't get on the bike." Deeg leaned in to try to hear what Sam was saying.

"Yeah, but—" Hank was unable to finish.

DeGarzia had jammed the point of his gun hard against Hank's chest. He yanked the phone away and hung up on Sam mid-sentence.

"What did I tell you?" Using the back of his hand, Deeg gave Hank a glancing blow across his head. "Didn't I tell you to not say anything? You can't keep pissing me off like that. Next time, I'll break your neck. Got it?"

Hank covered up for his gamble. "You didn't tell me not to say I was with you. What's the big deal anyway? I didn't say anything. He knows we work together. Why'd you hang up? Now he'll know something's wrong."

The phone rang again. It was Sam. "Don't answer!" Yvonne shouted. "Let him leave a message."

"He'll definitely think something's wrong if I don't answer."

"Shut up, and don't say another word," Yvonne ordered.

A minute later, the cell phone beeped, indicating Sam had left a voice message. Yvonne played it back on the speaker. "Hey, Hank, you okay? It's Sam. You must be in a bad cell area. Call me back about that ride."

"Larry, that cinches it. He told Emilio he was with you. I told you I didn't trust him. Let's get rid of him now."

Any sympathy Yvonne might have felt for Hank earlier had dissipated.

"All right, Yvonne. Take it easy," Deeg said. He held an open hand toward her, gesturing for her to calm down.

She whispered in Deeg's ear and motioned to him to move out of earshot from Hank. "I have an idea. Let's get Emilio to meet Mr. Kincaid at Walton Turner's ranch in San Ysidro."

"At the Circle-T? Why there?"

Hank heard the word Circle-T, and listened intently to hear what else they were saying.

"Keep it down, Larry." Yvonne shushed her brother and continued to whisper. "The ranch is in the middle of nowhere. The police won't find them for days. And when they do, they won't know why they were killed. Then we're done."

Larry slumped.

"What's the matter?" she asked.

"I can't be done yet. I still have a couple other people on my list I'd like to do."

"Like who?"

"Dahlia, Stephenson, for starters. And Captain Ellsworth. He pissed me off."

"We can talk about that later. Let's get these two taken care of first. Let me have Mr. Kincaid's phone."

"Who're you calling?"

"I'm going to send a text to Emilio asking ask him to meet at the Circle-T Ranch. When he shows up, we can take care of them both."

Deeg patted his sister on the face. He loved her creativity. Yvonne smiled at him and stroked his shoulder.

Hank observed the interaction between brother and sister. He felt powerless knowing only that their plan involved his fate and the Circle-T Ranch.

Yvonne spoke as she typed a message into Hank's phone. "On my way to Circle-T Ranch in San Ysidro. Meet me there in one hour. I know who the killer is. Can't talk now."

Within ten seconds, Hank's phone pinged back, *OK. See u there.*

"Who are you texting?"

"Shut up. You'll know soon enough."

"Let's go, Mr. Kincaid. We're going for a drive," Yvonne said.

"Where to?"

"The Circle-T Ranch. We're going to meet Emilio there." She turned to her brother and said, "I'll drive his car, and you take him in yours. Where are your car keys, Mr. Kincaid?"

Hank didn't answer.

"Don't make me ask again," she said harshly. "Where are your keys?"

"I don't know." He shrugged.

Deeg stepped toward Hank. He was still holding the revolver. With his free hand, he grabbed Hank by his shirt and pulled him up from the couch. With all his strength, he slung Hank face first against the wall. He frisked him and quickly located the keys in his jacket pocket. "Do what you're told, and everything will be fine."

Hank knew better, and concluded they were planning to kill him and Sam at Walton Turner's ranch. "What are you going to do with me?" Neither answered.

Hank realized there was no hope in trying to reason with them. He was going to have to fight his way out of this. He had been looking for an opportunity to escape, but Deeg and Yvonne had been vigilant. This was his best chance. When Deeg turned to retrieve his handcuffs from the foyer table, Hank lowered his shoulder and barreled into him from the side. Surprised by the sudden attack, Deeg fell against the table. He was stunned but unhurt.

His gun slid across the living room floor.

Hank tried to escape through the front door, but Deeg recovered quickly and grabbed him from behind before he could open it. He yanked Hank away from the door and flung him onto the foyer floor, kicking him hard in his side. "Now, why did you go and do that?" Deeg shouted.

Hank quickly got to his feet. In spite of Deeg's imposing size, he was ready to barrel into him again. Deeg fronted him with his feet set wide apart, daring Hank to attack.

"You're going to have to kill me here, because I'm not going anyplace with you." Hank clenched his fists and took a fighter's stance. He waited for Deeg to make the next move. From the corner of his eye, he saw Yvonne had retrieved Deeg's gun and stretched it toward her brother. "Here, Larry, here!" she shouted.

Deeg reached for his gun, but as he did, Hank chopped at his outstretched wrist. The gun fell to the floor again. Deeg went for it. Hank kicked it away and bolted again for the front door, but Deeg blocked him a second time. "What now, Hank?"

There was no place to run.

"Here, Larry, quick. Here's the gun." Yvonne retrieved the gun again and handed it to her brother.

"Turn around now or I'll shoot you right here," Deeg said.

Hank refused to comply. His eyes darted back and forth across the room as he tried to size up an escape route. "Go ahead and shoot."

"No, don't shoot him, Larry. Not here. Emilio knows he's here. We need to take him to San Ysidro and kill him there," Yvonne said.

Free of fear that DeGarzia would shoot him, Hank turned quickly and threw a punch that grazed his chin. The blow only served to further infuriate the big man. Deeg grabbed Hank with one hand and threw him hard against the wall again. Hank slumped to the floor. Deeg lifted him up and turned him around to put him in a hammerlock. "Get my handcuffs," he yelled to Yvonne. "What the hell did you think you were going to do, Hank?" Deeg was panting from the battle.

"Mr. Kincaid, you're going to San Ysidro with us, and that's final," Yvonne declared. "Did he hurt you Larry?"

"No, I'm good."

"Okay, catch your breath. We need to get going. We don't want Emilio to get there before we do." Yvonne headed for the stairs. "But give me just a minute. I'll be right back. I need to get a couple things." She ran up and returned a moment later brandishing a shiny silver pistol and a shopping bag with a bicycle helmet still packaged in its original box. "I'm ready now."

Deeg smiled at her. "Okay. Let's go." He jerked Hank by his manacled wrists and shoved him into the back of his unmarked police car.

Yvonne followed in Hank's car.

Chapter 63

Deeg and Yvonne arrived at the remote Circle-T in under an hour. Yellow police crime tape still hung stretched across the entrance with a warning not to cross. Deeg detached the tape, opened the gate, and drove slowly up the long dirt driveway to the ranch house, with Yvonne following close behind. He left the gate open so Sam could enter when he arrived.

Deeg parked his car out of view while Yvonne parked Hank's car in the front of the house. Deeg held Hank by his wrists and shoved him toward the front door. Deeg leaned his shoulder into the locked front door, and opened it with little resistance.

He nodded to one of the chairs in the kitchen. "Sit there." When Hank did not comply, Deeg took him by his collar and yanked him down. Yvonne set the bike helmet on the kitchen table and guarded Hank while her brother prepared for Sam's arrival.

It had turned dark. A luminous full moon spotlighted the ranch. Deeg stood at the doorway and didn't have to wait long for Sam to arrive. He saw headlights coming up the driveway and warned Yvonne of Sam's approach. "He's here. Keep him quiet."

Hank's phone beeped indicating a text message. Deeg retrieved it from his pocket. The screen said *Connie.*

"Who is it, Larry?"

"It's his wife." Deeg read her short message. "Hey, Hank. Wondering where you are. Give me a call."

"She's worried," Hank said. "Let me call her back."

"Shut up. If you say one more word, Mr. Kincaid, I will shoot you right now. Larry, turn that damn phone off."

Sam pulled up to the front of the house in his pickup and parked behind Hank's car. From where he was standing, Deeg was unable to see the inside the pickup. He peeked out the screen door. *I can't see him.*

Sam turned to Dahlia. "Honey, stay here, please, while I go talk to Hank."

"What the hell is he doing?" Deeg mumbled.

When Sam exited his vehicle, Deeg greeted him from the front porch. "Hey, Emilio, how're you doing?"

Sam was surprised to see Deeg. He looked at him warily and stopped a distance from the house. "Man, this place wasn't easy to find. I didn't know you were going to be here, too. Where's Hank?"

"In the kitchen. We found out who the serial killers are."

"Killers? There's more than one killer?"

"Yeah. Come on in. We'll explain." Deeg beckoned Sam with a wave.

Sam's cop instincts took over. *Something's not right.* There was only one light on in the rear of the ranch house. "If it's okay with you, I'll wait out here. Why don't you call Hank out," he said. He felt uncertain about the situation, and glanced back at his pickup.

Deeg insisted. "No. You've got to come in."

Sam heard a commotion from inside the house. Yvonne had turned to check on Deeg, and in that split second, Hank threw himself at her, knocking her to the floor. A chair toppled, and Yvonne screamed. Still handcuffed, Hank was unable to take full advantage of his surprise attack to disable her, but he had managed to separate her from her pistol. He fell on her, and held her down by the sheer weight of his body. He knew he couldn't keep her this way for long. She tore at his face with her fingernails, scratching, pulling his hair, digging into his eyes.

"Run, Sam, run!" Hank shouted. "Get help!"

Sam spun on his heels hoping to retrieve the 45-caliber handgun he had stowed under the driver's seat.

Deeg drew his service revolver. "Stop," he yelled, and fired once. The bullet whizzed by Sam's head.

Sam realized he couldn't get to the pickup in time and that his only chance was to zigzag his way to the safety of the barn. Once inside, he slid the large wooden door closed just as Deeg fired again. The bullet crunched into the door with an explosion of splinters.

*****

Dahlia was terrified. She didn't understand what was happening. Someone had yelled for Sam to run, and then there was a gunshot. Next she saw Sam run into the barn and heard another gunshot. She dropped to the floor, panicked, uncertain what to do. She was unaware Sam's pistol was under his seat.

Yvonne scratched and clawed at Hank until she was able finally to extricate herself from underneath his dead weight. She retrieved her gun, aimed it at Hank, and, fighting for breath, shouted at him, "Get up before I kill you."

Hank rolled onto his knees and with effort stood. His face was scratched and bleeding. Yvonne ushered him out of the house with her pistol aimed at his back.

Knowing Sam was holed up in the barn, Deeg turned back to check on his sister. "Are you okay?"

"Yeah, I'm all right. He knocked me over when I checked to see what was going on with you and Emilio."

"I should kill you now, you son-of-a-bitch." Hank didn't flinch. "Follow me, Yvonne, and bring him, too. If he does anything like that again, shoot him. Enough is enough!"

The three walked toward the barn. Yvonne asked her brother, "Are you sure Emilio is in there?"

"Yeah. I'm going in after him. There's only one way out. He isn't going anywhere." He was confident Sam had nowhere to run.

Through a crack in the wall Sam saw DeGarzia, Hank, and one other person walking toward the barn. The rising moon cast three long shadows ahead of them. As they neared, he was shocked to see his ex-wife. *Jesus, that's Yvonne. What's she doing here?* Sam also saw Hank was handcuffed. *What the hell's happening? Why do they have Hank in cuffs?* He looked toward his pickup, and in the moonlight glimpsed Dahlia peeking out over the dashboard. *Stay down, stay down, hon.*

Slivers of moonlight penetrated the darkness of the barn. Sam noticed a pitchfork hanging on the wall next to a ladder that led to the hayloft. He grabbed it and climbed to the loft.

From her vantage point, Dahlia watched as the three walked past the pickup. She recognized Deeg and Hank but not the woman. She heard Deeg mumble something and wave his gun toward the pickup. Again she dropped to the floor, unseen.

Deeg slid the barn door open. From his perch, Sam saw three silhouettes outlined in the entrance. One was holding a revolver. Deeg shouted, "Come out, *Papá*. I want to talk with you."

Sam didn't answer. *What the hell? Did he just call me Papá?*

Deeg called out again, "Come on, Papá. Come out! You don't want us to have to set the barn on fire do you?" Without his gun, Sam knew he was defenseless. He would only be able to use the pitchfork against Deeg if he were close enough. *Why did I leave my gun in the truck? And my phone.* He wanted to yell to Dahlia to grab his phone from the dash and call for help, but he couldn't. They would kill her if they knew she was in the truck.

DeGarzia heard the rustle of hay in the loft. "I hear you up there. Come on, Papá, Come on down. You don't want me to kill your friend now, do you?"

Sam's mind raced. *Why is DeGarzia calling me Papá? What does Yvonne have to do with all this?*

In a playful falsetto voice Deeg yelled out again, this time in Spanish. "Salir, salir, dondequiera que estés. Come out, come out, wherever you are."

Sam didn't answer. He looked around for another weapon, anything he could use to defend himself, but saw nothing.

"Remember all those beatings you gave me when I was a little boy? Do you remember, Papá?"

Sam shook his head. *What the hell is he talking about?*

"Remember how you used to hurt Larry, Papá?" Yvonne echoed. "Remember how you hurt him? Why? You always said it was for his own good. Remember that?"

They think I'm their father?

"Larry's here with me, Papá. He's all grown up now. You might not even recognize him." In her sweetest voice, she added, "We want to talk to you. Come on down, okay?"

Oh, Jesus, that explains it. DeGarzia must be Yvonne's brother Larry. Sam remembered her talking about him.

"Are you coming down, Papá?" Yvonne asked.

Finally, Sam answered. "I don't know what you're talking about, Yvonne. I'm not your father. I'm Emilio. I used to be married to you."

"I was never married to you. That's sick, Papá."

Deeg was losing patience. "If you don't show yourself now, I'll put a bullet in your friend's head. I'm going to count to ten then Kincaid's a dead man. And you know what else I'm going to do? I'm going to find your girlfriend. I know where she lives, and I'm going to hurt her. I will find her and I will hurt her bad."

Sam hoped Dahlia had found his cellphone and dialed for help. He would stall, and give her more time to discover it.

In a singsong voice, Deeg repeated, "Salir, salir,

dondequiera que estés. Come out. Come out, wherever you are."

"How do I know you won't shoot me if I come down?" Sam asked.

"I'm not going to shoot you. Trust me. I haven't seen you in so many years, ever since I left home. I only want to talk with you."

"Bullshit," Sam shouted back. "Why didn't you tell me who you were when I met you at the police station?"

Deeg fired a shot into the loft. "You're making me angry, Papá. I'm warning you, I'm going to put a bullet in your friend's head. One, two, three—"

Sam realized he had no other choice and that Dahlia was his only hope. "All right. All right. I'm coming down." He carried the pitchfork and climbed down the ladder.

"Drop the pitchfork," Deeg said. Sam didn't move. "I said drop it."

Sam leaned the pitchfork against the ladder. *I may still get a chance to use it.*

"That's good, Papá. Come here. I won't hurt you," Deeg purred, his gun aimed directly at Sam's head. Playfully, he chimed one last time, "Salir, salir, dondequiera que estés."

Yvonne lowered her pistol. Deeg glanced at her. Her expression reflected fear and incomprehension. "Yvonne—"

"That's what Papá used to say when he tried to find me. You sound just like him, Larry. Why are you talking like that?"

Deeg did not answer. Instead, he asked, "Okay, Yvonne, what do you want me to do with Emilio? Do you want me to shoot him?"

She ignored his question. "Larry, it wasn't Papá, was it?" Yvonne said.

"What wasn't Papá, sweetheart?"

"It wasn't Papá who hurt me, was it?"

"Of course it was," he answered. "Who else could it have been?"

"It was you, wasn't it?"

"Don't be ridiculous."

"Larry, it was you," she repeated. She started to cry and her shrill voice jarred them all. "Please tell me it wasn't you. Please."

"What do you mean?" Deeg used his sleeve to wipe perspiration off his brow.

"My God, Larry, it was you."

Deeg tilted his head. "What do you mean 'it was me?' I don't know what you're talking about. Stop saying that."

Sam inched closer to Deeg. If he could get within striking distance, he would throw himself at the bigger man and take his chances. And Hank, still in handcuffs, would somehow have to overpower Yvonne. Sam nodded his intention to Hank, who replied in turn with a barely perceptible nod of his own. They knew what they had to do.

Yvonne let out an unworldly scream. All eyes turned to her. "I used to hide from *you*! It wasn't Papá, was it? It wasn't Papá." She screeched like a scared animal. "Oh my God, it was you! I remember. *You're* the one in my nightmares. I thought it was Papá, but it wasn't. It was you." She sobbed. "Oh my God. Those eyes in my dreams—those evil eyes—they were *yours*. I see them now. They're following me now. Oh my God! Those eyes are your eyes."

"No, it wasn't me. It was him."

Over and over Yvonne cried, "Oh my God. It was *you*." She was hysterical. "You found me no matter where I was hiding— and Eric, too. You would say, 'Salir, salir, dondequiera que estés' to Eric, too. We would hide in the closet, but you always found us, didn't you?"

Deeg opened his mouth wide and shook his head slowly in a large arc, breathing hard. "Yes, okay. It was me. But then Eric ran away. Why did he run away?" Deeg asked in a child-like tone. "I wasn't going to hurt him."

"But you did. You hurt him and me both. I remember. I remember now." Yvonne screamed again.

Deeg's attention was focused on Yvonne. Hank shifted his direction toward Yvonne and nodded to Sam. The moment was now. Realizing this might be the only chance to wrest the gun away from Deeg, Sam lunged at him. He grabbed the larger man's wrist and the two grappled like summa wrestlers, each trying to throw the other to the ground.

Yvonne waved her pistol at Hank before he could assault her. He backed away. She turned to Deeg and Sam, who were in a life and death struggle of their own. She fired a shot. The two men fell to the dirt floor. Deeg's revolver landed alongside them. A second later, Sam shoved Deeg off him. He grabbed Deeg's revolver and aimed it first at Deeg, then at Yvonne, uncertain what had happened. Yvonne was not looking at him. She stared down at her brother, oblivious to Sam and Hank.

Deeg lay on his belly. Blood stained the back of his jacket, stretching slowly across his wide shoulders. He managed to roll over and look up at his sister with dazed eyes. He tried to sit up, but fell back.

"Why, Yvonne? Why?"

"Because it was *you* who did all those things to me. You used to say that to me and Eric. 'Salir, salir, dondequiera que estés.' I remember now it was you. You were the one who touched me all the time. It wasn't Papá. He tried to protect me. He would beat you when you did those things to me. Papá beat you because of what you would do to me. It was you, Larry. Oh my God, it was *you*. You used to touch me, and Eric, too. You touched me in bad ways. It wasn't Papá." Yvonne was delirious from the revelation. "You did bad things to me. I was only a little girl. Why?"

"No. It was Emilio, not me," Deeg pleaded. "Him. It was him." He lifted a finger to indicate Sam.

"No. You! You! You!" She was incoherent, babbling, frenzied. "You did bad things to Eric, didn't you? That's why he ran away. It wasn't Emilio. It was you."

"That's not true. I didn't."

"Yes, yes, you did. I remember now. 'Salir, salir, dondequiera que estés.'"

"Yvonne, let me have the gun. Please," Deeg said.

"No. I can't let you have it." She turned to Sam. "I'm so sorry, Papá. It was Larry who did all those things to Eric and me. It wasn't you, Papá. I'm so sorry."

Sam did not correct her. "That's okay, Yvonne. Now, let me have your gun." He was holding Deeg's gun behind his back, cocked and ready to use if Yvonne aimed her pistol at him.

"No, I can't."

She turned back to her brother, aimed, and fired—once, twice, again, and again. Deeg's body lifted and slumped with each shot. She pulled the trigger one last time. "It was you," she sobbed. Click, click, click. She tried to shoot him again but the gun was empty.

Chapter 64

Two police cars flew up the driveway with lights flashing and sirens wailing. Their headlights bounced erratically with each pothole they hit.

In the midst of the chaos taking place in the barn, Dahlia had found Sam's cellphone on the dash and called 9-1-1. She was standing alongside the truck and pointed to the barn when the cars pulled up. "Hurry, they're in there." The cops cautiously entered the barn with guns drawn. "Put down your guns! Put your guns down now!"

Sam complied.

The cops shouted, "Down on the ground. Now! All of you. Down!"

Yvonne was in a psychotic daze. She stared at her dead brother then turned to the cops with a vacant look. She was holding her gun loosely at her waist but then lifted it to her temple.

"It was him," she said.

Epilogue

Stacey Keenan pleaded guilty to aggravated manslaughter. She admitted to shooting Clyde after he had raped and beaten her. She contended he had threatened her with the same gun she used to kill him. The judge took into consideration the report of three psychologists who evaluated her and determined she was a victim of chronic physical and psychological abuse. She was sentenced to ten years in prison. With good behavior, she would be free in three years. She would realize her intentions of transforming the Circle-T Ranch into a haven and counseling center for abused and battered women.

Yvonne was committed to the Santa Fe Hospital for the Criminally Insane.

Sam and Dahlia were married. Hank served as Sam's best man.

THE END

About the Author

Tony Spallone lives in Pennsylvania. He has a graduate degree in psychology, was an officer in the armed forces, and a business executive. He and his wife, Patti, whom he met while he was stationed in the Army in Tennessee, have a love of travel, enjoy hanging out with their grandchildren, and are avid cyclists. *Murder at Breeze Canyon* is Spallone's first book. Visit him at www.tonyspallone.com.